REFLECTIONS OF WAR AND BLOOD

Lasheckia Lyons

R3M
MEDIAS
DR3AM DIFFERENT

For more information, or to book an event, contact:
info@r3mmedias.com
http://www.r3mmedias.com

Book design by Dave Chesson
Cover image by Patrick McGregor II
Jacket design by Idea Factory

First Edition: October 2024

1

Someone To Protect

At times, things can change faster than eyelids can touch and part ways. These moments can alter themselves with a greater velocity than snow flurries thrashed about by strokes of wind.

Gusts were accelerated through the narrow corridors of tightly packed skyscrapers. Mother Nature had turned against the world, her once smooth seasonal transitions cast out for alternating extremes. She battered what glass panes remained intact. Steel supports creaked under the weight of massive ice clumps and tightly packed snow. They would soon give way to gravity, as their surrounding brethren had.

The streets were silent and vacant, far from the Bogota of the past. Nothing was the same, nor would it ever be again, in this tainted future of humanity. The cold season had raided the lobby of a once posh hotel. Every surface had become frostbitten. Corners were packed with mounds of white, exposed metal rusting away between cracks within. A chandelier lay in shambles below its high-anchored perch.

Chris increased the tension on his compound bow until it locked into place. The feathers of the arrow's tail brushed against his scruffy beard. He held so still that the faint sound of the rub was nearly audible. One squeeze of Chris' fingers was all it would take to ensure the sharp tip would reach its mark. If the projectile didn't land home, he would likely go to sleep hungry. His shoulder was pressed up against the edge of a window frame, careful to avoid the jagged edges of protruding glass. The soles of his nonslip winter boots were planted firmly on the snow-dusted floor tiles, balance perfect.

The voice in Chris' mind said: hold steady. He must find the place between breaths, when air no longer traversed through his lungs. That place would ensure the ferret's demise. But it was not meant to be. The small mammal scurried from the street, vanishing into the infinite white. A sudden commotion had startled it away. Inwardly, Chris was frustrated, even angry. Prey was becoming increasingly difficult to come by. Hunting requires strength, and strength requires the fruits of the hunt, a never-ending cycle. Without the appropriate sustenance, Chris would gradually grow weaker.

Regardless of his feelings, Chris didn't show an ounce of stress on the surface. He panned his vision further down the cracked asphalt when his inner voice spoke up again. It said that they would likely not escape whomever or whatever pursued them. It wouldn't have been possible to outrun a kitten at that pace.

Even so, Chris found it best to avoid people in this new world. Too often, these kinds of displays turned out to be nothing more than elaborate ruses— theatric performances to draw hidden heroes out into the open for thievery or worse. He thought himself too smart for such simple trickery.

A quartet closed in on the unfortunate family. Chris wanted to slip away, but something kept him still. His bow remained taut, and his attention focused.

The fleeing male fell victim first, his begging rendered useless. "Please!" he yelled.

A long blade was shoved deep into his abdomen.

3

As he flailed about the cold ground in agony, the woman dropped by his side, slain by another member of the murderous group.

"Get the girl! And find the other little shit!" ordered the woman, seemingly the one in charge. "The boss wants them ASAP, and we need to stay ahead of the burn. I ain't dying out here in this piece of shit place."

The child hung on to the bodies of her dying protectors. "No! Tio! Tia!" she cried. Her fingertips clutched her uncle's jacket as long as she could, before the largest of her captors plucked her away. He flung her over his shoulder, kicking and screaming.

Her fight was futile. She was much too small to be any more than a minor nuisance.

Chris' inner voice was at it again. It said that this was no Broadway performance. Instinct made his next decision easy. The leader was always the first to kill when possible. It destroys morale and complex decision-making. A sickening crack sounded as the projectile pierced her back, ramming straight through her heart. Death was instant for her. Chris believed it was a cleaner death than she probably deserved.

The thud of the woman's body alerted her colleagues. They reached for their sidearms, only to find them missing. "What the hell?" said one man. It was as if their guns had magically vanished.

Having no weapons for defense, they bolted for cover, but there was too much distance to traverse from the open road to the nearest place of safety. A single pluck of the bowstring ended two more bodies' lives. The last man alive realized that he wouldn't make it much further, especially carrying precious cargo. He turned to face the direction from whence the arrows seemed to originate and held the child to his chest for protection.

"You don't know who you're fucking with, whoever the hell you people are!" he yelled, backing out of the street. Everything had happened so quickly that he believed there to be more than one culprit.

Chris stepped from the decaying hotel, his bow still tracking his last target. "Just me," he said.

The man pressed his blade against the girl's neck, continuing to creep backward. If he could just make the alley, he would be able to cut bait and run. "I don't know what game you motherfuckers are playing, but I'll kill the little cunt, I swear!" he said nervously.

Chris closed his eyes and breathed deeply. A cloud of visible air pushed through the checkered scarf wrapped around his face. His heart rate slowed to a fraction of what it should have been. Once his eyes reopened, everything was frozen, but not in the sense that it already was. This wasn't a winter's freeze. Time had slowed until it was nearly motionless. The scenery was now an ultra-high-definition still image. Snowflakes hung in the air, bound together with time. They melted against Chris' warm body as he walked his way through the suspended dots, leaving a silhouette burned in his wake. His eyes shifted metallic blue, shimmering like starlight on a night's canvas. Bolts of lightning ejected from his body, singeing the cool air. Gently, he plucked the blade from the man's grip and looked him deep in his eyes. He wondered if he would see his soul fade within them. The combat blade slid through the man's temple like butter. Chris didn't blink as he shoved it through. No light flickered inside. Chris wondered if the guy even had a soul to begin with.

Time broke loose, permitting the man and child to fall to the asphalt. It seemed she didn't notice any of the miraculous things that Chris had just done. Her attention was owned by love. She rushed to the lifeless bodies of her aunt and uncle and hugged them desperately. Her wails were heartbreaking. Chris believed that his own heart had long died, but it had only been dormant. There was no need for a heart in such a lonesome existence, but her pain gave his cold feeling a jump start. Chris was a protector. Now, it seemed, he had someone worth protecting. At least for the time being.

Chris searched the bodies for anything of use. There wasn't much—a couple of lighters, a pint of alcohol, a marked map of the area, and a photo of the girl with a young boy. The patches on their thick jackets caught Chris' eye. He filed them in memory, then stood silently at the girl's side. Maybe he was giving her time. Maybe he just didn't know what to say. Whatever the reason, he waited patiently.

The girl's cries subsided into whimpers after a minute or so. She remained in a crumpled heap between those she loved and asked Chris, "Who are you?"

"I'm nobody," he replied, gazing off in the distance as he did.

"Well, Mr. Nobody, my papa told me that everybody is somebody to somebody." The girl wiped the tears from her cheeks.

Chris thought it was best to change the subject. "I'm sorry about your parents," he said.

"These aren't my parents. They're my tios."

"Your what?"

"My aunt and uncle."

"Why didn't you just say that, midget?"

The girl jumped to her feet in defiance. "I'm not a midget! I'm a kid!" she shouted.

"Same difference. A short person is a short person." Chris paused in thought. "I guess I should take you to your parents then," he concluded.

"My parents are dead too. There's nobody else. They took care of us," she replied, pointing down at her last remaining bonds to the world.

"So, I'm stuck with a 6-year-old."

"I'm 10!" the girl yelled. She kicked Chris in the shin.

"You little..." Chris started to say while rubbing his leg. The pain must have refocused his thoughts. "Wait, did you say us?" he asked.

The girl's face scrunched into confusion.

"You said, they took care of us," Chris clarified.

Her face lit up, and her eyes bulged. "Yo olvidé! Mi hermano!"

"What?"

"My brother!" she replied, dashing off.

"This day can't get much worse than this," Chris mumbled to himself, trotting after the girl. The short dash concluded at a weather-battered sedan on the other side of the roadway. Chris peered through its windows. A small boy cowered in the rear floor with his head tucked between his knees. His head flung up when Chris pulled the door open. The child tried to back away, but there was no room to move. Panic was consuming him. He thought the bad people had found him for sure.

His sister popped her face into view. "Todo está bien hermano. Ven aquí," she said to him, with her arms outstretched. He climbed out and hugged her tightly.

"OK, enough with the gibberish. English please," said the annoyed Chris.

"Where's tío y tía?" asked the boy. He stared up at his sister as he spoke. She shook her head side to side. The boy then pressed his face against her torso and wept.

Chris thought the children were too young to perceive death at the level that they seemed to be, yet it was so. This was what this apocalyptic existence had reduced the human race to. Savages who recognized savagery before they could even protect or provide for themselves.

"Come on," said Chris. "I guess you're with me from now on. No one will ever hurt you again." The sky was dimming. He looked up and told them, "We gotta go now. If we get caught out here at sundown..."

"We'll freeze to death," the girl cut in.

"10 huh? A little smart for your age, ain't you?"

The girl smiled, still consoling the little one.

"What's your name?" Chris asked.

"Rosalia. My brother is Cory. He's only 5."

"How about I just call you Rose?"

She smiled again and nodded in agreement.

"Well, Rose, it's nice to meet you. I'm Chris." He stuck out his hand for a shake.

"I like Mr. Nobody better."

"Smart ass," Chris grunted as he pulled his hand away.

Rose's eyes bulged larger. "Hey! Don't say bad words!" she demanded.

"Whatever."

The trio headed through the hotel's front entrance

and out of the rear fire exit. Chris made sure to remain observant with every step. There was a very real possibility that the kidnappers weren't alone. As a matter of fact, it was more probable than possible.

The alley seemed to be clear. "Stay close to me at all times, got it?" Chris instructed. Rose nodded intently. Cory just stared blankly.

Chris hung his bow from his back, then equipped himself with a semiautomatic handgun from his holster, at the belt line of his cargo pants. He moved with his head on a swivel. The rooftops and the ground were the bulk of his focus. Tracks in the soft snow would alert of possible enemies, and high ground was always a significant advantage in any skirmish.

A dead end, about 50 feet down the back of the hotel, halted their trek. Chris tugged at a well-camouflaged tarp in the corner. With low visibility from blowing snow, its white tint made it virtually invisible from more than a few feet away. "Get in," he said, opening the door of a pickup truck that was hiding underneath. Its exterior continued with the icy white theme of his equipment. Once the children were inside, Chris flung the tarp into the rear bed, then shut the lid. A final scan of the alley assured him that it was safe to move.

The engine rattled to life. She wasn't Shelby, but neither was any vehicle left on the planet. As a matter of fact, Chris wasn't aware of any others that were functional at all. He drove away. Silence didn't last a second. Rose leaned over the back of the leather bench seat. "I can't believe you have a working truck! Did you steal it?" she questioned.

"From who? There's barely people left in the world. You think some dead person is worried about this truck? Now sit back," Chris responded.

Rose sat back and folded her arms. "Smart ass," she mumbled.

Chris slammed on the brakes, skidding the truck to a complete stop. "Listen little girl. Curse again, and you'll be walking!" he said.

"But, you just said the same thing!"

"I'm a grown ass man too!"

"Ay, adultos y sus reglas estúpidas."

"Hey, hey! Rule number 2. You speak English, not any of that shit that I don't understand. Now, shut up and stop being annoying." Chris started down the road again. "And just so you know, stupid sounds the same in both languages... smart ass," he added for safe measure.

"He's mean," Cory commented, grabbing hold of Rose's hand.

"Don't worry. He's all talk," she whispered into his ear.

Chris kept to seldom-used roads to avoid pileups of long-abandoned and overturned vehicles. Red tiles from the roofs of collapsed adobe houses poked from icy heaps alongside the roadside. They were once residences of some 50 million citizens of the growing country. Now, Colombia was a cultural haven withered to nothing, just as the rest of the world was.

"Where are we going?" asked Rose.

Chris kept his eyes focused on the road but answered, "To find someplace warm and safe."

Rose was excited. "We live in a place like that!" she exclaimed.

"Oh yeah? Where is that?"

"In a garage, under a really big building. There's a huge sign on top that says, 'Seguros'."

Chris had seen it before. "You got any food there?" he asked.

"Yep! My tíos hid it real good." The thought of Rose's aunt and uncle saddened her. She fell silent once more.

"If we go there, can you show me where it is?" Chris asked.

Happy to be of help, Rose perked up again. She loved to feel like she was part of something important. "Yeah, I can do it!" she replied.

Chris veered the truck around and headed back toward the center of the city. The target destination was just a few blocks away, so he was certain that they would arrive before sundown, which was closing in rapidly.

Having successfully settled Cory in, Rose climbed into the front passenger seat.

"What are you doing? Get back in the back," Chris demanded.

Rose ignored the latter part of his statement and said, "I've never been in a working car before."

"You still haven't. This is a truck."

"You know what I mean," Rose replied. Warm air trickled the exposed portions of skin around her eyes. She followed its path to a vent from which it escaped. What a foreign machine this was. Floral patterned gloves dropped to the seat at Rose's side. Airflow poured over them tenderly. It was such a pleasant experience.

Then, she pulled down her facial covering, letting it hang loosely around her neck. Her features were soft, her skin tan and youthful. Deep puddles of blue filled the gateways of her soul.

"Can you teach me how to drive?" asked Rose. She plastered her forehead against the side window to watch the scenery roll by.

Chris scoffed at the idea. "No," he responded.

"Why not?"

"There are several reasons, starting with your stubby little legs not being able to reach the pedals."

"What are pedals?"

Chris glanced at Rose briefly before returning his attention to the road. "Why are you so comfortable? Shouldn't you be scared of me, like your kid brother?" he pondered.

"I'm only ascared of bad people."

"Scared, not ascared," Chris corrected. A second of quiet followed, preceding his next words. "What makes you think I'm not a bad person?"

"Mmm... I just know," said Rose, her finger tapping against her chin.

"I killed four people right in front of you."

Rose stared at the floor and kicked her dangling feet. "Some people deserve to die," she said.

Chris felt heaviness in her voice. "You've been through a lot, huh?" he said.

Rose didn't give a response. She brushed her long, dark hair behind her ear. Chris was good with body language. The gesture told him a great deal.

"This the place?" he asked.

"Uhuh!" Rose said, relieved to reengage on something positive. "All the way at the bottom."

Debris covered the floor of the garage entrance. It was mostly concrete chunks from the collapsing roof, sprinkled with miscellaneous trash. Chris switched the pickup to off-road and drove over, careful to avoid protruding rebar and things liable to puncture a tire.

The truck swayed and rocked atop the suspension. Rose giggled, gripping the door to steady herself. Cory looked to her for emotional cues. The joy in her face shook loose a giggle of his own. It felt like an amusing carnival ride. Something they had heard stories about, but never experienced in their short lives.

An adjustment of the rearview mirror brought Cory into Chris' view. "So, he can smile," he mumbled to himself. Shadows engulfed the truck, plunging the interior into darkness. The automatic lights powered on. Both children were startled at the instant illumination.

"Whoah!" they said in unison.

The wonder of the children experiencing firsts was magical. Simple things, all of which we take for granted, were especially rare in those times. Maybe it was for the better, Chris thought. If it made people appreciate things as small as headlights on an automobile, the purchase may have been worth the price.

"Our tíos taught us about those," said Rose. "They said that fire wasn't the only light before the world broke."

"A lot of things were different before," Chris replied.

Layers of frozen water had accumulated over every surface inside the garage. So much so, that the remaining scattered vehicles were locked into place, rounded mounds of white accentuating the contoured shapes of their roofs.

The truck rolled to a complete stop. Chris eyed a downward slope. "We're going to have to walk the rest of the way," he said.

"Why?" asked Rose, raising her voice an octave.

"There's too much ice on the ramp. The tires won't be able to get any grip. We'll slide down and crash into something." Chris inhaled deeply, resting his forehead on the steering wheel. "Lord, help me. These kids don't know a thing," he grumbled.

Cory was confused. "Rosie, who is the weird man talking to?" he asked. She shrugged her shoulders, just as bewildered as her brother was.

"No, no, no. This is unacceptable," started Chris, wagging his finger at the children. "If you're gonna follow me around, you're gonna learn about the Lord. Ain't about to have you li'l heathens messing up my karma," Chris rambled. "Put your gloves on and cover your face. The temperature is dropping out there fast. We need to get down below and start up a fire before we turn into popsicles."

Rose opened up her mouth to speak.

"You better not ask me what a popsicle is, little girl," Chris interrupted. "As a matter of fact, no more talking. Especially you." He singled out Cory with his pointer finger. "You talk way too much."

The children were as confused as ever, and it showed on their faces. Chris left the vehicle running for use of light, but dismounted. "Let's go," he said to his new companions. Rose hopped out and walked around to the driver's side of the truck. Chris opened the bed's cover to gain access to a mounted equipment box. The hydraulic mounts hissed and held it upright. He rummaged around for a short moment before finding what he needed.

The temperature was plummeting, especially under the roof where what was left of the day's sunshine was absent. Cory wrapped his arms around himself. Rose held him to share her body heat.

A click powered on a flashlight. "Here," said Chris, handing it over to Rose. Another click. "And one for you," he added, handing a second to Cory. A final click illuminated one for himself.

Light danced around the roof as the children twirled

them about. Their attention left the cold conditions for a moment. Playtime was in session.

"Hey, c'mon with the lights," said Chris. "It's not like we can just buy some new ones if you break them." He checked the digital watch on his wrist. A timer was still actively counting up, its current reading at '36:27:32'. "The sun will be completely down in about thirty minutes. We gotta move quick," he said. With that, he killed the engine on the truck, and they made their way down the first ramp on foot.

The bottom floor was only five stories down. At a brisk pace, they would make their destination and start a fire with time to spare. There was a problem. Cory was losing his strength. The now sub-zero temperature was sapping the warmth from his body. He couldn't keep up.

Chris took notice. They couldn't afford to move too slow. "Up top, li'l man," he said, squatting down.

Cory was skeptical. Rose passed him a reassuring look. Satisfied, he clung onto Chris' back and they were off again. To the place that would grant them survival for at least one more night.

The sound of whipping air could be heard throughout the structure, even in the lower floors. The winds were approaching speeds of a heavy winter storm. Anything not bolted down, or heavy enough to withstand the pressure, was tossed around the empty streets.

The trio at last arrived on the bottom floor.

"Alright, Rose. Lead the way," said Chris.

Rose aimed her flashlight across the lot, weaving through the maze of vehicles with a sense of purpose. The cluck of their boots reverberated without end. Chris kept close. His right hand swung at his side, never too far from the handle of his weapon. Even when it seemed safe, it often wasn't. He treated every moment this way.

"Here!" said Rose. She pointed her light, revealing a row of dumpsters blocking off a corner. Chris lowered Cory to the ground. The boy was shivering uncontrollably. Time was of the essence. Long ruts in the ice around the wheels of one garbage bin told of frequent movement. A firm tug was all it took to slide it to the side. The area

REFLECTIONS OF WAR AND BLOOD

behind was compact, good for holding in heat from the open fire, which was oriented affront a hole in the concrete wall. The jagged gouge was barely large enough for an adult to crawl through. Chris pushed the dumpster back into place behind them.

"What's in there?" he asked, referring to the hole.

"That's where we sleep. The food is in there too," Rose responded.

"OK, good. We gotta get a fire going. I need you to keep that light on me, while I do this, alright?" Rose shook her head to confirm that she understood.

Chris took the earlier pilfered lighter from his pocket, along with a wad of dry material that he could use as tinder. He placed it in the center of a circle of rocks among the dead coals and ash of previous fires. A pile of collected wood was within arm's reach. He hoped that it was still dry enough to hold wick and stacked it in a cone shape around the tinder. Though there was no wind, the clump of dry brush had trouble igniting. After a few tries, very little remained to continue his efforts. There was more in the truck, but it would take time to go back for it. Time that Cory didn't have. Hypothermia posed a serious risk to the child.

A jolt of Chris' memory brought forth the flask he had also taken from the body of one of his earlier victims. One drop should be enough to give a flame the needed boost to maintain life, even in these extreme conditions, he thought to himself.

The blaze ignited quickly, spreading to the cold, stacked wood without issue. Cory clung to Rose. His shivers were now on the verge of violent. "Something's wrong," she said, with worry grasping her voice.

"Bring him close to the fire," Chris instructed her. He still worked to ensure that the blaze was stable.

The two children sat and embraced one another at the flame's edge. Chris went over to use his flashlight to search the crevasse in the wall. The area inside was wider than the entrance, but still small and enclosed. It was barely large enough to fit two adults and two small children, but that was actually an advantage. Heat from the fire would be trapped inside. The concrete acted as insulation, bringing the temperature inside well into the positive range.

Two rucksacks were far back to the rear. Chris crawled inside and unzipped them. He found that one was filled with canned goods and packs of jerky. The second contained a quartet of bowls, cutlery, and a cast-iron pot. He transferred two cans of baked beans and a pack of the jerky to the bag of kitchenware, then backed out with them in possession. "I'm going to make us something to eat," he said.

Cory wasn't looking well at all. The small blaze was warming, but not doing so fast enough. Chris walked over to the huddled siblings. A touch of Cory's forehead alerted him to how serious his condition was becoming. "He's still too cold," Chris said.

"The fire isn't working?" Rose was feeling the cold as well, but her concern kept her from noticing.

Chris turned his flashlight on again. "I got something in the truck that should help him," he replied, pausing on the way out.

"I'll be right back. Don't leave this area no matter what. And I mean no matter what."

"But, what if the bad people are out there? What if they get you, and you never come back?" Rose asked, her blue eyes twinkling with worry.

"The bad people should be the ones worried about me getting them." Chris slid the dumpster over just enough to squeeze out, shoved it back, then slipped away silently. More swift and agile movement was possible without the children, so Chris made it back to the ground level in no time. Conditions there had drastically deteriorated. Highway-speed winds blasted through the garage's open schematics, flapping his clothing about. Even he wouldn't survive out in the elements for too long.

Chris realized that his concern for the children's safety had caused him to abandon discretion. It was more important than ever to dot every I, with them now in his care. Their lives depended on it. That on his mind, he started his truck, then parked it between two mounds of frozen-over automobiles. When he killed the engine, the mechanical rumbling didn't die with it; however, the sound wasn't coming from within. Someone else was nearby. Chris exited the truck and eased the door closed, getting into a crouched position. There was a semiautomatic rifle strapped underneath the foot rail. He retrieved it, checked the magazine and side port, then stealthily made his way towards the noise.

The fallen concrete in the entryway was great cover. From behind it, Chris could see a convoy of vehicles traveling up the street. This was a sight he never expected to see again, but a militaristic presence was hardly a positive sign.

Blowing snow hindered visibility significantly. Even still, the collection of vehicles was close enough for Chris to make out a familiar symbol on the doors. It was a simple crest, two overlapping diamonds, one larger than the other. The very same design was on the uniforms of the people that had been after the children. Maybe they hadn't given up on the search yet. Maybe they had found their dead members and were looking for the killer. Either way, Chris began to wonder who the children were and why these kinds of people seemed to want them so bad.

Luckily for Chris, the heavy snowfall and wind had long covered his tire tracks that led into the garage. The convoy moved on without notice. Cory revisited his mind, so he shouldered his rifle and sprinted back to the truck. It was wise to keep the weapon in possession. He pulled it over his torso, moving for his primary task, which was to retrieve the necessary gear from the rear of the truck bed. Mission accomplished, Chris covered his truck with its white tarp and headed back to the children with urgency.

The grinding of the dumpster's wheels startled Rose, who was still clinging on to her brother's shivering body. Chris didn't waste a second. He took a lightweight cylinder from his back, then unraveled the binding cordage. Two sleeping bags uncoiled to the ground. Within the center was a bug net, a camo, waterproof sheet, and other cold-weather gear. With the more gaudy of the two sleepers, Chris went for the hole in the wall, then propped it up inside, facing the blaze.

"What's that for?" asked Rose.

Chris continued to work while responding, "I have to get his temperature back up before hypothermia sets in." A second trip to the pile of supplies rendered hand-warming pads. Chris activated them, shoved them into the bottom of the sleeping bag, then layered the waterproof sheet on top.

"What's hypothrulasia?" asked Rose, destroying the pronunciation.

"Rose, I will happily answer any of your questions later, but now ain't the best time." Chris carried Cory to the prepped heating bag, placed him inside, then zipped it up to the bottom of his chin. A few more sticks placed on the pile helped the fire remain a healthy size. "That should work."

"He's going to be OK, right?" Rose inquired.

"He'll be alright. He just needs rest and a little time, something we happen to have plenty of. Especially since the nights are so long."

Rose took off her gloves and put her hands close to the fire. The feeling was much different than the truck's heating. Natural warmth seemed to affect the soul, as well as the body. "How long were they before the world broke?" she asked.

Chris jammed his knife through the top of a couple of canned goods. "Depends on what part of the world you were in." An extra flick of the wrist gave easy access to the food contents. "There used to be only 24 hours in a day. A little less than half of that was dark in most places. There's about 37 in a day now."

"Cause the world slowed down, right?"

"Right." Chris poured the beans into the pot and hung it on a frame of sticks that he had rigged above the fire.

"My tíos said that the world slowed down because of a new weapon the bad people used at the start of the last war."

Chris sat on the opposite side of the fire. The past ran through his mind in mere seconds. Rose seemed to read his expression. "Did you see it?" she asked.

"I don't remember much from that day," Chris replied with a hitch in his voice.

Rose stared at the ground. "Oh," she replied, a little disappointed. A question that had been burning her since she met Chris needed to be asked. "Are you a superhero?"

"Superhero?"

"When you killed the bad people today, you disappeared. Before that, you shot two arrows at the same time, and they changed directions in the air. I saw it."

"Again, real perceptive for a 10-year-old."

"My tíos said they didn't really know my real birthday, 'cause of how different time is now, and all."

"Your tíos say a lot."

Rose brushed her hair behind her ear again. "They can't say anything now," she replied.

Chris felt pain rising up in her. "I had an accident," he interjected.

Intrigue replaced Rose's agony, as he had expected. "What kind of accident?" she asked.

"I was on a tour of a top-secret lab. Some guy was sneaking around, and I was the only one that saw him. I chased him, ended somewhere I wasn't supposed to be, then got shocked by some equipment. I passed out, but when I woke up, I was able to do some special things."

"Ooo! That's an origin story!"

"How do you even know what an origin story is, but not a freaking tire or a popsicle?"

Rose sprang up and ran to one of the rusty blue dumpsters. She slid the side door open, and three thin magazines sealed in plastic film fell onto the ground.

"Are those?" Chris began asking.

"Comic books!" Rose brought them over and took a seat next to Chris. After removing one, she carefully folded its protective casing, placing it in one of her many coat pockets. "This is my favorite. It's about this little girl that grows up to save the world. She's super strong, super fast, and super brave. I wanna be just like her when I grow up." Rose slowly turned through the pages. The artwork was beautifully unique. She had cared for them so well that the colors still popped vividly. Chris couldn't read the words, but the pictures told the story well enough.

"Maybe someone will write a story about you one day."

"I'm not as good of a person as you think, kid. Superheroes don't do the things that I've done." Silence fell for a spell. The setting was tranquil, a type once saved for camping trips and old western movie scenes. Only the crackling of wood could be heard over a layer of ambient noise. Smoke billowed upward before becoming lost in the underground maze.

Chris glanced over to Cory. He had become still, the gentle rise and fall of his chest his only movement. Redness had also returned to his cheeks. Rose noticed his improved condition. "He looks like a worm with a face in that thing," she laughed.

Chris shared a laugh with her. He was curious to learn more about both of them. "You've been asking all the questions. I've got one for you." Rose's body language said, go on. "What happened to your parents?"

Rose's nervous tell activated itself once more. Her hair fell over her ear, coaxed by her hand. "We're not really brother and sister, ya know," she said, effectively deflecting the question.

"I already knew. I just wasn't sure if you knew."

"How'd you know? Did you use your superpowers to read my mind?"

"No. I can't read minds. It's just that... well, you're obviously not the same race."

"Uh, what's running a race got to do with it?" Rose tilted her head curiously.

Chris found her ignorance on the matter beautiful. The children didn't know the differences of heritage because they hadn't been taught to. They saw contrasts in physical appearance as simply nuance. "Nothing important," he replied, not willing to poison her mind with stupidity. "Cory needs to eat though. You wake him up, while I get your bowls ready."

Rose did as she was instructed with spirit. Helping fulfilled her in the same way that protecting did for Chris.

She coerced a groggy Cory to the side of the fire. The toddler sat on the side of Rose opposite Chris, rather than between them. Chris reached to pass him a bowl, but Cory refused to take it. Rose interceded, grabbing, then handing it to him. "We've never been around anyone but our tíos," she notified Chris. "Sometimes they would meet people to trade things, but they taught us to avoid people."

"It's usually best. Now you know why."

Rose said nothing.

"He's lucky to have you," Chris said. The children's relationship reminded him of when things between him and his older brother had made sense. Gino was his protector during those early years, but Chris had failed to return the favor. He failed to protect anyone he loved from an apocalyptic end. "After you're finished eating, grab that other sleeping bag. You need to get some sleep. We've got a long day of traveling when the sun comes up."

"We're not staying here?"

"We can't. The planet's getting worse. If we stay in one spot, we'll die. The burn season is coming up, so it'll be too hot to survive here. We've gotta go north where it's cooler."

"Is that where we're gonna live?"

"Only until the Freeze sets in again. When that happens, we'll have to come back down here where it'll be warmer."

"Oh," said Rose. The task sounded both daunting and tiring. Besides, she longed for a home, even though she didn't quite know what a home really was. However, her instincts knew that this wasn't it. She finished her meal, then headed for bed with one last question on her mind. "Can you teach me how to fight, Mr. Nobody? Like La Maravilla in the story, so I can be strong like her."

"You'll be stronger than her," Chris replied, seeming to finally be getting the hang of being more tender with his choice of words. Rose smiled, dragging her sleeping gear towards the hole in the wall.

***

Dying sparks hovered away from the still burning

flame. Chris lay beside it, cloaked in his waterproof blanket. His dreams were lucid, maybe too much so. The water seemed so real that it overwhelmed his senses. It trickled up his shirt and down his pants.

Chris began to stir. The more he moved, the wetter he felt. Half-soaked, his eyes sprang open, and he jumped to his feet in about an inch-deep puddle of water. Droplets patted the fire, falling from above. It flickered on the verge of death. Chris pulled his flashlight, anticipating the darkness that would follow. As soon as he flicked it to life, the fire succumbed to its weakness.

The light of his flashlight touched virtually every surface of the area as Chris waved it around to determine where the water was coming from. All the ice was melting at a rapid rate. He raced to wake the children. They startled back from the land of dreams and into the real world.

"What's going on?" asked Rose, seeing the urgency of Chris' movements.

"We have to get out of here right now!" he said. There wasn't a second to waste. Leaving behind everything but his rifle, Chris shoved the dumpster to the side.

"My comic books!" Rose shouted.

Chris plucked Cory from the ground like one would a suitcase, and grabbed Rose by the hand, pulling her along. "We don't have time for that!" he responded. The water level was rising exponentially. Streams flowed down the ramps that led to the ground floor. Sunlight grew stronger as they traveled upward. Chris' assumptions had come true, but much sooner than expected. It should have still been dark and cold, but the burn was already upon them.

With one level left to climb, the flow of water burst into a full-on torrent. The children wouldn't be strong enough to traverse the final ramp. "We can't swim!" Rose exclaimed with deep concern. The floors beneath them were filling up fast. Drowning was certain if Chris didn't think on his feet. Cory was panicking. He was crying frantically and holding onto Rose.

Chris searched his mind for an idea. "The stairs!"

he shouted, then guided the children to a stairwell door. It was heavily rusted from years of hard weather, but Chris was able to force it open after a few kicks loosened the already melting ice in its joints. It didn't take long to climb the single flight of stairs to ground level, but a new problem had arisen. The exit door was blocked from the outside. A massive block of concrete had fallen against it. "We need to get to the truck before the water gets too high to use. I have to unblock the door from the other side," he said.

"You're gonna leave us here?" Rose asked.

"If you wanna be like the hero in the book, this is how it starts. You have to be brave." Chris backtracked rapidly down the stairway. The water had already risen knee level in the short time it took him to return to the floor below. Lapping waves threatened to push him off his feet, yet he struggled onward. By the time he reached the ramp, it had turned into a waterfall.

The sound of the heavy liquid bashing against the walls was deafening, amplified by the hollow corridors. At first, Chris couldn't think of a practical way to pass the obstacle. Fortunately, he had unconventional means of travel that only he had been blessed with. He looked down, hopeful to use nature's natural mirror, but the fast-moving current and debris wouldn't permit a reflection.

The next possible remedy found Chris' mind. He waded over to the nearest of the thawed vehicles. The outside mirror was attached too firmly to be worth the hassle, but there was a more easily accessible alternative. The brittle driver's window shattered behind the force of Chris' elbow. He reached in and yanked the rearview from above the dashboard. Stopping near the spewing ramp once again, he aimed the mirror so that it reflected the ground floor.

The bonds in Chris' body broke free. Each molecule glided above the waterfall, free from its bullying force. His body wasn't yet fully reformed when he made his first efforts towards the stairwell, blue particles stretching behind him like the tail of a comet. They would make chase until they were where they belonged, a part of his flesh.

Ice all over the city was melting. The resulting water searched out the lowest points, using the path of least resistance. A broad wave rushed into the underground structure. Chris was dunked by the churning, waist-deep water during his struggle to reach the children. Rose and Cory screamed out. They went up to the next flight of stairs to stay above water, but it didn't seem to be stopping its rise.

"Can you hear me?" Chris shouted, at last arriving at the door.

"The water is too high. We're gonna drown!" Rose responded, terror gripping her words.

"No you're not. I'm coming." Chris strained to push the hunk of rock away from the door, without success. It was far too heavy. Refusing to give up, he climbed on top of the block, hung from the pipes above, and used his legs in an attempt to shove it aside. It teetered an inch, however failed to go any further. "Fuck!" he yelled, angrily. Chris' exceptional peripheral vision saved his life. A flash of color brought his attention to a half-submerged sedan. He re-grasped the piping and lifted his body, wrapping his legs around it. The car narrowly missed him, smashed into the concrete obstacle. It rolled along in the accelerating, unpredictable rapids.

This solved the initial problem, but issues rarely come alone. The concrete was gone, but the water was moving too quickly for Chris to climb down. Furthermore, the truck was a complete loss. It would have to be abandoned, and a new plan formulated quickly.

Chris pulled himself into a straddled position on the pipes above, then removed the rifle from his back. "Stay away from the door and the water," he instructed Rose and Cory.

"We can't go any further. There's another door behind us, but it's locked. The water is almost here," Rose informed him. The water level in the cramped stairwell had risen higher than out in the open garage. It backed the children up against the door leading to the first floor of the office building. The tips of their toes were right up to the rising waterline.

"Cover your ears," said Chris. He gave the children a second to comply, then fired a shot into the door's locking mechanism. It jolted, but remained closed. A second shot did the trick. With nothing there to hold the door closed, the water flung it open violently. It continued to pour out until it was level with the water outside the enclosure.

"The water went down!" yelled Rose, but her and her brother stayed put.

"I'm coming in," said Chris, though he wasn't yet sure how he would accomplish the feat. He didn't have time to figure it out. Unexpectedly, the pipes gave way from the stress of Chris' additional weight, dumping him into the water. The current swept him away with the many swirling vehicles and dangerous debris.

"Mr. Nobody?" Rose called out. The ensuing silence rattled her to the core. Only swirling water and crashing objects could be heard. "Mr. Nobody!" she yelled louder, creeping down a couple of steps.

A ball of blue energy manifested above the steps in front of her. Rose screamed and dashed back to the inner door, frightened half to death. Rods of lightning extended from the center. The odor of scorched air added to the perceived horror, causing Cory to stuff his face against her torso, so that he couldn't see.

The dense circle of plasma began to spread apart, hollowing out in the center. It was so dark inside. The color black wouldn't come close to describing how dark. The children shrieked at the top of their lungs, until Chris walked from inside, dripping wet. The portal vanished. Chris fell to one knee, holding his head. It throbbed to the rhythm of his heartbeat. He didn't hear Rose calling out to him, "Mr. Nobody," because everything sounded like a low-frequency garble of random noises. The children hurried to assist him, worried about his precarious behavior.

"I'm OK. That kind of thing just takes a lot out of me is all," Chris reassured her, staggering to his feet. He breathed deeply to calm himself. "Let's get out of here before the water gets any higher."

"It's locked," said Rose, referring to the interior door.

"Not for long." Chris retrieved a small pouch from inside a pocket of his cargo pants. Inside were a set of small tools for picking various types of locking mechanisms. He had the door open within a few seconds.

The interior of the office building was not what the children expected. They gasped at the sight. The distraction was enough to draw their focus far away from the sound of thrashing water through the doorway behind them. "Everything is so new," said Rose.

Chris allowed the door to shut behind them. "The windows must be shatterproof. None of the weather could get in, so everything's the way it was the last time people were here."

Aside from scattered paper and a few overturned chairs, likely from panicked people fleeing in a state of emergency, the lobby was fairly pristine. That, plus a thin layer of dust accumulating over surfaces, were the only signs that something there had gone awry. There was a single, large desk closest to the main entrance, a small area for seating, and three hallways branching off in perpendicular directions in relation to one another. The decor was essentially simplistic with a warm color scheme, only disrupted by gray, stainless steel elevator doors down one of the corridors.

Just when the group was ready to explore for what hidden treasures may have been scattered about, they discovered that the soles of their footwear were submerged beneath a trickling sheet of water. "It's still rising," Chris said, more annoyed than worried. "We gotta go up, until the water clears." He found the door for the inner stairwell across from where they stood. The water splashed and rippled out, as he and the children strolled casually toward it.

A few meters away from perceived safety, Rose froze in her tracks. "What's that?" she asked.

Chris and Cory stopped short of the door. "What's what?" Chris asked.

"That noise."

Chris tuned his ear to scan his surroundings. A low-frequency rumble was beginning to vibrate the walls themselves. "Shit, run!" he exclaimed, plucking Cory from his feet. Rose hightailed it behind them, as they sprinted through the door and up the stairwell. They had nearly cleared the fourth floor when the building shook to the roots of its foundation. The quaking was accompanied by an eardrum-rattling boom. "Don't stop!" Chris yelled.

Rose responded by churning her legs with all her might. The resulting burst of speed allowed her to keep up with Chris, who was hauling Cory up the steps as fast as he could. The toddler clasped to his body with both arms and legs.

The thunderous explosion was from a wave of water that had crashed through the front of the skyscraper's lobby. The entire floor was submerged under several feet of water in a fraction of a second. However, fortune was once again on the side of the living. The weight of the crashing liquid held the door of the stairwell firmly shut, slowing the flood substantially.

Every fortune has a limit. The water assaulted whatever openings it could. Jets erupted from the slender spaces between door frames and ventilation ducts. It rampaged through every nook of one floor, then set its sights on the next. Each corresponding door of the stairwell burst open, like the geysers of Yellowstone.

"It's coming!" Rose exclaimed. She could hear the water fast approaching from below. As she passed the entrance for the twentieth floor, water shot from the perimeter of the door frame. The startle caused her to cry out and spiked her adrenaline furthermore, so much that she forgot how tired she actually was.

The door would hold. Chris' fear was sourced from the rising torrent below. Though he couldn't see it because of the solid cement staircase, the vibrations within alerted him that it was probably only a few flights beneath, and gaining fast. "Jesus! How much water could there be?" He said under his breath. He calculated that they could only stay ahead of the flood for a couple more floors before it caught up, but kept on running regardless.

The Lord must have heard his name. The rumbling faded away, then subsided completely. Chris halted, trusting his senses. In full fight-or-flight mode, Rose zipped around him without realizing. Only after the third ring of her name did she hear Chris calling out to her, "Rose! It stopped."

Light drippings were still audible, but it was clear that the immediate danger was gone for the time being. Chris was able to pry Cory from his body, following a few seconds of extreme effort. After coaxing him to the ground, he regressed the steps to see how close they had come to death. He needn't go far. Water lapped against the walls of the next flight down. They wouldn't have made it another five paces, had the meltwater continued its rampage. "Let's go," he demanded firmly.

"Go... where? I need... a break." Rose was barely able to get her words out. She panted heavily, folded over at the waist.

"We'll walk slow, but we can't stop. We need to get to the top."

"Why? The water already stopped."

"That's what we thought in the lobby. But, if you want to wait right here to see if it starts up again, then wait right here. I'm going up there," Chris pointed. He turned away and headed up.

Rose peeked around the corner at the dingy water. A large pocket of air escaped the surface. The sudden bubbling struck fear into the heart of the young girl. Up the steps, she dashed to safety.

***

The clatter of feet against the floor was the only sound that echoed in the hollow shell of the stairwell. Occasionally, loud creaks gave an eerie perception of danger, then dissipated in a series of dying reverberations. "I don't wanna walk anymore," Cory complained.

"Sometimes you gotta do things you don't wanna do," Chris responded, not slowing down.

Rose chimed in. She too had just about had enough. "How much farther do we have to go?"

"Penthouse."

"Penthouse?"

"All the way to the top floor. Rich people loved living at the top of the tallest buildings. This was an office building, so that's probably the only place in here to find a real bed. And, I'm sleeping in a real bed tonight." Chris was attempting to speak his wishes into existence.

"But, how far is it to the top?"

"Come on."

"Not until you answer my question!" Rose spoke with sass.

Chris shoved open the final door at the top of the steps. "If your smart ass was paying attention, you would have noticed that we ran out of steps," he replied.

Rose wasn't one to be defeated so easily. "If your smart ass was paying attention, you would have noticed there aren't any beds in here," she mumbled after exiting the stairwell. A portal blew open at her side.

"Say something else smart. I'll teleport your little ass to Timbuktu," Chris threatened.

"I don't even know where that is, and you probably don't either!"

"Try me."

The threat finally took hold, bringing Rose to silence. Chris closed the portal and moved toward the elevators. In the same motion, he pulled a large blade from a pouch along his waist, then shoved it between the doors to pry them apart. "Wait right here. And, I mean right here! Don't go over there, or over there. Stand right here in this spot," he instructed.

"You're gonna leave us here?" asked Rose.

"The only way to the penthouse is the elevator. I have to climb the ladder and get the doors open. It's too dangerous for either of you to go that way, so just wait and I'll come get you."

"How are you going to get us if that's the only way up there?"

"Just shut up and wait." Chris peeked his head into the elevator shaft, checking both above and below. As suspected, the lift itself was perched near the bottom of the seventy floors below, rather than the one above. This eliminated a major obstacle. A short climb was the only thing between him and a soft, plush mattress. He firmly grasped a rung of the service ladder, then shook it to be sure it was still in well enough condition to hold his weight. The steel mounts barely wiggled at all.

Satisfied, Chris pulled his flashlight from his pocket, powered it on, then slid it through one of the loops near the upper shoulder of his tactical vest so that the light shined upward. "Right there," he reiterated, with a finger gesture toward the floor under the children. Rose rolled her eyes and folded her arms across her chest.

The contact of Chris' boots with steel sent endless vibrations throughout the rectangular tube. Even the slightest sound was amplified in the tight, hollow space. The buildup of noise was nearly disorienting. Luckily, one floor didn't take very long to clear. Chris was jamming his Bowie knife between the penthouse doors a couple of minutes later. A few powerful wiggles pried them apart. The sudden opening caused Chris to lose his grip on the blade's handle. Gravity did the rest.

Curiosity killed the cat. In this case, Rose was the cat, only instead of death, she received an unsolicited haircut. Poking her head inside the shaft to see what was inside nearly cost her life, as the falling weapon sheared a tuft of hair from her scalp. She yanked her head back, thankful it was not severed from her body.

Obscenities filled the shaft as Chris berated Rose. She didn't hear him. His voice was drowned out by the rapid thump of her heart. The girl was as terrified as she had ever been in her entire life, and that was saying something, considering the way the last couple of days had unfolded.

A portal opened next to the children. Cory flinched and hid behind his sister. When Chris walked through, he peeked around her to see.

"Didn't I tell you to stay right there? I clearly said don't move. This is the type of thing that happens to hard-headed kids," Chris ranted.

"I'm sorry," Rose replied. Her voice was low and

dry. Fear had doused the flame of sassy retorts in her normal demeanor.

"Come on, let's go." Chris gestured through the pulsating doorway.

Fear has the ability to kill a flame, but it can also revive one as well. "Who? I'm not going in that thing!" Rose asserted.

"Well, we are. You can stay here by yourself. Come on, kid." Chris held his hand out for Cory to grab and made eye contact with him. Surprisingly, there wasn't much hesitation. Cory grabbed Chris' palm, allowing himself to be led through. Apparently, after Chris hauled him up a dizzying amount of stairs to prevent him from drowning to death, Cory learned where his bread was buttered. Survival was with the big guy.

Rose gasped audibly. "You little traitor!" she yelled, pumping her fist. There was no response, just silence, the echo of her own voice, and the sizzle of the portal's edge. She took in the lay of the land. Conditions were the same as the ground floor before—an undisturbed time capsule. The powerful sun radiated through large windows. Its glow glinted from office furniture, creating individual rays of light pointing in all directions. Airborne particles shimmered like glitter as they hovered through the golden streaks. It was beautiful. She imagined the hustle and bustle of the working class within the walls of that place. Why couldn't the world have waited to end until after she got to experience life, she pondered.

Creaking steel invaded tranquility. Having had enough adventure for a day, Rose thought it better to take her chances with her superhero and vanished through the portal. It took a second for her eyes to adjust to the low light conditions inside. Rose stood still, batting them for a moment, until she could make out the gist of her surroundings. "I can barely see anything," she notified her companions.

Chris started to walk toward the far side of the room. "I'm well aware," he said. "I'm in the same room as you." He slid back a thick velvet curtain, allowing sunlight to spill into the space. Both Cory and Rose shielded their eyes. The bold yellowish glow was powerful. Its warmth seemed to raise the temperature in the room in an instant.

"Wow, that's bright. Good thing the sun is on the other side of the building." Chris glanced around. He nodded his head and pursed his lips in a manner that showed his approval of their new place of shelter.

Both children followed with a, "Whoooooaaa," in unison. To them, the floors below were impressive. In contrast, the penthouse was grand. It was staged in a style between modern and futuristic. White trim accentuated smooth, silver counters, and glass-topped end tables. A large television hung above a stone electric fireplace. The wide screen was so thin that it appeared to be part of the wall that it clung to. Trinkets of all sorts were sprinkled about tastefully.

"What's all this stuff?" asked Rose.

"It's called furniture," Chris answered, over the top with sarcasm. He raised his hands skyward as if he were a wizard speaking of a forbidden secret.

"You're not funny," Rose pouted.

"Somebody thinks so."

Cory giggled with his mouth covered.

"You really are a traitor!" Rose accused him.

Surprisingly, the toddler stood up for himself. "Nu-uh!" he said, forcefully fist-pumping the air.

"I don't know where that came from, but I like it," Chris commented.

Rose wasn't having it. "Stay out of this! This is between me and him."

"Whatever. You stay here and argue with each other. I'm going to look around." Chris proceeded into one of two doorless entrances that led out of the central living area. He found himself in the kitchen. A faint stench encroached his nostrils. It was from long-spoiled food thawing with the swift invasion of the warm season. Luckily, the odor would remain bearable if the refrigerator remained shut.

Hardwood flooring gave a distinct sound to Chris' footprints as he passed the center island counter. He rubbed his fingers across the dark, mossy marble top. It was as smooth as the day it was installed. The cabinets creaked as he checked inside. They were empty. All but the one dedicated to liquor. Chris lifted a bottle of unopened Scotch from the shelf. "Definitely the good shit," he said. A quick mental review of his past alcoholism altered his train of thought. With a resentful lick of the lips, he placed the bottle back down and shut the cabinet door.

The following room was dim. The sunlight from the living room didn't quite reach to sufficiently get an eye on the inside. Nothing a slight curtain adjustment wouldn't fix. Illumination revealed contents of entertainment. Monitors, computers, and various game consoles surrounded a billiards table in the center. Chris pulled one of the balls from the leather corner pocket, then rolled it across the green felt. "Interesting," he mumbled to himself.

At last, Chris found what he was looking for. "Now that's what daddy is talking about," he said. The joy was short-lived. Among a puffy comforter, on a bed large enough to hold an extended family, were two mummified sets of remains. He inched closer and saw open pill bottles at their sides.

"Fuck!" Chris exclaimed. "Damn you, Jason Hilliard. This big-ass penthouse and you choose to kill yourself on a perfectly good bed." He stopped to get a closer look. "You nasty little suckers," he said, just realizing that the bodies were melded together in their final sexual positions. "Well, I guess it ain't the worst way to go out. Pop some pills, then go til' you're dead."

Small voices started to crescendo as Cory and Rose drifted closer toward the bedroom. The penthouse had curved around back to the living room. Chris hurried to keep them from entering. "You two still going?" he said. Rose glared at him with the intensity of starlight. He could almost feel the heat from her pupils. "If you wanna keep those beady little eyes you got, you'd better put them back in your head before I pluck 'em out," he threatened.

Rose saw through his distraction. "Why are you standing like that? What's in there?" she questioned, trying to get past.

Chris impeded her path each time she tried. "Nothing you need to see."

"Says who?"

"Says the only adult in here, now go sit on the couch."

Rose folded her arms over in submission. She took two steps toward the couch, then dashed back to the doorway. Chris went to block, but she spun around him like a running back dodging a linebacker. The maneuver completely caught him off guard. He started to count down, knowing what was coming next

"3... 2... 1..."

Rose shot past him screaming at the top of her lungs. She plowed into the couch so hard that the front legs nearly rose off the ground. Her face was buried deep into the cushions.

"See. What did I say? A hard head makes a soft ass," Chris chuckled.

"What's in there?" asked Cory, curious.

"Unless you wanna be crying next to your sister, you don't wanna know."

"OK," Cory replied in an imperturbable manner. He scaled the love seat and began to jump up and down, giggling blissfully.

Chris' face scrunched. "These are some weird ass kids," he muttered. Having had the full tour of the place, he refocused his attention outside the large windows. There were very few buildings as tall as the one they were in, and even less that were taller. This meant the skyline was only limited by the distant mountainous terrain.

Chris felt a slight bump at his right. Cory had abandoned his makeshift trampoline to get his own view of the scenery. "Can we go fishing in it?" he asked.

"I don't think there are any fish in there, kid. They live in bodies of water, like rivers and lakes."

"It looks like a river."

"Yeah, I guess it does." Chris recalled the river of his home. He thought of the words of wisdom his brother Gino had given him as they gazed upon the Mississippi. "The sooner you figure your shit out, the better things will get.

Things change, lil' brother. You gonna waste your time fighting against the current, or you gonna move with it?" he grumbled, not realizing he was speaking out loud.

Cory looked up at him. "Huh?"

Chris returned to the present from his mental time machine. "Nothing, kid. Just something somebody said to me a long time ago."

"I'm hungry," Cory complained.

"That's right. We haven't eaten all day, have we?" Chris paused in thought. "There's nothing in the kitchen, and we lost our food in the garage."

"There's gotta be something down there," Rose pointed downward. She had pulled herself together, joining Chris and her brother at the window.

"First problem is getting down there. Second problem is the time it would take to find a place likely to have nonperishable food at a high enough elevation to be above the water without a map."

"You do have a map."

"What are you talking about?"

"You took it from the bad people."

Chris felt embarrassed. The legendary combatant was beginning to regularly be outwitted by children. He took a deep breath before pulling the map from his pocket. It was laminated to limit wear and tear, especially from rough handling, along with the elements. It was an unknown blessing. Chris' pants were soaked from his rendezvous with the churning meltwater. Normal paper would be done for.

The map was loaded with essential information of the immediate area.

"What are all those red marks?" asked Rose. She stood on the tips of her toes to get a view.

"Looks like it's a bunch of locations where they set up camps. There's gotta be food at one of them."

"What about the water?"

Chris took heed of Rose's observation, using the map's key to determine elevation. "There," he said. "This is the highest point of all the camps. They're going to be there."

Rose clenched her hand into a tight ball. "Well, let's go!" she blurted.

"We're not going anywhere right now." Chris sucked the air right out of Rose's sail.

"Why not?"

"You can't sneak up to a base full of people in daylight, Einstein."

"Ein... what?"

Chris completely ignored Rose's ignorance on the reference and headed toward the bedroom. "I'm going to move that... thing out of sight, then find myself some dry clothes. Make sure your brother doesn't come in there until I'm done."

"What are we supposed to do?"

"I don't know. You're kids. Do kid stuff." Chris set out to complete the first of his tasks with a sigh. He stood at the foot of the bed, scratching his head. "I don't know what kind of conditions it took for you guys to end up like this, but what man wouldn't love to die and be mummified inside of his woman. I'm jealous," he said to the corpses. Sunlight bum-rushed the bedroom as the curtains were brushed aside. "Well, time to go," Chris continued as he ported them into the water below.

***

The bed wasn't salvageable, as Chris hoped it would be. Crusty clumps of God knows what had sunken deep into the fabric of the mattress. It joined its owners in the street below. "That's that on that." Chris dusted his hands as if he had done some sort of hard labor. "Now, let's see what kind of swag you're working with."

There weren't any drawers visible, so Chris went straight for the closet. Unexpectedly, there wasn't much of a selection. The only things present were a few simple dress suits and a lot of empty hangers. "I'm beginning to catch a pattern here," Chris said to himself. He grabbed a white button-down, pair of blue slacks, clean underwear, and got changed.

The kids were huddled around the glass coffee table when Chris stepped into the living room. Random items were piled on top. They seemed to be taking some sort of inventory. "What are y'all doing now?" Chris asked.

"Trying to figure out what this stuff is," Rose replied.

"Where did you even get all that?"

"Everywhere. There's all kinds of stuff in here."

Cory raised a rectangular object into the air. "What's this?" he asked.

"An alien number box!" Rose responded.

Chris couldn't help but correct her. "That's a calculator."

Next, Cory lifted a long, slender piece of plastic. "What's this?"

"Duh! That's an alien number stick."

That was about enough for Chris to shoot himself. "Really, Rose? That's a ruler."

"No. That's not a ruler. I'm a ruler. Ruler of the whole world. All hail la reina Rosalia!"

"I think the lack of food is eating away at your brain." Chris opened a smaller portal. He shoved his soaked clothing through, then closed it.

"What did you just do to your clothes?" asked Cory.

"I'm drying them." Chris could see that the children were clueless. "Come here," he instructed them. "Look out the window. You see that building right there?"

"Which one?" asked Rose.

"The one right across the street with the dark brown bricks."

"Oh yeah, I see it."

"Look on its roof."

"Your clothes!" Cory shouted with excitement.

"I'm using the sun to dry them so I don't have to wear this stuff for long."

Rose chuckled as she just noticed Chris' attire. "You look funny," she teased.

"Li'l girl, I look good in whatever I put on," he replied, popping the collar of his new dress shirt.

"Yeah, OK," Rose replied, sarcastically.

"Like you would know what swagger is. Looks like you've had that stuff on since you were his age."

The comment must have hit a nerve. Rose launched

the calculator at Chris' head. He ducked just in time. The device broke apart against the thick window.

"What the hell is wrong with you, you she-devil?"

"Don't make fun of me!"

"You started it."

"I'll finish it too!"

"You better finish your scrawny ass over there on that couch while you still got one to sit on. I don't know what your uncle and aunt did, but I will kick your li'l ass!"

Rose stormed out of the room toward the kitchen.

"What is wrong with that girl?" Chris asked Cory. The young boy shrugged his shoulders and returned to his table of gadgets to assess. Chris' intuition told him that there was something deeper to Rose's emotional explosion. Sure, she had been a firecracker from the moment he saw her attempting to kick her way out of the mitts of a kidnapping giant, but this particular reaction felt a little over the top, even for her. After giving her a minute to settle, he stepped into the kitchen. "What's up with you?" he questioned. "What was that about back there?"

Rose spoke without turning around. Her gaze was held outside the windowpane. "There aren't any pictures of the woman."

Chris had noticed and had his own assumptions why, still, he didn't expect Rose to know anything about the subject of wealthy men and their mistresses spending time in seldom-used real estate. He chose to divert. "What does that have to do with your attitude?"

"My tios said that people used to keep photos around their homes of the people they love. That woman isn't in any of the pictures. The man didn't love her."

Diversion unsuccessful, Chris decided to lie rather than have an uncomfortable conversation. "What are you talking about? She is in the pictures. She's right there with him on the refrigerator."

"That's not her."

"How would you know?"

"The dead lady had black hair, and look," Rose pointed, "there's no tattoo."

"She probably dyed her hair blonde and got a

tattoo."

"I'm a kid. I'm not stupid," Rose retorted.

"Whatever. What does this have to do with you acting like a maniac and throwing a calculator at my face?"

"I'm mad!"

"Mad at what?"

"At stupid people like him!" Rose pointed aggressively at the man in the photo. "He was supposed to love her, but he chose to die with the other lady! My parents chose to die without me. Maybe they didn't love me either." Tears flooded her eyes. The puddle at her feet was nearly deep enough to drown inside.

Chris was astonished. How could a preteen be perceptive enough to piece together so many hidden clues to come up with such a complex, and likely accurate, deduction? Most of the adults he knew would be blind to such notions, but there was only so much time for him to ponder the thought. "Don't think that way," he said, kneeling down to clear her tears. "I'm sure your parents loved you. A lot of things happened in the world. A lot of people died. Think of all the parents that were out working when the world broke, but couldn't make it home to be with the ones they cared for. This asshole might have chosen to be stupid, but not all of us had a choice."

"But Cory and me have nobody."

"Wrong. You have Mr. Nobody."

Rose grinned weakly. "You had a family?" she asked after a moment of thought.

"Yeah," Chris replied, with a hitch in his speech.

"Did they die too?"

"How about we change the subject? Death is too sad. We should be talking about stealing this food."

Rose dropped her jaw. "Stealing?"

"What did you think we were going to do, just walk up and ask for it?"

The look on her face signaled that she hadn't thought about it. Chris threw his hands up. "You mean to tell me you're smart enough to figure out all that other stuff, but you didn't think about how we were going to get the food?"

"Are you making fun of me again?" Rose was getting riled up again.

"You got any more calculators?"

"No."

"Then, that's exactly what I'm doing."

This time Rose laughed it off.

"So, we're good?" Chris asked.

"Yeah. We're good."

Cory didn't seem to pay much attention to Chris and Rose returning to the room. He had found wonder in what a stapler could do to a sheet of paper. "Careful with that. Don't stick your finger in there, unless you want a hole in it," Chris said to him, before he took a seat on the bleach-white reclining chair and unfolded the map again. He was eager to come up with a game plan.

"Whatcha looking for?" Rose asked from over his shoulder.

"I'm trying to figure out how to get there. Half the city is underwater. Can't just go on foot."

"Why don't you just teleport us there?" Rose suggested.

"I have to see a place before I can open a portal to it. You think I would be driving around, running from a flood, or climbing an elevator shaft like a regular human if I could just poof myself wherever I wanted?"

Rose scratched the tip of her chin. "You're looking at it on the map now," she said, as if it was the obvious solution.

"That doesn't count. I have to actually have been there."

"Ooh," said Rose, long and drawn out.

In that moment, it clicked. "There," said Chris. He smacked the back of his hand against the map. It was the hotel where the saga of Chris, Rose, and Cory had begun, and it was just a few clicks from the camp. It was also just high enough in elevation to likely be above water.

Chris' body language revealed to Rose that he had, at last, figured it all out. "So, when are we going?" she asked.

Not ready for another argument, Chris indulged her.

"After dark."

"Cool." Rose gave him the thumbs up.

Several loud clanks of plastic against glass rang out.

"Hey! Quit that!" Chris yelled.

Cory was smacking the stapler against the tabletop. "It's broken. Nothing's coming out anymore," he explained.

"It's not broken, it's out of staples. You know what, it's time to get some sleep anyway. It's gonna be a long night, and tomorrow's gonna be even longer."

"Where are we sleeping? The people are in the bed," Rose rationalized.

"People? What people?" asked Cory.

Chris gave Rose a look of disapproval. "She's making a joke," he replied. "You're sleeping on the couch. Boots off. Coats off. I saw an extra blanket in the closet. I'll be right back."

Chris returned to witness a pillow brawl had broken out. Rose and Cory pummeled one another with two-tone, decorative pillows. He watched briefly, with joy in his heart, until he decided enough was enough. "Alright, chill out. I told you, we have plenty of stuff to do tomorrow," he said, bouncing a third pillow off both of their heads in one accurate toss.

The children laid down on opposite ends of the main couch. Chris covered them with the blanket, then retreated to pull the curtains closed. He barely got seated and detracted the leg rest of the recliner before he heard snoring. The kids were exhausted. It had been a taxing day, but there were far more of the sort to come.

Complete darkness occupied every space. The Sun was gone, at least for the meantime. Chris eased out of his seat. He peeled back the curtain to gauge outside conditions. The water level had hardly changed. Moonlight gleamed from the still surface below. The children were still in a deep slumber. In fact, they dreamed so deeply that Chris could practically see thought bubbles above their heads. It was time, but first things first. He wasn't in the proper attire for this kind of operation. On the roof in less than a second, a touch of hand clarified that his clothing was sufficiently dried by the raging Sun.

He dressed quickly. Porting such a distance was a feat that was certain to take a tremendous toll on Chris' damaged mind. He filled his lungs with as much air as he could to flush his bloodstream with oxygen. Mind locked on the lobby where he watched Rose's remaining family slain mercilessly, space erupted open, and Chris stepped through.

There was a hitch in travel. Chris expected to step onto solid ground, or at worst, into a couple feet of water, but instead splashed down into what amounted to a slow-moving river. The flood had reached farther than calculated. To make matters worse, Chris' brain was pierced by pain. He was fighting to stay conscious beneath at least six feet of water. The absence of escaping air bubbles meant that there was none left in Chris' lungs. Nothing moved for a time, until his head exploded above the surface. He gasped for air. Violent coughs cleared his compromised respiratory system of moisture. As he had many times before, Chris had cheated death.

There wasn't time to dwell on the experience. The mission was to continue. Chris swam to the front doorway. He peeked out to scan both directions of the avenue. Nothing moved or made even the slightest sound, but there was a growing situation. The water seemed to stretch as far as the eye could see. If there was no camp, he and the kids' chances of survival would plummet. Not one to give up, Chris propelled himself across the water's surface. The map displayed a steep incline beginning the next block over, culminating exactly where the camp was marked. There were still great odds that it was clear, and whatever organization this was would be there. So, Chris kept on stroking for what seemed to be eternity. There was a great difference in the energy expenditure between jogging a city block and swimming one. His strategy was methodical and continuous, as to preserve what vigor he had remaining while limiting noise.

A glorious sight refueled Chris' resolve. A collage of lights flickered on the edge of the horizon. The camp was undoubtedly occupied. He picked up the pace slightly, but not so much as to sacrifice stealth. The water's depth gradually decreased in relation to distance from the destination. When Chris felt his feet touch the road below, he lengthened his body to keep all, short of his head, hidden beneath the shallows. His gears were turning. The map had absolutely zero detail on the camp's actual setup, so he would need to plan on the fly.

Chatter was audible and not far off. The tone of the voices was loud and unrestrained. The soldiers didn't seem to have any fear of being located or attacked, an advantage for a lone intruder. The small base of operations was in the center of an old park. Raggedy, rusty playground equipment was among the portable tents and light fixtures. A circle of vehicles and concrete barricades made up the outer perimeter.

Chris left the concealment of the floodwaters for that of nearby patches of shrubbery. From there, he mentally tagged each of the soldiers in view. He would keep track of their locations as he moved around. The first step of accomplishing his agenda was to locate the supply of food. It was probably the easiest task on his checklist. A plume of heated gas escaping the chow hall was equal to a large sign reading, "food here." It was his lucky day, indeed.

The tent was fairly close to the camp's boundary. Chris rounded it swiftly. He was sure to stay way out of sight, until he was directly behind the chow tent. Once there, he scanned for guards. Only one roamed around the perimeter alone. Chris timed his walk at roughly fifteen minutes. It was more than enough time to work with.

As soon as the guard began his next revolution, Chris went to work. He slipped from the bushes, dashing between the front and rear bumpers of two SUVs with armor plating, capable of deflecting small munitions. Curiously, Chris peeked through the rear window of the one on his left, and his jaw fell wide open. "I can't believe how easy they made this," he mumbled to himself. The rear compartment was stacked to the roof with boxes of food and water. The group of militants hadn't bothered to unload anything more than what they needed for the day. They probably didn't plan on staying long.

No matter the reason, Chris was about to kill two birds with one big rock. He had already planned on taking a vehicle, now rather than having to rob the tent and transport the goods to wheels, it was only necessary to hot-wire the ignition, then follow up with a clean getaway. The door was unlocked. Once in the driver's seat, Chris ripped away the panel hiding the electrical wiring and used the blade on his multi-tool to prepare the correct cord for splicing. The cord wasn't correct. It had been a long time since Chris had to hot-wire a vehicle. He erred, setting off the alarm. "Dammit!" he shouted, fumbling to get it right.

More shouting preceded, but not from Chris. Every soldier in the camp had been alerted, and no doubt were on the way. "Who the fuck is that guy?" the first on the scene asked his companion.

"Ask him when he's dead." The responding man let off shots into the SUV's window.

Chris flinched. After realizing the glass was bulletproof, he continued attempting to get the truck running.

"Bullets won't get through there you dumb-ass," yelled the first soldier. "Grab the RPG out of that truck." The command had come too late. "Fuck! Let's go," he ordered, as Chris got the engine started and peeled off.

A dozen others joined the pursuit, in half as many vehicles. Passengers emptied magazine after magazine, uselessly. Rounds bounced off the rear of the SUV with no effect. Chris fishtailed around corners with precision. Each turn was purposeful. He had memorized the elevation patterns of the map and was determining which roads would be safe to use, based on the water's current depth.

Everything was going as planned until a bullet finally made entry and zipped past Chris' scalp. The glass was more bullet-resistant than bulletproof. Enough smacks to the same spot were bound to give way to penetration. Exploding RPGs compounded the problem.

"Desperate times call for desperate measures," Chris quoted. He veered down a familiar street. Halfway down, moonlight glanced off the top, too reflective to be asphalt. Chris pushed the pedal to the floor. Suddenly, he vanished into darkness, leaving his enemies to crash into an urban lagoon.

A deafening crash violently separated Cory and Rose from their tranquil rest. They both screamed at the top of their lungs, dropping down to the floor for cover. The entire room shook heavily enough to knock the mounted television from the living room wall. The children whimpered helplessly when silence took root. "Mr. Nobody?" Rose called out. There wasn't a response. Finally, she mustered the courage to peer from behind the couch.

"No, Rosi. Don't go," Cory pleaded.

"I gotta see what it is," she responded, inching toward the source of the ruckus. An opaque veil of dust started to settle in the kitchen. Rose eased her way inside to find a truck parked on top of a series of crushed cabinets. "What the?" she uttered.

The door of the truck opened suddenly. Rose staggered backward, not knowing what or whom to expect. Chris stumbled out, barely able to keep his balance. He held both sides of his head tightly, his face scrunched in a painful knot.

"Mr. Nobody, what's wrong?" asked Rose.

Chris couldn't hear her, for he was in agony. Glass crunched beneath his feet. A small break in the pain allowed him to open his eyes enough to see what it was. Broken liquor bottles from the center island were scattered around the floor. One remained intact. Chris nearly toppled over as he attempted to pick it up. He struggled with the cork. Rose watched, totally confused. Eventually, Chris settled for cracking off the bottle's neck against the outside of the SUV. Adam's apple dribbled up and down his neck with each gulp. The goal was to avoid passing out, however, this time the effort would end in failure. Chris went completely limp.

***

What was left of the blurry kitchen slowly came into focus. The fridge was toppled onto its side, under a pile of cracked wood. Other appliances, such as the dishwasher, were also displaced far from their installed locations. Even the double-sided sink found itself impaled through a wall. Chris' body was numb, but the feeling in his face was returning. He could tell from dull pokes on his cheeks. A pool of saliva stretched from his mouth as he struggled to roll onto his back. "What the heck, Cory?" he sluggishly moaned. The poking was courtesy of the toddler and a stick from one of the crushed cupboards.

"I thought you were dead. Rosi said you weren't, but you looked like it."

"Well, I'm not, so cut it out." Chris mustered the strength to sit up. He looked around to check the damage he had done to the truck. Satisfied that it was still in working condition, he went to the next assessment. "Speaking of your sister, tell her to get in here. I don't have the energy to call her."

"Rosi's not here."

"What do you mean she's not here? Where is she?" Concern spiked Chris' adrenaline, driving him to his feet.

Cory pointed towards the elevator shaft. The doors had been pried open again. "Out there somewhere."

"What? Why would she go out there?" Chris hurried in that direction. On the way, he noticed sunlight creeping from the edges of the curtains. It informed him of roughly how long he had been out, and it was much longer than his previous spells.

Cory followed him to the entrance. "It's so hot. There isn't any water in here," he said.

Chris, then, observed Cory's appearance. He was dressed down to a T-shirt, and the legs of his thermal underpants were rolled above his knees. Beads of sweat pumped from his pores. The child wiped his forehead with the back of his arm.

"So, she went to get some," Chris inferred. "Both of you should know how dangerous it is for her to go out there by herself. She should have waited until I woke up."

"What if you never woke up?"

Cory had a fair point. Still, there was only one move from there. Chris had to find Rose's location before something bad happened, and there were about seventy floors worth of possibilities. He crouched down to meet Cory at eye level. "Listen, I have to go find her and bring her back here, but you have to promise me you'll stay here."

"Why? I don't wanna stay here all by myself."

"I can't risk using my powers right now. It makes me sick if I do too much. Climbing down that ladder is the only way out, and it's way too dangerous for you. Now, I need your promise, so I can go get your sister."

Cory crossed his arms with displeasure, something he likely picked up from Rose. "OK," he reluctantly agreed.

"While I'm gone, take those thermals off and put your pants back on. You'll feel a lot cooler without them on, plus I don't wanna see you walking around in your underpants anyway," Chris instructed, easing onto the service ladder.

The elevator doors closed under Chris' guidance. Leaving them open with a stubborn 6-year-old having access wasn't the brightest idea. Chris stared straight down the shaft for a view of color that didn't belong. Thankfully, there was only the cold steel of the roof of the elevator far below. Rose had, at least, made it out of the shaft.

Chris climbed out to the open floor. "Think," he told himself. "If I was a preteen, where would I look for water? Restroom? Employee lounge?" Immediately, he corrected his train of thought. Rose didn't think like a typical preteen. "Where would I go?" he asked himself. Now with the right question, the answer became obvious. "The flood." Into the stairwell, and down the stairs, he jogged.

As Chris approached the last few floors from where the water level had peaked, he slowed to a stroll. He pulled his service gun but kept it aimed at the floor. One could never be too cautious. Footsteps that were not his own echoed from the walls. They sounded hard and frantic. The person grumbled angrily under their breath. Chris shoved his gun back in the holster and leaned against the wall to watch Rose pace back and forth, voicing her frustrations aloud.

"Not what you thought, huh?" asked Chris. The

reaction he got wasn't the one he expected, but it was the one he should have.

"What are you doing here?" Rose questioned, aggression all over the tone of her voice.

This made it easy for Chris to pick a fight for his entertainment. "Me? I came to save your life," he replied.

"I don't need your help!"

"Clearly. Well, go ahead. Drink up."

The comment left Rose seething. She had come to fill her backpack of scavenged bottles with floodwater but instead found that it was a dark brown soup of disgusting muck. "I hate you," she menacingly spoke.

"Awww, how sweet," Chris replied, continuing his pestering. At last, he decided that he had enough fun for the time being. "Come on. Your brother is waiting on us in his underwear, and we've got somewhere to be." He glanced at Rose's legs. She was down to her thermals as well. "I see where he got the idea," he murmured. Rose resisted the urge to argue, so the two made their way back to the penthouse with urgency.

Chris divided the doors once more. He and Rose climbed out of the shaft before an awaiting Cory, who bum-rushed his sister with a hug. The show of love melted her salty mood. "I missed you too," she said, then asked of Chris, "What are we gonna do about water?"

"We already have water," he replied. Casually, Chris made his way to the SUV, popping open the rear hatch. Rearranging a few boxes ended with the desired result. "Here we go." He ripped open one of the many cardboard boxes. Afterwards, he held out two bottles of spring water for the children. They took them, then he broke the seal on one for himself.

Cory struggled to remove his lid, so Rose did it for him, then handed it back. Neither of the three wasted a moment. Each bottle was sucked dry within a few gulps. Rose inhaled deeply, after almost a half minute of breathless hydration. "Now, what do we do?" she asked Chris.

"Time to go. If we stay around here much longer, your brother's gonna turn into a baked turkey," he teased.

"A turkey? I'm not a turkey!" Cory emphatically stated.

"It was a...like you would know what a metaphor is. Just get in the truck." Chris saw that Cory had changed his pants as he was told, but Rose was still improperly dressed. "But first, you go change your pants. Don't leave those thermals either. Grab your brother's and put them both in your bag. You might need them where you're going," he instructed. Chris' words triggered something he had overlooked. "Bag? Where did you get that bag anyway?"

"Out there. It's cool, isn't it?"

"Yea, sure. Just change so we can go."

"What's wrong with these? I like them," Rose responded.

"Like I told your brother, they're basically underwear, now change. Your pants are on the floor, where you shouldn't have left them in the first place."

Rose finally did as asked. When she returned to the kitchen, Chris and Cory were already loaded in the truck, so she climbed into the passenger seat. "Where are we going anyway?" she asked.

"North. Put on that seat belt."

Rose fumbled with the strap. She had no idea how to use it.

"Like this," Chris guided her, using his own seat belt as an example. "One more thing. Getting this truck out of here is going to take a lot of energy. If I pass out again, don't move. Just sit here, until I wake up. Snacks are in that box, water in that one, but you don't leave this truck. Got it?" He leered into Rose's eyes.

"Why are you looking at me?" she asked as if innocent of any past transgressions.

"Don't play with me. You heard what I said."

"Alright, sheesh," Rose surrendered.

A similar gaze to Cory rendered an understanding head nod. Satisfied, Chris dropped the SUV into darkness.

***

Water trickled between the cracks of a paved

alleyway. Ice had squeezed and shoved chunks of cement in every direction, destroying what was once a uniform surface. Surrounding buildings blocked the rising Sun. This left the entire corridor in shadow. Light breezes matured into hefty gusts. Drastic changes in temperature were the likely cause. Abnormal amounts of small cyclones would manifest, then fade away just as quickly, leaving loose rubbish aloft in their wake.

The amount of trash littering the alley was about to take a spike. A mound of cherry and marble fell from thin air. A half second later, the SUV landed on top, flattening the kitchen decor even further. The three passengers bobbed up and down with the truck's suspension. Cory unbuckled his seat belt and leaned over the center console. "Is he dead again?" he asked Rose.

Chris squinted his eyes at Cory. "No. I'm not dead runt. Sit down and put your seat belt back on."

"How come you're still awake this time?" asked Rose.

"How am I supposed to know? I'm not a doctor."

"Duh. You're not smart enough to be a doctor."

"That's coming from somebody that thought underwear were pants." Chris started the engine to get going. The thick, heavy-duty tires rolled over the ruined cabinets, like a stack of harmless toothpicks. The rubber was far too thick for worry of damaging penetration.

"It's getting really, really hot," Cory whined.

Rose had the same feeling. "Why did it get hot so fast?" she asked. "It's never been like this before."

"The planet's orbit is getting out of control. This isn't even the worst of it. The bum is going to come faster and get way hotter. That's why we gotta get north, before it's too bad to survive here."

Smooth was an accurate description of the truck's ride, however, leaving the cover of the alleyway had consequences. The Sun beamed down, a large bulbous fireball. Almost every surface reflected its golden fury.

"It's so big," said Rose. She squinted her eyes, and used her hand to peek at the massive star.

"Don't look up at it like that," Chris demanded. "You

could go blind." He started to remove his long-sleeved shirt, while careful to maintain control of the vehicle. Down to his T-shirt, but still uncomfortably hot, Chris turned on the AC, with a few waves of the finger. Boiling hot air escaped the vents, before morphing into a moderate chill. "Good. It works," he said, relieved.

Rose placed her hand in front of the vent, as she had before in Chris' pickup. "It's cold now," she noted, surprised at the change.

"That's how it works. Hot when you need it. Cold when you need it." Chris kept his eyes peeled for trouble. Running into enemies at this point would be disastrous. He feared that they and the unknown army would more than likely cross paths again, but better late than now, in his deteriorating condition.

The affected areas of Columbia varied greatly. Shallow streams flowed over the highest hill crests, and deep swells sloshed through its valleys. Large chunks of road were washed away. Many homes and buildings collapsed into themselves. Others were completely ripped from their foundations, to float miles away from their origins.

Chris drove slowly, sure to choose his route out of town carefully. How bogus it would be to survive gunfights, plane crashes, bombs, and countless other death-worthy scrapes, just to die unceremoniously in a flash flood. People sang songs, and wrote stories about fatal ends to heroes, but nobody would write about that. Not unless they were making fun of him.

The further northwest that Chris drove, the more normal things seemed to become. With no speed limit in the degrading world, he was able to easily outpace the bum, putting hours of distance between them and its burning rage. At some point, Chris slowed his pace. He was sure it was safe to do so. The children had fallen asleep hours ago. This left him with a bit of time to think.

Clear blue skies and puffy white clouds were a rare sight during the cold season, but the Sun's heavy hand had cleared away the gloom on its march closer to the Earth. It brought to mind a game Chris used to play with his son. It was a game most people played with their children, at one time or another. "What does that one look like?" Chris would ask. He could still feel the blades of green grass ruffled against his neck, as they lay side by side in the yard. "A duck!" C.J. would reply, with his finger pointed to the heavens.

This would go on until Melissa ruined it with her orders. "If y'all don't get y'all asses off my grass, I swear before God!" she would yell. Chris thought she always ruined the fun. He missed her greatly.

Rose stretched her arms to the sky, and yawned so deeply that her jaw nearly touched the floorboard. "Where are we?" she asked, catching the hills rolling by her window.

"Does it matter? It's not like you would know if I told you."

Rose gave Chris the look that women have passed down to their daughters for centuries. The, 'answer the damn question that I asked you!' look. It was well interpreted. "Heading towards Panama. We need to cross into Central America before the pathway thaws and floods over. Now, go ahead and tell me you don't know what Panama or Central America is," said Chris.

"I know all the places in America, thank you!" Rose replied with an attitude.

"Well congratulations," Chris responded, sarcastically. Feeling belittled, Rose balled up her fist, and whacked him on the arm. "Ouch! That hurt, you... you short creature!" Chris shouted. Rose snapped her fist into his bicep again. She let out a grunt, signifying that she put everything she had into it. "Ouch!" Chris yelled again. He swerved the truck a little. "OK, OK, calm down and stop hitting me." Rose folded her arms in her usual form of frustration. Her eyebrows angled down, and her bottom lip protruded. "So, now you're gonna pout like a little girl?"

"I am a little girl!"

"I thought you were a superhero starting her origin story. You damn sure hit like one." Chris rubbed his tender muscle.

"I said, don't make fun of me!"

"I'm not. First, we have to get far enough north to survive the bum, then I'll teach you some moves."

"You mean it?" Rose was excited.

"Yea. Now how about we listen to some music."

"You're gonna sing?"

"Hell no... I mean no. The radio."

"The radio works?"

"When you have one of these it does." Chris pulled an mp3 player from his pocket, powered it on, and plugged it into the SUV's USB port. The soothing melodies of 90's R&B pushed from the speakers. Actual music, thought Rose. Her eyebrows arched with pleasure. It was nothing like she had ever heard before. "What is it?" she asked.

"It's called 'Fortunate'. It's from a time when artists made real music."

"What's the difference between real music and fake music?"

"Not real as in the sense of real or fake. I just meant good music. Music with a purpose. Something everybody can relate to in one way or another." Chris raised the volume a little, and began to bob his head to the rhythm. "Just listen to the words," he added.

Rose focused her attention on the lyrics. The words spoke of love, an emotion she had a very vague concept of, but enough to feel and comprehend it. Before she realized, her head was swaying to the sound as well. "I like it!" she announced with joy.

"Of course you do," said Chris. "Would have to be dead not to enjoy this song." He raised one of his hands off the wheel, and put his body into the movement.

"What are you doing?" Rose giggled.

"What do you mean, what am I doing? I'm dancing."

"That's dancing?" She laughed until a tear touched her cheek.

"Oh, that's funny? Like you can do better."

Rose waved her hands over her head to the beat. She closed her eyes and snapped her fingers, it was like activating dormant programming. She had never danced a day in her life, but it was there for her on cue.

"Yeah!" Chris encouraged. "Now we're getting it."

Cory peeled his eyes open, awakened by the party going on in the front seat. "What are you doing?" he sluggishly mumbled.

"Dancing!" Rose was smiling from ear to ear.

Cory rubbed the sleep from his eyes, still lost about what was going on. Chris and Rose just kept on dancing their way down the road to the perfection of Melissa's favorite playlist.

***

The Sun, in all its luminous glory, was at its highest point in the sky, but had lost its consistent grip with time. Climate and cycles of day were changing more and more sporadically. Chris couldn't understand what was causing things to unravel so quickly. He was no scientist, and it would take one to diagnose the world's condition. Ironically enough, they were probably all dead.

Chris continued driving northwest towards Panama, only stopping for bathroom breaks, to eat, and to search for abandoned cars, and stores for gasoline. So far, he had only been mildly successful, barely enough to keep the trip going. Something would have to change.

Still, Chris hadn't survived so long by wandering around aimlessly, depending on pure luck of the draw. He made educated decisions based on probability, and probability was high that untapped resources would be scattered around major cities. He could tell that the concentration of people left in the world was too low to plunder most places, due to the low concentration of people he had run into over the last few years. The world's population seemed so scarce that one could set off a nuke in the middle of Manhattan and would likely avoid more than a handful of casualties.

With that in mind, Panama City was the destination. Chris navigated what remained of the damaged highways carefully. Ice still clung tight to road signs and hanging traffic control devices. Overturned vehicles littered the roadsides. Most had been burned to a crisp, then frozen over several times, in a war of the most extreme temperatures.

The truck rolled to a crawl in a massive parking lot. Its wheels sloshed through growing puddles from slow-melting ice. Retail stores, as such, were the best locations to get lucky. A large star was the only remaining piece of a logo high on the storefront. All the letters had crashed to the ground to be reclaimed by mother nature.

The hundreds of vehicles piled up across the asphalt were in just as bad condition as most Chris had come across. It would be a waste of time to check them for fuel, but there was a beacon of hope in the form of a mechanic shop attached to the side of the supermarket.

"What do you think?" Chris asked, pointing in its direction.

Rose looked out of the window and scrunched her nose. "What do I know? I'm just a kid," she replied.

"Here you go again. You're not a kid anymore. You're my sidekick."

"Sidekick? I'm nobody's sidekick!" Rose informed Chris. "If anything, you're my sidekick."

"Oh really?"

"Yes really. This is my story. You're just in it."

"You really are something else, you know that?" Chris chuckled. "So, if I'm a sidekick, then what does that make lil' buddy in the back seat?"

"My other sidekick. He's sidekick number one, and you're sidekick number two."

Cory leaned into the front seat again. "Like the boy in the comic, with the yellow cape, that helps the flying girl beat all the bad guys?" he asked.

"Yep!"

"So, not only am I a sidekick, but I'm the least important member of the team too?"

Rose pointed her finger to the roof. "Exactly!" she exclaimed. "It's my story, so it goes how I say it goes."

"Well, in your story, I hope we get out to search that place."

"Smart a..." Rose began, before abruptly cutting her words short. She didn't want to be left walking after Chris' past threats.

"I don't wanna get out," Cory stated, fearful of

unknown danger.

"You have to," said Chris. "This isn't a movie. It's never safe to stay in the car alone."

Of course, Cory had never seen a movie before, but he understood what Chris was trying to say. After a second thought, he figured he'd rather be with the man with superpowers anyway.

Crossing the lot was like solving a maze. Chris was filling up with annoyance as he swerved between the beaten vehicles. He would drive into a dead end, then reverse out, only to drive into another. After getting nowhere fast, he decided it would be better to travel on foot. Besides, getting his truck trapped too far into the maze would be a rookie mistake, and a colossal one.

"Come on. We're walking from here," he said, opening the driver's door. He snatched his rifle from the truck. A check of its magazine and port only took a couple of seconds.

The children gathered their courage and followed him out. There wasn't much difficulty in traversing the debris field. All the cars, trucks, shopping carts, and scrap metal had been spread at random, leaving enough space to move practically unobstructed.

Surfaces were coated with loose tufts of snow and ice. Though fairly warm, the weather was much more pleasant than it had been in Bogota. Long-missing sights and sounds emerged around the trio. Nature's call transformed into something entirely different during the warm season.

"Birds are here," said Chris. "Must mean we're in a good spot for now." The rifle clanked as he slung it across his shoulder.

"Birds told you that? You can talk to animals too?" asked Cory. He seemed to be kind of weirded out.

"No. Birds can just sense things that people can't. If the Bum or Freeze was too close, they wouldn't be here. It's probably too cold north from here, and too hot south. If we stick with the birds, we should be alright."

Cory was silently eyeballing Chris' rifle from behind Rose. When it moved, his gaze moved with it. Chris noticed, as he did most things. "Don't worry," he said. "Guns don't hurt people. People hurt people. This one is to make sure people don't hurt us." The explanation seemed to placate Cory for the moment.

The closer they got to the building, the more odd things seemed to become. Chris started to notice things that shouldn't be. Even from afar, the windows looked too clean, the debris too sparse, and the ground looked to be trampled up with high frequency. He pulled the rifle from his shoulder, holding it at the ready, then prepared to turn back.

It was too late. Before Chris knew it, about two dozen rifles were trained on him. Some were from the roof, and others from behind the scattered patches of vehicles thrown about the parking lot. Red dots covered a large portion of his torso. Rose and Cory stood stiff as boards, leaving their eyes to do the panicking.

"I wouldn't do too much moving if I were you," said a rather rotund fellow stepping from the shop door. A radio cable coiled from his ear into the collar of his urban camouflage uniform. "Moving makes us nervous. Nervous fingers don't tend to stay off the trigger."

At one time, the military fatigues worn by the others would have given Chris comfort. Now, its meaning did the exact opposite. The powers that be were the ones who triggered the beginning of the end in the first place.

With this in mind, Chris ran calculations in his head, but the numbers weren't good. He might only take out half the group before a splitting migraine disabled him, even at full strength, so in his current condition he didn't have a chance. Might have been a good way to go out, had it not been for the children. They made his reaction far more diplomatic and sane. Chris released his grip on his rifle, leaving it to dangle from his neck by the strap, and slowly raised his hands high above his head.

"That's it. Just take it easy," said the man. He gestured to one of his acquaintances. A taller, slender fellow carefully approached and removed the rifle from Chris's shoulder. An efficient pat-down rendered nothing of particular danger or interest to them. Assured the threat was minimal, the man retreated to the side of his superior. "Who are you?" asked the leading man. He seemed genuinely curious.

"Mr. Nobody," Chris replied.

The man scoffed. "Mr. Fucking Nobody," he mumbled under his breath. "Who are the kids?"

"My responsibility."

The man chuckled this time. "Mr. Fucking Nobody's got a smart mouth, don't he?" He seemed to be speaking to all of his colleagues. They laughed. "Hey, chica," he said to Rose. "You and the little one OK?"

"They're fine," Chris insisted.

"I was talking to the girl."

Rose straightened her posture to exude confidence. She wasn't scared of a bunch of funny-looking dudes in funny-looking costumes. Not them, or their fat leader. "He said, we're fine!" she shouted.

"Who is he to you?"

"He's Mr. Nobody! He's a superhero, so you'd better leave us alone, or he'll kill all of you!"

"Well, if they don't have another thing in common, they got the attitude down," the man joked. Everyone laughed again. That is, everyone short of Chris, Rose, and Cory. "At least we know you're not Faction. They don't tend to keep kids around. Come on and get something to eat," he offered, walking back inside.

"Stick close to me," Chris whispered to the kids.

The shop interior reeked of fresh oil and rubber. Clanks of metal against metal ruled the atmosphere. Sparks showered from the chassis of raised armored vehicles on their high perches. Then there were the people. Chris counted six in classic mechanic attire, and four armed guards. That was more people than he had seen in one place in ages. Even further, there was electricity. The fluorescent lights above hummed, casting their glow on everything and everyone. There was so much here that Chris thought was long dead to the world. The wonder in his eyes was expensive. The wonder in the children's eyes was priceless, having never seen anything like it in their lives.

"Who are you?" This time Chris was on the asking end.

"Captain Foley," replied the plus-sized man.

"No, I mean YOU." Chris pointed around, signifying that he meant the collective you.

Captain Foley led them through the door that connected the shop with the supermarket. "We're the last hope of a sane world. There's the Faction, then there's us. They want control of the people. We want freedom for the people," he responded.

The hollow sound of jumbled voices bounced through the gigantic space. It was marvelous. The store had been converted to a compact utopian society. There was a gumbo of people—men, women, and children—black, white, and brown. Every citizen of what used to be the Americas was represented.

"There has to be a thousand people here," said Chris, in awe.

"Nine-seventy-eight on the head. Good eye though. Military?"

"In a previous life."

"Once a soldier, always a soldier."

"Who says that's a good thing?"

"Still alive, ain't you? Would've been a hell of a lot harder without your training."

"I guess," Chris replied.

Foley stopped for a brief moment. "Let me guess. Army Special Forces?"

"Ranger."

"Same shit."

"Spoken like a true jarhead."

"Close enough. Ten years as a SEAL. Twice as much in the Navy."

Rose and Cory didn't hear a word of the banter between Chris and Foley, not that they would understand any of it anyway. There were so many strange gadgets, people, sounds, and smells. Their senses were on overload.

"Look at all the stuff, Rosi!" Cory pointed all over the place.

Rose gawked around but still managed to keep the role of an annoyed big sister. "What do you think I'm doing?" she snapped.

Cory pulled away from her grasp. "You don't have to be mean," he declared.

"Stop being a baby!"

The toddler's response was a firm middle finger. Intent on instant revenge, Rose thumped him on the arm, making him cry out.

"Hey! Cut it out!" Chris demanded.

"She started it," Cory said in his own defense.

"Kids, eh," said Foley. "Why don't we take them to the entertainment area with the others, so we can talk turkey."

"Why do they like turkey so much?" Cory questioned.

During the walk, Chris saw that the camp was set up in pretty much the same layout as the store was originally. Food was stored and prepared in the grocery section, lounging was in the furniture and electronics sections, and physical games and entertainment in the toys and outdoor sections. There was even an infirmary, salon/barber shop, and beauty parlor in place of the pharmacy and hygienic departments.

"Whooa!" Cory and Rose exclaimed in unison. Before them was a small group of children seated together in front of several wall-mounted televisions. They had been rigged so that each of them was part of a whole. Six teens were engaged in a free-for-all battle on an action video game. Audible firing of weapons and cheers added to the perception of a good time.

"Go on," said Foley, gesturing toward the other children.

Rose and Cory looked to Chris for approval. He nodded, and off they ran. They were given a warm reception. New kids were a rarity, so whenever some showed up, there was tangible excitement.

"Special, ain't it," said Foley.

"What?" asked Chris. His eyes were still locked on Rose and Cory, but not for fear of their safety. The people there seemed happy, which said a lot about those running the show. He was entrapped by the glow on their faces. This was probably the most excited they had been in their short lives. It was certainly true for the brief time he had known them.

"The reaction of a child the first time they see a working television. Something we took for granted in the old days."

"True. Never thought I'd see one again myself. Too bad most people left in the world will live and die before they do," Chris replied.

"Not if we can help it." Foley led Chris toward the old stockroom.

"I don't mean to sound negative and all, because a few hundred people in one building is great for hope, but it's a long way from bringing the world back to this." Chris waved his arms to place emphasis on their surroundings.

"This? This is just an outpost. As a matter of fact, it's one of the smallest ones we have."

"You mean to tell me that you have more of these places?"

"From the shores of Chile, all the way to the States."

"Who are you people?" Chris asked again, requesting a more complete answer.

Foley pointed at a patch on his shoulder. "WTP," he replied. "We the People. We're the ones that are going to get rid of the Faction and bring the world back to what it once was."

"It can never be what it once was. The orbit's out of whack, and it's getting worse."

"Somebody once made the tech to break the world. We'll make the tech to fix it."

"At least one of us has confidence."

"I have been known to be a half-full guy. Got my reasons though," said Foley.

The stockroom was now a war room. Weapons racks covered most of the walls. The shelving had been cleared out to make use of all the square footage, but still, everything was a bit unorganized by military standards—a group of chairs here, a random table or workbench there.

Light chatter, though indiscernible, was prevalent. Soldiers indulged themselves in conversation while taking on a plethora of tasks. This included cleaning weapons, repairing electronics, and patching up tattered clothing.

Chris continued to follow Foley. He used his eyes to touch every part of the facility. Soldiers briefly disengaged from their conversations, nodding to acknowledge their captain as he passed.

"A little casual, ain't it?" Chris noted the relaxed state of it all.

Foley snickered. "We don't deal in pointless old traditions, like standing at attention just because an officer entered the room." Chris' face told exactly how he felt about the comment. "You don't agree?" Foley asked him.

"Old traditions like that showed the soldier's discipline," Chris replied.

"They used to teach soldiers that marching across a field of firing cannonballs and muskets was discipline too. The man next to you gets his head knocked off, but you just keep on marching. I'm sure you didn't experience that type of discipline during your years of service, did you?"

"That's not the same thing."

"Damn right it's not the same," Foley replied firmly. "The whole point is that it's not the same. Guerrilla warfare wasn't the same, but it won wars. The invention of the fighter plane won wars. Changes win wars, not stupid tradition. The time my soldiers spend standing up for me could be spent repairing a failing system or crucial weapon. Plainly put, fuck tradition." Foley stopped to look Chris in the eyes. "We have a war to win, and a world to fix." He turned to enter his office and offered his guest a seat.

"But, who are you really?" Chris asked again, this time with heavy emphasis on the word *who*.

The Captain plucked two glasses from a small wooden table, then filled them with cheap whiskey. "Considering you've asked that several times, I'm gonna assume you ain't got the answer you're looking for." He sat behind his desk. The chair squeaked beneath his weight. There wasn't much in the room, but it was too small to give much of an echo. Instead, loud sounds reverberated rapidly, presenting more of a doubling effect. The clanking of glass against wood did just that, as Foley sat down one cup affront Chris. "Ain't the best shit, but I'm sure you've had worse," he said. Chris took a sip, but said nothing.

"We're the good guys. They're the bad guys," Foley said as plainly as he could.

"Everybody's good from their perception," Chris responded.

"I take it you haven't met the Faction yet."

"Double diamonds?"

"Yep. That's them."

"Ran into them once or twice."

Foley smirked. "And what exactly were they doing when you did?"

Chris took another sip from his glass. It was the first time in quite some time that he drank for pleasure. The sip was also to buy a second of thought. Foley was winning their spar of wits. "Dying," he replied.

Foley leaned back in his seat. It creaked louder. "That either makes you a murderer, or they did something to deserve it." He already knew which was true.

"They were after the kids for some reason. They killed their family, so I returned the favor."

"That something the good guys typically do from your perspective over there?"

"Doesn't mean you aren't just as bad, or worse."

"Eh. Could be. You look like a betting man. What's your wager?"

There was a brief pause before Chris replied, "People look happy. Probably more good than not."

Now it was Foley's turn to inquire for a bit of information. "Where were you taking them to?"

"North."

"North ain't exactly the same North as it used to be."

"What do you know about it?"

"Everything there is to know. Alaska is direct North

from here nowadays, not central Canada. The planet's axis isn't the same. Best climate will probably be Washington state once the burn is in full season."

"How do you know all this?"

"We have our methods. What I don't know is why a loner type like yourself would take on the responsibility of some dead strangers' kids."

"What was I supposed to do, leave them to die? Let those Faction dickheads have them? I have to get them somewhere safe."

"And you have," said Foley. "They're safe here."

Chris sat his glass down, and leaned to the edge of his seat. "What are you implying?" he asked.

"Look," began Foley. He locked his fingers together, then placed them on the surface of his desk. "I can tell you're not planning to stay here, but there's no reason for those kids to have to go out there again. It's dangerous. They'll be safe here with us, and we'll take care of them. They'll be educated, have social relationships with other children their ages, and most importantly, we can protect them."

"Nobody can protect them the way I can," said Chris. His protective nature was taking over.

"Hey, the macho shit doesn't belong in a situation like this, OK? The girl might believe in that superhero talk, but you're just one man. We've got hundreds here. Our numbers win every time."

"Fuck your numbers!" Chris responded, standing to his feet. Before he could complete his angry tirade, an explosion shook the ground savagely. Shelves tipped on their sides, and the lights flickered.

Foley and Chris were on their feet in an instant. The office door flung open on its hinges, so hard that the knob crashed a hole in the wall. They sprinted back into the primary area with the group of soldiers from the stockroom at their backs, weapons hot.

"Get everyone in the vehicles!" Foley yelled.

Chris' only focus was Rose and Cory. He would protect them at any cost, something he couldn't do for his own family. As he dashed towards where he had last left them, a missile tore through the roof of the building. It plowed into the ground near the front entrance, sending shockwaves rippling outward. The explosion was deafening. The lights went completely dead. Total carnage had ruined hope. Hope for the children's future in a real society.

The pinging in Chris' hearing started to subside. He pulled himself from the ground to push forward. Desperation was kicking in. The more explosions, the lower the odds the children had of survival.

Sparks and fire were everywhere. Bellowing smoke blocked out the sky, as it pushed through the gaping wounds in the roof. Vision was sketchy at best. The screams were maddening. So many people were dying. So many were already dead, the smell of boiling flesh and blood replacing that of fresh-baked bread.

Chris' first thought was to freeze time, but he summed that it increased the chance of failure. Maybe he would find the children before he lost consciousness, but the likelihood that he would also get them clear before that happened was nonexistent. He would have to choose when to use his gifts wisely.

A few feet from what used to be the entertainment section, Chris noticed Foley on his six. He was pretty agile for his substantial girth. "We have to get the kids to the motor pool," said Foley.

For Chris, action was better than any response. Together they sifted through the overturned shelves and smoldering pieces of roofing that had fallen. They discovered four young bodies in the rubble, youth detached from the world prematurely. Anger swelled up inside of them both. Chris' affliction was befriended by worry. Thankfully, neither of the deceased were Cory or Rose.

The sound of relief came in the form of a series of coughs and weak cries.

"Rose! Cory!" Chris yelled, voice cracking.

"Help! It's dark and I can't move!" Rose called out.

"Is Cory with you?" Chris asked. He crawled over singed furniture. Even that task was risky. Flames were plentiful and were spreading exponentially.

"I don't know. I can't see, but I think I can hear him crying," she responded. Her voice led Chris and Foley to a location against the rear wall of the warehouse-type building. A large portion had collapsed into itself.

"How the hell are we gonna get under there?" asked Foley. He really didn't expect an answer, as there was no possible way to lift tons of steel supports and concrete. "Transport is waiting on us. If we can't get to them before another missile hits... I'm sorry, but you may have to say your goodbyes, or die here with them," he added, trying to be realistic.

"Shut up! None of us are dying," Chris retorted.

"If you wanna take this superhero shit to the grave, go..." Before Foley could complete his thought, Chris flung his arm across his body, as if throwing something across the room. The swift motion allowed him to briefly manipulate space. A massive chunk of the collapsed obstruction was ripped away, and sailed across the interior of the store.

"What the hell did you just do?" Foley's mouth was agape.

Chris didn't waste a moment. "Grab the kids, and let's go!" he demanded. Four heads popped from the hole left behind. Rose, Cory, and two others were saturated with so much dust and ash that their tear ducts couldn't function enough to cry.

Foley was initially paralyzed with shock. A moment passed before he snapped to. "This way," he said, coaxing the other two children to their feet. Chris pulled Cory and Rose along.

The group was able to make it near a corridor that led to the motor pool. Fire engulfed the path down it. Smoke inhalation was becoming almost unavoidable, meaning time was growing short. A powerful jet engine could be heard zipping overhead. Small arms fire followed, accompanied by heavy shells making landfall. The building couldn't take another direct hit.

"Hope you got something else up your sleeve, Mr. Nobody," Foley said sarcastically. He began hacking away, attempting to clear his lungs.

Chris searched his mind for the many ways he had concocted to use his abilities. So many laws of physics could be broken when one had control of light, gravity, and spacetime. The search only took a brief second. Chris held his arms out front, then parted them like pulling open a set of curtains. This created a vacuum in the hall space, successfully eliminating the blaze. He stared down Foley. "Nobody can protect them like I can," he reiterated, then led the group onward.

The doors flung open, and the group stepped out into war. Smoke oozed into the sky from every direction. Fire brandished its intense odor like a weapon, twitching against the shadows in the light of day. The rear of the store had been altered for just this purpose. Twenty-foot-high, reinforced cement walls ran well beyond the length of the building. Concrete-encased steel arches partially covered the top to give some protection from a potential aerial assault. Many of them had been bashed by the raining heavy ammunition. It wasn't a very wide area. A convoy of twenty vehicles fit snugly inside, single file. Engines rumbled down the narrow tube-like alleyway, causing Cory to cover his ears.

"It's too loud," he complained. He had no idea how much louder it was about to get.

Chris caught a glimpse of what was causing so much havoc in the skies. A stealth drone passed overhead at blistering speeds and dropped its payload. The protective structure took the brunt of the explosion, but there was still enough power from the impact to fling the group from their feet. Huge sections of concrete and rebar became missiles in their own right.

A cry of agony added to the soundtrack of battle. Rose had been hurt badly. A foot-long piece of rebar protruded from her thigh. It had pierced all the way through. Chris scrambled to her side, careful not to let her read the panic he was feeling.

"Damn it!" he exclaimed.

Foley was back on his feet. "Come on. We gotta get the fuck outta here!" he yelled to Chris, unaware of the current situation.

"She's hurt," Chris shouted in response.

The other children gathered around to get a look. Cory's eyes were large saucers. Foley cleared them away to get a view.

"Shit," he grunted. "The ambulance." Foley pointed at one of the vehicles farther down the line of the convoy. It wasn't a typical ambulance. An armored SWAT vehicle had been converted into a medical transport. As a matter of fact, every vehicle, including the passenger buses used for carrying non-combat personnel, had been outfitted in some kind of armored protection.

Not one to waste time, Chris grabbed Rose and sprinted toward it with the rest of the group on his heels. Foley lugged Cory along like an oddly shaped football, legs dangling and swinging.

The rear doors swung open upon approach, and everyone packed inside. Before the doors could be shut, Foley was on his radio ordering the convoy to move out. "Get us the fuck outta here!" he ordered.

Rose's cries subsided into whimpers. The pain was eating away at her consciousness. Violent bumps from the speeding vehicle jolted her body, sending pain surges that caused her to reengage with awareness. Blood drenched her denim jeans. When that job was done, it pooled on the floor beneath Chris's seat as he held her.

"Help her!" he angrily demanded.

"Get her on the table," said a woman.

Chris did as he was told.

"You know what you're doing?" he questioned. The question wasn't meant to be insulting, though it could have been interpreted that way. He genuinely wondered if there was anyone left in the world with the skills to perform an operation as serious as the one that lay ahead for Rose.

"Don't get much better than Dr. Stephens," Foley reassured him.

The physician worked quickly.

"I'm going to have to operate right now, or she won't have a chance. It looks like her artery might be compromised. She's definitely going to need blood.

What's her type?" she asked, while simultaneously prepping for surgery.

"I don't know, but I'm universal. Just take it from me," Chris replied. Everything was happening so fast. The driver swerved wildly, dodging missiles and rounds from mounted guns of pursuing vehicles. Weaponized WTP vehicles returned fire. They were trying their best to protect the convoy, even at the cost of their own lives—an effort that was beginning to look more bleak by the second.

Chris and the others rocked about the cabin, trying to keep their balance. Dr. Stephens helped Rose into a deep slumber with anesthesia, then attempted to start an IV drip.

"I can't work on her like this. It's too dangerous," she shouted, struggling to find a vein.

"Well, you can't just let her die!" Chris yelled back.

Dr. Stephens stood her ground. "I can't even get an IV in. There's no way I can do this kind of surgery. I'm not going to be responsible for killing a little girl," she stated.

"Fine. You want calm, I'll give you calm." Chris blasted the rear doors open. Destruction worthy of an action film was taking place all around. He watched. Everyone watched. Together they all watched busloads of innocents blown to fragments behind them. They witnessed men shot off their weapons, mists of red forced from their bodies.

Enough was enough. If it took peace for Rose to live, then Chris would make peace happen right then and there. The drone was the difference maker. Enemy ground forces kept pursuit, but there was no way to escape while the drone still stalked and picked them to pieces. As Chris readied himself, it made an about-face to set up another pass. He stood in the open door, with a hand against the interior wall to hold himself steady. The other reached out to the approaching craft.

Emotions trigger us to complete challenges we seem incapable of. Whether fear, love, hate, angst, or any other of the gamut of feelings we experience, we lose the thought of failure in those moments. It raises the ceiling of our capabilities. We sometimes like to believe our capabilities to be limitless. Chris's may have actually been so. His eyes glazed over in a fresh tint of blue. The doors pinned themselves to the side of the ambulance, then the heavens parted. A ball of lightning manifested in the path of the aircraft, another above the chasing Faction. They expanded into portals, one leading to the next. The drone plowed through the portal in its flight path, out the other, and crashed into friendlies, toppling end over end. It eliminated every automobile in its wake.

Deadly debris was propelled toward what few WTP vehicles remained. Chris ejected a gentle wave of energy, parrying it all away. Work complete, the whites of his eyes filled his entire sockets as he smacked the deck.

2

A Fatal Attraction

The wheels wobbled side to side, struggling to maintain stability at the speed at which they rotated. A sudden turn rattled the metal framework, causing joyous laughter to spill from the only passenger. Thrilling rides like this one really got him going. Another sharp turn, and he crashed to a stop. His body swayed back and forth, but he just kept on laughing.

"Boy, didn't I tell you to watch where you're going with that damn basket!" Melissa was irate.

Chris leaned in to whisper into his son C.J.'s ear. "There goes your momma again, trying to ruin the fun," he said.

"I got some fun for both of y'all. Now, hit me with that basket again."

"If your butt wasn't so juicy, I wouldn't have gotten distracted."

"I bet you somebody likes it."

Chris used his hands to cover C.J.'s ears. "Let me feel it to see if I like it too," he pleaded with Melissa.

"Boy, get away from me! You and that lil' brat of yours."

The family of three went on with their grocery shopping until completion. Well, Melissa did all the shopping while Chris and C.J. followed her around. Chris had told him that it was their mission to secure the mother.

A familiar face appeared on their way to the register. "Oh my God! Is that you, Lola?" said Melissa. "I haven't seen you since the wedding, and ooo you have been up to no good, I see," she added, referring to Lola's round belly.

"Girrrl," Lola replied with a drawn-out expression. She reached for Melissa, and they embraced. Afterwards, she shifted her attention to the men. "Hey, Chris!" she said, waving in his direction.

Chris's stomach was turning on the inside, but his poker face could have made him a world champion. "Hey," he replied. She was the last person on planet Earth that he wished to run into. Oh, the fun fate must have been having with him.

"And, look at this handsome man," said Lola. She lightly pinched C.J.'s cheek. He laughed, loving the attention. "He's a happy baby. Looks just like his daddy too."

"Mm-hmm. Acts like him too. Gonna have to beat 'em both up," said Melissa.

Lola rubbed her tummy. "I hope my baby doesn't look like his ugly ass daddy," she joked.

"Don't tell me it's Turner."

"Girl, no! That boy is too childish. I had to get me a real man."

"Amen to that! How far along are you?"

"A little over four months."

"Halfway there."

"Yes, and can't wait."

"Well, good luck, girl. I'll let you go, so you can handle your business, and get off them feet."

"Alright. You still have my number?"

"I do."

"Call me. We should hang out. Would be good for our kids to get to know each other too. They could be like brothers." Lola had just informed Chris of the sex of his other child. He couldn't tell if she did so intentionally but presumed so. She was growing well-adapted to playing shrewd games with him.

"Sounds good. I'll call you this weekend," Melissa assured her.

Lola went to hug Chris on the way past. "Bye y'all," she

said.

Chris felt her hand slide into the pocket of his jacket but didn't make any sudden movements. He reluctantly hugged her back. Lola's sweet fragrance nearly made his knees wiggle, but Chris was able to rebound from his trance.

"Bye, Lola. Be careful," he said cryptically.

Lola continued down the aisle, saying, "Careful is boring."

"That baby is doing Lola some good, ain't it? You see all that back there?" Melissa asked Chris.

"Wasn't looking," he replied.

"Boy, please. You'd have to have your eyes closed not to see all that. All I know is, seeing is the only thing you better be doing," she threatened, only half-joking.

***

Now with a family, Chris had left the comforts of his small condominium. It took just a few months for hired contractors to put the finishing touches on Melissa's dream home. His grandmother's land served as the perfect location to raise his son. It was a place with plenty of space, far enough from the ruckus of the inner city, yet close enough for reasonable travel when needed.

Their home was one of a kind. It was an artistic blend of concrete, glass, and stained lumber. Windows were long and plentiful, making it a welcome resting place for natural light. Its contours were accentuated and beautiful.

The sun started to slip below the horizon. Blue canvas morphed into rosy shades, soon to be replaced by pitch blackness, dotted with starlight. Shelby inched across the freshly paved driveway. Her doors flung open, allowing a rush of fresh air to flood the interior.

"It smells so good out here," said Melissa.

"You hated it the first time I brought you here. Didn't even wanna get out of the car."

"Why you gotta bring up old stuff?"

"I proposed to you right there. You want me to forget that old stuff too?"

"Shut up and get the stuff out."

Chris popped open the trunk, then headed to the rear of

the car. Melissa grabbed C.J. and headed for the door. She walked down the cobblestone path with him clinging to her hip. Her taste in clothing had matured with her new lifestyle. Long gone were the days of red, skimpy outfits. It was the time of elegant, professional gowns, pencil skirts, and heels designed for queens. The day's agenda called for something more modest, however. Shopping took a lot of time. Time pairs better with comfort than beauty. Jeans, a graphic t-shirt, and sneakers were perfect attire for the job.

Melissa had also become a professional mom. She pulled her keys, found the correct one, and unlocked the front door, all with one hand.

"Hurry up, Chris," she yelled out. "You know we have to go in at the same time to keep mosquitoes out."

Chris was becoming a professional father as well. For him, that meant getting all the groceries inside in one trip. He lugged four bags in each hand. The weight was never the issue with a man of his fitness. The problem was that no matter how strong he was, the plastic straps would dig into his fingers. This time, Chris didn't feel the nagging pain. He was stuck in his mind, wondering why he was so weak for Lola.

Melissa's yelling snapped Chris back to reality. The next moment, they were through the door, slamming it shut as quickly as possible to avoid a night's battle with stinging menaces.

"C.J.'s almost asleep. I'll put him to bed while you put up the food," she said, dropping her keys on the marble countertop. As she spoke, Chris's phone alerted him to an incoming text. He unlocked it, then recoiled in surprise. Melissa sensed something off.

"What's wrong with you?" she questioned.

"Huh? Oh, nothing. Just a problem at 047. I'll handle it in the morning," Chris lied.

"I guess. After he's asleep, I'm going to shower and get in bed. I'm tired."

"OK. I'll be up after I finish my last paperwork."

Melissa carried a dozing C.J. up the staircase and out of view. Past the maroon drapes, glass-printed family portraits, and homely decor, the patter of her feet lightly echoed into the vaulted roof, becoming lost in a decrescendo.

Groceries stashed away, Chris dropped a few ice cubes into a glass, grabbed a cola, and headed for his home office. The door shut behind him with a barely audible click. Motion sensors activated the lighting, revealing whom Chris had become. Not unlike his former Commander's, his large wooden desk was surrounded by family, accomplishments, and the one true God. Ironically, he didn't feel like much of a Christian.

"We all sin," he mumbled, "but this one…" The soda fizzled as it rolled over the ice, into a pool of bourbon at the bottom of Chris's cup. He slid off his shoes, using only his feet. The plush carpeting gave a semblance of comfort to an uncomfortable man. There was no real work to do. No papers, but only a cigar and a simple cocktail. Both were bad habits, sure, but one of his vices was a lot worse.

Chris unlocked his phone once more, scanning through the nude photos Lola had just sent. A heavy sigh pushed from his body. All he could think of was the stupid situation he had gotten himself into, but no solution would be had that night. He took a moment to admire the pictures. Even with child, Lola was as sexy as they come. Feeling the rise of his zipper, Chris shook from her web of lust, deleted the photographs, blocked her contact, then sank into his leather seat, puffing away at his cigar.

***

Early mornings no longer required an alarm clock for Chris to awaken. C.J. had taken on the duty. Excited to watch his favorite cartoons, he would plop down on his favorite seat—the side of his father's face.

"Move," Chris whined, pushing the growing toddler off his head. "We go through this every morning. This is a king-sized bed. You have all this room, but you still wanna bother me."

Melissa entered the room and flung a balled-up scrap of paper at Chris.

"It's time for you to get up anyway. You got work, and you need to drop your twin off at daycare on the way," she said. A similar speech was also common most mornings.

"Twin? This dude looks nothing like me," Chris replied, wrestling C.J., who was laughing goofily, onto his back for a prime tickling.

"Whatever. I just know that if I make it back downstairs before you, you're going to work hungry."

"So, you wanna make me breakfast, then threaten to eat my food? You're about to get this work, is what's about to happen." Chris bolted from the bed to chase down Melissa. She attempted a nimble escape but barely made it to the hallway before Chris took her down to the floor, dragging his tongue across her face.

"Eww! The food is downstairs, not on my face, you nasty whore!" Melissa cried.

C.J. slid from the bed. He let out his best war cry and pounced on his mother's attacker like a wild beast.

Chris feigned an intense struggle. Ultimately, he plucked the vicious child up by the belt of his pajamas. "You win. She's all yours," he said, laying C.J. across Melissa's abdomen before retreating downstairs to the kitchen.

Most of the curtains had been pulled open to permit the springtime sun to frolic around the house. The rural landscape was beautiful. Lush greens enclosed the property. A fig tree gently swayed outside the dining room window. It was planted by his grandmother years before even his parents were born.

Melissa dragged her fingers across the smooth-textured stair rails on her way down. She took in everything in range of sight, placed her hands on Chris's shoulders as he ate, and softly kneaded his traps.

"It still doesn't seem real," she said.

"What doesn't?"

"This house, us, C.J... I dreamed of this kind of life as a little girl, but I mean every girl does. But, it never happens. Not to a girl like me."

"What do you mean, a girl like you?"

"You know, the things I did. The way I grew up."

"Stop right there," Chris interrupted. "You're not your circumstances. You did what you had to do to survive. I didn't think this would be life either, but it is, and I love it. I love you."

"I love you too. Not as much as this house, though!" said Melissa, twirling around in circles with her arms wide.

Chris downplayed it. "It's alright."

"Better than that little ass apartment you had."

"It's a condo, not an apartment, that we happen to still

own. So, keep talking, and we can move your ass right back in there."

"You and what army?"

"You do realize I run the most advanced fighting force in the known universe, right?"

"Boy, please. Ain't nobody scared of them clowns."

"Aw, OK. I'll call them over so you can tell them to their faces."

Melissa leaned against the dining table. "I... ain't... scared! Now go get your son, and get out of my house!" she demanded, poking her finger into Chris's chest.

He wiped his mouth with a disposable paper towel. "Why are you trying so hard to get rid of us?" he asked, giving Melissa the side-eye.

"I got work to do. Y'all are keeping me from doing it." Melissa waved her pointer finger around demonstratively.

"What work?"

"I have three custom dress orders for the new Senator."

"Oh yeah? How much is she paying?"

"A wise man once told me that sometimes favors are worth more than money."

"That's what I'm talking about, boss lady!" Chris cheered. He raised his hand up for a high five.

Melissa clapped her hand against his. "There you go. Now get!" she exclaimed.

Chris stood up, grabbed her waist, and kissed her tenderly. "You're lucky you're sorta kinda fine," he said, "even with them stubby-ass legs."

"Ooowee!" shrieked Melissa, before chasing Chris back up the stairs.

***

Jeff greeted Chris at the gate of the repaired Project 047.

"Cringle," he nodded, while taking his weapon.

"Come on, Jeff. How long are you gonna be mad at me?" Chris asked him. "I said I was sorry. What I did wasn't personal. I mean, I tried to talk you down, but you didn't wanna listen."

"Yeah, yeah, yeah," Jeff's face remained rigid and serious. A few more seconds passed before they both broke into laughter.

"Man, why you always gotta bring that up? That was a year plus and seventy pounds ago."

"Yeah, Jeff! You look good too, boy. I see you," Chris replied. He was grinning ear to ear.

"I'll be ready for that ass next time you decide to go rogue."

"Haha. I don't care how good of shape you get in. You'll never be able to do nothing with me."

Jeff laughed, then waved Chris through and returned to his post inside the guard shack. It was the weekend, so the lower levels were lightly staffed. Chris greeted the few workers he met on the way to his office and used his phone to communicate with his automatic coffee maker. A steaming cup was ready by the time he opened the door.

With a couple of teaspoons of sugar to sweeten the deal, Chris was ready for the daunting task of a mile-high stack of paperwork. Since the trip to Atlas was delayed indefinitely, everyone was to stay prepared for a status change at a moment's notice. This meant that during the weekdays, Chris kept his growing battalion of ICA soldiers well-trained and in tip-top shape. The weekends were set aside for action reports, grievances, and whatever else required his signature to be validated.

Noon approached when a knock sounded at Chris's door.

"Come in," he said without looking up from his work.

The door opened but shut almost as quickly.

"Hey, baby daddy!" said Lola, diddling her fingers in the air for a salutation.

Chris locked eyes with her, pen still protruding from his grip.

"What are you doing here?" he questioned.

"I work here, remember?"

"Kill the bullshit. It's the weekend, and even if it wasn't, you're on desk duty in the Upper Four until you're in condition to train again."

Lola giggled. "OK, you got me. I just came to bring you lunch."

Chris looked at her empty, manicured fingers.

"Lunch? There's nothing in your hands," he noted.

Lola giggled again, pulled her dress straps from her

shoulders, then pushed it down until it dropped at her feet. "I am lunch," she informed him, posing provocatively.

"Look, I blocked your number for a reason. We can't keep doing this. I have a family."

Lola strutted over to Chris. She straddled his lap, kissing his neck. "And I got needs," she whispered into his ear. Still too weak to resist, Chris fell into her web of seduction all over again.

***

The doorbell of Gino's three-story mansion rang to his phone, rather than over a loudspeaker. He pulled up a display to the front door's camera. Recognizing his visitor, he used a phone app to unlock the door and spoke, "It's open. I'm in the theater." When the theater door popped open, Gino ordered his men to, "Clear da room." They did so with a trail of strange clouds lingering behind.

Inside was dark. Black walls and carpet added to the effect. Only light from a film projected onto a large screen helped visibility. Three rows of five leather recliners were spaced out in the center of the downward-sloping floor. Gino sat dead center. "What's good, lil' bruh?"

"You tell me," Chris replied. He took a seat directly beside his brother.

Gino was very perceptive. He also knew Chris better than he probably knew himself. That being said, he went on one of his rants that usually had some type of valuable lesson wrapped inside. "You see dat?" Gino pointed at the screen. Condensation dripped from the glass in hand. "You know why Ricky got shot?" He didn't pause to wait for a response. He answered himself. "Ricky got shot 'cause the nigga didn't hit da fence or lay his ass down. He prolly saw a thousand movies where da nigga run straight, and got shot in the back, but he still did the same shit."

Chris sighed heavily. "I know you're going somewhere with this, so just tell me."

Gino's glass was then empty, so he sat it in the cup holder. "Nigga, what da hell I tell you about patience?" He paused the film using the remote and looked Chris in the eyes. "Smart people see other people's mistakes and learn what not to do. You see all dese dumbass Memphis niggas wit three or four baby mommas on dey ass, and you got a fine-ass, good-ass woman at da crib, yet you couldn't keep yo Johnson der wit ha. Not only dat, but you dumb ass didn't even strap up. Now, I told yo ass the first time you came over here and told me bout dis, to go head and tell dat woman what happened while the shit could be fixed, but you here lookin' like a sad-ass puppy, so I know you ain't did dat yet. Don't worry bout it though. A hard head make a..."

"Soft ass," Chris said, finishing Gino's thought.

The following silence sparked Gino's intuition again. "Aww hell naw!" he exclaimed. "Nigga, you fell in it again? Mane, I need dat female's number. If she dat cold, I need her to slide through tonight!" Gino laughed loudly.

"I didn't come over here for this shit," Chris said angrily.

"You came over here because you fucked up again, but you ain't need me to tell you that. We cut from the same cloth, nigga. Ain't shit different but the stitches. Now handle yo got-damn biness, and get da fuck out of my house, so I can handle mine."

***

The ride home was dreadful. Chris drove below the speed limit for the first time in forever. Though the sky was brilliant with sunlight and the clouds were fluffy patches of white on a clear blue backdrop, the view, from his perspective, seemed dead and gloomy.

It was time to be a man. Being a man isn't always roses. Often it requires managing the happiness of those you love, even at the expense of your own.

Chris had created his own hell in this case. It was best to walk through the fire and take his burns. Maybe Melissa would forgive him. If she didn't, could he blame her? What would be his reaction if the shoe was on the other foot? The thought was unfathomable.

Even still, today would be the day he came clean. The knowledge that C.J. was spending time at his uncle Danny's helped his resolve. No chance of him being collateral damage if Melissa reacted too adversely.

Jangling keys struck the counter with a thud. Chris trudged down the hallway of his home. His feet felt heavy as lead blocks. The air felt thicker. Gravity pulled harder. It was as if the environment was as worried as he was.

"Melissa," Chris called out, trying to locate her in the house.

"I'm in the gallery," she responded. Her voice ricocheted from the many walls between them.

The door was already wide open. Melissa met Chris with a quick peck on the lips. Her hands were filled with pieces of richly colored fabrics.

"Hey bae. What you think?" she asked, heading back to an unfinished gown, draped across her model mannequin.

"I need to talk to you about something," said Chris.

"Don't you see me working? I think I asked you a question too."

Chris was thrown off the focus of his task. "Wow, that's cold," he complimented.

"I know, right?" replied Melissa. She took a moment to take pride in her work, though incomplete. "This should get her a few more donors and votes. And me some more money," she added after a pause.

A woman's voice came from the far side of the room.

"I know that's right, girl!"

Chris's eyes swung to locate the familiar voice. His heart skipped a beat. "You didn't tell me Lola was here," he said to Melissa.

Melissa rolled her eyes. "And I didn't have to," she said, giving him a dirty look.

"What if I decided to walk in here ass naked?" Chris was trying to prove a point.

"Why would you do that?" Lola questioned.

"'Cause this is my house," Chris firmly stated.

Melissa came to Lola's defense. "Uh, rude! You can yell at her at work, but when she's in here, she's my friend, so watch your mouth. And stop being so nasty all the damn time! Nobody wanna see you naked."

Chris shook his head in frustration. "Ooo, I have to go pick up C.J.," Melissa remembered, glancing up at a wall-mounted clock. She put down her supplies, then reached for her purse.

"Now, what did you want to tell me?" she asked.

LASHECKIA LYONS

"Don't worry about it. I'll wait till you get back."

"I'll ride with you, girl," said Lola. She stood from the couch, only to grab her waist with fatigue.

"You alright?" Melissa asked concernedly.

"Just a little tired and light-headed. This lil' boy is something else."

"I hope he's not as active as my baby. That's why he's with his uncle now. It's the only way I can get some work done."

"It sure feels like it. Draining all of my energy."

Melissa grabbed her car keys. "You just stay here and rest for a while. I shouldn't be much longer than thirty minutes. Someone needs to babysit this asshole anyway. If you need anything, just make him do it. Out there, he might be your boss, but in this house, you're his," she said.

"I like the sound of that," replied Lola.

Chris went on the defensive. "How are you going to volunteer me out like I don't have things to do?"

"Your pregnant friend is at your house. She's your problem."

"Aight dude. I'm going to my office," he replied, then left the room.

There was pure silence, aside from the low flutter of the AC. Chris sat alone, with his forehead resting on his hard, oak desk. His mind was overcome with frustration. This problem seemed to perpetually grow out of control. Lola walked through the door and pushed it shut behind her.

"No, no, no!" yelled Chris, almost jumping out of his seat.

"What's wrong?" Lola replied, pretending to be perturbed.

"Get out of here!"

"I'm not wearing any panties," Lola teased, inching up her skirt to show her fruit.

"Stop! I'm not about to do anything with you."

"Why not?"

"There's a million reasons, starting with this being the house I live in, with my wife and my son."

"Well, she told me to make you do whatever I needed, soooo..."

Chris slammed his hands down on his desktop, toppling

81

over everything with a higher center of gravity. "What the fuck is wrong with you?" he questioned. "You know I have a family!"

"Two."

"What?"

"Actually, you have two." Lola rubbed her stomach. "And unless you want your darling Melissa to know, then you do what I want."

Chris's eyes bulged with shock. "Now you're threatening me?"

"Shut up and fuck me!" Lola demanded.

The door swung open so fast that it smashed a hole in the wall. "Bitch! You gotta be crazy!" screamed Melissa. She aimed her handgun square at Lola's face.

Chris jumped between them, hands out, palms open. "Hold up, hold up, wait," he pleaded.

"Move, Chris!"

"You know I can't."

Melissa turned her fury toward Lola. "I invite you into my home, and this is what you're on, bitch?"

"Bitch?" Lola giggled like she was entertained. "Come over here and say that."

"The only reason I ain't already shot your ass is 'cause of that baby."

Lola seemed to be truly enjoying herself. "Oh, you mean *our* baby?"

"Lola!" Chris shouted.

"What?" she said, feigning innocence.

"Just leave!"

"She ain't goin' nowhere!" Melissa fired a shot into the ceiling, then re-aimed her gun at Lola. Trails of tears gouged through her eyeliner.

"Shit!" Chris yelled. "Calm down and give me the gun." Melissa's heart rate was through the roof. Adrenaline was taking over her better judgment. Chris knew he had to calm her down. "Breathe," he said, inching toward her. Slowly, he moved close enough to gently push the barrel of the weapon to the floor. "Lola, get out of here," he demanded.

She hesitated briefly. "OK. I'll leave," she finally agreed. Walking to the door, she waved one final salutation. "See you later, girl," she said, waving goodbye.

Melissa jerked, trying to escape Chris's grasp. Without success, she grunted, "Let me go!" Once Chris was almost certain Lola had cleared the house, he released Melissa. But he didn't expect what happened next. Melissa aimed her gun at him.

"Whoa, what the hell are you doing?" Chris was in full panic.

"Is it true what she said?" Melissa demanded answers.

"Put the gun down."

"Answer the damn question!" Melissa was beyond reason.

"Alright, alright," Chris paused. He didn't want to tell her this way, but what was done was done. "Yes."

"The baby?" she further interrogated.

"I don't know. I think so. Time matches," Chris tried to explain, but Melissa didn't want to hear any of it.

"You get your ass out too!" she ordered.

"But, let me—"

"Get out!" The gun trembled in Melissa's hands. "You're a sorry excuse for a man. I thought we were special. I thought *you* were special, but you ain't shit, just like the rest of them. So you get your ass out of my house, and don't come back here again. I don't wanna see your stupid ass face!"

"I just—"

"Get out!" Melissa shouted at the top of her lungs.

3

We Are Who We Are

Chris woke up in a cold sweat to completely unfamiliar surroundings. His ears sifted through the many layers of noise. A monitor audibly beeped in tune with his heart. The hum of fluorescent bulbs was reminiscent of honey bees, buzzing around nectar-rich blossoms. He squinted, waiting for his eyes to regain focus. When they did, he saw Rose gawking at him. She appeared to be chewing, unceasingly, on something.

"Where are we, and why are you staring at me like that?" Chris asked her.

Rose blew a bubble.

"A place like the one before. They said it used to be some famous building or something," she replied but chose not to respond to the second portion of Chris's question.

"Is that..."

"Bubble gum," Rose interrupted. "Foley gave it to me."

"He taught you how to blow a bubble?"

"No. I taught myself. I taught myself a lot of things,

like how to play the piano."

"The piano? What the hell? How long was I out?"

"A week," Rose hesitated before continuing. "One week, two days, three hours, thirty-two minutes, and forty-nine seconds to be exact."

"Real funny," said Chris, unamused. "The time thing was a little much. Besides, nobody can learn to play the piano in a week."

"I can. I did," Rose stated plainly. There wasn't a hint of humor in her tone.

Chris sensed something different about Rose. She seemed more aware, somehow beyond the oblivious little girl she was before he lost consciousness. She stood from her chair, walked to Chris's bedside, and grasped the rail.

"Your leg. It's healed?" Chris knew the question was stupid, but he saw her walk without a limp with his own eyes.

Rose jumped up and down as if to prove her point.

"Yup. Doesn't even have a scar."

"That's not possible. It takes more than a week for something like that to heal, Rose. Can you kill the jokes and tell me how long it's really been and where we are?"

"I'm pretty sure I'm a superhero now," Rose responded.

The statement jarred Chris's brain into action. "The blood transfusion," he mumbled.

"Same thing I was thinking," Rose replied, but her voice sounded as if it came from everywhere and nowhere at once.

Chris sat up taller in the bed.

"Your mouth didn't move," he noted, caught off guard.

Rose tilted her head in confusion.

"What?" she said aloud.

"I just heard you talk, but your mouth didn't move."

"What the heck is he talking about?"

"You just did it again!"

"Like this?" Rose spoke again, using only her mind.

"I gotta be going crazy," Chris said to himself.

"Hey, you can do it too!" Rose said excitedly.

"What?"

"You just did the mind thingy to me!"

Foley walked through the door, relieved to see Chris sitting up.

"You're awake."

"Has it really been a week?" Chris asked him.

"Give or take. You know how time works nowadays. How are you feeling, though?"

"He's good, weirdo!" Rose said, internally.

"Nobody asked you, smart-ass!" Chris said, gazing directly into Rose's face.

Foley was bewildered.

"Umm, I take it you two are having problems of some sort?"

Rose spoke to Chris on their newly discovered, private channel.

"He can't hear me, dum-dum."

"Stop reading my mind."

"I'm not reading your mind. It's obviously telekinetic communication, dum-dum."

"That's the same thing."

"No, it's not. Reading your mind means I would be able to know everything you're thinking. I can only hear what you say to me, dum-dum."

"Call me dum-dum again!"

Foley raised an eyebrow. From his perspective, it looked like Chris and Rose were having an intense, silent face-to-face stare down.

"Do y'all need time to sort something out?" he asked.

Chris removed the medical devices from his body.

"I just need to get out of this room," he said. He noticed there were no windows. Further observation of his surroundings brought notice to Cory. The toddler was balled up in a blanket on a forest-green futon. The room was chilly, as most medical facilities are. It also became evident that the children had spent a lot of time in the room. Toys and snack wrappers littered one of the two small end tables. Cartoons played on a muted TV mounted on the plain, white walls.

Chris got up, but the room spun. He took a second to gather himself.

"Clothes?" he requested, ready to get out of the uncomfortable hospital gown.

"In the living quarters. Take a walk with me," replied Foley.

The hallway was long and thin, almost too clean and pristine. The walls were white, the floor was white, the ceiling was white, even the light emitted had a pure white appearance. Windows, however, were still absent.

Foley and Chris walked at a fair pace. Cory and Rose followed, able to keep up without issue. She held Cory's hand, her senses locked onto the conversation, thirsty for every ounce of information she could obtain.

"What is this place?" Chris asked.

"Our Dallas facility," Foley responded with a bit of pride.

"Dallas?"

"It was the closest place we could get to that had the right equipment to get you and girly back to peak condition."

"I guess I should thank you."

"Didn't take you for the thanking type."

"Not for me. For saving her life."

"Don't know if we can take credit for that. By the time we stopped the bus, her wound was already healing." Foley looked for a sign from Chris, to gauge his reaction. There wasn't one. Chris hid his thoughts well.

"So, what's with you two?" Foley asked.

"Nothing. She's just being her regular annoying self."

"Not that."

"I'm not catching your meaning."

"You took down a drone and an entire convoy of gunners without a weapon. That little Barbie healed a flesh wound that went through an artery, nerves, and deep tissue in less than a couple days."

"Oh, that. I've got a few abilities. Had them for a while. Her, on the other hand, something new is going on."

"Don't tell him that!" Rose yelled into Chris's mind.

"Quiet!" he responded.

"Interesting. So, it may be possible to transfer those abilities from person to person." Foley mumbled to himself, then spoke up to Chris, "We took some bloodwork earlier in the week to make sure you were OK. We'd like to run some more tests, if that's fine with you."

"Don't trust him," Rose advised Chris.

"I don't."

"Can't you see grown folks are talking?"

"No, but I can see your butt," Rose replied, using her mind, but laughed out loud.

Chris clenched the rear of his gown tightly and scowled at Rose before turning his attention back to Foley.

"Right now, all I want is a shower, some clothes, and something to eat," he said, successfully dodging Foley's request for more tests.

Not wanting to press the issue, Foley continued guiding them to what he hoped would be their long-term living quarters.

"Okay, your place is down the hall here," he said.

The door to the room was made of thick stainless steel. Foley swiped his fingertips across a touch panel on the wall beside it. Its square LED light turned from red to green, and the door parted from the center.

"Make yourself at home," said Foley. "The few things you had on you are in the storage space. We gave the children the option to sleep here, but they didn't want to leave your side. Hell of an impression you made on 'em. Anyway, do what you need to get comfortable. I'll send someone back around for dinner. We're having burgers and fries," he said, targeting the children with the last bit of information.

Cory jumped up and down with excitement at the idea of eating something other than beans for once. Rose didn't flinch, nor did her demeanor improve.

"Okay, bye," she said.

Foley laughed. "That one's a real firecracker," he said, retreating.

Rose cringed inside. Her intuition sent all sorts of

red flags. She would keep close tabs on Foley until he could prove trustworthy.

Both children followed Chris inside. The space was cozy, with a modern feel. The living area was small but adequate, with hardwood floors running wall to wall. At the center, a single couch sat atop a small handmade rug, facing a wall-mounted flat screen above a long, thin, dark-stained table.

Three doorways lined the far wall. The outer two led to bedrooms, barely large enough to fit beds and a single storage drawer. The left room contained a full-sized mattress, and the right had twin-sized bunks, one stacked atop the other.

Chris immediately felt a sense of comfort. It had been years since he stayed in a place that actually felt like a home. Memories invaded his consciousness—images of his son and wife playing a game of chase, scuttling about, faded away as Rose's voice interrupted.

"What are you smiling at?" she asked.

Chris shook off the hallucination. "Nothing," he replied. For the first time, he took note of the children's clothing. Both sported similar black sweatpants and matching shirts. Their black sneakers were laceless, with a solid white strip along the midsole. The material looked incredibly comfortable—like cotton, but with a synthetic blend.

Reaching out to touch the sleeve of Cory's shirt, Chris asked, "Where did these come from?"

"A drawer in the room. They put more in there," Rose replied.

"You've been in here before?"

"Only for a little while."

"Why? This place is nice. You'd rather stare at me, sleeping in a hospital bed?"

"We had our reasons."

Cory interrupted before Chris could press further.

"I gotta pee," he announced, crossing his legs.

"You know where the restroom is," Rose pointed out.

"I don't wanna go by myself. It's scary here."

"Ugh. I'll stand right outside the door, but I'm not going in there with you. You're not a baby anymore."

Rose grazed her fingers across the door's touch pad, and it gave the green light, sliding open. The bathroom was the smallest room of all. There was just enough space for a toilet, sink, and standing shower.

"Hurry up," she ordered, leaning against the wall.

"Where's my stuff?" Chris asked.

Rose pointed at the other bedroom. "There's a storage space in there too."

Chris went inside to take a look. On the wall, there was a slightly different texture, barely noticeable from a distance. He stroked it, and a drawer protruded outward, slightly above waist level.

The few items that remained on his person were inside—a 9mm handgun, a half-empty metal flask, a Zippo lighter, and about ten feet of coiled 5/50 cord. His ratty clothing and rifle were absent, replaced by an empty flak vest, a pair of lightweight combat boots, and dark-colored cargos. The apparel was made from the same strange fabric as the children's clothing.

"What the hell is this stuff?" Chris mumbled to himself, rubbing the material between his fingers. It felt cooler than room temperature, just like Cory's had. Pushing the thought aside, he grabbed the gear and returned to the living room.

By that time, Cory and Rose were scrolling through channels on the television. For a moment, they looked like a family. Maybe they could be one in a place like this, Chris thought—at least as close as one could be.

Chris placed his gear on the small, wall-mounted shelf in the restroom. He swiped his finger across the pad to close the door behind him. The shower knob squeaked lightly as it turned. It was a bit primitive for what otherwise seemed to be a tech-heavy setup.

Once the water started to fall, it sent Chris into a trance. He drifted back to the time he and Melissa had first touched, that moment when she floated through the confines of his shower and into his arms. He deeply missed her, but she was gone. Everyone he had ever loved was gone. He knew better than to believe it was entirely his fault, but he recognized that he held a lot of the responsibility. The real culprits were probably dead too. Chris was the only one left from his past, or so he believed.

The water felt wonderful. It wasn't about getting clean anymore—warm, running water wasn't a luxury people were blessed with anymore. Chris decided to enjoy it. It was yet another reason to consider staying. His mind wrestled with itself, torn between suspicion and the comfort of this temporary normalcy. He forced his worries to wash away with the water down the drain.

Quite a bit of time passed before Chris emerged from the restroom. When he stepped out, he felt a warming sensation from the fabric of his clothing. It seemed to adjust to the coolness of his moist skin.

Cory had fallen asleep on the couch, and Rose was fighting her own case of sleepiness, nodding her head up and down.

"If you're tired, why don't you just go to sleep?" Chris asked her.

Rose snapped fully awake. "I have to watch Cory," she replied.

"Watch him? Nothing's going to happen, Rose. It's safe here."

"No, it's not!"

Chris took a seat on the end of the couch next to her.

"Why are you thinking that way?" he asked, curious.

"I don't know. I just have a bad feeling."

"Have you seen anything? Has someone treated you badly?"

"No. Well, when we got here, some people poked you with needles and stuff."

"That's normal, Rose. They were just making sure I was okay."

"That Foley man whispered something to a lady. After that, they brought us here to shower and put on these clothes. They wanted us to stay here, but I didn't want to leave you by yourself. I watched you and Cory the whole time."

Chris's eyebrow arched. "When was the last time you slept?" he asked.

Rose took a moment to think.

"Uhh, I slept a little bit, like, two dinners ago."

"What the hell, Rose! You have to sleep. It's not healthy to stay awake that long, especially at your age."

"Okay, but only for a little bit, and only if you promise to watch us." It was clear Rose was seeing a picture Chris wasn't.

"Watch you?"

"Promise me, or no sleep!"

"Alright," Chris relented. "Go get in bed. I'll carry little man in, so you both can rest until dinner."

Rose lumbered into the room drowsily. By the time Chris laid her brother down beside her, she was already out. He took a blanket and laid it over them. How wrong he hoped Rose was about this place and its people. It wasn't his old life, but it was something. Something all three of them needed. It was normalcy.

***

A few hours ticked away in Chris's mental clock. Although time was off-kilter, his body still adhered to the feeling of a 24-hour cycle. Mostly, he had spent that time flipping back and forth through the television channels, never finding anything worthwhile.

At last, a knock at the door saved Chris from his boredom. It opened before he had a chance to invite the person in.

"Excuse me? Do you always just walk into people's spaces like that?" he asked, still seated on the couch.

A young girl, seemingly around Rose's age, shyly stared at the floor between her feet.

"Sorry. It was unlocked, so I... I can leave..."

"No, no. You're already here now. What is it?"

"Um, Mr. Foley sent me to get you for dinner." As the girl replied, she lifted her head slightly to scan the room.

"Oh, I get it," said Chris. Foley had done what any smart person would have done. He was very aware of

Rose's skepticism. If she made a friend, maybe her mind would be swayed to stay.

"One second. I'll get the kids up, so we can go."

The room was silent, aside from Cory's light snores. Memories of C.J. floated to Chris's mind until he quickly shoved them back deep down into his subconscious. It wasn't the time to feel sorry for himself, but was there ever a time?

Chris reached to shake them awake. Before his hand made contact, Rose's eyes snapped wide open, nearly making him flinch out of his skin. Rose said nothing. She remained as still as a lifeless corpse, staring blankly into Chris's eyes, only blinking after Chris waved his hand in front of her face.

"What the hell is wrong with this kid?" he thought to himself, though he was convinced it was internal.

"I heard that!" Rose exclaimed. She sat up, immediately returning to her charming self.

"I didn't say anything."

"You thought it!"

"I can think what I want in my own mind. You stay out of it!"

"It's not my fault you can't control your own powers! I'm a better superhero than you!"

Cory sat on the edge of the bed, rubbing the sleep from his eyes.

"Why are you yelling?" he asked.

"Sorry," Rose apologized. In the same instant, she spoke to Chris telepathically.

"This isn't over," she assured him.

Chris responded in kind.

"Like I'm scared of a ten-year-old midget girl." He scoffed at the idea, provoking Rose to jump off the bed, her fists balled up tight at her sides. Her face was scrunched into a tight ball. An invisible force popped Chris in his sternum, throwing him off balance just enough to require a step back to regain it.

"What the? Did you just hit me?" he snarled.

"Keep making fun of me, and I'll do it again!"

"Oh, so now you've got some little powers, you

think you're tough, huh?" Chris worked his own bit of magic to lift Rose into the air by the rear of her shirt collar, the way another canine would lift her puppy.

"How do you like it now?"

Rose squirmed around, throwing her hands and kicking her feet.

"Let me down!" she shouted. Blood rushed to her cheeks, turning them the rosy color of embarrassment.

Cory moved to intervene.

"Will you guys stop fighting?" he pleaded.

"She started it," answered Chris.

A giggle came from the doorway. Rose dropped to the bed, finally released from Chris's teasing spell.

"My daughter told me there was a man and two kids arguing in here," said an amused woman. She had a round face with long, flowing dark hair. Her large, engaging brown eyes gave Chris the impression she was probably from Southern Asia—India was his best guess.

Rose was still seething.

"He's not a man. He's a kid that likes to pick on little girls," she hissed.

"Haha. The relationship you have with your daughter is cute," laughed the woman. Her words seemed to bring a calm over the room. The comfort level the three had with one another led her to believe they were a family. An incomplete family, but a family nonetheless. Strangely, they didn't correct her. The children needed a parent as much as Chris needed someone to give him purpose. The fit was natural.

"I'm Yesha, by the way. This is my daughter, Ari," added the woman, furthering the conversation. She reached out her hand with the introduction.

Chris took it and introduced himself and the children.

"I'm Chris. That's Rose, and that's Cory."

"Are you new to the Dallas settlement or moving from a different segment?" Yesha inquired.

"This place is that big?"

"What do you mean?"

"I just thought everybody would know everybody in

a place like this."

"Oh. This location is about ten thousand strong, and people come and go all the time, so it's hard to keep tabs on everyone. We haven't been here that long either."

Chris was both surprised and impressed. He didn't think ten thousand people were even left alive in the world, yet here they were, not only surviving but thriving.

Yesha read the look on his face.

"Human nature always finds a way," she said.

Cory had had enough of the chatter.

"I'm hungry," he announced.

"You haven't eaten yet?" asked Yesha. "We were about to get dinner now."

"That's what I'm here for. Mr. Foley asked me to come get them," Ari informed her mother.

"Okay then, Chris. We can walk you down to the dining area if you want," Yesha suggested.

"Alright, cool."

Everyone filed out into the hallway. They barely made it ten feet before Yesha stopped the party in their tracks.

"Let me grab my purse, then we can head down," she said. She and Ari lived right next door.

"Guess we're neighbors," Chris said.

"Looks like it. I'll be right back."

Rose's behavior was still a bit skittish. With Ari remaining in the hall, Rose used the more discreet method of communication with Chris.

"Do you think she saw us?" she asked.

"What are you talking about now?"

"Our powers. She sure isn't acting like somebody who just saw a kid floating in mid-air."

"Maybe that's because she didn't."

"Ugh! ¿Por qué son tan estúpidos los adultos?"

"You want some more of what you just got?"

"Don't talk about it, be about it!" Rose challenged.

Ari broke the silence to ask Rose,

"What settlement did you guys come from?"

"We didn't come from one of those."

"You mean, you lived out there on your own?"

"Yeah."

Ari was impressed.

"Wow. You must be really tough. Everyone talks about how dangerous it is out there."

Rose thought of her aunt and uncle being murdered right in front of her.

"Sometimes," she replied, downplaying her feelings.

"Well, you'll like it here. There are games, good food, and TV. They protect us too, so it's always safe here."

"I don't need protection," Rose clarified.

Chris cleared his throat loudly to show disapproval.

"What?" Rose questioned, in a manner that meant Chris should get off her case.

Before another argument had time to brew, Yesha exited her home. "All ready to go," she said with a big smile.

The hallways were full of people walking in every direction, on their paths to complete daily tasks. Though fashion was diverse, everyone's clothing was largely composed of the same, odd fabric. The facility had the feel of an indoor metropolitan area. Chris wondered what the entire place looked like. He figured it might have been underground, due to the lack of windows, but that was as much information as he could gather from his current perspective.

Yesha led the group to a large steel staircase. There appeared to be natural light coming from the top. Cory squinted his eyes and covered them with his arm. It had been a few days since they were in actual sunlight. It would take a moment to adjust.

Rumbling voices grew louder. A slew of other sounds and smells fused with them, forming a new atmosphere.

"Whoa!" gasped Rose and Cory, a reaction that was becoming a common theme. The living community was extravagant. There were restaurants and boutiques, convenience stores and novelty shops, courtyards with fountains, and tables for dining. Green trees partnered with shrubbery to add a homely feel to the environment.

Chris was just as flabbergasted but for a different reason.

"Isn't this the Dallas football stadium?" he asked, even though he already knew the answer. The one-of-a-kind, retractable roof was a dead giveaway.

"Used to be," replied Yesha. "Rebuilt and repurposed."

The WTP had burrowed deep beneath where many games had been won and lost. They built the living quarters and operations center underground, spreading far beyond the perimeter of the stadium, under the parking lot, and many of the neighboring structures. The reinforced concrete below their feet was poured on top to protect from bomb threats, and the overhead dome had been sealed shut to protect from extreme elements. It was just thin enough for the sun to pierce through.

"I was expecting a cafeteria, not an open market," said Chris.

Yesha laughed. "Maybe you should raise your expectations. So, what'll it be?" she asked, leading them forward.

"The fat man said we were having burgers!" Cory informed Yesha.

She laughed at the description, knowing children hardly minced words.

"Only if that's what you guys want. You don't have to have it just because he said so," she replied.

"You're pretty. I want what you want."

The compliment brightened Yesha's day. She kneeled down and gave him a peck on the cheek.

"Aww, thank you, handsome."

Cory giggled bashfully.

"You're pretty too," he added, trying to manipulate a kiss from Ari as well. He figured that if his scheme worked once, it would work again. It did. Ari laughed, placing a peck on his other cheek.

Chris attempted to suppress his desire for anything not cooked on a stick over an open fire, but his cravings were difficult to hold back.

"Can you stop flirting with the ladies so we can

eat?"

There was finally something for Rose and Chris to agree on.

"Yes, because I'm starving. I'll eat anything, as long as it's not beans or people. Ew." She winced visibly at the idea.

"Why would you even think about eating people?"

"I don't know these people. They could be weirdos."

Chris held the bridge of his nose between his fingertips and shook his head in disbelief.

"I want one of those, and one of those, and ooo! I want two of those," Cory announced, unable to choose just one.

"You're sick," Chris said to Rose, "and you're greedy," he added to Cory.

"How about we just start simple and do pizza," Chris suggested, pointing toward a shop with an old brick oven.

"Ooo! Tia told us about pizza!" Rose exclaimed.

Chris gave her a look.

"I thought you wanted to leave," he communicated.

"This doesn't change anything."

"Let's see if you feel that way after you taste pizza for the first time."

"They can't buy me!"

"Then don't eat."

"Oh, I'm gonna eat the pizza!" Rose assured Chris, hand on her hip.

The baker greeted the group as they approached the pizzeria.

"Hello. Can I help you guys?" he asked.

Yesha took the initiative.

"Do you have any fresh pies?"

"Sure. Only pepperoni though. Anything else, I'll have to cook."

"Pepperoni's fine. We'll take two." Yesha looked at her new friends' eager faces.

"Make that three, with five colas," she added.

"Whose account will I be charging?"

Yesha handed over her identification card. It also acted as a form of currency, similar to a credit or debit card in the world before. The clerk scanned it and then returned it to her.

"Thank you. Enjoy your meal," he said.

Chris took the three large boxes, with a small stack of paper plates on top, and Yesha grabbed a six-pack with a single soda missing from its plastic rings. The group took seats at a long picnic table. Happy to be of service, Chris took the liberty of distributing the meal.

"Can I say grace?" asked Ari. Her mother nodded yes.

Rose and Cory didn't know what Ari was asking. They both stared at the others, then mimicked them as they bowed their heads. Ari began to give thanks.

"Lord, we thank you for this meal you have provided for us. May we all enjoy it. And, thank you for answering me and mom's prayers. We asked you for good friends, and you sent us three. Amen."

Feelings of compassion barreled into Chris's heart, but he became aware that it wasn't his own. The emotion came from beyond his own being. When he opened his eyes to follow its source, he realized that he was feeling what Rose was feeling. It was a feeling of fondness linked to Ari's sweet sentiments. The blood transfusion had connected him and Rose in spectacular ways. They were separate, yet they were now one.

"That was really nice, Ari," said Chris. He smiled generously.

"Thanks," she replied.

Rose wasn't sure if it was okay to eat yet. Cory wasn't either, but toddlers don't usually put much stock in manners. He took a bite, then another, and another. Since no one gave him any flak, Rose figured she was good to do the same.

"Mmm! This is so good," she said, still chewing.

"Do you have to talk and eat like that?" Chris chastised.

Rose swallowed and wiped her mouth clean with her sleeve.

"Sorry," she apologized. "I've never tasted anything this good before. What is this stretchy stuff?" A bit of mozzarella was strung between her fingers.

"That's cheese, Rose. It's cheese," Chris answered, reluctantly. He reached out to hand her a napkin.

Yesha pursed her lips in thought.

"You're dressed like a WTP soldier, but you're obviously not," she said to Chris.

He wiped the grease from his hands and lips, then glanced down at his attire.

"This? Foley left this in the room for me. Just needed some clothes."

"Then, you really are Campers?" Yesha's initial theory was confirmed.

"Campers?"

"I'm sorry. I didn't mean that to sound offensive, if it did. It's something we call people who are neither WTP nor Faction."

"Why Campers?"

"Everyone that's joined us from out there usually has a similar story. Without technology, they have to bounce around making camp wherever the Freeze and the Burn allow them to. Thus, Campers."

"Makes sense. I never heard of either of you before a few days ago, though."

"Really? So, where have you guys been? I mean, how have you survived with all the freezing, thawing, and burning?"

"We were on our way up through Panama when we ran into your guys. Settled in Colombia for a while, but the burn came early this time, so we were heading north. You just find a sweet spot in the weather pattern and move around with it. Gets cold, go south. When it warms up, head north again."

"I'm thirsty," Cory interrupted.

Chris held up his can of soda. "That's what this is for, kid," he said.

Cory picked up his own can, then turned it about. Curious as to what was inside, he shook it around to feel the liquid sloshing inside.

"Whoa, hold up." Chris took the can from Cory and set it down on the table. He popped the seal on his own can. The snap and hiss made Cory flinch. Rose laughed, highly amused. "Never shake these up, then open them," said Chris, handing Cory the open can.

Rose took the liberty of opening her own soda. The sound of the cracking seal pulled another giggle from within. Condensation rolled over their fingertips as she and Cory took their first sips of cold cola. They couldn't believe what was happening to their taste buds. A burp slipped from Cory's mouth, inadvertently. The look on his face swayed laughter from everyone.

"Did you always have this kind of food before?" asked Rose.

"Uh-huh," Yesha replied. "We had a lot of things that we took for granted in those days. Luckily, the WTP were able to help us get some of those things back. Maybe we can appreciate them more this time around."

"What exactly is this whole WTP thing?" Chris questioned.

"We're the ones that are going to get rid of the Faction and bring the world back to what it once was."

Chris didn't like the response one bit. He had heard those exact words once before.

"Not the canned reason you use to convince people that you're the good guys. Gimme what's real."

"They told us that big ship up there was supposed to take humanity to a new world," Yesha pointed towards the heavens. "They said that once they got to a safe distance, they could fire up the engines, and it would be OK. Do you remember that day? I do. Those bastards turned that thing on right above the atmosphere. There was so much wind. It was because the planet changed directions so fast, but I just remember flying. I was up so high, for so long. After that, I blacked out. They said I was out for months. When I woke up, I was in a makeshift hospital with a lot of other people in bad shape, most worse than me. I made it out with just a knock on the head and a broken arm. Over the last decade, we've managed to rebuild a portion of society to something we can be proud of, but that damned Faction is always in the way. We want freedom and a new life. They want control. So, to answer your question, the WTP is the only thing that stands in the way of the death of democracy."

Chris did remember that day. He knew what had really happened. In some ways, he was even culpable. He wanted to tell Yesha but wouldn't. It was a secret he may have to die with in the long run.

Foley came into the picture, just in the nick of time.

"Heeey. There you are," he greeted, propping his hand out for a handshake from Chris, who took it. "I sent Ari to bring you down, but I see you've already met her lovely mother, Yesha. She's one of our resident scientists. Once we find out where that ship crashed, they might be able to figure out what actually happened."

Chris got a little nervous.

Rose felt it.

"What's wrong?" she asked him.

"Nothing's wrong. Why would you think something's wrong?"

"Cause I can feel it."

"Hush. I'm in the middle of a conversation here," Chris replied, trying to pay attention to what Foley was saying.

By that time, Foley had finished rambling and was ready to be off.

"Anyway, I'll let you guys enjoy your meal. Continue to get the feel of things around here, and if you like it, maybe we can talk about a permanent fit," he said, bidding farewell.

Tension swelled in Rose again. She did not get a good read from Foley.

"Will you calm down? You're making me feel all weird," Chris said to Rose, after sharing her vibes. He pulled the tab on the soda he had confiscated from Cory, totally forgetting its shaken state. It hissed loudly, spraying a stream of suds into his face and up his nostrils. He breathed in and coughed violently.

Everyone laughed hysterically at Chris's misfortune. Rose's worrisome mood was even chased away, for the moment. A small win for Chris, but still a win. The trade-off was definitely worth a wet, sticky beard.

Silence brought on another serious engagement. Yesha looked Chris in the eyes as she spoke.

"Your children's mother?" she asked. "What of her?"

"Almost everyone we knew died that day," Chris replied, answering the question without actually answering it. He didn't break eye contact to avoid revealing deception.

"Her father?" he retorted.

"I don't remember. I assume he died that day as well. I have vague flashes of memory, but I can never see his face, just a T-shirt with a tiger on it and a dark sports car outside a restaurant. I know the memory is real, but it doesn't feel like it's mine. It's like I'm watching the story of someone else in my dreams. I wouldn't recognize him if he were sitting at this table."

"Maybe you'll remember one day."

"Maybe it's better if I don't," replied Yesha. She was ready to change subjects.

"How about we get out of here?"

"Sounds good to me," said Chris, standing to his feet.

Rose held Cory's hand as they filed back down the stairs. Something held fast to her mind.

"Why didn't you tell her that we aren't your kids?" she asked Chris.

"I don't know. I guess, the same reason you didn't." Chris's response was pleasant for Rose. She paused to gift him a hug.

Yesha smiled and descended the steps, pulling her own daughter a bit closer.

Idle conversation accompanied the group back to the living quarters. They were outside their doors before they knew it. Though the introduction and everything after flowed naturally, the goodbye was rather clunky.

"I guess we'll see you guys later," said Yesha, breaking the awkward silence.

"I guess we will. I mean, you will... see us, I mean. We'll see each other." Chris was stumbling over his words like a rookie bachelor. It had been years since he last had been in the presence of a woman, nonetheless, one he was attracted to.

Rose rolled her eyes, embarrassed.

"You suck at this," she said aloud.

"See, here you go," replied Chris. Annoyance overtook his nervousness.

Yesha couldn't help but laugh.

"Are you always this way with each other?" she asked.

"Always," responded Cory. He smacked his hand against his own forehead, signifying his patience with the two had long ended.

Yesha used her thumbprint to unlock her door.

"Well, if you need anything, you know where to find us," she said with a pleasant smile.

"Bye, guys," waved Ari, before disappearing inside.

Goodbyes given, Chris swiped the door pad to get inside his temporary residence. Rose followed, with Cory trailing behind.

"Why doesn't our door lock?" she asked.

"Probably because this isn't our place. Besides, we don't have anything to steal," Chris replied.

"Good point." Rose bee-lined for the television and began to channel surf.

Chris's first stop was the restroom. A brief search paid dividends with a cabinet of towels and hygiene products beneath the sink.

"This should work," he mumbled to himself, retrieving a bar of soap and a small washcloth.

The faucet squeaked lightly as it turned between Chris's fingers. Hot water pattering against the porcelain bowl sounded familiar, from a time before the beginning of the end.

'The only thing old-school in the entire place is a raggedy sink handle and shower knob,' he thought. With the towel soaked and lathered, Chris scrubbed the dried, sticky soda from his stubble. His peace was cut short when his peripheral caught movement from the bathroom doorway.

"I gotta go," said Cory.

"All yours," Chris replied. He left the room, still scrubbing the towel across his face. Images flashed on and off the television screen as Rose continued to flip through, searching for something that interested her.

"I hope you find what you're looking for," Chris said to her.

Rose replied without taking her eyes off the screen. "I don't know what I'm looking for. Never used a TV until we got here."

"Kids usually like cartoons. Try that."

Rose ignored his suggestion. "Someone's been in here," she said instead.

"What? How would you know that?"

"There's stacks of clothes on the beds."

Chris looked in the children's room, then his own. There appeared to be about a week's worth of clothing for the three of them. He shuffled through the piles meant for himself. There were a couple of combat outfits identical to the one he was currently wearing, some comfortable civilian clothing, and sleepwear, all made from that strange material. It was cool to the touch and far more comfortable than any cotton he had ever felt.

"Those are fresh clothes for us. You guys should shower and get comfortable. I'll go after," Chris suggested, now back in the living room.

"Uhh, how?" asked Rose.

It hadn't dawned on Chris. The children had grown up in an apocalyptic world. They probably never used a shower before.

"Didn't you shower before I woke up?"

"Some lady turned it on for us."

"Well, look. It's easy. I'll show you how to turn it on, so you won't need someone else to do it next time."

"Next time? You mean we're staying here?" Rose was disappointed.

"I don't know," replied Chris. "I'm just taking this one step at a time, Rose."

"I just don't like it here. I mean, I like the stuff, but something doesn't feel right."

"What about Ari and Yesha? They seem OK."

"Yeah, but... I don't know." Rose fell silent, caught between the things she liked and hated about the place.

Chris sensed her inner conflict. Their emotional status was, once again, meshing together. It was far beyond empathy. He actually felt what she felt.

"Let's not worry about it right now. We can make a decision after we know more. Together," he said, using his arms to emphasize the word "together."

"Alright," Rose responded.

"Come on, so I can show you how to turn this shower on and set it to the right temperature."

Cory was sure to tag along. He wanted to learn as well. Neither Rose nor Chris had any idea how much of a sponge he was, always silent, always learning. Always.

***

An hour later, Chris stepped out of the restroom, swirling a towel around inside his ear to dry any remaining moisture. His large biceps flexed the sleeve of a tight-fitting, black long sleeve shirt. On this particular article of clothing, the special material had been woven thin enough to accentuate the contours of every muscle fiber of his chiseled torso. The matching black pants were looser fitting.

He barely made it a couple of steps before a knock at the door altered his route. Rose and Cory ignored it altogether. They were dressed in pajamas, sitting on the floor, attempting to put together an adult puzzle. Amazingly, they were very successful. Over half of the eight hundred pieces were already in place.

Chris wasn't aware of any peephole or other method of seeing who the visitor was, so he just went ahead and opened the door. Yesha and her daughter Ari were standing on the other side. They had changed into their comfort clothing as well.

Awkwardness made another brief appearance. Yesha's eyes traced every rounded arch on Chris's person. His chest bulged out, two rounded orbs above his brick-like abdominals. The nappy stubble was groomed into a smooth, coarse carpet, lining a swooping C from his mustache to his sideburns. His eyes even seemed a bit browner, as did his skin.

After a few seconds, Yesha cleared her throat and spoke up.

"Interested in movie night?" she asked, tilting her head to sway a preferred answer. She held up the case of a once-popular mega film.

Ari stood in silence. She couldn't speak at the moment, even if she wanted to. Her mouth was busy chewing through a fistful of buttered popcorn. The bowl she held was about as wide as she was.

"What's that?" asked Rose. The children had finally pried themselves away from their task to see who had come by.

"Popcorn," Ari attempted to say with her mouth full.

"What?" Rose's eyebrows furrowed in confusion.

"It's popcorn," said Yesha, filling in the answer for her preoccupied daughter. She then redirected her attention to Ari.

"Don't speak with your mouth full," she mumbled.

"Can I try some?" asked Rose.

Ari reached the bowl out to her.

Rose popped a few kernels into her mouth. "Do you have any more stuff like this over there?" she asked, definitively pleased with the response of her taste buds.

"Yup! We have chocolate candy bars, chips, and a lot of other good snacks," said Ari.

"We're in," said Rose.

"Guess that's your answer," Chris responded. He wanted to say yes just as much, but it was more comfortable for it to be the children's idea. There was one flaw in his plan for secrecy. He no longer had a monopoly on his feelings, whether joyful or otherwise. As long as Rose was nearby, she could detect his overall mood. She turned to give him a wink on her way out the door. He pretended not to see her, but she knew he did.

The hamper near the restroom door clunked as Chris's towel landed on top, forcing its way through the revolving lid.

"Let's go, Cory," he said. "We're going to watch a movie at Yesha and Ari's."

Cory skipped out the door. A final scan of the room brought the puzzle back into Chris's view.

"What the hell?" he said to himself. The entire thing was complete. He put away the observation, entered the hallway, and followed the group to Yesha's door. He did his best to keep his thoughts clean, but it had been so long—about five years—trapped alone in a deserted world. Yesha wasn't helping at all. She wasn't a thin woman by any stretch of the imagination. She was full-figured, yet fit, and it was clear that she took care of herself well. Yoga pants had been the downfall of man since the invention of spandex waistbands and stretchy synthetics. Hers hugged her hips, her thighs, her everything, as best they could, in a struggle to fulfill their purpose.

***

The interior of Yesha's place was much different from the one Chris, Rose, and Cory were currently staying in. Its feel was more homely in comparison to the laboratory-like decor of their space. There was wood trimming, art on the walls, and a palette of colors on the furnishings. It was also about twice as big.

Ari headed straight for the beanbag chairs in front of the television. Rose and Cory followed suit, giggling at the wiggly, cloud-like seating.

"What are these things called?" asked Rose.

Ari seemed to glow with happiness.

"It's a beanbag," she replied.

"Beans? I hate beans," said Cory. He had had enough of those to last the rest of his life.

"It's not beans like the kind you eat," laughed Ari.

"Ohhh. Well, what are they for?"

"To sit on. It's like a chair, but more comfy."

"It's weird, but I like it," said Rose.

Chris found his way to the couch. It was a dark, earthy color. His fingers rubbed across the surface. There it was again—that material was everywhere.

"What is this stuff?" he asked Yesha.

"What's what?" she questioned, popping the disc into the player.

"This fabric. It's everywhere. The couch is made of it, the clothes, even the tablecloth at the pizza place."

Yesha sat on the couch and picked up the remote. "Oh, it's called Thermalight. You get hot, it gets cold. You get cold, it gets hot. Moisture-wicking too, and lightweight," she replied.

Both Rose and Cory looked down to feel the hem of their pajamas. It was the first time they had paid it any mind at all. Chris, however, had just realized that he hadn't been hot or cold since he had gotten dressed. No matter where they had been, the temperature always seemed moderate.

"You make it here?" Chris investigated further.

"Not here. The WTP has control over the project facility that was responsible for its design before the world broke. They make it there and ship it to the bigger colonies, like this one."

"Project facilities? I used to live near 047." Chris didn't know why he didn't tell the whole truth.

"Really?" Yesha's eyes nearly popped out of her head. "I used to work there!" she said with enthusiasm.

"Mom, the movie?" Ari interrupted.

"Oh, sorry," Yesha said, apologetically. "We'll talk later," she whispered to Chris, pressing the play button.

***

All three children were out by the end of the second film. Empty packaging from various snacks littered the room. Cory lay with his mouth wide open, and a candy bar wrapper stuck to his chin. They had eaten themselves into a coma-like sleep.

"And then there were two," joked Yesha.

Chris laughed. Her personality was refreshing, nonabrasive, and light. She was a gentle soul. Still, he wasn't one to take advantage of her kindness.

"I should get them to bed," he said.

Yesha had a suggestion.

"How about they just sleep over with Ari?" she asked. "Looks like they're becoming good friends already."

Chris looked at them. They were happy. It was written all over their chocolate-covered lips.

"OK, cool," he replied. "They sure look cool with it."

They shared a laugh as Yesha walked Chris to the door.

"Tomorrow then," she said, going for a friendly hug. It only lasted a brief moment, but time felt malleable. She smelled so good, like honey and wild berries. It wasn't lust like it had been for Lola. It was deeper. He had felt this sort of instant connection only once before. The thought made him pull away. Years later, he still missed her, as if it were day one.

"Tomorrow," he said, heading out.

* * *

Chris kicked off his slippers, removed his shirt, and sat on the edge of the bed. What a mind job he was doing on himself. In all likelihood, Melissa had been dead since before the Earth was dying. He just wanted to be loyal to her, the way he hadn't been when he had the chance. Of course, that chance would never come again, and being alone the rest of his life wouldn't make up for what he had done.

Knocking pulled him back to the present. So much for that, he thought. Chris figured one or both of the children had woken up, wanting nothing to do with a sleepover. Rose didn't seem to trust anyone but him, as it was. Cory was even less trusting.

He opened the door, with his line of sight already set to look Rose in the eyes. There were no eyes there, but mahogany skin between the hems of an unbuttoned pajama top. He looked down. There were those dreaded yoga pants. His gaze then met Yesha's eyes. She stepped inside and closed the door behind her.

* * *

Nearly another hour passed by. Yesha sat up to regain her composure. The shaking of her legs faded away as her adrenaline dissipated.

"I should be heading back over there," she said.

"Right now?" asked Chris.

"I thought you were so intent on making me fall in love."

Yesha smiled.

"Don't need the kids waking up alone. Besides, I think that's already accomplished," she replied.

"That sounds good."

"Just wait on it. It'll kick in when I'm gone."

Yesha started to get dressed. Her identification card dropped on the floor. Chris remembered her using the card to pay for their meal, as well as open her door. There must have been something else to it.

"What exactly do you do here?" he asked.

"I'm a structural engineer."

"What did you do at 047?"

"Unfortunately, I helped build the stupid ship that caused this whole catastrophe."

"And here?"

"Made something more worthwhile. This entire place is actually my design."

Chris was impressed.

"Wow. You're really great at your job," he said.

"Thanks," replied Yesha. "You know, it's so ironic that you lived that close, yet we never met. We probably walked past each other a million times in Memphis." She had no clue they were certainly in close vicinity to one another, more often than not. As she worked on the LOGOS, Chris trained soldiers a floor beneath her feet.

"Probably best, considering we were both in relationships at the time," he replied.

"Fair point." Yesha was back in her sleepwear, ready to leave the room.

"One more question before you leave."

"What's up?"

"How many of the project facilities were you able to recover?"

"Not many. Most of them belong to the Faction."

"Them again. I wonder where they came from."

111

"I promise you one thing," said Yesha. "You'll find that out sooner or later." Having given her response, Yesha leaned over the bed, kissing Chris like she was contemplating an additional round. Suddenly, she pulled away, bug-eyed.

"What's wrong?" Chris asked.

"A mem... I just remembered...," Yesha was too flustered to complete her thought.

Chris sat up, sensing something off.

"Remembered what?" he asked.

Yesha's eyes darted back and forth, but she quickly regained her composure.

"Nothing, just work stuff. I'll see you later," she replied, heading for the door.

Chris was left stumped by the ending to what was otherwise a beautiful day. It was rare to find a woman he liked on more than a physical or platonic level. He hoped he hadn't ruined this one before it even began.

***

Chris was woken up by yet another knock at the door. This one sounded heavy-handed. He was exhausted. There certainly wasn't much sleep had that night. His size ten slides scrubbed the floor as he approached the door, too tired to lift his feet fully.

It opened to a fully energized Foley.

"My guess is you either had a great night or a completely shitty one. Either way, you don't look too well," he said.

"Just tired is all," Chris replied.

"Fair enough. I need you to walk with me. How long would it take you to get ready?"

"I don't know, fifteen minutes, maybe. The kids are at Yesha's though."

"Don't worry about them. You just get dressed. I'll go over and ask her to take them to the center with all the other youngsters. I'll walk you over to get them after we're done."

"Alright, fine," Chris responded.

Less than half an hour went by. Chris rinsed, spit

into the sink, and came into the living room, fully geared, including weaponry provided courtesy of Foley, who sat on the arm of the sofa in wait.

"Mr. Fuckin' Nobody. Let's go," he said.

The two coasted down the corridor into an area that Chris had never been. They soon approached a moderately sized room full of computers manned by employees in blue jumpsuits. Chris recognized what was on the many monitors scattered around.

"Cable television," he said. "I was wondering how you pulled that off."

"Over the years, we compiled films, shows, plays, and whatever else we could find, digital or physical. We even have a place where we shoot our own daily news." Foley pointed at a small offshoot with a desk and live camera.

"A bit much."

"Nothing's a bit much when it comes to providing for our people. We want to give everyone a shot at normalcy. Eventually, we want to spread that normalcy across the globe. You could help us with that."

"By fighting a war I don't understand?"

"Look around you," said Foley, guiding Chris further down the hall, pointing around. "We have agriculture here, tech advancement there, restaurants with real food, air conditioning, running water—hell, we even have people making chocolate candy bars."

"Yeah, everything looks good here, but I'm sure that if I were with the other guys, they'd show me the same type of things to convince me their fight was worthy."

"We've shown you who we are. If you don't trust your own senses, that's on you, but this is a working society. Everyone here has a job. Jobs are assigned by skill. Children are trained in skills based on their attributes and natural talents. Nobody stays here with a free ride."

Chris laughed. "There it is," he said. "The give and take."

"We're adults here. Society has always been this way. You earn your keep."

"I'll pass. I was good on my own."

"And the kids? You'd take them away from a good life?"

"Don't worry about them. They're my responsibility."

"Says who? They're not even your kids."

"You know what, we're done here. Take me to my kids, and we'll get out of your hair."

"Don't be like that," Foley thought for a second. "How about this? You stay for one more night. Sleep on it. Talk it over with the little ones, and if you're still sure you want to leave, we'll give you a few supplies to help you out."

Chris didn't want to spend any more time there, especially after what he had just heard. He felt forced. He also suspected that Rose had been right all along—there was something more to the WTP. Still, the supplies intrigued him. Not sensing any immediate danger, he agreed.

***

The rest of the day was rather uneventful compared to the last. On the way back to their temporary residence, Chris and the children stopped by the food court to get a bucket of freshly fried chicken. From that point forward, they sat in front of the television, dozing in and out of sleep. By late evening, Chris began to wonder if he would see Yesha. He assumed she would stop by when she was free, but she hadn't. His next thought was to take the initiative—he really wanted to see her before they left.

Chris knocked at her door. Only the sound of the television was audible through the door. He knocked again. Still nothing. Was she not home? Was she avoiding him? Uneasiness began to spread through his mind.

"Rose, I need you to pack up all the clothing they gave you. Cory's too," he said after returning.

"We're leaving?" she asked, part relieved, part disappointed. The place was growing on her. So were Yesha and Ari.

"Yeah," Chris replied. "You were right. There's something off about Foley and this place, and we're not sticking around to find out what it is."

"Does that mean we have to go back to eating beans?" asked Cory, still holding a greasy chicken bone between his fingertips.

"Not anytime soon. We're staying the night. In the morning, I'll get some supplies from Foley, then we'll leave and find our own place."

"What about Yesha and Ari?" asked Rose.

"I went over to say goodbye, but no one was there. I'll try again in the morning," Chris replied.

Rose did as she was asked, taking a backpack from the storage in their room and shoving as much clothing as she could fit inside. A puzzle or two also found their way into the side pocket.

Chris also took the liberty of clearing out the bathroom cabinet. Hygiene products would be put to good use out in the uncivilized world. However, the night would be a cautious one. He decided it best to keep his weapons on and for them all to sleep in the living room. What wasn't clear to him was whether this choice was due to his own uneasy feelings or those transferred from Rose through their telepathic abilities.

Decorative couch pillows served as makeshift beds. Very little sleep came to Chris until the early hours of the morning. Yesha hadn't reached out to him at all. He replayed the previous day in his mind, searching for something he might have said or done wrong. He concluded that he had done nothing—it was her, not him. He even felt foolish for losing sleep over a woman he had known for only a couple of days.

At last, he drifted into a state of deep rest. It wouldn't last. Loud hissing woke him from his slumber as soon as he had arrived in dreamland. Rose and Cory flinched so hard they fell from the couch.

"What the hell is that?" yelled Rose.

"Language!" Chris chastised.

"Really? That's what you're worried about right now?" Rose exclaimed.

Cory was scared. He started to cry out in full panic as a white mist shot out of hidden nozzles throughout the room. Coughing soon overtook his wails of despair.

"They're trying to gas us!" Chris yelled.

"What are we going to do?" asked Rose, panic rising in her voice.

Rather than respond, Chris sprang into action. He focused his mind to find each individual molecule of gas in the air. The visible white cloud started to swirl away from them, leaving a small cocoon of fresh air enveloping the trio. The remaining gas filled the room so heavily that visibility was reduced to almost nothing.

Chris, Rose, and Cory all gasped for oxygen. A few more heavy coughs purged their lungs clean enough to function properly.

"Now do you believe me?" Rose asked.

Chris shushed her. There would be time for her to gloat later, but the trouble hadn't passed.

"Quiet," he whispered. "They're about to come in, and they won't be expecting us to still be awake."

The door slid open without a sound. Five WTP soldiers entered, wearing gas masks. Their handguns remained holstered. Gassed prey couldn't fight back, so precautions weren't taken. What they didn't know was that Chris was hardly ever prey, no matter the situation. The soldiers entered at a casual pace, with nothing but looped zip-ties in hand. As the gas escaped through the door, visibility gradually improved. Once the dark uniforms of the soldiers faded into view, Chris sprang into action.

An open palm strike to the throat of the first soldier dropped him to his knees. He barely had a chance to gasp for air before Chris roundhouse-kicked him into unconsciousness. The thud of his body hitting the ground alerted his partners. They all pulled their sidearms, but were bewildered when their weapons flew from their grips, seemingly on their own. It was another of Chris's magic tricks. Simultaneously, he spun around, driving his elbow into the temple of the nearest adversary. It was a thing of beauty, comparable to the twirl of a seasoned ballerina. The soldier joined his companion in slumber.

The air was now clear enough for everyone to see. Rose and Cory took shelter behind the couch, clinging to each other tightly. Three soldiers remained. Rather than one at a time, they surged together. Chris parried the lone man's punch and ducked under one woman's kick, but the second woman's heel struck him square in the chest. He stumbled backward as they sized each other up again.

The more aggressive of the women led the next assault. She kicked high and swept low. Chris blocked the first attack and jumped over the second, but as his feet touched the floor, a fist crashed into his jaw, sending him careening into the mounted television, which cracked open and fell to the floor.

"Mr. Nobody!" Rose screamed. He was losing, and she had no idea what to do.

Chris slowly got up, holding his hip with one hand and wiping blood from his mouth with the other.

"I got this," he reassured her, though it sounded almost like a joke.

The first woman lunged again. Chris ducked her punch but kept his eyes up, waiting for the next move. When a spinning heel kick came from the second woman, he caught her leg mid-air and violently slammed her into her male counterpart. Their masks clanked together, and they joined the others in unconsciousness.

And then, there was one. Though Chris couldn't see the woman's face, her body language showed fear. He feigned an attack to watch her flinch. She nearly tripped over her own feet, clearly rattled. It upset her, causing all rationality to fly out the window. Going on the offensive so thoughtlessly was a bad decision. Chris sidestepped and drove his fist into her stomach. Every ounce of air must have left her body. She didn't even notice Chris pluck the zip ties from her belt loop as they fought. He slipped one around her wrists and cinched it tight, rolling her onto her face to bind her ankles together, then used a third to link both ties. She was now bound, like an amateur hog-tie job.

Chris glanced at Rose, who looked at him with intense disapproval.

"Too much?" Chris asked. Rose didn't need to reply. He pulled his blade and cut the third tie, leaving the soldier to lay somewhat comfortably.

The purpose wasn't entirely clear, but for whatever reason, Foley wanted Chris and the children alive. Chris had no doubt the kidnapping order had come from him. He would figure it out later. Right now, they hadn't escaped danger just yet.

"Grab your bag, and let's go," Chris ordered Rose. His voice had a hint of rasp in it. Rose had learned that when his voice took that tone, he was all business. She slung her backpack on her shoulders, and Chris followed suit with his own.

The hallways were eerily empty. That wasn't normal. This society functioned much like the old U.S. — people always coming and going, even at night. There should have been night owls, third-shift workers, someone. Chris suspected there was more going on. His time with Yesha might have meant nothing to her. He was just a pawn in a larger endgame. Whoever orchestrated this clearly thought the takedown would be easy. No backup appeared to be nearby. Chris moved silently through the halls, with Rose and Cory close behind, their footsteps dampened on the hard tile.

Chris peeked around each corner before leading the children forward. It wasn't long before he saw what he expected: two guards posted at the end of the hall, ensuring no one interrupted.

Rose, realizing something crucial, communicated telepathically, "We don't know our way out."

"I do. The old entrances to the stadium. I saw them when we ate there. They're gated off, but there's gotta be a way through. That's our best bet," Chris replied.

"What about them?" Rose asked, referring to the guards.

"I'll take care of them. Once I do, we have to run for it. Don't stop."

In a split second, both guards were down. But the plan fell apart almost immediately. A squad of soldiers rounded the corner, fully geared for combat.

"Shit! Run the other way!" Chris yelled. They sprinted back the way they had come. As they ran, Chris swiped at every door pad, praying one would open.

Locked. Locked. At last, a door slid open.

"In here!" Chris ordered. Rose and Cory nearly ran past, but adjusted to squeeze inside. Chris locked the door of the small ten-by-ten supply closet. He knew it would only buy them a few minutes, at best. If any of the soldiers had a key card, even less.

"Can't you just teleport us out of here?" Rose asked, her voice shaking.

"I told you, it doesn't work like that. I can't open a portal to a place I haven't seen. And it has to be close. Too far, and I'll pass out again."

Seconds of silence followed, then Chris had an idea.

"Wait, didn't you see the outside of the building when we arrived?"

"Yeah, but how does that help us?"

"If you have the powers I have, then you can get us out of here."

"What? I don't know how to do anything but talk in your head. Sometimes I can feel what you feel, but I don't even do that on purpose. It just happens."

"Exactly!" Chris said, snapping his fingers in a eureka moment. "Words and feelings might not be the only thing we can share."

"I don't get it."

"What did it look like outside?"

"I don't know. There was a little snow, a few trees... ooo, and some old buildings. I remember the outside of the big dome thingy too."

"That's good, Rose. Now I need you to close your eyes and concentrate on that."

Footsteps grew louder outside the door.

"They're coming," Rose panicked. Cory remained scared silent, his wide eyes speaking for him.

Chris grabbed Rose by the shoulders.

"Ignore them. I really need you to focus for this to work," he said, though he wasn't sure if it would.

Rose closed her eyes again and pictured the outside world. It was almost as if she was already there. She could feel the chilly wind on her nose. The crunch of snow underfoot. She could hear the breeze rustling through leafless branches.

Chris closed his eyes too, searching for a connection with Rose's mind. Nothing. He tried again. Nothing... then, bingo. He could see himself standing next to Rose in her memories. Their eyes opened, glowing a brilliant shade of blue. Rose's eyes were already blue, but this was different—quasars upon white orbs. Cory couldn't bear to look at them, but he couldn't look away either. Trapped in a middle ground of fear and admiration, he thought to himself, 'A real superhero.'

Lightning-like rods formed as atoms split, creating a portal through space and time. The outside world appeared within, their way out. Without hesitation, the three of them stepped through. Moments later, the door to the closet burst open, but it was too late. All that remained was the faint scent of burned ozone.

***

Light flirted with the sky, but dawn had not yet fully arrived. Bright stadium lights illuminated the perimeter of the old stadium. Chris, Rose, and Cory appeared in a shaded area, just off the main entrance road.

"It worked!" Rose shouted, her eyes wide with joyful surprise.

Cory took in the area around them, still trying to grasp the concept of changing locations without a real door. Chris, however, wasn't looking so good. He dropped to his knees on the cold, snow-patched ground, clutching his head as a piercing migraine racked his brain. There wasn't a word strong enough to describe this kind of pain. Rose felt it too, though less intensely. She squinted and pressed her hands to her temples. After a few seconds, she was able to shake it off.

"What's wrong, Rosi?" Cory asked, his voice full of concern.

"Nothing, I'm fine," Rose lied. She knelt beside Chris, offering her hand in support. The moment her hand touched the fabric of his shirt, everything became clear. In the blink of an eye, Rose's eyes glowed even brighter, and blue sparks danced around both their bodies. These sparks were different—far more passive than the violent portals Chris created. The sight was so mesmerizing that Cory reached out to grasp at the ones floating into the air.

Gradually, Chris's heart rate slowed, and his muscles relaxed. His grunts of agony turned into deep breaths, and eventually, calm.

"How did you do that?" Chris asked, wiping sweat from his forehead.

"I don't know. It just happened."

Chris stood up and knocked the snow from his knees. Rose was perplexed, trying to understand.

"What did you do?" she asked.

He had no idea what she meant.

"Excuse me?"

"You broke your mind. What did you do?" Rose clarified.

"I didn't do anything."

"You're lying. You told me."

"I didn't tell you anything," Chris said, becoming defensive.

"Not this you," Rose insisted, pointing at his chest. "The you in there."

This was an uncomfortable conversation. "Look, we've gotta move before they decide to come looking for us out here," Chris said, trying to redirect the focus.

Rose wasn't having it. "I'm not going anywhere until you tell me what you did!"

"Fine, if it's that damn important to you!"

"Language!" Rose shouted.

"Do you want us to get caught?"

"We disappeared in a mop closet. Nobody is looking for us out here."

Chris's evasive tactics weren't working, so he gave in. "Look, I tried to go back," he admitted.

"Back where?"

"In time. I tried to go back to before we broke the world. I had done it before—turned back time. I saved someone really important to me, but that was only for a few seconds. I don't know how long I was out after the planet spun out of control, but it was too long. I saw it, though. I saw the past. I just didn't have enough power to get there. Something in my head snapped, and ever since, I've had limited use of my power. Too much, and this happens."

"I patched it," Rose revealed, content with his explanation. "It didn't feel permanent, but you're better for now. So, what are we going to do?"

"Put some distance between us and them. Let's hope the weather in this area is stable enough to survive. If we can get through the next few nights, we'll be alright."

***

Footprints stretched back for miles in the melting snow. At random intervals, Chris would double back or even triple back to confuse anyone attempting to track him and the children. The smell of approaching spring made him fear that the burn could reach as far north as their current location, so he guided them towards true north.

The terrain was rugged, at a minimum. Many buildings had begun to crumble, while others were overgrown with vegetation that had been dormant during the Freeze. Now that warmth was spreading, vines and shrubs were awakening, further claiming what used to be a civilized world.

Texas's climate was unpredictable, no longer the dry, arid land of the past. Long spells of ice and snow clung to the region for brief periods, followed by spiking humidity and elevated temperatures. Heavy rains turned the land into a breeding ground for plants of all kinds.

Nightfall was approaching. Chris decided it was time to make camp while they still had daylight to work with.

"This is probably a good spot for us to stop for the night," he said.

Cory agreed, "Good, 'cause I'm tired."

"That's 'cause you have those itty bitty legs."

The surrounding area had once been a small but pricey Dallas suburb. A few of the houses still stood rigidly, with vines, moss, and superficial damage telling the story of their battered history.

"So, where do you wanna live?" Chris asked Rose and Cory.

"Uhh, that one," Rose pointed.

"I wasn't talking to you." Rose balled up her fist and whacked Chris on the arm, hitting the same spot as usual with pinpoint accuracy.

"Ouch! Why are you so violent?" Chris rubbed the stinging sensation from her needle-like fist.

"Porqué eres tan estúpido? Viejo," Rose mumbled.

"Aye! I heard you. What did I tell you about that? Keep on, and... you... you..." Chris struggled to find a kid-friendly insult. Finally, he settled on, "You're ugly, you know that, right? Like a little fruit fly without wings."

"Ha! You wish," Rose replied, flipping her head back dramatically.

"Was that supposed to be a hair flip?" Chris laughed, catching up to them.

When they reached the house Cory had chosen, Chris saw what had caught his eye: all the windows were still intact, though some were cracked. Initially, it put him on edge. The only way this could be possible was if someone had replaced them after the world broke. But upon closer inspection, he realized they were thick, shatterproof windows. It would take far more time and force to break them than they had endured.

This introduced a small problem—they would need a more creative method of entry. Chris delivered a couple of heavy kicks to the door, but its stout frame held fast. He readied for a third kick, but Rose stepped in front of him.

"You think you can do better?" he asked smugly.

Rose turned the knob, and the door squeaked open on rusty hinges. There was no need for a reply.

The inside was orderly. The only signs that it hadn't been lived in were a thin layer of dust and scattered spider webs in the corners of walls and furniture. Cory wrinkled his nose and pinched it off with his fingers.

"It's stinky in here," he complained.

"It's just stale air," Chris said. "I'll open some windows."

He chose windows in the back of the house, where

it wouldn't be visible if someone passed by. The kitchen was his next planned stop anyway. It took quite a bit of effort to force the windows open—the wood frames had swollen and jammed in place. Even with all his might, Chris only managed to get about five inches of clearance.

"That'll have to do for now," he muttered.

Rose and Cory had already started exploring the kitchen. Rose made the mistake of opening the refrigerator, unleashing the foulest stench of long-rotten food and dead creatures that had crawled inside. The smell hit her so hard that she vomited all over the floor.

Chris quickly slammed the door shut.

"Let's not open that again."

Cory hesitated before opening a cabinet, remembering Rose's unfortunate experience.

"I see you're a fast learner," Chris reassured him. "Pretty sure it's safe to open that one."

The cabinet contained only cleaning supplies and chemicals. Cory closed it and moved on.

A few more minutes of searching produced a satisfying amount of still-viable canned and dry food. Even better, the rats and pests hadn't reached the pantry.

"It's untouched by scavengers. I bet most of the neighborhood is like this. Especially the ones built like this. Nothing can get in. I think we found our home, kids," Chris said, pleased with what he was seeing.

"Let's bring as much stuff here as we can. We can set traps for protection and live here as long as we stay out of sight. If the Burn and Freeze don't touch here, we could last a long time."

The children were ecstatic. There was finally a possibility of a true home, away from evil people, and with food other than beans. But there was still one thing left to address.

"I couldn't help you in there," Rose admitted. She felt defenseless.

"It's not your fault," Chris said confidently. "You're only a kid."

"I'm not just a kid. I'm a superhero."

Chris nodded. "True," he agreed.

"What good is a superhero who doesn't know how to fight?" Rose's eyes dropped to the floor.

"I made you a promise." Chris lifted her chin with his finger.

"Take off your backpack."

"Right now?" Rose asked.

"Better now than later."

Chris picked up Cory and set him on the kitchen island counter. Rose dropped her bag to the ground.

"Stand like this," Chris instructed.

Rose did her best to mimic his stance.

"Now I want you to use your rear foot to kick here." Chris raised his hand, chest level, as a target.

Rose swung her foot but lost her balance and fell to the floor, her face turning red with embarrassment.

"Nobody gets everything right on the first try," Chris reassured her, helping her to her feet.

"Get in your stance again."

Rose did as he said. Chris steadied her shoulders and used his foot to slide hers further apart, widening her base.

"Again," he commanded, his voice firm.

This time, Rose's foot made it slightly lower than Chris's hand, but she managed to keep her feet. Chris caught her leg mid-swing and lifted it to his chin.

"Aim high. Most people will be taller than you. And straighten your support leg."

Chris used his hand to guide her into the correct posture, then released her foot.

"Again."

The next kick landed on its mark, but barely made a sound. It wouldn't knock over a fly. Rose adjusted her stance. Chris lifted her guard higher.

"Hands up here," he said. His next instruction was about power. Chris used his hands to help Rose rotate her waist.

"Your strength comes from here, not your legs or feet. Now kick like you mean it."

The snap of Rose's foot against Chris's palm was audible.

"Again." Rose kicked so hard a grunt escaped her lips.

"Again!" Rose twisted her hips with fury.

"Put all your pain in it. Everything you've lost is a tool. Use it. Kick with your soul!"

Rose yelled at the top of her lungs and drove her foot into Chris's palm with everything she had.

4

We're Not Kids Anymore

"Again!" Chris belted once more. Rose responded with a low kick to high kick combination, followed by a flurry of fast, snapping punches. Chris blocked the low, ducked beneath the high, and parried her fists, but she was relentless. A flying knee nearly grazed Chris' nose, but his reflexes were as sharp as ever. After dodging the attack, he attempted a front kick to Rose's midsection. She spiraled around it and threw a back fist aimed for the rear of Chris' head. He blocked, but it only seemed to anger his student. Rose executed a back handspring to create space, then opened a portal. Cory dived through, unleashing a barrage of precise attacks, yet Chris evaded every solid connection.

The two worked in unison, keeping Chris on the defensive. Rose layered the use of her powers between maneuvers seamlessly, and Cory had become one with her intentions, dancing in tune. It was art—beautiful, even. But Chris was better. He dropped both of them on their rears.

"That's enough," he said. "Rose, you're too aggressive—too much emotion, not enough strategy. Cory, you're the complete opposite. No fire, and you think way too much. You complement each other well, but what happens if someone good enough catches you alone? I didn't use my power once, and I still beat both of you at the same time."

The statement wasn't entirely true. Chris hadn't used any active abilities, but he had learned to extend his senses. Not only could he observe movement by sight, like everyone else, but he could also feel pressure fluctuations in the fabric of space, making him aware of an incoming attack before his eyes registered it.

"Here he goes with the lectures," Cory complained.

"Shut up! You're the one that let him beat us again!" Rose argued.

"How is it always my fault? You're the superhero, remember? I'm just the sidekick."

"Ugh! I hate both of you so much!" Rose stormed off toward the house, slamming the door behind her.

Chris chuckled. "Don't look at me. She's your sister," he reminded Cory, who headed straight for the fridge as soon as they were inside. He retrieved a pack of frozen peas and pressed it against his ribs.

"Why do you always hit the same spot?" Cory asked.

Chris leaned on the kitchen counter, reaching into the cookie jar. "Because you keep leaving the same spot open."

Cory decided to change the subject before Chris launched into another hour-long lesson. "What's her problem today?"

"What are you asking me for? Ask her."

"You know she won't tell me anything, but you can get into her head and feel what's going on."

"Nope. Not doing that again. Last time I tried, I ended up wanting to cry, laugh, and hunch my own leg all at the same time." Chris shook his head. "That's probably it."

"What's 'it'?"

"There aren't any boys around," Chris concluded.

"I'm a boy."

"Boy, to be so smart, you're not that bright," Chris said, finishing off his cookie.

Cory finally caught on. "There aren't any girls around, and I'm fine."

Chris leaned closer and pointed at Cory's face. "You won't be for long. That peach fuzz on your lip? Give it a few weeks, and you'll be slamming doors and humping stuffed animals."

Cory rubbed his upper lip. "You know you're on generator duty today, right?" Chris informed him.

"Why don't you ever do it?"

Chris stroked his scruffy beard. "See these gray hairs? They mean I'm a grown-ass man. In fact, *the* grown-ass man. Ain't another one in this house."

"Man, that's your excuse for everything."

"I don't need another reason. Tell you what—when you can whip my ass by yourself, you can make the rules. Until then, get down there and make sure the tank doesn't run dry."

Cory threw his hands up and went to do his duty. As he opened the basement door, Rose's door shot open down the hall, catching his attention. Chris stood in the middle of the hallway, staring her down.

"What are you doing?" Chris asked.

"That's not you?" Rose replied.

Cory felt left out. "Can somebody tell the one normal human being what the hell is going on?"

"Language!" Chris and Rose yelled in unison. Cory had just about had enough of them.

"If that's not us, then someone is coming," Rose said.

Cory frowned. "I thought you two could only sense each other. How can you sense someone else?"

"Guess it's new," Chris reasoned. "Go cut the generator. Hurry, before they hear the appliances."

Cory leapt down the stairs and hit the kill switch. The house went dark. Rose and Chris moved into the living room, their senses heightened as they prepared for whatever came next. If the WTP or Faction had found them, they were ready to fight.

But the most surprising thing happened. Someone lightly knocked on the door. By that time, Cory had rejoined them. They exchanged puzzled looks until the knock came again.

"Check the peephole," Chris directed Rose.

Rose shook her head. "Haven't you seen the movies? When someone looks through the peephole, they always get shot in the face. How am I going to find a man if I get shot in the face?"

Cory, tired of the back-and-forth, checked the peephole himself.

"It's some girl," he whispered. "She's pretty... real pretty."

"She could have shot you in the face!" Rose whispered back.

"This isn't a movie, Rose. Nobody can tell when you're looking through the peephole."

Rose felt embarrassed. "Smart-ass," she mumbled.

"The girl," Chris interjected. "Is she alone?"

"Looks like it," Cory replied.

Impatient, Chris decided to confront the situation head-on. "To hell with it," he said, opening the door. The girl looked young—somewhere between Cory and Rose's age, not yet an adult, but already blossoming into a young lady. Her dark, curly hair bobbed on her shoulders in the breeze, and her large brown eyes matched her creamy tan complexion.

Chris yanked her inside, checked for anyone else outside, then shut and locked the door.

"It's me," the girl said before anyone could question her.

Chris's aggression faded as soon as he heard her voice, though he didn't yet know why.

Rose's eyes softened too. "Ari?" she said, her voice rising.

"Yeah!" Ari replied excitedly, glad Rose remembered her.

"What are you doing here? Where's your mother?" Chris asked.

"She doesn't know where I am. I snuck away yesterday."

"Why?"

"Something bad is going on there. People have been coming up missing. Nobody knows why, but my mom has been acting really strange. She's afraid of something. She tried to hide it from me, but I could feel it. I was hoping you could help us."

"How did you even find us?"

Ari's voice shook with nervousness. "Well... I felt you. Both of you."

"What do you mean, you felt us?" asked Rose.

Cory had already figured it out. "You're like them, aren't you?" he surmised. Ari nodded, yes.

"Wait. That can't be possible. I got this way because of a specific accident. Rose has my blood in her veins from the transfusion. Some random kid can't just catch it like a cold," Chris explained.

"She's not just some random kid... are you?" Cory spoke suggestively.

"He has a point. We both felt her," Rose reminded Chris.

Chris was completely bewildered. "Who are you?"

Ari looked him in the eyes, then said, "I'm your daughter."

Chris laughed. "I don't know what world you live in, kid, but I met your mother the same day I met you."

Ari didn't have a response, but Cory did. Information was his thing, so he wanted to gather as much as he could. "How else can you explain it?" he asked.

"I can't, but I'm not her father. Based on what Yesha said, Ari had to be conceived right before the day the world broke. I know exactly who I was with at that time and it wasn't her mother." Lola passed his mind briefly, but he shook her away.

"One way to find out what's going on," Cory said.

"And what's that?"

"Get Yesha and ask her yourself."

***

Rose, Chris, and Ari filed down the steps behind

Cory. The wooden boards creaked under their weight.

"I can barely see anything," Ari complained.

"Give me a second," Cory responded. He reactivated the generator. It rumbled to life, then puttered to death. He pressed the primer a few times before trying again. This time, it started and remained running. The overhead light gradually brightened until the entire basement was well lit. It was a spacious area, spanning the width of the four-bedroom home.

Ari couldn't believe her eyes. "Whoa!" she exclaimed. "Where did you get all this stuff?"

"Just found a few things laying around here and there," Chris replied. The room was stocked with food, water, medical supplies, and weapons. Most of them bore familiar emblems.

Ari became visibly upset. "That was you? The supply chains were getting hit hard. We thought it was the Faction, but the whole time it was you? You killed a lot of innocent people!" Ari was disgusted.

Cory quickly defended his family. "Wait, we never killed anyone," he clarified. "We didn't have to. Not with Rose and Chris. A little distraction, and the supplies were gone before the guards even realized someone was there. Besides, there are only three of us. A few hits were more than enough to get what we needed, including the times we hit the Faction. The number of raids you're insinuating doesn't match us at all."

Ari's body language showed relief. She had almost believed she came to the wrong people. Unjustified murders went against the very core of her principles.

"Are we done with the questionnaire, so we can get this over with?" asked Chris.

Rose walked over to a wall of mounted firearms and tactical gear. "We going light, heavy, or in between?" she asked Chris.

He was already sliding a vest, equipped with pre-loaded magazines, over his sleeveless top. "Let's go light. We need to be able to move quick, so we can get in, get out, and get lost," he replied.

Rose put an identical vest over her form-fitting tank

top. She checked one of the magazines to ensure the 9mm rounds were fully stocked, then snapped a holster to her waist, with a black handgun already inside.

No seconds were wasted as she tossed Cory his own equipment. He was dressed and ready to go just as quickly.

"Grab your rifle too, just in case," Chris instructed on his way up the steps.

Rose flipped open the lid of a wooden crate and took out a hardly used M4 Pro. A row of five magazines lay underneath. She grabbed two and slipped them into empty slots of her tactical vest.

"I got the support bag," said Cory. He slung a small pack on his back, filled with medical supplies and dried packages of meat.

"You have enough stuff?" Ari asked sarcastically.

"What did you think, we were going to walk in empty-handed and politely ask for your mom?" Rose retorted, leaving the basement.

Cory was the last one out. He gave Chris a report on the generator. "If we kill everything but the fridge, the generator should last a couple days at best. Too much longer and whatever's in there won't be any good," he informed him.

"Alright, let's get to it then."

They all spread out to cut the power throughout the house, while Ari waited in the living room. She flinched when everything went pitch black. The windows had been sealed so well that no outside light got in. A few seconds passed, then flashlights re-lit the immediate area. Ari covered her face. "Can you guys point those anywhere other than my eyes?"

Chris redirected his light toward Cory. Something Cory was attempting to hide in his hand caught Chris' attention.

"Are those the cordless trimmers?" he asked. "You're bringing hair clippers on a combat mission?"

"I might need a little edge up, ya know. In case we're out there too long," Cory replied bashfully.

Chris turned his flashlight to Ari, who covered her

eyes again, then back to Cory. "I'm guessing that mustache is finally starting to kick in, huh?" he joked. Cory was caught off guard, his eyes widening. Rose failed to hold in her laugh.

Ari looked around, dazed and confused. "I don't get it," she said.

"Ignore him. Hardly anything he says makes sense," Cory replied. He stuffed the trimmers deep into his bag.

Rose continued to laugh. "Makes sense to me," she announced. Chris snickered with her, heading for the front door.

***

Texas had been cast into a perpetual spring, and remained so for a period extending years. The climate was more than pleasant. Temperatures hung in the seventies to eighties range, which was more irregular than the dramatic shifts from hot to cold, right after the planet was thrown out of orbit. Nature faded into an artful blend with the remains of civilization. Trees and shrubbery had reclaimed nearly all the empty land beside highways, but— though heavily cracked and largely overrun with grass— the roadways were still present. The asphalt and layers of rock beneath delayed the growth of larger plants, leaving mazes of open paths between the developing forest.

The group followed the interstate system but indirectly. They stayed just far enough into the surrounding wilderness to avoid easy detection. The complicated movement slowed progress greatly, turning a thirty-mile journey into a twenty-four-hour effort.

"I swear this is so weird. The world was ending at first, then all of a sudden it fixed itself," said Rose.

"Something must've happened to the orbit again. That's the only explanation," Cory concluded.

"Like what, know-it-all?"

"Assuming it was a natural fix, the only thing with enough force to change the course is another planet. If Earth got the right distance from one, at the right angle and speed, it could be nudged onto a more stable orbit."

"Impressive," said Ari. "That's exactly what happened."

"And how would you know?" Chris asked.

"I heard my mom talking to another scientist. He told her that the LOGOS ship knocked the planet so far off course that sometimes it would get as close to the Sun as Venus and as far out as beyond Mars' orbit. If it kept going, it would've spiraled into the Sun, but we got close enough to Venus to get a good enough tug to change things. He said that the orbit is now more like a circle than an oval. That's why the weather is almost always the same."

"That sounds like classified information. How'd you get close enough to hear that?"

"I have my ways," Ari replied. A hint of deception was detectable in her voice.

"Told you," said Cory. He loved being right, almost as much as he loved rubbing it in his sister's face.

The thing is, Rose hated it a bit more than he loved it. "Shut up, you nerd!" she snarled.

"Don't get mad at me because I actually read the stuff that Pops gave us."

"Don't get mad at me because I actually read the stuff that Pops gave us," said Rose, mocking Cory in an exaggerated tone. "You're such a damn suck-up."

"You only talk to me like that 'cause of your little ass powers."

"I don't need 'em to whip your..."

"Hey!" yelled Chris. He didn't care if he gave away their position or not. His heavy voice carried through the trees, scattering birds in all directions. "Stop acting like babies and watch your damn language. I'm the only one here with permission to curse."

"I'm not a kid anymore," Rose argued.

"Hell, I can't tell. You think 'cause you went through puberty, that makes you a woman? You're sitting here arguing with a ten-year-old about nothing, but I'm supposed to treat you like an adult?"

"I'm pretty sure I'm at least thirteen," said Cory. He regretted it the moment he said it.

"Boy, shut up when grown folk talkin'," said Chris, who had a tendency of slipping into his southern accent when he was upset. He redirected his gaze back at Rose. "Grown folk, without an -s. As in singular. As in just me. Am I making myself clear?"

"Yes," Rose was visibly embarrassed and angry, but there were no doors to slam in the outdoors, so she folded her arms and replied.

***

As night approached, the team of four searched for a place to make camp. Chris usually found it best to use what was left of houses and buildings that remained standing. The location of these places was predictable. The pricier the neighborhood was, the stronger the materials and construction methods were used, therefore, it exponentially improved the likelihood that structures remained, more or less, intact.

"Wait... You guys hear that?" Rose stopped to get a clear listen to their surroundings. Everyone else tuned their ears to the environment, as well. Light chatter was audible between the rustlings and chirps of nature.

"Someone's out there," Chris whispered.

A few hand gestures directed Rose and Cory to take precautions. They unholstered their handguns, then dropped into crouching positions, facing the direction of the voices. Ari wasn't sure what to do besides mimic their postures.

Movement was subtle and quiet. They walked on thick grass, softening the noise of each step, until Chris' toe clanked against the side of a piece of metal hidden beneath the brush. Luckily, it wasn't loud enough to draw attention. He moved away some of the grass with his feet to see what it was. The rusty alloy was a sign for an exit ramp with most of the lettering faded and flaking away. Chris led them around it, using the treeline of a large clearing, next to what used to be I-20, as cover. A large circle of fencing created a perimeter for a camp. Several tents were adorned with a familiar logo.

"Good old Faction," Rose whispered.

"What do you think they're doing?" Chris pondered aloud, ready to accept a response from anyone.

As usual, Cory was the first with an opinion, only this time it wasn't what everyone expected. "I don't know," he said.

Rose couldn't let a second pass without addressing it. "Did he just admit that he didn't know something?" she asked.

"I wasn't finished. I don't know, but I know how to find out."

"Please, inform us, genius."

"The big tent in the middle."

Chris started to laugh but held most of it in.

"What are you laughing at?" Rose somehow yelled and whispered at the same time.

"You've been waiting on him to be wrong about something for like half your life, yet he's right again."

"We don't know that yet!"

"Well, I'll go find out. Y'all watch my back. Rose can tell me if something happens out here."

"No."

"What do you mean no?"

"You're not going. I am," Rose stated.

"You actually believe that?" Chris responded.

"There's nothing you can do that I can't, and the last thing we need is you having one of those little episodes and passing out in the middle of a Faction camp."

"She's got a point," Cory said.

"Oh, so now y'all wanna be a team when it's against me," Chris complained.

Ari added her say. "You said he was always right," she commented.

"You too? You know what, just go ahead and do it. If you get caught, I'm letting them keep you." Chris was visibly annoyed.

Rose turned to Cory. "What am I looking for?" she asked.

"Anything that needs a key. A drawer in a desk, a

file cabinet, a safe. Once you get inside that, look for paperwork with a red stamp. Don't know why, but everybody uses red stamps to highlight something that's supposed to be a secret."

With that, Rose handed off her rifle to Cory, kept a low profile, and made her way to a neglected portion of the fence. Darkness swallowed the area, so it didn't take much effort to remain concealed. The only lighting was from raised poles within the perimeter, but she would deal with that once she was able to gain entry. Rose reached her hand out to touch the fence. Her icy iris' began to fluoresce. Where her fingers touched, the steel turned a rusty tone, then blew away with the wind, as thin as talcum powder. She slipped through the hole left behind, disappearing from view.

Ari looked down at her own hands. "I can do that?" she questioned with astonishment.

"If you're really Pops' daughter, you can do a whole lot more than that," Cory replied.

***

Rose silently moved through the maze of tents and idle soldiers. She quickly formulated a plan in her mind and executed it. Improvisation was a cakewalk for her swift, creative mind. There was only a single generator running power throughout the camp. Cables stretched out in every direction. Rose followed them with her eyes to the location in which they originated.

"I'm about to take out the generator. That should draw out whoever is in the tent," said Rose, informing Chris of her next action. They took full advantage of being human radios.

A few seconds later, all the lights and equipment shut off. Light chatter morphed into heavy conversations. "God damn it! If one of you tripped over that cable again, none of you are sleeping tonight," erupted an angry woman from the main tent. The sleeves of her uniform were covered in stripes, the Faction's way of notifying rank.

"That's the one," Rose said to herself. She was already looping around towards the tent entrance. Her timing had to be flawless. The soldiers' eyes hadn't adjusted to the dark yet, but if she ended up in direct view, things would get violent rapidly. "I'm in," Rose relayed to Chris. It wasn't what she imagined, exactly. She pictured some luxurious amenities fit for an evil general, like in the action thrillers she had become accustomed to watching. Instead, it was dingy, dirty, and practically empty. The only things inside were a portable desk, a small cot, a standing fan, and a steel safe. "I found the safe."

"That was quick," said Ari.

Chris looked at her, dazed. "You heard that?" he asked.

"Yeah."

Cory wrote an imaginary check in the air with his hand. "I don't know, Pops," he said.

"Shut up, Cory," said Chris. "If it was possible, which it isn't, that would make her your sister." He was trying to make Cory as uncomfortable as he was, and Cory fell into the trap.

"You're not my real dad! He's not my real dad. He's just trying to... uh..." Cory didn't know how to finish his thought without alerting Ari of his personal interest.

"Uuh... Uhh." Chris mocked Cory. "I'm just trying to what?"

Cory thought fast on his feet. "Aren't you supposed to be paying attention to Rose?" he asked.

Rose knew that she was pressed for time, so she went to work on the safe at once. The steel was much thicker and denser, and it took much longer to rust away. She was accelerating hundreds, even thousands of years on something meant to last forever. The increased time manipulation also demanded more energy. Rose's body started to heat up. Sweat ran down her face. She became hungry and thirsty. Her body was a machine on full throttle, burning away its reserves.

Just when she began to think she'd need a new plan, there was a pop from the locking mechanism. Rose had finally eroded through. She wiped away the sweat before it could fall into her eyes, then pulled open the door.

The inside had two shelves. The lower contained several folders stacked on top of one another. A black case rested on the other. Rose's curiosity got the best of her. The paperwork was the goal, but she had to know what was in the box. She thumbed the two latches apart to take a look inside. It was a classic revolver. Rose rubbed the dark wood finish on top of the blemish-less, shiny metal surface. It intrigued her, like an abstract painting might intrigue an art lover. "Bonus points," Rose said. She stuffed the gun into a cargo pocket, along with the six golden bullets resting in velvet-lined slots.

The generator puttered, then leveled out. Power was restored to the camp.

"Shit," said Rose, knowing she was pretty much out of time. She fumbled through the stack of folders, almost losing loose pieces of paper in the process. One for logs, one for personnel, another for communication information, and at last, the one with a big red "Classified" stamp. Rose removed the folder, then pushed the door shut. Its lock re-engaged, good as new. Undoing time manipulation took far less effort than creating it, and the woman in charge wouldn't notice anything amiss until she opened the safe. By then, Rose and the others would be long gone—if she didn't get caught first.

The camp leader continued to yell at her subordinates as she returned to her tent. She walked in backward to finish her insults, just as Rose stood up to leave. When the woman turned around, they were face to face. She seemed to be looking right through Rose's eyes, frozen in her tracks. She sensed someone was there but didn't see a thing. Her eyes scanned back and forth, trying to figure out a solution to an unknown problem. Unsatisfied, she turned around and stuck her head out of the tent. "If I find out one of you assholes has been in my tent, I'll kill you!" she yelled angrily.

Simultaneously, Rose stepped to the side. When the woman re-entered, approaching her desk, Rose slipped out of the tent and back to her waiting companions.

"Shit. She's not answering me," said Chris.

Cory was more observant and patient, for he didn't have any supernatural communications to depend on. "Give it a minute. If they spotted her, there'd be a lot more commotion going on," he pointed out.

"I'm not about to sit around here until they do catch her. Wait here with Ari."

Rose appeared out of nowhere and slapped the folder against Chris' chest. "Don't bother. I'm done," she said. Cory and Ari nearly jumped out of their skin.

"Where the hell did you come from?" Cory asked, a little spooked.

"Found a new one. I can turn invisible."

It made perfect sense. "Light onto gravity onto space. LOGOS," Chris muttered, unwittingly revealing more than intended.

"Wait, so what happened to you had something to do with the ship that broke the world?" Cory figured.

Chris had never discussed much of his past, especially his connection with Project 047. The words had slipped his tongue, but the cat was out of the bag. Still, he would at least postpone the conversation. "That's a long story for another day," he said. "Anyway, let's get away from here while we still can."

***

The quartet trekked nearly three miles further to ensure they were a reasonable distance away from the Faction camp. Every step they took increased the potential search radius by an exponential factor, had their intrusion been discovered prematurely.

An old hotel would serve as the night's stay. It was rundown, as expected, beaten by intense weather, and carved into by strong root systems and ever-growing vines.

Experience, however, was the greatest source of information. Anyone who had done enough exploring knew that the centermost parts of large structures were usually fine enough protection from predators, as well as the elements.

The group selected the driest room to make camp. Rose and Chris activated a few glow sticks, spread them around the room for lighting, then picked a corner to sit and rest their heads against their backpacks. "Wonder what this place looked like before," said Rose, imagining the five-star suite in its pristine condition.

Ari stood in the center of the room with her arms folded across her chest, obviously uncomfortable. The rest of them were used to slumming it wherever they could, but Ari had lived her entire life in the sheltered confines of a WTP settlement.

Cory noticed. He took a tightly rolled bag from his pack, then unraveled it on the floor. It expanded, much bigger than it seemed it should, the moment he removed the coiled binding. "You can take this, Ari," he said. She pulled the puffy foam mat perpendicular to the wall furthest from the window openings, then climbed inside, sitting with her back against it. Cory took a seat on the floor next to her, asking, "Where did you sleep when you came to find us?"

"I didn't. I just followed... well, I don't know what to call it, but I followed it to you. I sat down to rest sometimes, but other than that, I just kept walking."

Cory was impressed. "You walked thirty miles straight with no sleep... alone... in the heat... on that terrain?" he said, speaking with his hands.

"Yep."

"Hope that mat helps you sleep, then. You're going to need it," said Rose.

"Compact foam, courtesy of Project 78... I think," Cory added.

Chris rummaged through his backpack to retrieve the stolen documents. "Let's see what these assholes are up to," he said.

"Ugh. He's such a hypocrite," Rose complained.

"I heard that."

"You were supposed to!"

Chris ignored Rose's further prods so that he could begin reading. He skimmed through page after page. Most of it was a bunch of seemingly random orders and an inventory of supplies that the leaders of the Faction didn't want known to those in the lower ranks.

"What's it say?" asked Cory.

Chris kept reading, growing more troubled with each page.

Rose lost all patience. She got up and snatched the file from Chris' hand. Oddly, he didn't resist. Rose read aloud. "Orders for 3rd Regiment to deliver cyanide canisters into fresh water containment of WTP Dallas. Mission time Sol3 3200 in synchronization with Regiments 4-10."

"They're going to poison everybody," said Chris.

Rose became very animated. "We're not going to let them, are we?" she asked.

"What do you expect us to do? There are at least six more camps out there somewhere. We don't even know when this is supposed to happen. Sol3 3200, you tell me when that is. Could be tonight for all we know."

"It's about a couple of months away. There's only summer now, so Sol3 represents the third quarter of the new year," informed Ari.

"A couple months is plenty of time to do something," said Rose.

"We'd still need a hell of a lot more people than us. Besides, who are we actually risking our lives to save? The people that tried to kill us when you were kids?"

Ari went on the defensive, saying, "Those are good people. Everybody's not like Ron. I've been to other settlements, and they're different."

"Who the hell is Ron?" asked Chris, oblivious.

"Foley. But, that's not the point. My mom's in there, and so are a lot of other good people."

"I don't trust her either, after the shit she pulled!"

"Chris!" said Rose, still filled with passion.

"Alright, Jesus. How about we just get your mom out of there and deal with the rest after?"

"Fine," Ari pouted.

Rose unraveled her own sleep gear, then laid down, signifying her acceptance of the peace treaty. A soft bulk of something smacked Cory on the side of the face. "What was that for?" he whined.

"For being slick. You and that peach fuzz on your lip. Now, go over there and get some sleep, 'cause you're taking second guard. Rose, you're after him," said Chris.

Cory picked up Chris' sleeping mat and took it to a wall, away from a blushing Ari, where he would sleep.

***

Sweat droplets trickled down the bridge of Rose's nose. She tossed and turned, until she jumped into a sitting position, fully awake. The dream was heavy, soaked with emotion, but it didn't feel personal. She knew why. Chris was unwittingly projecting again.

Rose stared at him, as he stared at the orders they had lifted from the Faction camp. Something was off. Chris was hiding something, and Rose was determined to find out what it was.

Cory and Ari were fast asleep and had been for a few hours. It was already getting close to time for second shift guard duty. "Dad," whispered Rose, trying to get his attention. She would do so several more times before he heard. "Dad," she whispered louder, shaking his shoulder.

He flinched, then shoved the papers back into his bag. "Huh? Sorry, I was going over the documents again, making sure we didn't miss anything," he explained.

"Uh-huh. Well, I can't sleep. I'll take Cory's guard. He can go last."

"What's wrong with you?"

"Nothing. Just not that tired, I guess." Rose was lying through her teeth.

Chris' eyes were red from fatigue and stress. "Alright, I'm taking your mat then." He tossed his backpack next to the yellow rectangle.

Rose sat with her rifle across her lap and pulled a file from her pocket to fiddle with her nails. She was always expecting a fight. Long nails weren't conducive. It was also a ploy to bide time until Chris fell into a deep sleep. After a while, she tossed the metal file on the floor near his head. It pinged against the exposed wood, between patches of damaged carpeting. He didn't move, so she knew she was free to do her snooping.

Years of stealth training, ironically from Chris, gave Rose the skills to rummage through his things without detection. Maybe another once-over of the paperwork herself would reveal what he was hiding. Rose had her hand on the folder when something else caught her attention. It was an old zip-up binder with a dirty, beat-up fabric cover. She had seen it several times over the years, but private things normally remained private between them. It would still be so if she didn't believe Chris was holding information that could affect more than his own life. She slipped out of the room, with the binder in one hand and a glow stick in the other. There was an overturned steel chair in the lobby. Rose attempted to unfold it, but it was rusted together, so she settled for standing, opening the binder atop the counter.

The pages inside were covered from top to bottom in writing. As she flipped through the pages, she could see different shades of ink, where one pen went empty and was replaced by another. At first, there were dates, but then there was no sense of time. Once Chris had lost track of the world's new cycle, he just continued to write without specification.

Rose wasn't aiming for Chris' innermost secrets. She decided to flip to the last entry. The ink was still fresh. He must have just written it that night, she figured. The words spoke of a name he had found on the stolen documents. A Louis Steed. He wondered what the person had to do with the former Director of Project 047, Jane Steed. Was he a husband or son? Was she herself still alive and pulling the strings of the Faction?

Chris also wrote of his friends. He reminisced about Scott and Sasha, about how Ramirez endlessly pursued uninterested Candy. Even Turner and Lola's strange dynamic made an appearance. He longed for the days when they would train until they had nothing left in their bodies to give. But most of all, he held memories of how they foiled the destruction of the world, only for it to fall victim anyway.

Tears flooded Rose's eyes, so much so that they started to drench the pages of Chris' journal. She was heartbroken, but heartbreak turned into unbridled, irrational anger. The soles of Rose's boots thudded as she pounded them into the floor, headed straight for Chris. She cocked her arm back as far as she could and slammed the journal in his face. Papers flew all over the room and slowly rained back down.

Chris jumped up, aiming his handgun at her face. Rose used her power to fling it out of his hand, pinning it to the wall. "What the fuck, Rose? I almost killed you!" he screamed, realizing it was her instead of an intruder.

Cory and Ari sprang awake to a mad display of confusion.

"Who the hell are you?" shouted Rose.

Chris scrunched his eyebrows and asked, "Are you serious right now?"

"How did you find us? You knew who we were the whole time, didn't you?" Rose pulled her gun on Chris.

Cory scrambled to his feet. He held his hands out as a gesture for Rose to calm down. "Rose, what the hell are you talking about? Put the gun down," he pleaded.

"He didn't just happen to save us. He knew who we were the whole time."

"What's she talking about, Pops?"

"Hell if I know!"

Tears ran rivers down Rose's cheeks. "Well, explain why our parents' names are in your journal!" she demanded.

"What? I don't know who the hell your parents are, and why were you in my shit anyway?"

"I saw you, and I felt it. You were looking at that paper like you were hiding something from us, so I went in your bag to see if I could find out what it was. That's when I saw it. Sasha and Scott Truman. Those are Cory's parents. Thought maybe it was a coincidence, but then there it was. Candy and Arturo Ramirez. My parents' names are in your book. You wrote about them last night!"

Chris' eyes widened. Rose's ocean blue eyes, round face, and brash fearlessness, Cory's bold jawline, brawny physique, and uncanny intelligence, they certainly fit the bill, but again, the time frame didn't mesh. "That can't be right," Chris attempted to reason. Tears of his own began to fall.

Rose lowered her gun. "You really didn't know?" she asked, desperately wanting to believe that the only person in the world she trusted, aside from Cory, wasn't some weirdo that hunted them down, then raised them with some hidden agenda.

"None of them even had children before the world broke. I would know," Chris responded. Rose didn't have to take his word for it. The tangle of their spirits told her that he was being sincere.

"So there's a five-year discrepancy in our births, then there's Ari's situation," Cory calculated. "Something's off."

"I have an idea who would know," said Chris.

"Who?"

"The man on the Faction papers, right?" Rose concluded. "Louis Steed."

"Yeah. The problem is, I don't know who he is, or where he is," Chris responded.

Until then, Ari had just watched the drama unfold without interrupting. "We could ask my mom," she suggested.

Chris thought it was a great idea. "Well, let's go get her," he said.

5

More Than My Watch Is Wrong

The group of four arrived outside the Dallas WTP facility around midday. They took cover inside of an old restaurant in visibility of the repurposed stadium. Dense clouds were moving in above. Wind speed also started to pick up, foretelling of incoming bad weather.

"What's the plan?" asked Rose.

"Should be simple," said Cory. "You port us in, we get Ari's mom, then you port us out."

"I can only port places I've been."

"We've been there already, haven't we?"

"That was one time, years ago, when we were kids. I don't remember what it looks like."

All of their eyes swung to Chris. "It's kind of far away. His head might explode if he tries too hard," said Cory.

Rose didn't agree. "I patched it again before we left. He'll be fine."

"You talk like I'm crippled or something," Chris complained. He was annoyed, but traced a large circle in the air with his finger, leaving a trail of blue lightning in its wake. The portal stabilized with Chris still conscious and absent any pain. Rose's handy work with his damaged mind was holding fairly well.

Yesha and Ari's living room appeared on the inside of the glowing ring. It was just as it was, all those years ago. Not even a piece of furniture had been shifted, to give a feeling of fresh decor, as we humans often like.

"Your house. You first," Chris said to Ari. She stepped through, careful not to touch the portal's edge. It was a controlled band of lighting, yet it was still lightning, so the sound and sight of it were frightening. The smell of burning air added to the intensity. Safe on the other side, Ari's heart rate slowed to a state of calm. She briefly scanned the house for her mother, but Yesha was absent, so she waved the rest of them through.

"What if this is a setup?" asked Rose. She didn't quite trust Ari.

"I don't know about you two, but I've been thinking setup since she found us. I only came 'cause I need to know how she got my power and where she came up with this daughter bull crap," Chris replied. He didn't trust Ari either.

Cory didn't seem to share their cautionary feelings. "What did her and her mom ever do to you guys?" he asked, in her defense.

"Set us all up to get gassed and probably murdered when you were a kid, but other than that, nothing," Chris reported with sarcasm.

"So stop thinking with your wee wee, and keep your guard up. Most likely we'll have to fight our way out of here," Rose added.

Chris stepped through the portal. He noticed the place was unchanged. "Not big on decoration, I see," he said.

"Rude," Rose giggled, pettily.

Cory was ready to get down to business and asked, "So, what now?"

"We have to find Yesha," Chris answered.

"No need," said Ari. She picked up a wall-mounted phone and spoke with someone on the other end. When she hung up, she informed the group. "She'll be here in a minute."

They didn't have to wait long. Yesha rushed through the door like rockets were attached to her feet. "Where were you? Nobody could find you for two days! You better have a good explanation for disappearing on me like that, and it better not be some damn boy!" she fussed at her daughter.

"A man actually," said Chris, being the smart aleck that he was. "And a boy... And a girl."

Until then, Yesha was so angry with Ari that she hadn't seen that she had company. "What's he doing here?" she asked.

"I went to get him," responded Ari.

"Why would you do that, especially after how he left us?"

Chris' own demeanor went from casual to angry, in a moment. "I left you? You got some damn nerve accusing me like you didn't have a part in what happened," he yelled.

"Great. Not only are you the type to steal supplies and leave without saying a word, but you're also the type to blame other people 'cause you chose to be a dick, not to mention, turning your kids into criminals."

"Excuse me!" said Rose, feeling offended.

Chris held up his hand to silence Rose. This he wanted to handle himself. "I don't know what you think you know, but obviously you were misinformed. I met with your dear Ron Foley the morning after you and I last saw each other. He gave me an ultimatum. Either I fought his battles for him, or we had to leave. Of course, I chose the latter. He promised us supplies to get us started on our own, which is why we didn't leave immediately. We waited on you all day, to say goodbye. I even knocked on your door, but nobody answered. Ironically enough, that night we were gassed. They were trying to capture us, for who knows what reason. Coincidentally, you never showed up. But, let me guess. You didn't know anything about it."

Yesha was awe-stricken. "He sent me on a diplomatic run to the California settlement. He said that he would tell you I was gone. When I got back, he told me that you had just run off with a bunch of food and clothes."

"I told you there was something wrong with him," Ari said to her mother.

"What could he possibly have wanted from you? You came in with practically nothing," Yesha wondered.

"I know what he wanted," said Ari. "I can show you. I found a hidden lab. I think it has something to do with all the missing people."

"How are all of us supposed to get near a lab like that?" Chris questioned.

"Do the mind thing with your daughter. She's been there," Cory suggested.

"You told him?" Yesha's response radiated her disapproval.

"Told me what? She's not my daughter."

"She is," said Yesha.

"Am I the only one here not going crazy? I don't even know you. We only met the one time, and she was already almost Rose's age," Chris argued.

"Call it what you want, but she's yours. I told you I had memories of her father, but I could never see his face. The night we were together, I finally saw his face. Your face."

"Is that why you left like that, because you thought you saw me in a dream?"

"It wasn't a dream! It was a memory. They're all memories. I remember everything. That Shelby car that you love so much, that big stupid silver gun you always carry, and your son C.J.."

"How the hell do you know about him? I don't talk to anyone about him!"

"Because I was there. We were there with you, except not in this world. In my memories, things are how they used to be. She has them too. The older she got, the more vivid they became. Memories of the three of us, together."

"None of it makes sense. It's not possible." Chris couldn't grasp what was going on.

"Actually, it is possible," Cory surmised. "In the same way it's possible for you and Rose to alter small pockets of time, and manipulate space. I have a theory," he added. All ears were open. "Time doesn't move in one direction, at least not the way we typically think. Whenever there is a decision to be made, theoretically all decisions are always made, but time splits into parallel realities. The thing is, you can only live in one of those realities. I believe that somehow their minds are experiencing a flow of memories from an alternate, parallel timeline. The hard part is figuring out how that happened."

Chris looked into Ari's eyes. His pulse quickened, as he saw a familiar face within hers. A face he hadn't seen in a lifetime, but had longed to that entire period. In Ari was the likeness of his long-passed mother.

Rose felt a sensation of grief, with love and sadness. "You're doing it again," she said to Chris, with a bothersome undertone.

"Sorry. I just need a minute," said Chris, taking a seat on the couch.

"Look, I know there's a lot of personal stuff going on, but what are we going to do about this lab situation?" asked Rose.

"I've sneaked in there before, but I don't know how to do what you guys do," said Ari.

"You don't have to," said Cory. "Chris can do the work. All you have to do is see the place in your mind. Are the labs ever closed?"

"There's only a few scientists, so that wing is usually closed off and guarded at night," Yesha responded.

"Then, we wait until tonight."

"I can't just stay here. I'm supposed to be working. They'll come looking for me if I don't show back up."

"Then go. Do what you would always do, and we'll wait here until you get back."

Yesha agreed. Rose's observant nature kicked in. She asked her, "Does anyone else know that Ari's back?"

"No. I didn't tell anyone. She could get in big trouble, so I needed to know what was going on before I said anything to anyone."

"Good. If they're suspicious that she's back, they'll be snooping around, which we don't need."

"I understand," said Yesha. She took in deep breaths to calm herself, then left.

***

Yesha returned a few hours later to a house of sleeping people. Rose and Ari were stretched out on opposite ends of the couch, with their legs tangled like loose cordage. Chris and Cory were each bowed over a beanbag chair, mouths open wide enough to park a truck in. "Sooo, are we sleeping or trying to figure out what's going on here?" she said, projecting her voice loudly.

Everyone startled awake. "Sleep? Who was sleeping? Maybe they were asleep, but I wasn't," Chris denied, with his speech slurred. It brought a smile to Yesha's face, however brief.

Rose launched a couch pillow, walloping him on the side of the head. "You're up, Mr. Nobody," she said, using the name she loved to wield when her purpose was to pester Chris.

He threw it back, but Rose ducked. The soft square of cushion plopped Ari, who was still half-asleep, in the face. She was so drowsy that she didn't seem to notice she was caught in the crossfire.

"Not me. You," Chris said to Rose.

The response snapped Rose fully alert. "What do you mean, me? I've never pulled information from your mind and used it like that. I don't know how," she complained.

"Well, you better figure it out."

"How come you can't just do it?"

"Two reasons. It's the only way you're going to learn, and it takes a lot of energy to do it. We don't know who or what's in that lab. The last thing we need is me having an aneurysm on the other side. If those reasons aren't good enough for you, then I got one better. Because I told you to do it."

"I'm an adult now. You can't just boss me around," Rose fussed.

"Every time you get a year older, I get a year older. Compared to me, you'll always be a little girl. So, how about you adult your ass over here and figure out how to get this portal open," Chris demanded.

Chris gave Rose plenty of leeway to joke around and press his buttons, but she knew what her limit was, as children seldom do with their parents and/or guardians. She rolled her eyes, then gathered everyone and asked, "What's the plan when we get in there?"

"We don't know anything about the lab or what we're looking for, so I say we just wing it. Search will go faster if all five of us just look around," said Cory, until a new factor entered his mind. "Any special security features we might need to know about?" he asked, intending his question for Yesha.

"I can't say for sure about this lab. I didn't know it even existed. But, if it's similar to the others, then no. There aren't any cameras because of the classified nature of some of our work," she informed him.

Ari had input of her own. "There were two guards outside the door when I went, but that was all."

Rose was intrigued and asked, "How did you get that far without getting caught?"

"I turned invisible."

"Invisible? How is that possible?" asked a perturbed Yesha.

"I don't know. I was following Ron when it just happened. He almost caught me when he turned around, but he looked around like he couldn't see me. When I looked down at my hands, I couldn't see them either."

"What I don't understand is, if she was born with it, why can't she already do more? It only took me a couple of years to master the simpler things. Same with Rose," Chris pondered aloud.

Cory had a viable answer, as always, this time with a clever analogy. "Let's say you were born as the only member in your community that can use your legs, so to fit in, you never walked. What do you think would happen if someone asked you to stand?"

"You couldn't."

"Well, let's teach her how to walk," smiled Cory, peering into Ari's eyes. They were colored like fresh ginger. Ari blushed and looked away.

"Alright, enough of that," said Chris, snapping his fingers.

Rose giggled. "Pretty protective over someone that's not your daughter," she said.

"Are we going to stand around and get cute with each other all day, or what?" Chris was practicing the art of misdirection but had a point.

"Give me your hand," Rose instructed Ari, still shaking off a case of the giggles. Now calm, she remembered the way Chris would guide her as a child when he needed to lift a target from her mind and mirrored his steps. "When I open the doorway on this side, I need you to close your eyes and imagine the inside of the lab in as much detail as you can. I'll try to search your mind for it."

Ari nodded that she understood. Rose traced open the portal in the air with the tip of her pointer finger. Upon completion, Ari did as instructed, closing her eyes to use her imagination to bring the lab to life. Everything seemed to be going to plan until Rose was swept off course, deep into Ari's mind. Both of their eyes lit into blue infernos, so intense that their companions had to shield their eyes from the radiating glow. Electricity pulsed rhythmically, encircling them all.

Scenes played to Rose, one by one. She stood by, watching Chris hold his Baby Girl for the first time, then coach her to take her first steps. He shoved her higher on the swing set, then coddled her after her first fall from her bike. It was all there. Any doubt that Chris could be Ari's father was dead to Rose.

Garbled voices began to crescendo in the background of Rose's mind. As they cleared, she could hear that it was the others pleading with her and Ari to focus. The blue rings surrounding their pupils dimmed to the likeness of a calm ocean. So did the electricity firing from the portal's edge. A second more, and the innards of the lab blossomed into clear view. Both girls unlocked their hands, faces bursting with an indescribable expression.

"Are you guys OK?" asked Cory.

Yesha was visibly shaken beyond words.

"Uh, Dad... we should talk," Rose stuttered.

Chris knew, by her choice of a specific word, that Rose meant to talk about a very pressing matter, yet there was a higher priority at hand.

"It'll have to wait," he expressed, pointing at the open, temporary doorway.

The lab was dim, but there was enough light emanating from idle equipment and monitors with bouncing screensavers to see sufficiently. A steady, cool stream of air swept through the portal, a sign of a large temperature difference.

"Why is it so cold in here?" Rose whispered.

"Cold and creepy," Cory added, one-upping the notion.

Chris compiled the layout of the lab in his mind. "I'll run point this one," he said to Rose. He had begun to empower her to lead, taking advantage of her natural skill set, but lives other than their own were at stake this time, unlike the hundreds of supply raids they had previously been on.

"What's the call then?" Rose asked.

"You take Ari and look around, while I search the other side with Yesha. Cory, see if you can break into the computer system and find anything."

With that, they all moved to complete their prospective tasks. Cory took a seat, cracked his knuckles, then worked to find a way inside the lab's database. The initial login was child's play, but getting deeper would take time.

Everyone else did their best to move quickly, but with caution. Chris suddenly urged Yesha down into a kneeled position, behind a bookshelf. "The guards are outside that door," he whispered. She peeked over the top to see. Outside the glass pane were two heavily geared men, facing outward. Neither should have been a problem, as long as no one gave them a reason to turn around.

Rose and Ari inched their way around the far side of the room. There were several microscopes on tabletops, and loads of electronic equipment designed for experimentation down to the microscopic level.

A light scratching sound alerted Ari to something nearby. She turned around to see a bulletproof glass enclosure. Her eyes ballooned as large as their sockets would allow. "What do you think all this stuff is for?" whispered Rose, unwise to Ari's discovery, who only answered with more silence. "Ari! I was talking to... holy shit," Rose exclaimed in a soft voice, forced to change her thought process mid-sentence. Ari remained still as a statue.

"Uh, you guys should get over here, like right now," Rose communicated to Chris.

He and Yesha approached the girls quietly. They were equally surprised at their discovery, Yesha holding her hands over her gaping mouth.

"Holy shit!" Chris exasperated.

"Same thing I said," Rose replied.

A quartet of people were huddled together inside the encasement. Two additional bodies lay lifeless, off by themselves. The state of the corpses should have been an impossibility. "What did they do to them?" Rose questioned.

Cory delayed his hacking to come over and give the bodies a thorough once-over, then said, "They've been mummified."

"Doesn't it take like hundreds of years to do that?"

Yesha was disgusted with what she was seeing. "Whatever happened to them didn't take hundreds of years. It didn't take one year. That's Janice. Her face is unrecognizable, but the piercings are unmistakable. She's been missing for about six months," she pointed out.

The fluorescent overhead lights began to power on, one section at a time, starting with the ones inside the glass enclosure. The three huddled people scrambled to their feet and bolted to the glass front, faster than humanly possible. They left a trail of their own multiplied bodies to gradually fade away into clouds of smoke and lightning, only stopping because their prison let them move no further. The phantom-like humanoids pressed their faces against the glass in a constant state of change—old, then young, then somewhere in between, perpetually.

Chris and his collage of a family were spooked to the point of nearly tripping over themselves. Ari covered her eyes as Yesha grabbed hold of her, holding her close. The remaining group drew their sidearms, ready to empty the contents of their magazines, but flinched backward so hard that they tipped over the bookcase behind them. It slammed to the floor with a thundering boom.

"Finally back with us, Chris?" said a known voice, from all directions.

The group swung their weapons around in search of Foley, before realizing he was speaking over a PA system. "What is this, Ron?" Yesha inquired. Terror had latched onto her voice.

"Yesha, I must thank you and your wonderful daughter Ari for bringing me these marvelous specimens. Been looking for years, without as much of a sniff. The other kid looks well too. They grow up so fast."

"What did you do to these people?"

"Something I wouldn't have had to do if your friend there would have helped us."

"What is he talking about?" Rose asked Chris.

"He wanted me to help him fight the Faction. I told him no. That's why we had to leave here, when you were younger. Judging by all this, I'm pretty sure I made the right choice."

Foley laughed until he coughed. "I don't need you to fight. Hell, I've got a couple hundred soldiers to fight, and I can get a hundred more on a whim. What I need is your blood," he corrected.

"Blood?" Yesha was clueless.

"The girl got her power from his blood. We took a couple of vials from him when he was unconscious. Tried to use a bit of it, with genetic engineering, to enhance our soldiers. Didn't work exactly the way we planned, as you can see from the test subjects, but nothing a little time and work won't fix, now that we've got those two."

"What do you think is going to happen here? You're not touching either one of them," shouted Cory.

"Oh, don't feel left out. You, Yesha, and Ari are

going to make great test subjects."

Yesha became inflamed. "Why are you doing this? You're sick!" she yelled.

"I'll do whatever it takes to kill off those Faction bastards. That's the mission I was given, so I'm going to do whatever the hell I have to do to get it done. They don't fight fair, so why should we? You have these wonderful weapons that can turn the tide of this war, yet you want to keep it to yourself."

"They're not weapons, they're people!"

"Tomato, tomata. You can make this easy for me. Surrender and live, or I can kill you, then get what I need from your corpses."

"If you think it's that easy, come do it yourself," Chris challenged.

Foley was amused. "Better if I didn't let my last few subjects go to waste. They really are intriguing creatures, but they don't last long. After a few weeks, they go feral, then turn into those ugly statue things."

Rumbling pulled everyone's attention back to the glass chamber. The front of it was sliding open. "Take Ari and hide," Chris ordered Yesha. She took her daughter as far as she could from the brewing trouble.

"So, what's the plan here?" asked Rose, her handgun still at the ready.

"Shoot first, then shoot again," Chris instructed.

"What? You want us to kill those people?"

"Look at them, Rose! Do those look like they're still people to you?"

"But, what if they're in pain?"

"Then put them out of it! Or, you can just stand there and see if they wanna have a conversation."

When the cage was open enough for the poor souls to break out of its confines, Rose was still unsure about where she stood with firing on the innocents. The decision was quickly made for her. Chris and Cory fired several rounds as they backpedaled. The bullets passed through what seemed to be ghosts and ricocheted off whatever was behind them.

"What the hell?" Cory panicked. "The bullets are

going straight through!"

"I can see that!" yelled Chris, still shooting.

Foley started to rant over the loudspeaker to further amuse himself. "Funny thing, isn't it," he said. "I couldn't figure out which was the real one either. My scientist buddy eventually figured it all out. It's like they exist in more possibilities than one. Past, present, future—hell, every single possibility of existence, all at once. Isn't that crazy? The key is, most of them you see are just smoke and mirrors. Only one of them is the real thing. Can't hurt what you can't find though."

The creatures moved more like apparitions than physical beings. One of them could appear to be as many as ten individuals at once, leaving replicas of themselves leading from where they once were to where they were going, or could be going. Chris was the first to feel their wrath. While reloading, one of the phantom pursuers covered the distance between them, then flung him across a tabletop, wiping out everything on its surface on the way to the floor.

That was enough to convince Rose to separate friend from foe. She was preparing to help Chris by firing at his assailant, but her weapon was smacked from her hand. One of the other creatures had grabbed hold of her arm. Rose kneed it in the abdomen, then hip-tossed it to the floor.

"I don't know. This never happened before. I'll try harder," Rose replied, trying to remain calm. She placed her hands on Chris' head again, straining to focus her efforts. The toll was greatly draining of her own reserves, but Rose wouldn't give up. Without a say in keeping her birth parents alive, she wouldn't lose a loved one while she had breath in her lungs.

Yesha grabbed hold of Chris' hand, a comforting tactic, but something unexpected and unintended happened. Her eyes and palms emitted a familiar energy. Something tugged at Ari's spirit. She was being drawn in, by an unknown magnetism, and enveloped Chris' free hand within her own. The link propelled starlight to burst from within her.

The air became so statically charged that every hair on Cory's close-cropped head stood erect. He recoiled from the tingling sensation. "Guys?" he uttered, but neither of them seemed to hear. Figuring that if Yesha, who seemed to be as normal as he was, could get in on the experience, Cory extended his hand, only to be zapped with enough electric current to make him yelp from the pain.

The collective power of the three women was building rapidly, with a violent display. It was dangerously glamorous. Cory backed away, worried for his own safety. "Guys!" he yelled again, to no avail. When he was just about ready to vacate the premises, there was a decisive change in the behavior of said energy, produced by Rose, Yesha, and Ari. The view was more marvelous than anything Cory had ever imagined. The rings surrounding their pupils had settled into calm ripples of sapphire. Liquid droplets of the glow cascaded from nothing and nowhere, anywhere and everywhere. Chris' mind was being made whole again, and this time, for good.

6

I Just Remembered That I Love You!

"It's a girl!" said Dr. Allison, carefully cradling the baby. A nurse handed Chris a pair of sterilized scissors. He cut the umbilical cord, like the experienced father he was, after being there for the birth of his son, C.J. A chill brought goosebumps to his skin. He couldn't be certain if it was the cool hospital air or excitement in the moment.

Dr. Allison delicately popped the newborn on the bottom, teasing out a lung-clearing cry. It was the one moment a parent found joy in hearing their baby wail away. She handed the child off to a nurse for cleansing, then checked on the mother.

Yesha was exhausted, and it showed. Her long dark hair pointed in every direction. Sleep was the only thing in the world she wanted, aside from the touch of her baby.

"I know this is the part where I'm supposed to say she looks just like you, but she doesn't," Chris joked.

"Who is she supposed to look like, you?" Yesha responded, lazily.

"No. Her real father."

"OK, comedian," muttered Yesha, pursing her lips.

Chris took advantage and placed a kiss on them. When he stood up straight, something was different, but he couldn't place his finger on it. Yesha's hair was beautifully pressed. It flowed beneath a pointy party hat, and her face was also powdered with a light layer of makeup. Still, he wasn't sure why that was an oddity.

Chris glanced behind himself, to check if Dr. Allison was returning with his Baby Girl. Instead, he found the hospital had become a children's party center. A puffy-cheeked toddler smiled at him. Other children flanked her on both sides, but they were faceless individuals. Again, something weird was definitely happening, and again, Chris had no clue what it was.

The logical course of action seemed to be to ask Yesha if she was noticing anything funny, but when he turned back around, she was gone. "Bae?" he called out. The pet name seemed like a normal thing until it passed beyond his lips. "Why did I just call her that?" he mumbled to himself.

Yesha walked from a hallway with a black dress bunched up around her waist. After she pulled the straps over her shoulders, she turned around for Chris to zip it up. "Go start the car. I just have to put in my earrings, then we can drop Ari off at my mother's, so we can make our reservations on time."

They transitioned seamlessly from indoors to driving down the highway. Yesha maneuvered to the off-ramp marked by a sign reading, "Bartlett, TN." She was always beautiful, but Chris thought she was particularly ravishing that evening.

"Do I have to be at grandma's all night?" asked an annoyed Ari in her full teenage stubbornness. "You should've let me ask Melissa if I could go over there."

"You're over there often enough. Besides, your grandparents want to spend some time with you," Yesha replied.

Chris questioned how Yesha and Ari even knew Melissa, and more so, what Melissa felt about such a complicated situation. By the time his focus returned to his surroundings, Chris and Yesha were seated at one of the most exclusive restaurants in the Tri-State area. She gazed at him with such admiration. At once, he felt what she felt. He loved her, in the manner he had only loved twice before, yet deeper still.

"So, Mr. Cringle. How does it feel to be with the same old hag for thirteen years and counting?" Yesha teased.

"Thirteen years?" Chris mumbled under his breath. It couldn't have been real. Was he dreaming? He thought that he must have been, but dreams were never clearly dreams until you woke up. Chris closed his eyes, urging himself to do just that.

His eyes opened to yet another abrupt scene change. The bedroom was none other than his own, but the decor was completely altered. Even the scent filling the air was unfamiliar. Yesha reappeared, wrapped in revealing negligee. She was such a curvy woman that the sheer outer dressing draped over her smooth midriff, then bulged drastically around her peach and thighs. Chris was confident that she would put any plus-sized model to shame.

The aroma of her perfume was captivating. The best Chris had smelled to date. Yesha noticed his nose searching out more of the hypnotizing fragrance. "It's the one you said was your favorite. I saved it for our anniversary night, and here we are," she said, dancing provocatively to R&B that began playing from no apparent source. Chris may have finally concluded that he was, in fact, in a vivid dream, if not for being fully distracted by Yesha's enticing performance. She shoved him backward. Chris' back should have made contact with the mattress, but it never did. He continued to fall into a bleak darkness, for what seemed to be eternity.

7

The Training Wheels Are Off

Sweat beaded in bunches on Chris' forehead. After several attempts to wake him, Rose and the others gave up, deciding to talk out a new plan. "So, Ari's his daughter. I don't understand it, but I saw it myself, so whatever. What I wanna know is, how you became one of us," Rose said to Yesha. She was suspicious that Yesha was a product of Foley's inhumane experimentation.

"She's her mother," Cory explained, speaking for her. "If it transferred from Chris to Ari by genetics, and you by blood, it only makes sense for Yesha to receive the benefits as well. Mother and child exchange many different types of organic material, fluids, and such throughout pregnancy."

Yesha wanted to clear the air. "I understand that you guys want to be protective over your father, but reality is what it is. I can't explain how it happened, but Chris is Ari's father too. That's the truth."

"He's not," said Cory.

"Excuse me?"

"Our father. Chris isn't our real father."

Yesha didn't verbally respond, but her expression showed that she was indeed unaware. Rose changed the subject, eager for further cross-examination. "You mentioned someone named Sasha to Foley. Who is she?" she quizzed.

"The leader of the WTP. What does that have to do with anything?"

"Cory's mother's name was—is—Sasha. His real father is—"

"Scott?" Yesha interjected.

"You've got to be joking," said Rose.

Cory couldn't find words worthy of the situation. The chances that he would lose his parents, then wind up being raised by their friend and mentor, only to find his mother alive and running the organization that was trying to kill him, were microscopic. Yet it seemed he had hit the lottery of life.

"They're alive!" exclaimed an excited Rose. If Cory's parents were alive, then hers could be too.

Yesha spoke softly, careful not to sour the moment. "Not they. Only Sasha. Scott was killed in the war with the Faction." Suddenly, she connected the dots. "You're them!" she pointed.

"Huh?"

"You're the two heirs of the WTP!" Rose and Cory were dumbfounded. Yesha elaborated, "There were five founders of the WTP. Four of them coupled together and had two children. They were supposed to lead the next generation, to rebuild the world. They would be taught by the best teachers, trained by the best soldiers, and serve as living inspirations to the remaining people of the world. They represented hope. The problem came when the dictator of the Faction found out about them. She's an evil woman, who cares about nothing but power. As long as the heirs were alive, the people wouldn't follow her own child, so she called for their deaths. In the midst of all the fighting, all but one of the founders died, and Sasha sent the children away with trusted friends to save their lives. If you're her son, then that means your parents are Candy and Ramirez!"

Rose's heart tore in two. In the amount of time it took her to regain hope that her parents were alive, she discovered that they were both dead, with one hundred percent certainty. Cory's emotions, however, split the difference. He was ecstatic to learn that he may be able to meet his mother, but devastated that his father was lost, along with both of Rose's parents.

Rose was a strong woman. It was in her blood. That attribute, coupled with her being raised by Chris in a post-apocalyptic world, gave her the strength to compartmentalize her heartbreak and progress the situation. "Where is she? We have to get to her," she said, speaking of Sasha.

"Project 002. It's the capital of the WTP, deep in the valleys of California."

"It'll take weeks to get there. Not to mention, we don't know when Chris will be back on his feet," Cory expressed.

"Maybe on foot, but if we had wheels, that wouldn't be a problem."

Rose caught on to what Yesha was insinuating. "You want to steal one?"

"If you're up for it."

"We've never done a full operation without Chris," Cory stated.

"Then it's time we do. Time to take off the training wheels," responded a very determined Rose.

***

"What you got?" Rose directed, charging Cory to come up with a plan.

"Do you know exactly where to find one?" he asked Yesha.

"Yeah. There's a motor pool full of vehicles in an underground wing, but it's where all the soldiers spend most of the day."

"OK then. Rose can pick your mind for the exact spot to port into. From there, she can get a vehicle and port out. Should be simple enough, if she's up for it."

Rose nodded yes.

Error

167

"I should go with her," Yesha suggested, "in case it doesn't go so smoothly. I'm the only one of us who knows the way around in there."

"She has a point," said Rose.

Cory was also in agreement. "It's settled then. Ari and I will stay here with Chris, until you guys get done."

Rumbling from far off captured everyone's attention. They rushed to the boarded windows, to peek through spaces large enough to view outside. A series of headlights bounced in the distance.

"That's gotta be Foley," Yesha inferred.

"A dollar says he's going to see my mom," said Cory.

Rose smirked. "Shut up. You've never even seen a dollar," she retorted.

"Whatever. Let's just hurry up and get this done before he does something crazy."

Ari had hardly made a peep throughout the entire discussion. Her eyes darted back and forth to whoever happened to be speaking. "I'll be right back," her mother said to her.

"What if you don't come back?"

"Don't think that way. I'll be fine. I've got Rose with me. You'll be fine here too. I'm confident that this young man will make sure of it," she reassured, embracing her daughter.

With a solid plan in play, Yesha sent her mind to the motor pool. Rose opened a portal and plunged into Yesha's mind. Experience gave her a deeper control this time around, so she was able to see the desired destination quickly and accurately. She sailed around the still-image of Yesha's memory, in search of the perfect spot for insertion. The last thing the duo wanted was to walk into the middle of a group of armed soldiers, throwing the possibility of stealth right out of the window.

The open layout of the motor pool didn't give many promising options. In the end, they settled on a locker room several floors above. Noting the time of day, they figured it likely to be unoccupied.

The portal sealed shut behind Rose and Yesha. Initial silence led them to believe the place was indeed empty. They were wrong.

"Hey! What are you doing in here?" yelled a male soldier from behind them.

Rose's reaction time was superb. She picked up a Kevlar helmet from a nearby bench and flung it as hard as she could. The guy flinched to bat it down, giving her sufficient time to close the distance between them. She shoved her foot forcefully into the side of his knee, dropping him down to it, then shoved his head into a steel locker. The blow rendered him unconscious.

Yesha was impressed by the explosion of power by such a small-framed young lady. "Definitely didn't expect that," she commented.

"Neither did he," Rose replied. She started to examine the innards of each locker.

"What are you looking for?" asked Yesha.

"A girls' locker probably has uniforms our size. We can use them to blend in."

"Military only uses last names, but I know a lot of the soldiers here." Yesha scanned the nameplates on the lockers. "There. M. Johnson and B. Hewitt. Those should work." Moving quickly, Rose rusted the locks open. "Wait. I'm sure someone will recognize me, and strangers stand out here. What's the point in wearing uniforms if we'll be made the moment someone sees us?" Yesha pondered.

Rose was already slipping the fatigues over her current attire. "If we keep our distance, they can't see our faces." Yesha and Rose advanced from the locker room with their appropriated hats low. They moved down the hallways and flights of stairs with purpose, passing several civilian workers on the way. So far, no one batted an eye. "What's our best option?" asked Rose. "Since the roads left out there are bad, we'll need a heavy-duty truck to make the long distance. They're parked on the far side. The good thing is, the keys are kept inside." "Perfect. As long as we can get there clean, this should go smoothly."

The motor pool was loaded with soldiers. Most were actively engaged in conversation or busy with equipment maintenance. "Almost there," Yesha apprised. She and Rose weaved through the random pockets of people, nodding their heads at the few that bothered to look up for acknowledgment. Before they knew it, they had crossed the divider between the lighter transports and heavy armored vehicles. "There they are. All the way down on the   left."

Anxious to get the job done, Rose committed one of Chris' cardinal sins. Never break character in lack of patience. She picked up her pace to a steady trot, and Yesha followed suit. "Hey! You know there's no running on the shop floor," shouted a fast-approaching man. His many patches alerted the women to his high rank and combat experience. The women summated that it was best to attempt talking their way out of the situation rather than starting an unnecessary fight. "Sorry, it won't happen again," said Rose, keeping her head low. Yesha also tried to keep her face   hidden.

"You must be a couple of the new recruits," assumed the soldier.

"Yes, Sir," Rose replied. Yesha knew it was a mistake the moment the words came from her lips. The WTP was a very   casual   organization.

The man turned his eyebrows and replied, "Sir?" His senses now looking for deception, he became aware that Yesha was trying her best to not be recognized, so he lifted her head with his hand under her chin. "It's you!" he exclaimed. The soldier pulled his sidearm and held Yesha and Rose at gunpoint. With his offhand, he called out over the radio, "Foley, you still in radio range?"

"Yeah.   What   is   it?"

"I found Yesha. She's here in the motor pool with some girl."

"Mexican,   with   blue   eyes?"

"Yeah."

"Kill Yesha, but lock the girl up until I get back. I'm turning the convoy   around   now," Foley ordered. The soldier was shocked. "What?" he questioned.

"That's an order, now do what the hell I told you to do!" Rose could read the hesitancy in the man's body language, but wasn't willing to gamble that he wouldn't follow orders. She lunged, taking hold of his weapon, while pinning his trigger finger to the side of it, preventing him from firing. He grabbed Rose's arm with his other hand in response, attempting to pry it away. She swiped down hard at his elbow joint, weakening his grip. The fight had devolved into turn-based combat, one move made after another. The soldier's next chess move was to kick Rose to the ground. Her back hit the concrete hard, but she used the momentum to flip over backward into a kneeled position, then put a round in the flesh of each of his thighs. The third was meant for his brain, but Yesha shoved the weapon to the side, causing Rose to miss her target   completely.

"No! Don't kill him. He's a good man. He has a family," she pleaded.   Footsteps   of   alerted   servicemen   and servicewomen fast approached. Rose ended the encounter by crashing the butt of the gun to his skull, then sprinted for   the   truck.

"Look what they did to Pun. Kill 'em!" someone shouted. Sensing that bullets were about to fly, Rose tackled Yesha behind a concrete barrier before the first one zipped past. "What are we going to do now?" shouted Yesha, trying to speak over the loud gunfire, which was deafening inside the   enclosed   concrete   structure.

Rose's eyes twinkled with joy as she looked up from her back. A humongous chunk of steel had gotten her attention.   "What   the   hell   is   that?"   she   asked.

"They   call   it   the   shell."

"Oh,   we're   stealing   this!"

"I   had   something   lighter   in   mind."

"Nope. This is it. Get in," said Rose, already climbing inside.

The shell was the Frankenstein of engineering, covered in thick armored plating. There was a cab-over-styled cockpit attached to a SWAT passenger compartment. Two steering wheels gave it the ability to be driven from either side, if necessary, therefore stopping wasn't required to change operators. Between the two segments was a fully protected, fifty-caliber turret. "Incoming!" yelled a soldier, after seeing the barrel of the turret swing in their direction. The entire group scattered in every direction, like roaches when someone turns the kitchen light on. Rounds the size of salt shakers punched through steel and concrete where they had just stood.

"Shit," said Rose, after pausing her fire. Yesha asked, "What happened?" not sure of the reason for Rose's reaction.

"I can't port us out from here. We've gotten too far from the surface."

"Are you sure?"

"Yes. We would be able to sense Dad and Ari."

"So, what do we do?"

"Drive!" Rose cried out. The diesel engine cranked up under Yesha's touch. She threw the turtle-shaped rig into reverse, smashed the gas, then whipped it into the aisle. Rose revved the mounted rifle up again for cover fire until it clicked empty. "Can you just drive us out of here?" she asked.

"No. The doors are like three feet of solid steel."

"Well, you have to get us close enough for me to get us out of here, or we're dead."

"I'm trying, but the ramp is back that way, with them."

"There's got to be a way to... I have an idea!" Rose said, after quickly calculating their options. "Hurry up, 'cause I'm running out of places to drive." Yesha fishtailed around to the next aisle. The soldiers had blocked the far end off with other vehicles, so she jammed the brakes, bringing the shell to a complete stop.

"We need to get up the ramps," said Rose.

"Hello!" Yesha used her hand to alert Rose of the obstructions ahead.

"Just drive! I'll handle them." Yesha pushed the pedal all the way to the floor. The massive, super-single tires screeched into motion. The soldiers fired barrages of ammunition, but the vehicle was designed to take direct hits from explosive devices, so small arms were virtually useless.

"Rose!" Yesha squealed, voicing concern. "Just keep driving!" As soon as they were in range, Rose used a hanging convex mirror to catapult the shell to the other side of the blockade. They burst into a cloud of particles, then reassembled at her direction. "Holy shit! What did you just do to us?" "Dad said it was his first power. I never tried it before but figured it was easy enough." "Figured? What if it didn't work? We would've crashed." "Woulda, coulda," Rose mocked. "Just drive to the top, and don't stop." Chase was given by the squadron of soldiers. Rose fended their faster vehicles off with hails of gunfire. Yesha rounded the final turn. The ramp led right up to the huge metal door. It was the only obstacle remaining between them and the outside. "I hope you're sure about this," she said, with the gas still to the floor. "Me too," Rose responded. She was greatly worried on the inside. It was only her second try at an instant port, and being on the move only complicated the maneuver exponentially. "One... two... ahhhhh!" Rose shouted out, sure they would die, if she failed. Only feet from the door, the shell vanished into oblivion.

Rose and Yesha realized the danger wasn't over. Rose had mistakenly ported them directly to the marketplace. They were on course to smash through all of the shops and food reserves. Both women screamed as Rose made an effort to pull off an additional, miraculous feat. Civilians scrambled to avoid becoming roadkill by the rampaging tank. In the nick of time, Rose managed to blow open another portal, and they drove inside, just short of causing any real damage. That is, until they crashed through the side of the abandoned restaurant, narrowly missing Chris, Cory, and Ari. Dust from the wrecked storefront was set aloft by the open breeze that sifted through its broken wall. Wood and brick crunched under the feet of Rose and Yesha as they stepped out of the vehicle, hair upended by electrical disturbances from the portals interacting with the steel-enveloped truck. "What the fuck?" Cory shouted angrily.

"What? You didn't poop your pants, did you?" Rose teased, carefully working her way over the rubble.
"I hate you."
"Stop being a pussy!"
"Oh, so now you wanna talk crazy because Pops can't hear you."
"I'm not scared of him," Rose peeked from her peripheral to verify that Chris was still out.
"We'll see when he wakes up."
"Snitch!"
"Yeah, sure. Just fix your hair, dust mop head-ass girl." Embarrassed, Rose did her best to smooth down her dark locks. Yesha took the insult as applicable to herself, raking her fingers through her own.
At last done pestering his sister, Cory turned his focus on the truck. "I was expecting something... more practical," he said.
"We ran into some unexpected problems, so we made do," Rose replied.
"Problems are always expected. Rule number eight."
"Ugh! I can't with you," Rose dismissively spoke. She walked over to where Chris still lay, then asked, "Any change with the old man?"
"Not much. I checked his pulse, and it's back to normal though, so that's a good sign."
Ari spoke of her own observations. "He kept saying me and Mom's name. What does that mean? You think he's thinking about us?" she queried.
A familiar rumble killed the chance for any response. The convoy was returning to the facility. The group was fortunate that night had fallen. Darkness, in a world no longer dominated by electricity, or a light-reflecting body like the moon—ejected from its planetary orbit the day the world broke—was just that: true darkness. It was nearly impossible to see still objects from moderate distances.
"Guess they weren't going to see Sasha," Cory surmised.
"No, they were," said Yesha. "We just changed their plans a little."
"Good. If we leave now, we should be able to beat them to my mom. Let's get Pops in the truck."

"How are three tiny women and a half-grown boy supposed to lift him that high off the ground? He's over two hundred pounds of dead weight," noted the always observant   Rose.

Cory couldn't wait to unleash a barrage of sarcasm. Making his sister feel less than intelligent was his superpower. "Oh, I don't know. If we lived in a comic book, and there was some ravishing, handsome, smart, muscular young man, with a mediocre, basic, angry—and I mean really angry—borderline evil sister with the ability to magically move things from one place to another..."

"I'm going to kill him, I swear," threatened Rose, seething.

"I hate to interrupt your fun, little sibling thing, but if we plan on getting to Sasha before they do, we need to get out of   here,"   said   Yesha.

"We'll finish this later," Rose grunted, digging her pointer finger   into   Cory's   chest.

Yesha pulled open the rear doors. They were weighted down with armored plates as well, but the heavily oiled hinges allowed them to be moved without too much strain. The only sign that bullets had even touched them was glints of silver, where the black paint had been gouged away. Cory flung the three packs of survival gear and supplies inside, then assisted Ari up. She thanked him with a smile and took a seat on one of the two benches that straddled   the   side   walls.

Ready for her task, Rose flagged Cory over for aid. "You know the old man is gonna castrate you if you keep fawning over his daughter like that?" she muttered at a volume   that   only   he   could   hear.

"I'm so scared," Cory used his entire body to gesture his lack   of   concern.

"Mmhm.   We'll   see   when   he   wakes   up."

"Now   who's   the   snitch?"

"Just   pull   him   through   when   I   open   this   thing."

The portal opened level with the bed of the truck. Cory dragged Chris inside by his arms, then Rose followed them through. She took a seat on the passenger side of the vehicle next to Yesha, who asked, "Are we ready to go?"

"Yeah, as soon as he closes the door, we're good," Rose

responded.

Cory secured the doors, then took a seat opposite Ari, then slapped the wall to notify Rose and Yesha that they were good to go.

"Seatbelts, everybody. Ride's gonna be rough most of the way," Yesha responded, as she threw the truck into reverse. The wreckage crunched beneath the multi-ton behemoth, backing out into the roadway. Its ten-inch rims were wrapped in massive fourteen-inch thick rubber tires, so there was no chance of deflation due to puncturing debris. A steel encasement protected them from gunfire. Ari was still fiddling with her buckle. She wasn't familiar with the harness-style belts commonly used in military-style vehicles.

"Here, I got you," said Cory. He stood up, careful to keep his balance in the lightly rocking vehicle, and walked over to sit beside her. "Untangle this first. This is supposed to be upright. Now, put these over your shoulders, and this around your waist. Clamp the big buckle together first, like this, then slide the two smaller ones in the bottom. That's it," he instructed while demonstrating how to complete the task.

"Thanks," Ari said shyly.

"I'm here to help whenever you need it." Cory was getting up to retake his seat on the other bench, but Ari grasped his hand.

"You don't have to," she said, so Cory remained seated, buckling his own harness while trying to keep his excitement hidden inside. He could see Rose pointing to Chris and sliding her thumb across her neck from his peripheral, but pretended not to see her at all.

A number of miles into the drive, the color began to drain from Rose's face.

"Are you alright?" Yesha asked her.

"Just a little tired, is all."

Cory unbuckled his safety harness and scoured through his bag for nourishment.

"She needs to eat. Using her power like that takes a lot of energy," he said.

A bag of deer jerky rustled as he pulled apart the resealable opening.

"Gimme that!" Rose grunted, snatching the entire pack from his hands. She shoved the pieces of cured meat down her throat so fast, the others wondered if she had eaten them   whole.

Cory had already uncapped two bottles of water and held them within her reach. Only equalizing pressure prevented Rose from gulping them down any faster. Heavy gasps calmed into smooth breaths. Now satisfied and at rest, Rose observed the concerned glances from Yesha and Ari, both   avoiding   eye   contact   with   her.

"Sorry," she apologized for her animalistic lack of manners, as if she could control it anyway.

"You have any more of that?" asked Ari. It had been a while   since   she   last   ate.

"I've got something better," Cory responded, once again scrounging through his pack. He retrieved a rectangular brown package from inside.

It's a meal ready to eat. You don't have to cook it, but it has this heater in it, so you can warm it up without a fire. It's not as good as the food you're used to, but you can't   beat   it   when   you're   on   the   move.

"That thing heats it up?" Ari was curious about how a primitive-looking tea bag could heat up a packet of food. Cory demonstrated, "Yep. Just put the food in the plastic bag   with   it,   then   add   a   little   water."

"Wow," Ari exclaimed, feeling the increasing warmth with her   fingertips.

Cory pulled the packaging away after a moment. "Careful. It'll get hot enough to burn you," he warned, sitting the contraption on the seat next to him. "It'll be ready in a few minutes.

Northern Texas had primarily become an expansive woodland. Rose, Cory, and Ari had spent the bulk of their lives there, so new scenery was a rarity for them; however, that fact was actively changing. The dry, thirsty familiarity of New Mexico had also changed into a similar type of ecosystem. Daylight cast itself, uninterrupted, across vast grasslands,   separating   dense   jungle.

Fatigue weighed down on Yesha. She had driven constantly through the night, hoping to stay ahead of Foley's, who she was sure wouldn't be too far behind. "You look exhausted," said Rose, watching her yawn several times.

"I   am."

"Why   don't   you   take   a   break?"

"I can't. Not here, while we're in the open like this," Yesha replied, when an idea presented itself to her, and she asked Rose,   "Can   you   drive?"

"No. I wanted to learn, but Chris said it was safer if we moved around on foot. Harder to get seen that way."

"Take the wheel," Yesha instructed. Rose looked at the extra steering wheel in front of her, as it rocked slightly side to side, mirroring Yesha's control on the other. She didn't often feel genuine nervousness, but this time it found its way out. "Go ahead. I've got your back if you need it,"   Yesha   reassured.

Rose slowly grasped the wheel, but firmly. After a few seconds, Yesha relinquished full control of the steering to her. A chuckle found its way from Rose, a sign of jittery excitement.

Yesha gave further instruction. "The left pedal is for stopping or slowing down, and the right is to speed up. If you keep it steady, it'll maintain the same speed. The key is to ease into the pedals, rather than jamming them down. I'm about to take my feet off, then it's all you," she said, then released the gas, giving Rose a supportive nod. The large vehicle lurched forward. Rose gasped and quickly removed her foot from the accelerator. "Easy," Yesha reminded her. A second attempt resulted in the desired reaction. The truck smoothly quickened to a safe thirty-five miles an hour, and held fast. "Good, now make sure you hold the wheel steady, and don't go too fast. These roads are really bad in spots. One bump can make you lose control."

Rose was a quick study with most things. Driving was no different. After only a few miles, she was dodging potholes, slowing to climb buckled sections of asphalt, and swerving around rusted frames of unattended vehicles.

Once comfortable enough with Rose's skills, Yesha was ready for a nap. "Can you handle things?" she asked. Rose responded, "Sure. Get some rest," so Yesha permitted her eyelids to close.

Ankle-high grass fields stretched to visual limits in every direction. Grazing herbivores kept things controlled and tidy. Very few trees were near the shabby road. The lack of cover made the area particularly dangerous for anything without sharp canines and strong jaw muscles. "Can we stop? I need to use the restroom," said Ari, after another hour of travel. "You do know there aren't any restrooms out here? You wanna just use it out in the open?" mocked Rose. "There isn't one in here either." Not to be outwitted, Rose responded, "Well, if you find somewhere to stop out here in the middle of nowhere, let me know," aware that neither she nor Cory could see much from the windowless rear. Cory found a solution in the roof above. The gunner's nest was the perfect vantage point to view things as they appeared on the horizon. "Up there," he pointed. Ari's body language said that she was game. They shed their safety harnesses, then found balance in the rocking truck. Luckily, its large tires and heavy suspension system dampened much of the more violent jerks. The gunner's platform was only meant for a single adult soldier to stand in, but the two teens managed to squeeze up next to one another, very little room to spare. A circular, glass globe covered the head area in completion, with the fully automatic rifle mounted with the long barrel poking through precisely cut port holes. Not a single enemy round would likely squeeze through. Ari and Cory were intoxicated by the scenery before them. They had been injected into what amounted to an African safari. Families of elephants moved together, shaping the landscape to their will. Deer were plentiful, mounted by small birds that hitched rides on their backs. Even a couple of giraffes picked at the limbs of high vegetation, out of reach to most other species.

"I am so confused," said Ari. "I studied the zoology of the world in school. Most of these species shouldn't be here."

"Zoo animals," Cory figured. "It must have been."

"Wouldn't they be scattered all over the country then?"

"Maybe not. Animals have a way of sensing things that we never could. All they would have to do is find the climate best suited for them, and they would all end up in the same places. Breeding without interference from people would get numbers up pretty quick."

"What about in the beginning? Why didn't the extreme temperatures kill them off?"

"That I can't answer. But, life always finds a way," Cory replied. He thought for a second. "They didn't teach you any of this stuff at that school you were talking about?"

"Not much. My teachers, Mom, and Foley didn't say much, except how dangerous it is. They rarely let me travel between settlements, and when I did, it was usually in the back of one of those RV things with the protected windows." Ari drew in more of the view. "I imagined something more... dead and damaged."

"Sounds like that's what they wanted you to think. That everything you needed was in that place." Just then, Cory eyed a cluster of trees and thick brush near the edge of an off-ramp. Chris had taught them that this usually was a sign of degrading man-made structures. He said to Rose, "I guess we could stop there. May not be a restroom, but at least nobody could see the truck from the road." Her vantage point was not as good as his from where she sat, so she asked, "Where?"

"Coming up on the right."

A short while later, Rose exited the old freeway. Though she was a natural, inexperience led her to take the curb with a little more speed than desired. Cory and Ari were tipped off balance, and fell onto the double triggers of the mounted weapon. A burst of rounds spun from the long barrel into the air.

Trilling booms scared Yesha awake, causing her to smack her head on the roof. "Shit! What the fuck!" she screamed at the top of her lungs. With her footing regained, Ari peeked down from the gunner's nest. "Ooo momma!" she exclaimed, floored to hear her mother use such colorful language. "Don't momma me, people are shooting at us!" "That was us." Yesha was further confused. "Why would you be shooting a gun?" "It wasn't on purpose. We fell into the thing." "Get out of there before you hurt yourselves or give me a heart attack."

Cory's assumption was spot on. A few square miles of old buildings were shrouded in leafage. The ruins had become part of nature and would one day be entirely reclaimed by Mother Earth. The deep-grooved tires slid across the ground when Rose punched the brakes down. Her passengers were thrown forward, violently. "What happened to nice and easy?" asked Yesha. Rose looked back to see Cory and Ari piled in a heap, with Chris' limp body. They all slid across the floor until they met the wall. "My bad," she giggled, halfway between apathetic and amused.

The air was ripe with strong odors, most unpleasant. Yesha was the first to get out to survey the surroundings. She walked over to the opposite side of the truck to get a better view of the ragged commercial buildings.

"Did something die out here?" Rose questioned, after dismounting the vehicle. Yesha looked down at the young woman's feet. "No. Something went number two, and you just stepped in it." "Ew! That's so disgusting." Rose did her best to wipe her foot clean on the shin-high grass at the walkway's edge. Ari and Cory were stepping from the rear doors by this time. They enjoyed watching Rose be the victim of instant karma. "That's what you get," Cory teased. Waving him off, Rose elected her focus was better spent on thorough reconnaissance. "Where are you going?" Cory asked her. "Just looking around."

Yesha wasn't as calm as her younger companions seemed to be. "Be careful. There's a lot of wildlife around here. No telling what could be hiding." "They're the ones that should be afraid of me," Rose replied, rounding the corner of the nearest building. Not to miss out on an exploration, Ari and Cory followed behind her.

"Ari, where are you going? I just said it's not safe out here," said Yesha.

"You also told me how bad things were out here. Doesn't look bad to me." Ari was upset that her mother lied to her about the state of the world for so long. "Besides, Rose is the most dangerous thing out here and she's on our side." Both her points were valid. Yesha glanced between her feet, feeling a bit guilty. Rather than arguing further, she shifted her attention elsewhere. Chris, though unconscious, was alone on the floor of the truck. She climbed up, closed the door, took a seat at his side, and spoke out loud, as if he could hear her. "I don't know what you're dreaming about in there. I mean, I'm sure you have to be thinking about something. Now would be as good a time as any for you to wake up. We could use a little bit of help... I could use... The kids are so brave. You did a good job raising them. Ari too. Sometimes she's a handful just like you. I know you don't remember, but we do... That has to mean you'll remember one day. I hope." Tears rolled down her cheek. Her voice trembled, as she went on. "I think I messed up really bad. I only wanted to protect her... our baby, but... I didn't tell her the truth about the world out here. I was only trying to protect her, but... I don't know. I don't think she will ever forgive me. I don't know if I'll forgive me."

Elsewhere, Ari and Cory caught up to Rose. She was standing still, staring off into the distance, using her hand to shield the sun from her eyes. "Books don't do this type of thing justice, do they?" she said.

"Not even close," Cory replied.

The distinctive sheen of water was visible only a short walk away. The brownish bush grew greener on the path toward it. "You think we could check it out?" asked Ari. Rose didn't feel much like it. "Maybe later. I'm tired and hungry. Let's go back to put some real food together, cause I'm not eating an MRE today." She headed back for the Shell. They followed, though lagging behind a little.

The rear door latches clicked as Rose pulled them apart. Yesha was still sitting with Chris' hand clenched in hers. "Any changes with him?" Rose asked her. "No. He mumbles something every now and again, but I can't make out what he's saying." Yesha laid Chris' hand at his side then stood. "Ready to go?" "I think we should make camp here for a bit." "What about Foley? We can't let him get ahead of us." "I don't know about you, but all that bumping around is killing me. I need some peace. Besides, that was a convoy of eight trucks. I highly doubt they'll drive clear across the country without taking a break themselves." "I suppose you're right." Yesha exited the truck. She took in a deep breath of fresh air, regretting it immediately. "Girl, you really need to do something about that poo on your shoe," she added. Rose looked down at her ruined boot. The excrement was still moist, which meant the effort to clean would be easier. "Poo?" she mocked. "You have quite the colorful vocabulary for an adult." Rose reached into the truck, reeled in her backpack, and retrieved a bottle of water. "How bout' you get a fire going and cook something," she instructed Cory, walking off to wash away her troubles. Cory gathered supplies together, then headed for an awning that, though full of holes and leaning, still remained firmly attached. Combined with the tree branches above, it would act as a filtering chimney, making it more difficult for the smoke to be spotted from a distance.

Homemade stew bubbled in a cast iron pot above open flames. The aroma of wild-caught boar blended perfectly with fresh vegetables and spices. The plastic vacuum seal packaging that once held the tastefully prepared dish blew away on a swift breeze. Smaller and lighter were always the rule of thumb for traveling soldiers, so cups would serve in place of bowls. Each was dressed in a thin rubber protector that would prevent hot contents from scalding hands.

"Mmm. This is really good," Ari complimented. "Why does it taste so familiar?"

Yesha blew a cooling breath over a spoonful and ate. The flavor was definitely one that she recognized. "It's your father's recipe." She pulled the thought from memories of a life that they had never lived. "He made it about a week ago, after our last hunt," Rose informed them.

Silence took hold of the group for a moment, as they all thought of Chris. Some of them had to fight away thoughts that he may never wake up again. That he had saved their lives one last time at the cost of his own. Yesha was the first to break the silence. "So, what was it like all this time?"

Rose smiled, an unexpected sign of fond recollection. "Hard, but worth it."

"You really have a good life out here in this?" Yesha waved her hand to the savage wilds of the land.

"Better than good. We don't have all the technology that you guys have, but we don't live as primitive as you guys might think. We found this house after we escaped. It was in surprisingly good condition. Dad taught us how to fix it up. We found a generator, then stocked up on fuel, so we had power. After that, we planted a garden in the backyard. He taught us how to grow whatever we wanted and we would go on hunts and scavenge. We trained and learned how to protect ourselves. We survived. But, more than that. We had fun. He learned who we were, then let us be us. Who can ask for more than that?"

A new quiet fell upon the group. All of them had their own stories of Chris; most pleasant, some annoying, others angering and painful. He was a polarizing father, friend, and lover, but he tried and he was always present as the glue to many pieces.

The four of them went on talking for several hours, but to them it felt like mere minutes. Chris would always say that time flew during a good time. This was an example of how true the saying actually was. Crackling popped from the controlled blaze when Cory added fresh wood. It wasn't needed for warmth, as heat was atmospherically abundant, but as a predator deterrent and light source. The sun was fading away, leaving burnt orange markings in the sky. Night would soon wrestle the day away for a time. "You guys OK out here? I'm going to go sit with Chris for a while," said Yesha. Rose made herself comfortable near the fire. "Yeah. You alright with leaving at first light?" Though impatient internally, Yesha didn't want to ruin the night by forcing the kids back into the cramped truck. They deserved to rest without bouncing about the cab endlessly. "That's fine," she responded. It didn't take long for Rose to fall asleep. She snored horridly on a tarp she had laid out on the soft grass. Only Cory and Ari remained to enjoy the twinkling stars overhead. They learned a great deal about one another through shared stories and discussions of likes and hobbies. The consensus between them was that they were the same, yet different. Both were intellectuals in their own right.

Ari had the best education available in a time where most were not afforded one at all. Cory was naturally gifted, and fed his thirst for knowledge through material scavenged out in the world over time. "Wanna go for a walk? We could check out that watering hole we saw earlier," Cory suggested. Ari was skeptical. "I don't know. It could be dangerous out there."

"We'll be alright. It's not that far, and we've been here all day, but haven't seen any big predators around." "My mom and dad wouldn't like it."

"You always do everything they say? Live a little. They can't be mad at what they don't know. Besides, nothing will happen to you long as I'm around," Cory convincingly reasoned. He pulled his sidearm from the holster as a show of power, but dropped it in the pile of dirt and ash surrounding the fire.

Rose shifted positions in her sleep, disturbed by the sudden noise.

"So, that was supposed to make me feel protected?" Ari taunted.

"Did it work?" Cory picked up his weapon and returned it to its holster.

Ari stood up, dusting off the back of her clothes. "Nope," she teased, still falling victim to pure pressure.

Rose was fast asleep in clear view, so their first step was to get an eye on Yesha. The pair peeked through the two long, oval windows on the rear of the truck. She was also sleeping, her head resting on Chris' chest. "See. Nothing to worry about," Cory pointed out.

Ari turned to walk away and Cory followed. She rubbed her fingertips across crumbling stacks of brickwork as she rounded the corner. The abundant sounds of nature whisked through the ruins as insects played a symphony. Though dark, the starlit sky was enough for fair visibility on such a clear night. Cory broke out a flashlight anyway.

Dozens of paths zigzagged all the way to the water's edge, created by the many creatures that called the vicinity home. They would travel for a drink or to cool off during the hot hours of the day, then return to their respective dwellings. Ari and Cory walked those trails surrounded by knee-high grass, retracing the steps of those native animals. They didn't speak for some time. Silence and adoration of the scenery was a language all its own.

A cluster of bioluminescent bugs erupted outward, lighting the way. It was as if they were lamps of life, guiding anyone or anything taking the night venture to the life-sustaining body of water. "It's breathtaking out here," said Ari, finally breaking the silence.

"It is," Cory replied.

"Living on your own, do you guys see things like this often?"

"Like this... no. There's a lot of beautiful scenery in Texas, but none of it compares to this." Cory hesitated a second, then countered with a question of his own. "How is it living with two realities? It's gotta be confusing."

Ari pondered the question. There wasn't an easy way to explain something that no one could fully comprehend. "It isn't really," she said. "I guess in a lot of situations two things can be true at once, the way a dessert can be sweet and salty. Everything kind of just blends together. For instance, I'm here with you now, but I'm also home with my parents. I can see the yellow wallpaper in my room, and feel the soft carpet between my toes. I'm living there, just as much as I am here."

"It hurts my brain just thinking about it." Cory rubbed his head.

The conversation led them within a few feet of the water's boundary. Ari grabbed Cory's hand, guiding him closer, until the soles of their boots were submerged. "You think fish are in there?" she queried.

"One way to find out." Cory's tough upbringing made him much stronger and larger than one would expect for his age. This enabled him to dangle his light-framed counterpart in the air with ease. He plucked Ari from her feet, pretending to be about to toss her in. She flailed her feet around, laughing intensely, pleading, "Wait, wait, wait!"

"What's the safe word?" Cory heckled.

"I don't know!" Ari laughed even harder.

"Nope. Not it."

"Mercy! Mercy!"

"Well... if you're going to beg me." Cory finally returned Ari to her feet. She responded with a kick to his shin.

"Ouch!" Cory yelped, surprised by the attack.

"That's what you get!" An audible ruffle in the surrounding brush abruptly halted the flirtatious fun. "What was that?" asked Ari.

"What was what?"

Ari's facial expression read full panic. "Cory," she muttered, pointing at a moving figure.

"Shit." Cory recognized the threat for what it was. He pulled his gun slowly to avoid sudden movement and coaxed Ari behind him with his offhand. "Stay between me and the water."

More movement signified that the danger had increased by a factor of four. The lionesses were on the hunt. Cory and Ari had become prey. Not one to panic, Cory pieced together a strategy on the fly. His first step was to attempt to scare the beasts away. He aimed in the air, pulling the trigger twice. Only one bang sounded. The gun had jammed.

***

Chris fell into a state of unrest. His eyelids twitched and his face scrunched with discomfort, as his hands clenched involuntarily into tight fists. The jerking of his body disturbed Yesha enough to shake her into the place between sleep and wakefulness. "Chris... stop moving so much. You're waking me up again," she said, unaware of what she was really saying.

A gunshot rang out loud. Rose snapped awake, pulling her weapon. She scanned around for enemies. The truck's thick shell, however, muffled the sound to the point of inaudibility, but the next sound would penetrate deep into Chris' soul. Ari let out a bloodcurdling scream. Its effect on Chris was powerful and instantaneous. His eyes vaulted open. His body imploded in on itself, evaporating into a plasma of white-hot and blue.

Yesha's face planted the rubber-lined floor, no longer supported by Chris' broad torso. The collision jarred her awake in enough time to see the last of Chris' particles dissipate. "Why can't I just have a normal freakin' life?" she complained, picking herself up from the floor.

A turbid haze of energy condensed together from nothing, swatting the pouncing cat mid-jump. It tumbled, but quickly recovered to its feet. The formless figure disappeared as fast as it had coalesced.

"What in God's name is that?" Ari was terrified. She didn't have much time to worry, nor did Cory to respond. The initial threat still remained. The hunting pride flanked them on all sides. Cory tried desperately to free the caught round from his weapon as the animals closed in. This time they all attacked in close succession, but the mysterious cloud again phased into existence. It pulsated, at times taking on a human-like silhouette, battering the wild felines from their purpose.

"Dad?" muttered Ari, feeling the connection to his aura in the ever-changing ball of lighting and smoke.

Cory didn't hear her. His mind was running calculations at a staggering pace, until an opening finally made itself available. "Come on Ari. Run!" he yelled, pulling her by the hand. They dashed across the open field, heading back towards camp, when a new obstacle presented itself. A gigantic male lion leaped from his place of hiding to claim them as his own meal. His powerful legs propelled him at speeds they couldn't escape.

Time slowed down. Cory and Ari were left in an impossible state. They themselves, along with all around, played at a fraction of the speed normally experienced, but their minds still worked in real time. They felt like prisoners of the moment in their own bodies. A bolt of lightning manifested from the ground, snaking its way towards the sky like a growing sprout captured in a time-lapse. An orb of debris rotated around the rod of electricity. It blackened until it took on its true, natural form, then Cory saw him.

The cracking explosion of the storm-like presence narrowly missed the lion, but injected it with sheer terror. It vacated the premises as fast as it could, along with the rest of its family of hunters. When time found its regular pace once more, Chris was standing inches from Ari. The glow in his eyes was more mighty than it had ever been, yet she didn't fear. There was no malice in his powerful display. Chris outstretched his hand, brushing her hair behind her ear. He ran his thumb across her cheek.

A blue ring glinted in Ari's eyes. "I know you," she said.

"Better than you know you," Chris responded, completing a special saying between father and daughter. A sudden gust of wind battered them into a waft of smoke and carried them away, leaving Cory standing alone.

8

Home Is Where The House Is

Leaves tinged in yellow dangled by their stems, riding temperate breezes. Perpetual autumn left the trees frozen halfway between a state of life and dormancy. Large sections of paint were gouged away from the house's exterior by the wilds of nature. An owl perched above the main doorway hooted into the vastness of night. It flew away, surprised at the arrival of other living souls.

Chris and Ari materialized from a fog of their blended bodies. The place was one of great familiarity, though a decade of deterioration marred its pristine memory. "This was our house," Ari recollected. She approached the main entrance. Her feet crunched through dead herbage piled on the wide steps that led up to the porch.

Chris followed behind her, but stopped at the base of the stairs. "Still is," he replied. Ari twisted the door's handle. It was unlocked. The hinges squealed. A sudden pop resulted from wood around the topmost hinge cracking from the door's shifting weight. "Careful," said Chris, aware that the withering structure could be unstable in places.

"Everything's so old." Ari mentally compared the place to the way it looked in its prime condition.

As they passed through the foyer into the living room, Ari dragged her fingers across the walls, furniture, and decor. Her favorite sensory language was touch, so feeling around was often her go-to. Textures told her far more than sight alone was able to. Chris continued to tag along as Ari explored what she had already known so well.

The doors and windows leading to the atrium had been long shattered. Ari's boots rested on broken glass. Her eyes met with an important item from her youth. Its essence tugged her over, as if magnetized. She stepped through the framework, careful to avoid jagged pieces still jutting from its perimeter.

A broken-down swing set was the element of Ari's focus. Its gravitational pull on her soul was equal to that of a black hole. "This was my favorite," she recalled.

Chris could sense that her spirit called for one last swing. He was blessed with the ability to grant this wish, so he rolled back the clock in the confined space. The chains regenerated from the rusted maroon weaklings they had become, and the poles straightened to their former glory. Even the wild blades of grass beneath reverted to green, tamed versions of the past. "Go ahead," he said.

Ari took a seat on the leather base. Now much bigger, she sat back further so that her legs didn't drag the ground. Chris pushed her, at first lightly, then with more vigor. Ari giggled with the spirit of adolescence. Years of this practice played in their minds. They again felt the love their alternate lives provided. "How much do you remember?" she asked him.

"Everything. The day you were born all the way til' now. It's like you and your mother were there the entire time."

"We were."

A moment of silence preceded Chris' next statement. "It's funny that I still can't remember anything before. I don't know how I met your mother and I still don't understand how you can be as old as you are, but be born when you were. None of it adds up."

"I don't know. Maybe we'll remember things one day."

"Maybe."

The others returned to Ari's mind. "Don't you think we should go back? Everybody is probably worried about us."

Chris reached out his hand and connected it with hers. "They can wait a few more minutes. I just got my Baby Girl back and I want to enjoy it a little longer."

9

He's Only Human

Cory scuttled back to the campsite, nearly tripping over his own feet. Rose targeted him with her pistol. "What the hell is going on?" she yelled, toggling her weapon back onto safety.

"Some lions attacked us out of nowhere..." he began to explain.

Yesha interrupted, entrenched with fear. "Where's my daughter?"

"I think Pops took her."

"What do you mean 'think'? Is she with him or not?"

"It was him, but it could've not been."

"What the fuck are you talking about?" Yesha's language lately had become more and more vulgar, but for good reason.

"You know that movie when people die and then the cemetery brings them back to life, but when they come back, they're evil killers?"

"Really! You're bringing up movies right now?" Rose shouted.

"Well, how else am I supposed to explain what I

saw? He had this crazed blue look in his eyes and—"

In the midst of Cory's argument, Chris and Ari silently appeared in the same manner they had vanished. Their arrival was dead center of the disputing trio, who all pointed their guns at Chris' face. "Dammit it's me!" He threw his hands up in submission.

Guns remained aimed. "Are you you or the evil you?" Rose interrogated.

"What?" Chris raised a single eyebrow.

"Like in the movie when people die, then the cemetery brings them back to life, but when they come back they're evil killers."

"Pet Cemetery? No... Fuck no!"

"That's what he would say if he was evil," Cory concluded.

"You know you're not too old to have a well-whipped ass, right?"

The line was all it took for Rose and Yesha to put away their guns. "He's normal," they said in sync.

Cory finally put away his own but still had a bone to pick with Chris. "If you're really you, then why did you leave me out there with those lions by myself? They could've come back and killed me!"

"Why did you have my daughter out there in the first place?"

"Well, uh..." Cory failed to come up with an explanation.

Rose dragged her finger across her neck, again signifying an upcoming murder. "Told you," she teased.

"Wait. So, you remember?" Yesha nervously questioned.

"Everything that matters," Chris replied.

A faint whistle grew louder, catching the attention of the quintet. They all turned their eyes to the sky in search of the source until it became obvious. "Get down!" Chris shouted at the top of his lungs.

Fire and brimstone rained from overhead. A number of mid-range missiles plowed into the earth, sending everyone careening. Luckily, the ruined buildings took the brunt of the first round. Rose and Chris used their abilities to shield the group from the following impacts. "Get to the truck!" Rose called out.

They scurried, dodging falling rocks and flames from the crumbling shelter. Yesha hopped into the driver's seat and started the diesel engine as everyone else piled into the already open rear doors.

"Turret," Rose said, alerting Chris to its presence. She then took the passenger seat, ready to give Yesha whatever assistance she needed.

The bulky tires flung dirt every which way as Yesha plowed her foot through the throttle. Chris was barely up top before the vehicle fishtailed toward the main highway. He checked the belt-fed ammunition, then searched for targets to engage.

Foley's convoy had set up shop about a mile off. Aware of the special abilities of his enemy, he had chosen to attempt a surprise attack at a distance. Now cognizant that they had failed to terminate their target, his convoy went on the move to give chase. In no time, the smaller, more nimble vehicles closed the distance between them.

Chris fired in staggered bursts, careful not to overheat the barrel. He had seen the results of one exploding in his past, and it wasn't a pretty sight. The armored plating on the chasing fleet of Humvees and repurposed sedans was significantly thinner than the Shell's. The fifty-caliber rounds were capable of punching through, so they swerved about trying to avoid direct hits, then fell back to a safer distance.

Rocket-propelled grenades whistled past the swerving Shell. Chris was able to phase it and its passengers out of the line of fire by mere thought.

"How the hell are you doing that?" Rose shouted.

"I don't know. You and your brother have a problem asking questions at the wrong time. And watch your damn mouth!"

"Shit!" Yesha cursed on cue.

Rose took notice of what worried her. "You'd better have something else up your sleeve," she said to Chris.

"Really? Am I not doing enough already?" he responded sarcastically.

"We're almost out of fuel."

"You didn't put fuel in this thing?"

"We stole it from them!" Rose pointed at their enemies. "Where do you think we could get fuel?" She looked to Yesha and asked, "How far are we from the 002 place?"

"Not even close," Yesha responded.

"Did you say 002... as in Project 002?" Chris questioned.

"Does it matter? It's not like we can make it anyway," Rose argued.

"Shut up and strap in! I'm going to try something."

"Oh Lord. When he says that, it's never something good," Cory complained. He rushed to help Ari buckle her harness, then his own.

The last time Chris had tested the limits of his mind, it was left in shambles, preventing him from completing even the most basic maneuvers without the risk of losing consciousness. He had only been whole for what amounted to a few moments, but was being forced to take that risk again already.

One was the number of times that Chris had been to Project 002. His memory of that instance was fleeting at best, but there wasn't much of an alternative. A direct hit from an RPG was more likely the longer the chase was active. He focused as best he could, then phased the six-ton truck and its five occupants across an area spanning states, all without taking the time to open a portal.

The location was spot on, but unfortunately, Chris misjudged the terrain. The truck regenerated several feet above rolling hills, nosediving into the ground. It rolled over countless times. A wheel ripped away along with the mounted weapon and large chunks of the outer shell.

Smoke billowed from the crumpled wreckage. Not a soul moved among the mangled debris. Then, a siren called out, an ambient track to a scenery of carnage. Rose willed her eyes open. It was the only movement she could manage. Until blinded by darkness, her eyelids collapsed under their own weight, to remain closed for an indefinite spell.

***

When Rose's eyes opened again, a bright light forced her to shut them. She squinted, shielding her face with her forearm until they could adjust to the illumination. "What is this place?" she grumbled, inspecting her whereabouts. The room had the appearance of a modern prison cell, blended with a low-expense hotel. It was very small, about 10ft x 15ft, with blank white, windowless walls. There was a single door with a small, rectangular window, but no handle to toggle it open.

Rose sat up straight. She felt the comforter covering the twin-size bed beneath her. It was of great quality, odd for a jail cell, she thought. Attempting to stand up wasn't as easy a task as Rose thought it would be. She grabbed hold of her sore rib cage, squinting from the pain, which was a nuisance, but not what she expected after such a gruesome crash.

"Where's everybody else?" She spoke to herself, the wreck now at the forefront of her mind. Worried about her family, Rose focused her mind to reach out to Chris telepathically. With no response, she tried for Ari and Yesha with the same result.

"What the...?" Rose pondered out loud.

Trying not to slip into full panic, Rose concluded escaping would put her in better condition to find them. She summoned all of her willpower to blast open a portal to anywhere but where she was. Nothing happened. Rose couldn't even feel her mind connecting with the outside world. Panic finally took over. "Let me out of here!" she yelled over and over, banging on the door. "If you hurt my family, I'll kill every one of you fuckers!"

A group of approaching footsteps caused Rose to step back from the door. She dropped into a three-point stance, ready to pounce like the wildcat she was. The door swung open and a male soldier started to speak. "Ma'am..." was all he was able to utter before Rose began her attack. She drove her knee into his abdomen with a running start, then hip-tossed him onto the bed. He landed atop it with so much force that the wooden frame cracked, rolling him onto the floor.

The next man that entered was more expectant of her reaction. Rose threw a wild hook, not paying much attention to her target. He knocked her fist away, using her own momentum to counter, then whacked her on the forehead with the center of his open palm. The maneuver was one Rose hated with every fiber of her being, but was also seared into her brain. During her lifetime of combat training, Chris would correct every error or predictable move with a counter that usually ended with the same irritating smack on the noggin. Not very painful, except to her ego.

"Ugh! I hate it when you do that!" Rose was oozing with venom.

"Well, you shouldn't be so predictable. That, plus you shouldn't hurt people when they're trying to help you," he responded, pointing at the man who was stumbling to his feet.

"How was I supposed to know he was helping? You can't lock people in a prison cell and not expect a reaction!"

"Funny that out of all of us, you were the only one with that issue. I keep telling you to do something about that little attitude of yours."

"So, everyone else..."

"Fine. Well, for the most part."

"What do you mean by that?" Rose's eyeballs grew tenfold.

"Cory lost both of his toes and big thumbs."

Rose was livid. "Why the hell would you joke in a situation like this?" She pumped her fist in the air to the rhythm of her words.

Chris ignored her, turning for the hallway. The guard escorted him and Rose down a series of corridors. Every few steps, he would rub a knot forming on the top of his head from his collision with the floor. "Sorry about that," Rose apologized, softening the tone of her voice to demonstrate sincerity. The soldier rolled his eyes, refraining from speaking.

The hallway opened up to a lobby area. Yesha

and Ari were talking among themselves when they saw her. Ari met Rose with a sisterly embrace. "I'm glad you're OK," she said.

"The feeling's mutual. It's just hard to believe all of us got out of that without a scratch."

"Not all of us," said Yesha. She nodded her head in the direction behind Rose.

Cory was leaving a room, hounded by a doctor for pushing a wheelchair rather than using it. "Hey kid. You really should use the chair," he pleaded.

"One, I'm a grown man, not a kid. Two, you can keep it. Roll down a hill in it for all I care," replied the stubborn teen.

The doctor gave up, flinging his submitting arms in the air, then retreating.

"Oh my God! Look at you!" exclaimed Rose, hugging her brother a little too tight.

"Ow, ow!" he shrieked with pain.

It was a wonder Cory was standing at all. His right leg was strapped in a walking boot, and the left wrapped in bandages to protect broken skin from infection. In addition, his left arm was in a cast and sling. His ribs were tightly wrapped as well.

She looked into his eyes, both encircled with black rings. "Oh my God! What are you going to do without your thumbs and..."

Cory's face shriveled. "What?" He held both his thumbs in the air. Rose stared at Chris viciously. Cory caught the purpose, smiling as wide as he could. Two top teeth were missing, and a few bottom ones were broken at odd angles.

Rose turned back to Cory in just enough time to see his ruined smile. The two broke into hysterical laughter, folding over in pain from their sore mid-sections, which caused them to double down, laughing even harder.

"Those are some weird-ass kids," Chris commented.

Yesha smacked her lips. "You raised 'em. What does that say about you?"

Finally able to bring herself under control, Rose was ready for answers. "Where are we?"

"Project 002," Chris replied. "We crashed right outside the gates. They brought us in right after. I was the first one of us to wake up."

Rose's mouth dropped. "Cory's mom?" she quizzed.

"We're about to meet with her now. Man, I haven't seen her in forever."

"I've never seen her," Cory mentioned.

Silence robbed the group of their voices momentarily. Nobody had a proper response, until Chris discovered one. "Well, let's go change that." He squeezed Cory's shoulders. The pain caused his mouth to shoot open, but nothing would come out. "Aw, suck it up. You're a grown man, remember?" Chris mocked.

***

The passage appeared to elongate the closer the nervous group drew to the door. Rose couldn't tell if it was because of the fascinating architecture, or that the gravity of who Sasha was contorted their perception. She was Chris' first protégé, Cory's lost mother, the link to the story of Rose's parents, and the leader of the organization responsible for giving Yesha and Ari such good lives during the worst time of the world's modern history. There may not have been a more collectively influential person alive as far as Rose was concerned.

Chris barely made it through the doorway before Sasha bum-rushed him. She squeezed hard enough to mesh every hug that should have been passed between them since the last time they saw one another into one. "You have no idea how good it feels to see you. I thought you were dead a long, long time ago." Her eyes were soaked thoroughly.

"I think I have a good idea, considering I thought you were dead too." Chris reciprocated the embrace.

Sasha's view settled on an unfamiliar, but intimate face standing behind Chris. "Is that him?" she asked.

"That's him."

Cory became the next target of Sasha's heat-seeking passion. She wrapped her arms around her flesh and blood for the first time in well over a decade. "Easy, easy." Cory braced for the pain that would never come. The undying love between a mother and child overcame his wounds and bruises.

"Wow. Look at you. You're so big." Sasha looked up to Cory, who was taller by a few inches, and heavier by plenty. She smoothed out his shirt with her hands, a habit of most every nervous mother in the world. Sasha's sights changed again. "That makes you Rose. I'd recognize those blue eyes anywhere," she said, shelling out another hug.

While wiping the tears from her face, Sasha's last two guests came into view. "Yesha, what are you and Ari doing here?" she questioned curiously.

"Long story, but she's my wife," Chris interposed, "and Ari's..."

"Wait... what?" Sasha calculated. "Ari's the same age as Rose. That means..."

"No, it doesn't mean that. I'm not that much of a dick. Everything's all messed up, which is why we can't know their ages anyway."

"Ari is seventeen. Rose is nineteen. Barely though. Her birthday was like a month ago."

"How would you know?"

"We still have atomic clocks. Doesn't matter how the orbit changes. We can still keep time on a 24-hour scale."

Chris was floored. "What about boy genius here?" he asked with curiosity.

"Sixteen."

"What? With a flimsy mustache like that?"

"Leave him alone!" demanded Sasha, fist raised.

"Alright! Alright! I'm sick of all you violent women."

Rose and Cory laughed, at last seeing someone put Chris in his place.

"So how long has it actually been since the ship

crashed?" Chris pondered out loud.

"Seventeen years. Which is why it's so weird that Ari was conceived around that time, considering Melissa..." Sasha was insinuating treason of the highest order.

"Look, that is a long, complicated story that I don't fully understand myself yet, but it's not what you're thinking."

"Yeah, whatever," Sasha replied dismissively. Aware of his thriller with Lola, she wasn't buying his excuses. Passing the topic off for a later and more private setting, she took a seat at the long conference table and everyone followed suit.

Rose was the next to break silence. "Anyone else wondering why Cory is the only one that got hurt last night?" she asked.

Cory had the answer himself. "Because I'm human."

"What the hell is that supposed to mean?"

"Calm down. Why do you always take offense to everything? You all have powers and I don't. Your mind probably did something to protect itself at a subconscious level."

Sasha needed some things clarified. "If Ari's really your daughter I guess it makes sense about her and Yesha, but Rose?"

"Yesha probably got her abilities through childbirth. Rose got hurt bad when we were kids. She took a blood transfusion from Pops and boom, superpowers."

Sasha giggled. "Pops? That's cute."

"Don't start with the cute and cheesy shit." Chris looked to the sky and sighed, not wanting to be chased down some sentimental, conversational pathway.

"Speaking of powers," Rose interjected, bringing the subject back where she wanted it, "I wasn't able to use mine when I woke up. I think the crash messed me up."

"The place is lined with lead," Sasha replied.

Chris was stumped. "Huh?"

"Your abilities and radiation have similar qualities. Neither travels well through lead. We insulated the whole place with it to keep that evil bitch Lola from porting in and out of here."

"Wait... Lola's alive?" Chris yelped.

"Yes. Her and her kid. By the way, did you ever find out if it was yours? Speaking of which, three kids by three women in less than two years! You are a low-down, dirty, nasty mother—"

"Damn it, Cory, will you please explain this situation to your mother in a way that she can understand, so that I don't have to deal with this verbal abuse!"

Yesha blushed with embarrassment. Ari's eyes bobbed back and forth in their sockets. She was starting to feel a little hurt and angry at Sasha's insulting accusations.

Cory kept it simple. "Parallel realities."

"Parallel realities?" Sasha tilted her head as if she understood the concept.

"Yep."

"Their abilities are spacetime based, so... makes sense," she replied, as if it were common sense.

Chris was frustrated. "You know about this stuff?" he blurted.

"Of course. I'm not a dummy."

Rather than wasting his breath with an argument he would ultimately lose, Chris transitioned the topic of discussion. "What does Lola have to do with anything anyway?"

"You've heard of the Faction, I'm sure."

"We've had our run-ins. Last time, we actually took some documents from them. This guy Louis Steed's name was all over them. He has to be related to Jane, right?"

"Loo-is? You mean Low-is?" Sasha corrected Chris' pronunciation. "That's her name. Lola is just a nickname. Turns out, she's Jane's daughter."

Chris smacked his forehead, as if he blamed his own brain for being too stupid to put together the pieces. "I can't believe it," he said, even though he believed every bit. Everything made perfect sense now.

"It's true. She runs the Faction. Your daughter is her right hand."

"Daughter? We were having a son."

"Nope. She definitely had a girl."

"That doesn't make sense. I was at the hospital for every checkup until the eighth month. I saw it with my own eyes."

"Well, I don't know what to tell you, 'cause I saw your daughter with my own eyes. Cypress is one hundred percent girl. Actually a woman now. Every bit of her mother too."

Chris let the moment sink in. "Now, everything she said the day we crashed the LOGOS makes sense," he mumbled.

"You?" shouted Sasha. "You're the stupid fuck that did this to the world?"

Everyone else was just as appalled.

"No... she did. I just tried to stop her, but I..." Chris sounded both desperate and disappointed in himself.

Sasha got in Chris' face and dropped her voice to an almost demonic pitch. "Don't stop now. We're listening."

Chris took in a deep breath, then began, "It all started a couple of months before the wedding, when you gave me a ride home..."

10

How We Broke The World

The sex was unbelievable. Of all the lovers that passed through Chris' life, Lola was hands down the best. It was nearly an hour before they were finally able to pry themselves apart. Sufficiently satisfied, she slipped back into her caramel, leather parka, cinching its wide black belt around her waist. Next, she went into his personal restroom to fix her hair and reapply her maroon lipstick.

Chris fumbled to refasten his own belt. The task would have been easier had he been sober, but with enough effort, he was able to complete it. "What the... is this blood?" he mumbled after noticing fresh, red stains across the hem of his shirt.

Leaving the restroom, Lola noted what Chris was referring to. "Relax. I was a virgin about five minutes ago." The clicks of her heels were muffled by the shaggy gray carpet as she headed for the door. "I knew there was something special about you," she added on her way out.

When the door closed, Chris threw a small tantrum. He kicked his desk and chugged down a debilitating amount of alcohol straight from the bottle. He couldn't believe he'd cheated on his bride-to-be mere months before their wedding day. In addition, he had taken Lola's maidenhood in a shabby work office, with no intention of making her an honest woman. This type of behavior was below his moral standards, albeit he dipped below them for selfish pleasure at times.

Chris felt it was best to get home before he managed to get himself into any more trouble. The fob to his car fell from his desk as he attempted to grab it. "Where are you going?" he slurred, bending over to pick it up. He lost his balance and smacked his head against the desk.

On the other side of the door, Sasha was preparing to knock when she heard a blunt slam. She opened the door to find Chris on his knees, rubbing the top of his head. "What are you doing?"

"Fighting with my desk. He's winning," Chris replied.

Sasha read the situation almost immediately. She was already aware that it was the anniversary of Jalil's death and could audibly hear the alcohol in Chris' voice. "Oh Lord. I'm taking you home," she said, walking over to help him up from the floor.

"I got it."

"No, you don't."

"My car practically drives itself. I'm good."

"Don't argue with me. Let's go." Sasha braced the drunkard on her shoulder, leading him into the hallway.

Chris wrinkled his face. "You smell good," he said, pointing at Sasha's nose.

"And you stink," she complained in response, before whacking his hand down. She continued to assist him towards her car.

At last, they arrived at the side of Sasha's beige, four-door sedan. She opened the passenger door, helped Chris in, and buckled his seatbelt for him. "Is that blood?" she asked herself, after seeing the stains at the bottom of his shirt. Unable to find a source, she settled on the assumption that he probably spilled red wine in his drunken state.

Chris was already snoring by the time Sasha

rounded the driver's side. "This man is a mess," she mumbled, putting the car into drive.

The ride was quiet and uneventful. Sasha parked in the closest open space she could find and called Melissa down on her cellphone. Melissa approached the car groggily, the wrinkles from her pillow still engraved on her face. Sasha met her outside the passenger door. They greeted one another with a hug.

"Hey girl. Sorry to wake you up this late," said Sasha.

"I should be the one thanking you for getting this idiot home safe."

Sasha chuckled. "Take it easy on him, will you? I can't imagine how hard it is to not only lose your best friend but have to kill him yourself. Not to mention how tainted his memory will always be. No matter how good of a person he used to be, Chris will always remember him as the man that tried to hurt you and destroy the world in the process."

"Yeah. It is a hell of a story, isn't it?"

"Worthy of a feature film."

Melissa sighed, her shoulders drooping a little. "Can you help me get him up?"

"Sure. Let's hit his head on a few things on the way, so he regrets this a little more in the morning," Sasha joked.

"Sounds like a plan to me."

Having assured Chris was home safe, Sasha waved goodbye to Melissa and pulled away, though her intuition still sensed an oddity. It was uncommon for Lola to still be in the building so late. Sasha had passed her on the way to Chris' office. They greeted each other, but Lola seemed uninterested in conversation, rushing the meeting to a quick end. Though curious, the two events seemed to be unconnected, so Sasha drove on, letting the thought fade into the night sky.

***

Time passed on, and yet again, Chris was searching for peace at the bottom of a bottle. This time, however, he had dug his own pit of misery. Weeks had gone by and Melissa had yet to return any of his calls. Lola, on the other hand, flooded his phone with an exorbitant amount of texts and calls, to which he reciprocated none.

Chris woke up with his mind in a foggy state. The hard floor beneath him didn't feel anything like the comfy bed he was aiming for the night before. Somehow, he ended up passed out in the hallway outside his bedroom. The odor of sizzling bacon in the morning invaded Chris' senses. It was the first good omen since Melissa found out Lola was having his baby. Cooking breakfast had been her morning ritual from the start of their relationship and continued throughout.

"She came back!" Chris scrambled down the steps, calling, "Melissa!" several times. He rounded the corner only to be greatly disappointed.

"Nope. Melissa's a little busy. It's just us," said Lola, rubbing her engorged tummy.

"How the hell did you get in my house?"

"What do you mean? I just unlocked the door, silly." Lola held up a cellular phone, illuminating the application she used to gain entry to the house. The case containing it was plastered with unique stickers around a family portrait.

"That's Melissa's phone. What are you doing with that?"

"We'll get to that. First, you should eat your breakfast and drink your orange juice. It'll help with that nasty hangover."

"Lola, I'm not playing with you!" Chris shouted, smacking the counter with his clenched fist.

Lola pulled up a photo, then calmly slid the cell phone into Chris' view. "That wasn't a suggestion. I worked hard to make all this for you. Now sit down and eat your breakfast. Don't be ungrateful."

Chris couldn't believe what he was seeing in the photograph. Melissa and C.J. clung together, cowering between two large, armed guards, while Lola posed with a peace sign, smiling ear to ear. "You're fucking crazy!" he yelled.

Lola became unhinged. She picked up a 9mm from the counter, waving it around without any weapons discipline. "Call me crazy again, Chris! Go ahead, I dare you. I'll kill you, then go kill that bitch too," she threatened.

"Look. Just tell me where they are and we can forget this ever happened."

"Does that ever work? Like, seriously... Do you really think we would be here if I wanted to just forget about it? A person doesn't go through all of this hard work, then just quit because you asked nicely? Sit down, shut up, and eat your damn breakfast! Or, I can call my men to get started without me. And don't try me. If they don't hear from me by a specific time, they both die."

It wasn't Chris' first rodeo dealing with these types of negotiations, so he knew it was necessary to yield control to the opposition. If they felt any amount of power slipping from their grasp, things could spiral into chaos. Out of options, he sat at the kitchen bar and quietly nibbled on the spread of bacon, eggs, and blueberry pancakes.

"Much better," said Lola. She sat opposite Chris, eating from a plate of her own. Wiping syrup from her lips with a napkin, she began her expected rant. "My mother always wanted me to have a family. A husband, some kids, you know the whole bit. I always wanted to make my mother proud. In most ways, it was a lot easier, but the whole lesbian thing really made it difficult, you know? I can't tell her. It would break her heart. But, you fixed that, didn't you," Lola continued, pointing her fork at her baby bump. "First time too. Definitely not shooting blanks with that gun," she laughed.

Silence, mixed with the sound of silverware scraping plates, endured a moment, as Lola took another bite of her food. She took time to chew before speaking, "At first it was just a means to an end. The baby would shut my mother up for a while. Probably wouldn't like the disappearing father part, but she'd at least have her coveted grandchild. Who in the hell would have guessed that I would fall in love with you, a man... A man's man at that. Not a feminine bone in you. I sure as hell didn't.

"Can you just get to the point Lola?" Chris asked

impatiently.

"That is the point. I love you and I'm going to marry the man that I love. I'm going to make my mother proud, and we're going to live happily ever after."

"What are you talking about? You know Melissa is my wife, and..."

"And that's the problem. But." Lola paused for dramatic effect, raising her pointer finger in the air, "I have the solution." She stood to her feet. "I don't think I could trust you to be faithful, as long as she's around, so I'm going to give you a choice. You come live with me on the LOGOS, until it's ready to launch, then we move to Atlas together. The moment we board the ship, I'll send them back to Earth, where they can live a normal, full life."

"You expect me to abandon them? You think I would leave my son without a father?"

"At least he'd be alive, right? The other option is," Lola took another break mid-sentence, "I kill them both."

"No. Fuck you!"

"Fine." Lola retrieved her phone to make a call.

There wasn't a good play from Chris' current position. He needed to bide his time until the situation would lend him a way out. "Alright, alright," he relented.

"That's what I thought." Lola put away her phone, picked up her purse, then headed to the door. "Let's go. We have a shuttle to catch."

***

In a matter of hours, Lola and Chris arrived at the launchpad of Project 047. It was designed as an inexpensive means to transport supplies and people to the LOGOS on a regular basis, as they repaired components to make the voyage to Atlas possible. The passenger section of the small, bullet-like ship was empty, aside from Chris, Lola, and four of her paid guards. This led Chris to wonder how a soldier under his command had enough pull to make such paths open, without so much as a hitch.

"Who are you?" Chris asked Lola

"Don't worry. We have forever to get to know each other my love."

"Can I see them?"

"Sure. I need you to have no doubt of their safety, so I know you're going to behave. At least long enough for me to make you forget about them."

"I'll never forget about them."

"I wouldn't be so sure." Lola licked her lips suggestively.

The rocket-propelled pod convulsed, as it rode a violent jet of flames past the stratosphere. Once it broke through into the vacuum of space, it became still, floating in a gravity-free state. A thousand thoughts passed Chris' mind, and a million more would do so in the many hours it would take to reach the ship, perched well beyond the orbit of any satellites. He would find a way to snatch his family and get off the ship the moment they were close enough.

The automated pod docked with the LOGOS on its own. The door slid open to release its few passengers. "Follow me," said Lola, leading Chris and her security detail through the intricate ship.

The interior heavily resembled a typical city on the inside. There were shops and businesses lining streets of concrete, with railways for passenger cars to escort people around the tens of miles of living space. Below deck hydroponic systems, coupled with artificial lighting of the proper wavelength, supported live vegetation on the space vessel. There were flawless ferns and manicured lawns tastefully placed around the space.

The group boarded a rail car for a destination unknown to Chris. He was doing his best to focus and not be amazed by the beautiful creativity of the monster ship. His attention could not be divided if he was going to successfully rescue his family.

They dismounted in front of a set of massive windows. It was one of the areas designated for enjoying the amazing view of space from inside. "Where are they?" Chris asked, noticing it was empty.

"Look out the window," Lola instructed, pointing in a specific direction.

In the adjacent hallway, Chris could see Melissa and

C.J. being escorted to a pod similar to the one he had just left. They were close enough to see him as well, their eyes briefly locking.

"Wait, wait, wait! You told me I could see them," Chris said.

"You just did. Do you think I'm stupid enough to let you get close enough to pull one of your little mirror tricks? They're safe, and they'll stay that way, as long as you hold up your end. If not, I'll have someone fetch their heads and bring them to us in one of those silver things. I always wanted to be served with one of those. It looks so... fancy."

"How am I supposed to know that you're not just going to have them killed once they're out of view?"

"You'll just have to trust me."

Chris looked at Lola with a gaze of pure reproach.

"Fine," she said, throwing her hands up in submission. "I'll have someone send weekly video, if it shuts you up."

This time Chris was outwitted, but of course, he wouldn't give up. The moment he found a way to escape, with assured safety for his family, he would take it.

The pod disembarked for its earthbound journey. Chris could no longer see his family, but he felt their spirits drifting away. He glared from the window, lamenting the fact that all of it was his fault. Suddenly, a low-frequency hum reverberated through the hull of the LOGOS. It increased gradually, accompanied by a high-pitched buzzing. The vessel was priming up for its first jump.

Chris whipped his head around and shouted, "Lola, tell me this thing isn't about to take off!"

"OK. I won't tell you."

"You can't. You're going to kill everybody down there."

"Not everybody. All the people that matter are already here."

"You just sent my family down there."

Lola rubbed her tummy. "Your family is right here. Now, shut up and stop complaining!"

The ship's AI started its audible countdown.

"I'll kill you," Chris threatened.

"While I'm pregnant with your child? I doubt it. You're too self-righteous for that."

The countdown had reached its end. Desperate, Chris summoned all of his inner strength to stop time. He had only done it once before to save Melissa's life, therefore he figured he could do it again. The wave of electricity from his body interfered with the building current of the ship. Wiring and circuitry exploded from the walls throughout the LOGOS.

"You dumb-ass! What did you do?" Lola screamed.

Time no longer moved forward. The universe had become an infinite still-life. Somehow, sound still found a way to exist. Chris shrieked with agony, his body overloaded with energy. Unable to handle the load, he blacked out.

11

There's A New Problem, But We Can Fix It

"When I woke up, I was laying in a field of what was left of the ship. There was fire everywhere. The smell of the burning steel and bodies... There aren't words for it. I tried to stop her. I did, but I couldn't," Chris explained, ending his story.

"I knew that little witch was up to something that night," said Sasha, clenching her fists.

Chris saved the blame for himself. "It's my fault. If I would've never been with her..."

"Nope," Sasha interjected, "we're not doing that. Yeah, you fucked up, and I mean real bad. You really cheated on Melissa with that short, squeaky-voiced, no good... succubus!"

"Do you have a point? Because, you're not making me feel any better."

"My bad." Sasha took a deep breath. "There was no way you could know the woman would go psycho and try to destroy the world. I sure as hell didn't see it coming, as long as I worked with her." Sometimes Sasha had a tendency to get off track, which she did again. "She is pretty though. Like reeeeaally pretty. She could have anybody. Why would she be stuck on you like..." She caught herself crossing the line into inappropriate commentary. "Never mind. We should probably talk about our mission to fix the planet."

"Fix it? The weather has been steady for years. I thought it fixed itself," Cory said.

"We thought so too. Here, look at this." Sasha tapped her fingers on the surface of the table. The glass finish illuminated as a large, flat monitor. A few more selections, and a holographic display projected upward.

"Whoa! This is crazy!" said Rose, waving her hands through the hologram to see if she could feel it. Cory was just as captivated, having never seen such advanced tech.

The display morphed into a three-dimensional model of the Solar System. The planet Earth was highlighted with a yellow, circular border. "This is where the Earth was when the LOGOS first knocked it off course. The ripple in space shoved it off course, but not by as much as the models predicted before. I'm assuming that's because you disabled the ship before it could fully activate," Sasha explained. The model Earth's orbit was represented with a wide, elliptical ring. It elongated as the path of its revolution became more extreme at its closest and farthest points, in relation to the Sun. "This is what happened a few years ago."

The world caught an astronomically lucky break. At its furthest distance from the Sun, Earth came in close enough proximity to interact gravitationally with Mars. The brief jostle was hardly noticeable, but prominent enough to allow Earth to settle into a near perfectly circular orbit. Sasha continued on. "This is where it gets ugly." The planetary joust saved the world, only to put it to death. After sixteen revolutions, Mars and Earth collided.

"Holy shit!" Chris exclaimed. "That's going to happen?"

"Calculations say we have about six years left."

The air was sucked out of the room by its gasping occupants.

"We can fix this right?" Rose questioned.

"With the same tech that broke the world in the first place and enough time. The problem is, it's stored at Project 001."

Yesha's optimism was sapped. "The Faction's home base," she announced, sulking.

"How do you suppose we get it?" Chris asked, ready to get into action as soon as possible.

"That's what you're going to help us figure out. There's somebody dying to meet you, then we can get started," said Sasha.

"Who?"

"You'll see. I'll walk you over, then I'd like to spend some time with my son... if that's alright with him."

Cory met eyes with his mother. A nervous shudder came over him. "Sure," he said, able to hold it together, though he was internally in turmoil.

Rose felt left out. "What about the rest of us?" she asked.

"I'll have someone show you to where you'll be staying and give you a tour of the place. You're welcome to anything we have. You're family."

***

Sasha left Chris outside of an office, then bid him to enter before heading off with Cory. The entryway consisted of large, oak double doors. He twisted the brass knob and walked through.

"No fucking way," Chris blurted out, unable to hold in his astonishment.

"Hahaha. Look at your face. You really thought I was dead, didn't you, you ugly shit," Fields responded, laughing heartily.

"One could dream."

A light whir was audible, as Fields drifted around his desk. The wheels of his motorized chair were silenced by the cushion of a priceless and elegant Persian rug.

"What the hell happened to you?" Chris asked.

Fields looked down at himself, as if he was puzzled, and said, "What do you mean? I was born this handsome."

"Look... Can we not do this already?"

"Awww. Poor Cringle in a bad mood? I thought Santa Claus was always happy."

"You know what. I don't have time for this. I'm leaving," said Chris, turning for the door.

"Relaaaax. I thought you'd be happy to talk a little shit after all these years."

"Things change."

"You got that right. I'm paralyzed from the waist down. That's a damn change for your ass."

"How'd it happen?"

"The day of the crash, I was pulling out of the garage at 047, when the planet's rotation shifted. Turns out, air and water don't like to change directions so easily. Land went one way, but the rest of the elements just kept on pushing. Floods killed a lot of people. Wind too. Threw the car back down the garage entrance. It flipped over a few times and I cracked my spine. So, here I am. The most handsome cripple left in the world."

Chris pondered a while at the amount of destruction Lola had caused. In some places where the wind was strongest, trees were uprooted, cars were turned into missiles, buildings were toppled, and people were flung hundreds of feet away. The number of dead and injured amassed to an uncountable measure. Survival was retained only by those lucky enough to be underground or in small pockets around the globe that were subjected to winds at low enough speeds for small structures to stand firm. Larger buildings with wide surface areas and high centers of gravity hardly stood a chance.

"How'd you get out?" Chris asked.

"The team got me out. What was left of them anyway. Turner, Gypsie, and Rudolph weren't in the building that day. We assume they're dead, but then again, we thought you were too."

"I don't think my body will let me die."

"Ah, yeah. That weird superhuman shit. Don't think that makes you special, cause it doesn't. I made you special."

"I will hit a disabled person," Chris threatened. The

conversation left the bitter taste of loss on his tongue. According to Rose, his friends had survived a near extinction-level event only to be killed at war. "How'd they die?" he asked.

"That bitch picked 'em off with her own hands. I hope you can do more than mirror tricks, cause the things that woman is capable of are scary. The kid too."

"My daughter..." Chris mumbled with embarrassment.

"Yeahhh. I would congratulate you on your successful sexual endeavor, had your dick not caused the end of the world this time."

"Here we go again."

"Look, God put a whole lot of fine in that tiny package, so I get it. If I had a choice between the world or tappin' that ass, I would've blown the planet up my damn self."

"You just can't help yourself, can you?"

"You just make it so easy."

Chris was nearing the end of his rope. "Can we just talk about getting that tech from the Faction?"

Fields spun his chair around, heading back behind his desk. "Fine. Take a seat. And, grab that bottle of Scotch and some glasses on your way. Maybe a couple drinks will loosen your tight ass," he said.

***

Early morning painted the horizon a gorgeous blend of oranges and violets, reds and blues. Birds chirped symphonies, signs they had begun their daily, ritualistic activity. Nectar scavenging insects scattered from their perches atop the colorful petals of a plethora of flowers, shooed off by approaching souls.

"I love coming here around this time of morning. It's beautiful, isn't it?" said Sasha.

Cory continued to follow but only offered a single word in response. "Yeah."

There were a series of wooden benches off the dirt path that spanned the garden. Sasha took one near the center and offered Cory a seat next to her. He sat quietly.

The breeze carried sweet aromas from nearby patches of lavender, giving a calming effect. It settled the many queries cluttering his mind, morphing them into more manageable thoughts.

Sasha found her words. "Hey... I know you're probably upset with me for sending you away, but..."

Cory cut her apology short. "I'm not upset," he interjected. Though silence followed his statement, Sasha could sense that he wasn't done speaking and waited patiently for him to continue. "We had a garden like this. Not as big, but just as beautiful. I remember when we first started, me and Rose hated it. It was so much work to till the ground, plant the seeds, and water everything every day. Plus, Pops made us do it all on our own. I was barely big enough to hold a shovel. Then, something crazy started to happen. Things started to grow. I can't describe how it felt, even at that age, to work that hard to see results. To see with your own eyes that if you put in the time, you can create something special. We were so proud of ourselves. Pops could have planted the garden himself, with a lot less effort than two little kids, but he didn't. He wanted us to learn what we're capable of doing on our own, and that you get out what you put in. He trained us how to protect ourselves, and how to protect each other. He taught us how to have fun. In however many years it's been, there hasn't been a single day that we haven't laughed together. I was where I needed to be, and I'm alive because you sacrificed our relationship for my safety, so no. I'm not mad at you. I'm thankful my mother loved me enough to protect me, even if that meant losing her only child."

Sasha's eyes pooled over with tears. Cory's heartfelt speech murdered her fear of rejection. She hugged him, this time careful to avoid aggravating his injuries. "My son," she whimpered, then laughed. "Where did all this wisdom come from? And don't tell me Chris, cause I'm not buying it," she teased, wiping her eyes.

"Pops might be annoying, but he knows his stuff."

Sasha smiled wider, if that was even possible.

The conversation was about to dive back into a place of pain, and they could both feel it coming. They braced themselves for impact, then began the inevitable. "What was my real father like?" Cory asked.

Sasha spaced out. Cory could tell that she was seeing her late husband, as if he were there in front of her.

"He was special. Your father knew me better than I knew myself. He would bring things out of me that I didn't know were even there. Early on, during our training, we had to go up against Chris and his team in war games, and I'm sure you know how intense he can be."

"Oh my God, yes." Cory's body language spoke louder than his words.

"Well, Chris put your father in charge of our team. We got beat bad, and I mean real bad, for days. Scott convinced me that I could be the difference in us winning and losing. From that day on, I knew he was a person I could lean on. That's who your father was. Everything I needed him to be and more. So handsome too. You look just like him."

"Pops always says that."

"That Scott was handsome?"

"No. No. That I look like him."

Sasha went from a little weirded out to relieved. "See for yourself," she said, removing a photo from her pocket.

The picture was of the entire ICA unit. She pointed out each member, telling stories of who they were, and where they ended up. All but four were dead. When Cory's eyes at last rested on his father, it was like looking into his future. He imagined that's what he would look like in twenty or so years. "He does look like me," said Cory.

"Correction. You look like him. He's your daddy, not the other way around," Sasha joked.

"Is... I like that. Sounds a lot better than was."

The mother and son conversed for hours about everything under the Sun. When they thought that a topic ran dry, another would appear from thin air. Though it could go on for hours more, they both sensed that the day would call for other things.

"One more question," said Cory, as they headed back inside. "Why aren't you dressed like your people?" he questioned.

Sasha looked down at herself. She was dressed very casual-like, with tight blue jeans, a gray scale graphic T-shirt, and navy blue running shoes. "What's wrong with what I have on?" She was appalled that her son was questioning her sense of fashion.

"Nothing... It's just that everybody else is wearing that weird Thermalight stuff."

"Oh, not me honey. Only in the field. This is what I was comfortable in before the world broke, and it ain't broke, so I ain't fixing it."

Before they could make it inside, Chris exited the door with Fields rolling beside him. Sasha could already tell by his face that Chris was fighting the urge to punch him, as it was their usual ritual when they hadn't seen each other in a while. The day was still young, however, she thought. "So how'd it go?" she asked.

"Eventful," Chris responded.

Fields was as flagrant as always. "He's still got a vagina."

Chris inhaled deeply and managed to ignore him. "We've got a basic idea of what we should do, but we'll need your expertise to tighten details," he said.

"Great," Sasha answered. "But, we can work tomorrow. Today, we're going to party!"

"Party? For what?"

"What do you mean, for what? You're not dead, my son's not dead, I'm not dead, Fields isn't dead."

"You could have left the last one off."

"In this case, you're correct. I'm not clubbing in a wheelchair."

"Aw, come on Luke. Don't be like that," Sasha begged.

Fields was already riding back to his office. "Nope. You two have at it. Just make sure you're ready tomorrow," he said.

Sasha shrugged her shoulders. "Guess it's just us."

Chris had an idea. "What about Yesha? She might wanna come."

"Oh yea, thanks for reminding me. She volunteered

to go on a mission to check sea levels. It's only a few miles from here, but the scientists are staying in the field overnight to gather data at different times of day. Since there's no moon, the tides are different, and with all the glacial ice gone, sea levels could have increased as much as 230 feet, globally. She wanted to tell you herself, but you were with Fields most of the morning. You should be able to catch her before she leaves if you go now."

"OK cool. Where is she?"

"Just follow the signs to the lab area and ask for her. I have to show this big head boy where his room is."

"I'm coming to the party, right?" asked Cory.

"No," Sasha replied.

"Why not?"

"Because you're eleven years old, that's why," Chris interjected.

"I'm not freakin' eleven."

"And you're not going either," said Chris with the final word.

The comical banter was a pleasant sight for Sasha. Her family was together again. At least, what remained of it.

***

Chris zigzagged down the corridors of the facility, following the posted signs to the lab area. Once he arrived, he asked the desk clerk for Yesha's exact location and was guided to her.

"Hey babe. I was hoping you made it in time," she said, greeting him with a peck on the lips.

"I was hoping we'd get some personal time tonight," Chris replied with emphasis on personal. He cupped her bottom, pulling her close.

Yesha giggled, then smacked his hands away. "Boy, stop it."

"But, it's been years."

"It's been just as long for me. We've waited this long, we can wait another day," Yesha fussed.

"What about Ari?"

"She's going with me."

"Why doesn't she just stay with me? It's dangerous out there."

"We have security. Besides, she wants to learn what we do in the field."

"Yeah, I know. Baby Girl wants to change the world."

"And one day she will," Yesha reassured Chris. "You just enjoy yourself. Sasha says she has a small celebration planned for you guys."

"I know, but I'd rather spend my time with you and Ari."

"That's sweet, but we're always going to be here for you." Yesha moved forward to whisper in Chris' ear, "One more day and you can do with me as you please."

"No take backs."

Ari approached from an adjacent room. "Ew. Nobody wants to hear that," she complained.

"Well, mind your business and you won't," Chris replied, kissing her on the forehead.

"If mom actually knew how to whisper, that would make it easier."

Chris found an avenue to change the subject. "You are rocking that lab coat, though," he complimented.

"You think so?" Ari twisted, posing as if on a runway.

"Yeah, but you do know you don't wear that in the field, right?"

"Uh, yeah. I knew that. I just wanted to see how it looked." It was obvious Ari was lying through her teeth.

"Looks great to me," said Cory, placing his arm around Chris' shoulder.

"If you want to keep those eyes, you'd better find something else to look at," Chris responded.

Ari was embarrassed. "Dad!" she exclaimed.

"Don't dad me. Now, go put that coat up. I need to talk to Mr. Observant alone."

Ari did as she was told, though she wasn't happy about it. She mumbled under her breath all the way out of the lab. Yesha accompanied her, leaving Chris and Cory to their business.

"Sup Pops?" said Cory.

"You know about the field mission?"

"A little bit. My mom told me about it earlier."

"You're going with them." Chris' words were clearly a statement rather than a question or suggestion.

"I am?"

"Yes, you are, and you have one job. Protect my daughter. I don't care what happens out there, you don't leave her side, you understand me?"

"Relax Pops. I got you."

"You better. And, keep your hands to yourself. I see how you look at her. Don't catch these hands," Chris said, showing his fist in a threatening manner.

Cory couldn't tell if Chris was joking or serious. He parried the awkwardness by switching topics. "Does my mom know?" he asked.

"I'll fill her in. How did that go anyway? With you and her, I mean."

"Better than I thought it would. She gets me. Makes me feel like we're not strangers, ya know?"

"Glad to hear it. Well, looks like Ari's waiting on you. Once she leaves this building, she's your responsibility."

Cory was heading off but paused with a question. "Why'd you pick me? Rose has all the power. Don't you think Ari would be more safe with her?"

"No. Rose has her gifts, but you have your mind. That's your gift. Plus, you have another advantage. A man in love would die for the woman he's in love with. Trust me, I would know."

"It's not like that, I promise."

"You really want to piss me off, by lying to my face? I was your age once. I get it. You won't see me become this tyrant that's always yelling for you to stay away from Ari. It's obvious you care about her and she cares about you. Both of you are almost adults. All I ask is that you be a better man than me. Make good choices and protect her heart. You see where my bullshit got us. The whole world is dying and it's my fault."

"This isn't on you."

"It is. If I had kept my johnson in my pants, and cherished the heart of the woman I loved, all of this could have been avoided. Don't miss out on your forever chasing after a few minutes. Remember that, and you'll be OK. But, if you do break her heart, I'll still kill you."

Cory cringed at the violent ending to a beautiful speech. "OK... I'm gonna go over there and uhh... start protecting. You should probably check with a therapist about that anger thing. I hear they have a couple of good ones here," he said, scurrying away.

***

A forest green heavy bag trembled violently, as Rose smacked her foot against the side of it. The chains from which it hung pinged loudly, but held firm. Sweat that dripped onto her MMA-styled gloves, flung off with each solid blow. Her form was perfection in its most perfect state, not a bit of wasted motion between strikes. She popped her fists and legs in a series of eye-catching, complex combinations.

Many of the gym's guests stopped their own workouts to witness Rose's spectacular skill set. She hadn't noticed. Her focus and intensity were just as marvelous as her fighting ability.

"Hey you, newbie!" yelled an older gentleman, leaning over the ropes of one of four boxing rings. His face was as wrinkled as his unpressed jeans, and his posture shrunken by father time.

Rose stopped her workout to see if she was the subject of his attention. "Yeah?" she responded, seeing that she was.

"My grandson here thinks he can take you. My money's on you."

Rose walked over to the edge of the ring. She glanced momentarily at the young stud, then refocused her attention on the senior. "Your grandson like to hit women, or something?"

"No. At least not that I know. You versed in jujitsu, right?"

"Yeah. How'd you know?"

"A person that good with their hands usually is. He suggested take-downs and submissions only. One point per. First to five wins."

Rose declined. "No thanks. Not interested in being treated like a baby," she said, turning to get back to her work.

The young man called out to her himself this time. "I'll fight you," he said. "But, if you get hurt, it's on you."

"If you hold back like I'm some little weak, defenseless woman, I promise you'll be the one hurt."

"What's the game?"

Rose worked her way inside the ring. He was much more handsome up close than she realized. She didn't know if it was his sculptured form, his perfectly barbered, dark hair, or the way the stubble complimented his boyish grin. Her heart fluttered and beat a bit faster. "Touch the mat, a point. Five to point out. Submission, game over. KO, game over," she informed him after clearing her throat to compose herself.

"Sounds good to me."

The older gentleman remembered that they hadn't introduced themselves. "I'm Bobby, by the way. My grandson is..."

"I don't need his name," Rose interrupted. "It's still to be seen if he's worth remembering."

"Nothing in the world like a feisty woman," Bobby replied.

The two youths squared up in the center of the ring. The young man was distracted almost immediately. "Wow. Your eyes are beautiful," he said.

Rose swept his legs from beneath him with so much force that his back crashed into the mat with thunder. "One, zero," she said.

By then, the entire gym had worked their way over to ringside. This was the best action they had seen in a while. Bobby's chuckle carried throughout the gym. "I'll take my money in cash," he said.

The young man got up to his feet and settled back into his stance. "You like cheap shots, I see."

"I like to win," Rose replied, going back on the

227

offensive. She feigned a right hook, then quickly switched to southpaw, landing a clean left straight to his ribs. When he dropped his guard to protect the body, Rose slipped her foot behind his legs again, dropping him to the mat in identical fashion as before. "Two, zero."

Murmurs passed across the crowd. They were impressed with Rose's showing. Bobby was ecstatic. "Ohhh!" he yelled out.

His grandson hustled to his feet, faster than before. "Alright," he said. "Let's get serious."

"Two points too late." This time Rose played defense. With her male opponent thoroughly frustrated, a mistake was coming. All she had to do was take advantage.

He threw a left jab. Rose parried it away but felt the snap behind it. She now knew that she couldn't take a clean power shot, or she'd be out before she touched the mat. The dance went on. The young man threw a left jab, left hook, right hook combination. Rose redirected the jab with her hand, then slipped both hooks, but he managed a stout front kick to her midsection. It was strong enough to lift her off her feet, then drop her to one knee.

Her opponent smelled blood in the water. He lunged for the finish, which was the mistake Rose was waiting for. She countered using his aggression. Missing the power punch, he extended too much. Rose gripped his arm, perched both her feet on his abdomen, tugged backward with all her might, and used his momentum to flip him head over heels. He bounced off the mat and slid through the ropes onto the floor.

Much of the crowd reacted as if they felt the pain themselves. Some of them resorted to laughter. The rest applauded. Bobby was of the laughing sort. He nearly keeled over as his grandson squirmed in agony.

"I'm sure his shoulder's dislocated. Game over," said Rose, leaving the ring.

"You come here and beat up on him anytime you want young lady. He needs every bit," said Bobby, laughing to the point of coughing.

"Bye Mr. Bobby," said Rose, grabbing her gym bag, a gift courtesy of Sasha.

The young man scraped himself from the floor as Rose left the door. He stopped to his grandfather, holding his disconnected arm. "I'm going to marry that girl," he said.

Bobby scrunched his face. "Are you kidding me? Why would a woman like that want a boy like you? She's way out of your league. Way, way out."

"Thanks grandpa. I really appreciate the vote of confidence," he replied, leaving to go after Rose. A few moments later, he caught up to her in the hallway. "You walk pretty fast," he said, still clutching his injured shoulder.

Rose didn't say anything.

"I'm Justin," he added.

"I didn't ask."

"Are you like this with everybody?"

Rose stopped walking. "Not with people that interest me. Different is interesting. What makes you different, Justin? You look like the average, pretty white boy that sits in the gym all day thinking just because he pumps a few hundred pounds, women are supposed to swoon over him. Well, I'm not swooning, Justin."

"Wait... you think I'm pretty?"

Rose rolled her eyes, then continued walking.

"I'm kidding, I'm kidding," said Justin. "Why don't you just give me a chance to take you out? If you don't like me after one date, I'll leave you alone. I swear it."

"Your swear means nothing to me. I don't know you, and I damn sure don't trust you."

"C'moooon," Justin pleaded.

"Ugh, so annoying. Ask my dad if you can take me out. If he doesn't kill you, then you get one date to prove you're... interesting. One!"

"Deal," Justin replied without thinking. His brain caught up eventually. "Wait, why would he kill me?" he questioned.

Rose walked on without responding.

Justin hesitated but decided Rose was worth the risk tenfold. "How do I find him?" he asked.

"Don't worry. He'll find you," Rose replied, leaving

Justin alone to ponder.

**

Rose entered her newly acquired living quarters, then placed her bag on the couch. She was relieved to finally have a place of her own. An eternity of living with Chris and her younger brother was a test all its own. The moment her bag touched the leather surface, Rose rerouted back to the door and opened it. "Yes, daddy?" she said in a kid-like voice.

"Don't do that," said Chris. "You always do that when you want something."

"You're the one that wants something. You came here... why?"

"I could feel your giddiness from my room. What the hell are you so happy about?"

"Daang, I can't be happy now?"

"Don't play with me. Something's up with you."

"Why are you so grumpy, is the question. I felt you coming down the hall."

"I don't know. Maybe because I haven't had any in almost a decade, and just when I think I'm about to get some, my woman leaves on an overnight mission," said Chris, frustrated.

Rose recoiled. "First thing, ew dad. Second thing, it beats never having any at all."

Chris squinted his eyes, detective mode activated. "That's what this is about. You met some boy, didn't you?"

"Why would you ask me that?" Rose turned for her dresser to retrieve clothing for a shower.

"Don't you walk away from me. I knew something was up. You only start that dad shit when you want me to say yes to something!"

"Why are you yelling? Calm down. You're so intense over nothing. It's just a date."

"Just a date, my ass. Next thing you know, there will be little Roses running around here driving me crazy. But, they won't have a mom or dad, cause they'll both be dead."

"Whoa, whoa, whoa. First of all, ain't no kids

messing up this figure, and you're the only one thinking about sex." Rose put her clothes on the table, grabbed Chris' hand, and guided him to sit with her on the couch. "My father happened to teach me my worth as a woman, so just because we're somewhere with boys doesn't mean I'm going to forget that. It's just one date, and if he tries something, I'll kill him myself."

"Promise?"

Rose kissed Chris on the cheek, then grabbed her clothes. "Sure. You can still make him sweat though. Besides, it's Ari you should be worrying about. If Cory gets a hold of that girl, you'll be his real father."

"Don't make me change my mind."

"Well, Mr. Nobody, I'm getting in the shower, so get out."

Chris got up to leave. "See, that's the shit I'm talking about. Daddy when you want something, Mr. Nobody after you get it," he complained.

"Language!" Rose shouted, shutting the bathroom door.

"Whatever. I know I better see that boy before you go anywhere or don't come back," he yelled on his way out.

12

A Night None Of Us Will Forget...Ever!

Later that evening, Sasha tapped on Chris' door, ready for a night of fun. She wore a maroon cocktail dress with black, high-fashion heels. Her fine brunette hair was tied together elegantly with a diamond-encrusted clasp. Her long legs and tastefully oiled, cream-colored skin highlighted her thin yet powerful body.

Chris complimented her, "Wow. Gorgeous."

Sasha playfully gave a curtsy, then returned the favor. "Rather handsome as well, my dear sir."

Chris wore a sky-blue button-down, dark pants, and classy loafers with golden buckles, courtesy of the WTP. His hair was freshly lined and wavy on top, with tapered sides. Every flexing muscle bulged underneath, begging to be set free. He entered the corridor, shut the door behind him, and gave his friend a hug.

On cue, Rose turned the corner with her companion for the evening. She approached first, giving Sasha a hug, then Chris a peck on the cheek—her usual greeting. Rose's gown was a statement of her robust personality. It hugged her curves, splitting below the knee on one side to reveal her bronze leg. The neckline dipped just low enough to be sexy without entering the territory of promiscuity. A rounded diamond shape was cut out from the base of her sternum, extending slightly below her navel to reveal her polished core. Her full Hispanic grace was on display.

"Oh my God, Rose, you are so gorgeous. Just look at you. I wish your parents could see you," said Sasha.

Chris wasn't as composed. "Yeah, I'm reconsidering this whole date thing. I was more comfortable when you looked like a tomboy."

"Daddy, stop it. Be nice," Rose demanded.

Her choice of words and tone of voice told Chris how important this night was to her. He also detected her nervous mood through their special connection, deciding to give her a break. "You going to introduce us, or what?"

"This is Justin. Justin, this is my dad. I'm sure you already know Sasha, considering she runs the place."

"Hi, Mrs. Truman," he greeted Sasha. "Nice to meet you, Mr., uh... Rose's dad."

"Well, at least he has manners," said Chris, inspecting the young man. Justin looked like he walked straight out of a magazine. His double-breasted suit was tailored perfectly to accentuate his lean, muscular body. It was toffee-colored with dark brown, cross-patterned stripes. His loafers were almost an exact match to Chris', but with silver buckles. "Good taste, too," Chris noted.

"Thank you, sir," Justin replied, happy that things seemed to be going well so far. Then, the grilling began.

"How old are you?" asked Chris.

"I'll be twenty-one next month."

"You drink? Smoke?"

"No, sir. It would mess with my fitness."

"Good answer. Good answer."

Rose used her eyes to signal Chris to hurry up.

"So, what do you have planned for the evening?" Chris asked.

Justin cleared his throat before he spoke. "We have reservations at a restaurant designed for people our age. It's one of the best here."

"It's called Jovenes. We created it for new adults so they have a place to mingle, make friends, and maybe even find love," added Sasha. She had secretly booked the reservation after Rose asked her, once she managed to shake off Chris' snooping aura.

The heat was about to turn up. "Okay. Okay. What are you planning for tonight?"

Justin knew exactly what the insinuation was and dodged the landmine. "Nothing! Uh, nothing, sir. After dinner, I'll get her back here safely, then go home... alone... by myself."

"Another good answer. Sharp boy." Chris smiled at Sasha, slapping Justin firmly on the shoulder. "This boy's sharp, Sash'."

Justin cringed from the pain—Chris had happened to hit his newly reset shoulder joint.

Chris' smile evaporated instantly, replaced by a crazed glare. "You seem like a nice, bright young man. I'm very kind and very generous to my friends and family. You want to be my friend, Justin?"

"Yes, sir."

"You want to be my family, Justin?"

"Yes, sir... I mean, uh, not like that. I mean, we just met, so..." Justin stumbled over his words.

"You ever been with a woman, Justin?"

"No... uh, no, sir."

"You sure about that? You didn't sound so sure, Justin."

"I'm sure, sir."

"Well, tonight ain't the night, Justin. As long as you understand that, we can be friends. Who knows, if she likes you enough, maybe we can become family. But you have to live long enough, Justin. We on the same page?"

"Yes, sir."

"Alright then. Bring it in." Chris embraced his daughter's suitor tightly. Justin tried his best not to cry from the agony in his shoulder. At last, Chris released his grip. "Okay, sweetheart. You go enjoy yourself. I'll see you in the morning."

After a farewell kiss, Rose was off on her first date.

"You didn't tell me you were THE Rose," said Justin as they walked away.

"What do you mean 'THE Rose'? I'm just Rose."

"Your family started this entire society. You're a legend around here."

Rose didn't care for the reputation, "I guess."

Chris and Sasha were still standing outside his door. "You familiar with that kid?" he asked her.

"Yeah. He comes from a good family. His mom and dad died when he was Cory's age. The only person he has left is his grandfather. He runs the gym here."

"Cool... Now, where are we going?"

"A nice spot with a hole-in-the-wall vibe. Food, booze, blues, and a lot of dancing."

"When did this white girl start liking blues?" Chris asked, leaning back in surprise.

"Before the world broke, I started hanging out with Scott's father. That man knew how to kick it."

"Let's go kick it then!" Chris presented his arm for Sasha to hook onto. She clasped on, and off they went.

***

The atmosphere was electric. A live band filled the house with the eccentric tones of Memphis blues. The lighting was dim, giving the wood-accented decor a calm, homely feel.

"Where'd you find a live band to play blues, Sash'?" Chris asked. He had to speak up to be heard over the music.

"The lead singer is the only true bluesman. He bounced around a few of our other camps but ended up here about five years ago. The rest of the band plays whatever. It's the way they pitch in. Everybody has a job around here. Keeps things running smoothly when everyone lifts their own weight."

"I heard something like that before from your guy Foley."

"Sorry about that. Cory told me everything. I can't believe I didn't see it. I sent word to bring him in, but apparently, he and some others went missing."

"Must know you're onto them."

"I assumed as much, but we're not here to talk about work. We're here to have some fun!" Sasha took a seat at the bar. "Shots for everybody, bartender!"

He grabbed a few bottles from the shelf to pour up. "You got it, boss."

"Hey everybody. Before we really get things going, I want to introduce you to a very important person in my life. Without him, I wouldn't be the person I am today, and neither would any of the founders be who they were. Candy, Ramirez, Scott, and I all owed our lives to him. They died to protect us and paid their debt. So tonight, let's celebrate their sacrifices. And let's celebrate the man that made us." Sasha raised her glass skyward. "To the return of Chris Cringle, the baddest fucking Santa in the world!"

The entire place hooted and cheered. Chris was a little embarrassed, but his first shot took the edge off. They drank well into the night before dancing, while dancing, because they were dancing. Any reason to drink was a good enough reason. Before long, half the patrons were plastered beyond plausible deniability.

Sasha was well past inebriated, so she had taken off her heels to retain the ability to walk. Even then, her balance was a bit compromised. Still, she kept the party alive, until it was no longer feasible.

**

It was approaching the middle of the night when Chris and Sasha stumbled out of the venue. They laughed at old stories, eventually managing to get to the residency wing. Chris stopped outside of Sasha's quarters, making sure she got in OK. He was about to go on his way, when she asked, "Where are you going?"

"To sleep."

"Oh yeah, sleep. The thing when you use the pillow to um... to um..." Sasha bolted for the restroom, unable to complete her thought process. She barely made it before puking into the toilet bowl.

Chris staggered in to check on her. "You good?"

"I'm fine," she said, scrambling to the sink. She took a swig of mouthwash, gargled for a minute, then washed it down the drain.

"Nasty," said Chris.

They both laughed as if the moment was the funniest thing that had ever happened in the world.

***

The fun of the night had long ended. Chris rolled over in his sleep, pulling the blanket with him. "Stop hogging all the cover," said Sasha.

"Oh, my bad," Chris replied, relinquishing his monopoly on the comforter.

A few seconds of silence let reality sink in. Both parties sprang up from the bed, like the mattress had burned them. "What the hell are you doing in my bed?" Sasha shouted. Realizing she was naked, she attempted to use the blanket to cover herself, but Chris had the same idea.

He nearly yanked the entire thing away from her, trying to hide himself, exclaiming, "I don't know. You tell me!"

"Oh my God... Did we?"

"This was your idea. I knew we shouldn't have drunk that much."

Sasha hustled to find her undergarments. Without success, she retrieved a new set from her drawer. "Owww! My nana hurts," she complained, struggling to put them on as fast as she could.

"Shit! We did, didn't we. This can't be happening," said Chris, racing to locate and put on his own clothing.

"The security footage!" Sasha thought, desperate to know what really happened.

"You have a camera in your room?"

"I have them in my entire living space. There are a lot of valuable things in here, so I need to keep tabs on my housekeepers and look out for break-ins. This is still a normal society. Thieves do exist, ya know." Sasha sat at her laptop, then pulled up the saved footage, rewinding it to when they first entered the room. She saw herself bolt to the restroom, as well as everything after. "No, no, no," she repeated, holding her head in denial. "Why did you let this happen?" she whined.

"Me? Why is this my fault? Your choices count just

as much as mine. Besides, did you not just see yourself pounce on me like some kind of wild animal?"

"Maybe it's not that bad." Sasha tried to convince herself. Reality quickly dashed her hopes. She skipped ahead nearly an hour, and not only were they still going at it, but things got much more interesting. "Are we floating... like in the air? Oh God... that position shouldn't even be possible," she continued complaining.

Chris watched intently. "I don't remember any of this," he said.

Sasha skipped a few more times, searching for the end. "What the hell, Chris! Four hours and thirty-six minutes! Really?"

"Explains why your nana hurts. Man, look at you go."

"This isn't funny!" Sasha blurted, punching Chris in the arm. Just when they thought things couldn't get any worse, there was a knock at the door. "Shit! Shit! Someone's at the door," Sasha yelled and whispered at the same time.

"I can see that, Captain Obvious!"

Sasha scowled at him. "Who is it?" she asked, trying to sound as normal as possible.

"It's Rose."

"Um, hold on a sec. Let me throw on some clothes," Sasha replied, trying to stall. "Hide somewhere, you big dummy," she demanded.

Chris headed for the restroom. "Not there, genius," she said. "What if she asks to use the restroom?"

"Then you let her use the guest one."

"Oh yeah. Wait, can't she sense you?"

"Not if I keep my energy suppressed. Just go and stop distracting me." Chris waved his hands to remind Sasha she was still standing there in her lacy undergarments.

Sasha threw on a fluffy, pink robe, then made her way to the front door, closing the bedroom behind her.

Rose was the happiest form of herself when the door opened. "Hey Sasha!" she said, going for a hug. "Whew! You smell like you had too great of a time last night. That hair could use some attention too."

Sasha giggled reluctantly. "We drank a lot and danced a lot. I passed out before I got to shower. Come in, though." Sasha invited Rose inside, trying to act as normal as possible.

"Whoa. This is a nice place," Rose said, walking inside.

Sasha lived in the largest quarters at the facility. The living room was spacious and well-decorated. It had ruby red carpeting, wood-paneled walls, and warm lighting. Two bedrooms were on opposite sides. The guest bathroom was centered in the rear, and the master bath attached to the master bedroom with a Jacuzzi tub. "Thanks," she replied, taking the compliment well.

"You're welcome. I just wanted to talk about my date yesterday, but I can see you're not in the condition for that."

"I'll tell you what. Give me time to freshen up and get myself together, then I'll come find you."

"OK, great," Rose replied. "By the way, have you seen Dad?"

Sasha was quick on her feet. "He's not in his quarters?" she asked.

"No. At least, he didn't answer the door. I can't sense him anywhere either."

"He's probably still passed out. He drank more than I did, and I was hammered."

"Probably," Rose agreed. "If you see him before I do, tell him I'm looking for him. If he doesn't hear from me, Justin is done for."

"OK, honey. I will. See you in a little bit."

Sasha returned to the bedroom. "I'm getting in the shower. When the coast is clear, you have to sneak out of here," she told Chris.

"What did she want?"

"To talk to me about her date and she was obviously looking for you."

"Talk to you? Why would she wanna talk to you over me?"

"Because you're a man, and because you overreact

over nothing."

"I guess... Anyway, I'll give it a few, then I'm outta here."

"I'm deleting the footage. Damn it! It had been so long since a man touched me... plus the drinking. Why did it have to be you? You better not tell anybody about this!" Sasha threatened.

"Why would I tell anybody? I'm the one in a relationship, remember?"

"Oh my God! Poor Yesha. I didn't know what I was doing."

"From the looks of it, you knew exactly what you were doing."

"Ugh, shut up! Just get out and go take a shower. If Rose smells me on you, we're finished. I'm never partying with you again. Ever!"

***

Sasha arrived outside Rose's door, preparing to knock. Wars and battles had never made her nervous, but the thought that Rose may be perceptive enough to read through her was nerve-racking. She reworked her ponytail, removing the rubber band, then putting it on again to be sure her hair was smooth. She took a deep breath, then proceeded.

Rose answered the door. "Hey," she said, greeting her with a firm hug. Having a woman in her life, after only Chris and Cory, was just about as big a deal as her first interaction with a potential suitor.

Sasha wondered if Rose had been replaced by an impostor. She looked her up and down. "You really don't look like the Rose that came in here."

Gone was the rugged combat gear of old. Rose had on a red and black, long-sleeved flannel. Rather than buttoned, it was tied in a knot below her bosom, in a manner that exposed her shapely midriff. Her hugging jeans were high-waisted, just covering her belly button. Stylish, shallow shredding revealed a bit of her thighs, and black, leather-strapped, six-inch heels tied the outfit together.

"Is that a good thing?" she asked, twirling around to give a view from all angles. "You said we were welcome to anything, so we stopped by this fashion boutique."

"We? He took you to shop for clothes?"

"No. I made a friend last night at Jovenes. It was her idea to go. She picked out a few outfits for me. I don't know anything about fashion, but she said the styles she gave me would accentuate who I am as a woman."

"Let me guess. Tiffany?"

"Yeah. How'd you know?"

"She's one of the more promising kids around here. Fashion's her thing. Real talkative though."

"So true, but do you like it?"

"Yeah. You're gorgeous. I'm not just saying that either. I really mean it."

"Thanks," said Rose. She realized how inconsiderate she was being. "I'm being so rude. Come in and have a seat with me. I could really use some advice."

Sasha took a seat. "So, what's on your mind?" she asked.

"Well, I guess I should start by telling you about my night."

***

Resplendence was the theme of the swanky restaurant. Just like the rest of the underground facility, windows were an absent pleasantry. Several illuminated fish tanks were built into the walls, then framed with shutters as faux replacements of what would normally be an outside scenic view. Peaceful tones of piano played softly in the background. It soothed the diners and deadened the travel of conversations from table to table.

"I've only seen places like this in movies and books," said Rose, as she and Justin neared the hostess booth.

"Me too. I've never actually been here. This is my first date too," he admitted.

The hostess became aware of their presence. "Hi, I'm Tiffany. Can I help you guys?" she asked. Tiffany seemed to be about Rose's age. Her smile was radiant, and she hardly stopped flashing it. Freckles dotted the skin below her thin, rectangular frames, and her naturally curly, coarse hair was pulled into a puffy ponytail. Her fashion sense was top-notch. Even the way she wore her work uniform made her stand out from her co-workers.

"We have a reservation," Rose responded.

"Your name?"

"Rose Ramirez."

The hostess scanned her list. "I'm not seeing it here. You sure your reservation was tonight?"

"Um... It was supposed to be. Sasha called ahead for me earlier."

Tiffany's eyebrows raised. "Oh, you must be her niece. All everyone around here has been talking about lately is you, her son, and Chris Cringle. We learned about you guys in school. Especially him. The man that made the founders. He is so sexy, o-m-g! And, he's here. I hope to get to meet him. What's he like in person?" she asked, beginning a full-on rant.

Justin cleared his throat as a way to signal to her that she was being rude.

"Oh, I am so sorry. Please forgive me. You hardly get to meet your heroes. I'll get you a private table on the balcony. Follow me."

Tiffany led them toward the base of a staircase. As they walked by, half the patrons paused their conversations to gawk at Rose. It could have been because of her stunning beauty, but it was probably just as likely due to her legend. Two bulky men moved to the side, permitting them to pass. At the top was a small area with a rounded booth. It contained a single table with a white tablecloth draped over the top.

"Is security really necessary?" asked Rose, curious about the men.

"Unfortunately, yes," Tiffany replied. "You're famous and Sasha has a few political challengers. Some years ago, one of them tried to attack the son of a lawmaker on her council. Ever since then, the leaders and their guests are shielded, especially in public places like this."

"Wow. This place sounds more and more like a movie."

"Yep. But, I'll have someone come wait for you. Menus are on the table. I hope you enjoy your dinner," said Tiffany, making her way back out to her post.

With a chance at a social life, Rose had an idea. "Hey, Tiffany," she called out.

The young woman turned to see what she needed. "Can I help you with something else?"

"Well, sort of. I was just wondering if um... you wanted to hang out sometime."

"Seriously? With you?" Tiffany was stunned at the offer. "Of course. I'll write down my user for you." She pulled out her order pad and pen to scribble down the information.

"User?" Rose had no idea what she meant.

"Oh, you don't have a comm-watch yet?"

"What's a comm-watch?"

"It's a little device you wear on your wrist to talk and send messages to people. It keeps track of your balance, so you can use it to buy stuff too. Well actually, now that I think about it, we use it for almost everything: doctor's appointments, logging into computer systems, and stuff like that. It's kind of like cell phones from the old days, only it doesn't work outside the building. I would show you what it looks like, but we're not allowed to use them at work. This one time, I got caught and almost lost my job, so I keep it in my bag."

Justin cleared his throat again.

"Oh, I'm sorry. Listen to me rambling again. Here. Take this paper, and when you get a comm-watch, use it to reach me. We can hang out anytime I'm not working or schooling."

"OK, I will. Bye," Rose replied, taking the paper.

Finally glad to be rid of Tiffany, Justin spoke up, "She's a talker, isn't she?"

"I think she's nice." Rose checked out Justin's wrist. "Why don't you have one of those watches?"

"I do. I just left it back at home. Didn't want any distractions."

"Smart man," said Rose, giving the idea that Justin was under scrutiny for worthiness of her affection. She grabbed the menu and immediately spotted something eye-catching.

"Ooooo, steak! I've never had it before, but my dad swears it's the best thing in the world. I'm definitely getting that."

"That's too expensive for my pockets. You see how many units it costs?"

"Units? That some kind of currency or something?"

"Yeah. Two hundred units is an entire week's pay for me."

"Oh wow. Well, Sasha said I can have whatever I want, and I want steak. You can get whatever too. I'll take care of it."

"So, you're willing to pay for my food on our first date?"

Rose tilted her head, curiously. "What? Too manly to let a girl pay the bill?" she interrogated.

Justin responded with his hand up in submission, "Not at all Miss Rosie. Pay away."

"Ugh," she grunted, rolling her eyes. "Don't call me that. My annoying little brother used to call me that."

"Fine, Rosalia." Rose scowled at Justin. "What? That is your name, right? Or do the legends lie?"

"Call me that again, and you'll become part of the legend."

"Duly noted," Justin replied apologetically.

The waiter arrived as the conversation was in full swing. "Sorry to interrupt. I'm Devon, your waiter for tonight. Are you guys ready to order?"

"Steak and chips for me," said Rose.

"Same," Justin added.

The waiter scribbled in his pad. "How would you like them?"

Rose pondered. "I've never tasted one before, but my dad says it's best medium rare, so I'll try that," she rationalized.

Justin wasn't as bold. "I'll take it well done," he said.

"Anything to drink?"

"Water's fine for me." Rose was keeping with her ban of liquids without the molecular makeup of pure H_2O. Justin nodded in agreement of the same.

The server verified that he had the order correct. "Two steak and chips, one medium rare, the other well done, and a pitcher of iced water. I'll bring it over as soon as it's done. If there's anything else, just let me know."

Alone again, a time for the serious questions had arrived. Rose was the first to break the truce, as she often was. "Earlier, you said this was your first date. Is that true?"

"It is."

"Why? You're twenty-one already. You never thought about girls before?"

"Not really. I mean, I like girls, of course, but I guess I was so busy helping my grandpa keep the gym going and training that I never paid much attention to them."

"Why now then? What makes me so special?" Rose truly didn't think anyone would look at her in the way Justin did. Self-confidence was a rare commodity for a girl growing up with zero social cues to know whether or not she was a catch.

"Are you kidding me? You're easily the most beautiful girl I've ever seen in my life."

Rose blushed. It was the first time a man, other than the ones in her family, had told her that she was beautiful. Furthermore, it was the first time she actually believed it. Still, she remembered what Chris had drilled into the fabric of her being. She was to never become someone's eye candy. "Is that all I am? Something pretty to look at?" she queried.

"No. That's not what I'm saying. My life is being a fighter. It's what I love doing the most. My dream is to become a soldier for the WTP. I want to fight for our people, you know? Women don't usually understand that, but I know you do. Anybody that fights the way you do has to know. Besides, my grandpa says you can tell everything you need to know about someone by the way they dance or fight. I knew I was going to marry you from the first kick

I saw you take."

"Marry?" Rose laughed. "You're getting a little ahead of yourself, aren't you?"

"Eh. When ya know, ya know," Justin joked. "Might as well skip dinner and get straight to the I do's."

Rose displayed her fist. "I do wanna hit you again."

The meals arrived without too long of a wait. Presentation was flawless. The steaks sat in shallow bowls of their own juices, and the crispy fries accompanied them in separate dishes.

"Oh my God! That is the best thing I have tasted in my life," Rose said, wide-eyed.

Justin would trust the opinion of his own taste buds. "Man, that is good," he agreed. "I see why it costs so much."

The further the evening went on, the more Rose felt her protective walls crumble. Conversation felt natural with Justin. He understood her humor and seemed to relish in her abrasive nature.

"Can I ask you something?" said Justin.

Rose could tell the question would be something she might not want to answer but felt opening up was probably a good step to take. "Sure."

"Why do you call Mr. Cringle your dad? I thought Arturo was your father."

Rose answered, though reluctantly. "He is, but I never knew him. Chris raised me. Cory too," she said.

"That makes sense." Justin took a second to think. "Are all the stories they teach about you and your family true?"

"Depends on what they teach."

"That Mr. Cringle was the greatest soldier in the world before he died. Well, obviously that part was wrong, because he's still alive. They also said he trained the founders of the WTP and that they had to send you and Cory away, but one day you would return to lead the fight against the Faction."

"What else did they tell you?" Rose could sense that Justin was holding something back.

"They said that Mr. Cringle was a literal Angel. That

he could do magical things in combat, and one hundred men would fall at the stroke of his hand."

Rose chuckled. "The angel part is a bit much, but there's always some truth in legends."

"You mean he really does have powers?"

"Yeah, but not as good as mine."

"You? No way!" denied Justin, leaning in with surprise. "You're playing with me, right?"

"Wanna see?"

"See what?"

"Watch this." Rose's glass vanished, falling through a small portal that she opened beneath it. A second later, it fell from above, landing in her already cupped hand. She never glanced at it once.

"Oh my God, I love you," said Justin.

Rose laughed heartily. "You are so dramatic," she said.

After dinner, Justin walked Rose to her place of dwelling. On the way out, they managed to avoid a lengthy conversation with Tiffany. "Don't forget to reach out!" she blurted, as they passed.

The comment gave Justin an idea. "Let's pass by the market area on our way back. The stores are closed, but there are vending machines nearby. I want to get something for you," he told Rose.

"For me? OK, I guess."

The machine in which Justin referenced was one with electronics available for purchase. They stopped in front of it and Justin flashed his watch across a panel. It illuminated its stock of items. He tapped a few buttons to make his selection. The machine beeped, signifying that it had deducted units from his account, and dropped a boxed product about the size of the average human hand.

"Here. A much-needed comm-watch," he replied, handing the box to Rose.

"You didn't have to do that," she replied.

"How else would I get to talk to you when you're not around?"

"This has to be expensive. I could have just gotten one from Sasha."

"I know, but I wanted to do it for you. And don't worry about the money. I was saving some units up to upgrade to a fancier one for myself, but I'd rather you have one."

"Aww. That's sweet. Thanks." Rose rewarded Justin with a peck on the cheek. His knees nearly buckled.

"You're welcome," he said, voice wobbly.

"How does it work?"

"Here, I'll show you."

Justin opened the package to retrieve the small electronic device. Its band was synthetic rubber. The digital screen on its facing, being about the diameter of a soda can, was made of a flexible material that hugged the wrist, stretching and twisting in harmony with its movement. "Give me your hand."

Rose held out her arm. Justin slipped the watch on her wrist, allowing the self-tightening strap to secure it to her arm, so that it was snug but not restrictive. Her stomach fluttered from the touch of his hand. There was definitely a spark between them.

"It's a lot more comfortable than it looks," she said, showing her girlish intrigue.

"After a while, you barely notice it's even there," Justin replied. Once the device powered on, he instructed Rose on the next steps. "It should be asking you for a login. It works by a retinal scan. All you have to do is line your eye up with the camera and click the button on the side. Since you don't have an account, it'll automatically recognize that and let you create a new one. After that, you just type in your name and it locks you in."

Rose activated the eye scan, and the device said, "Welcome back, Rosalia."

Justin took a look at the screen. "That's funny. It's saying you already have an account."

"How would that happen?"

"I don't know. It's weird." Justin tapped the screen to check her account details. "Holy shit!" he exclaimed.

"Umm... language," Rose chastised.

"Sorry. It's just that your account balance says twenty million units. You're rich, and I mean rich rich."

"What? That doesn't make sense."

"Maybe Sasha has something to do with it."

"Maybe. I'll have to check with her tomorrow. Can you walk me back now?"

"Sure. Let's go."

Outside Rose's place was the most awkward part of the night. Neither had any experience with telling someone goodbye after a date, but they had seen plenty of films and shows that emphasized how important this moment was. The wrong action or reaction could ruin a relationship before it started.

"So, I'll see you tomorrow?" Justin asked, bashfully.

Rose decided to play coy. "Maybe."

"Maybe is better than no."

Rose laughed.

"Oh, before I forget," Justin tapped the screen of his comm-watch a few times. Rose's lit up, then pinged loudly. "I just sent you a contact request. Accept it and it'll automatically link our users so we can message or call each other."

Rose tapped the accept button. "Done."

"Soooo... another kiss for the road?" Justin requested, pointing at his cheek.

"Nope. You get what you earn. What do you think, I'm easy?" Rose teased.

"No, ma'am," Justin replied. "I'll earn my keep. Goodnight," he said, then left in good spirits.

***

"Sounds like you like him," said Sasha.

Rose held her pointer finger and thumb centimeters apart. "Maybe a little," she said, minimizing her interest.

Sasha wasn't fooled. "Girl please," she said. "I'm a woman. The way you were glowing when you were just talking about that boy, I'm surprised you didn't attack him yesterday."

"Is it that obvious?"

"Afraid so."

"I can't help it. He's so yummy!" said Rose,

covering her face from embarrassment.

"Careful now. If Chris finds out you like him that much, he might castrate the boy," Sasha teased.

Rose rolled her eyes. "Ugh! I don't know what to tell him. Can you talk to him for me? He's so intense."

"He just wants to protect you."

"I know, but I'm an adult, and there isn't a man alive that can take me on."

"You hear, Rose. He's trying to protect your heart. There are lots of things for you to learn about boys. Some of them will tell you anything you want to hear. They'll treat you like a queen just long enough to get in your pants," Sasha explained.

Rose's facial expression showed disappointment.

Sasha peeped her concern and advised further. "I'm not saying that Justin is one of them. He seems like a good kid. All I'm saying is that you need to take your time. Don't go falling head over heels too fast, and definitely don't give him anything you won't be able to take back. Love is something that takes time to grow. Your virginity is sacred. Treat it that way."

"How will I know?" asked Rose.

"You're a perceptive young woman. Pay attention to your instincts. Everyone gives red flags. We just choose to ignore them. If you sense that a person is being deceitful or disingenuous, get yourself out of the situation before it hurts too much to do so. Trust yourself and you'll be OK."

Brief silence was the birthing ground for an awkward question.

"What is it like?" asked Rose.

"What's what like, honey?"

"Sex."

Sasha was thrown for a loop by the unexpected question. "Um, um... wow. I wasn't ready for that one. Um... Chris hasn't had this conversation with you already?" She was a few steps past uncomfortable.

"No. Whenever the subject comes up, he acts all weird. Kind of like you're doing now," Rose pouted.

Sasha regained her composure. "You're right. I'm so sorry. Ask me anything."

"OK, great." Rose looked around the room suspiciously and whispered, even though she knew no one else was there, "When was the last time you had sex?"

Sasha's face went flush. "Um... that is a good question. Yep... a good question that I will answer as soon as I get some water. Can I get some water?" she rambled.

"Uh... sure," Rose replied, detecting evasion.

Lucky for Sasha, Rose's attention was redirected to something that would suppress her talents of insight. Her comm-watch started to ring. "It's him!" she blurted after viewing Justin's name across the screen. "What do I say?"

"Calm down," Sasha advised. "Just act normal. Imagine you're talking to Cory."

Rose's nervous angst immediately dissipated. "Ew. So annoying," she said.

"It worked, didn't it? Now, hurry up and answer the damn thing."

"OK, OK, OK." Rose tapped the answer key and was yet again surprised by the outcome.

Justin appeared on the screen of her comm-watch, flaunting his irresistible smile. "Hey, what's up?" he said.

Rose recoiled, covering the camera on the front of her watch. "I didn't know he was going to be able to see me. Why didn't you tell me?" she asked Sasha.

"I'm just now finding out you even have one of those, remember?"

"He is so gorgeous! When I look at him, things start to happen down there. Is that normal?" Rose confessed.

"Uh... you do know that covering the camera with your hand doesn't stop him from hearing you, right?"

"Shit!" Rose mimed with her mouth. She was beginning to make a habit of embarrassing herself. Attempting to salvage what remained of her dignity, she spoke into the camera. "Forget what you heard, or else!" she ordered in a menacing tone.

"You know what? My ears were in my pocket. I had taken them off to clean them before I called and I forgot. Didn't hear a thing," Justin explained.

Rose squinted her eyes, sizing Justin up through the device.

"I love your hair," he stated, moving the conversation along to save his own skin. He thought a compliment would be a good place to start.

Rose's hair had a healthy shine permeating through every strand. It was styled with a single part, separating two thick, French braids that traced the contours of her head, and flowed over each shoulder. "Really? Tiffany did it for me this morning." Rose fiddled with the tip between her fingers.

"That girl is best taken in small doses," Justin criticized.

"Be nice to her. She's my friend!"

"Friend? You've only known her since last night."

"You're one to talk. You practically proposed to me last night."

"He did what?" Sasha mouthed, pantomiming with her entire body.

Rose waved her away with her offhand, then moved farther away for a little bit more privacy.

"In my defense, you can't see yourself from my view," said Justin.

"Don't try to sweet-talk your way out of being a hypocrite."

"I'm actually trying to talk myself into seeing you again."

Rose laughed. "Ooo. Smooth comeback," she said.

"I'm serious. Can we hang later?"

"I already have plans. Tiffany and I are going to the Lazer War Arena today."

"How'd you talk her into that? She doesn't have an active bone in her body."

"I've been told that I can be a bit persuasive."

"That, I can believe," Justin confessed. "How about we make it an event then? I'll bring four friends from training."

"Riiight. Tiffany and I versus you and your four lackeys... that's a fair match."

"I'm sure Tiffany can help you scrounge up some competition for us to beat on."

"I guess I would enjoy kicking your butt again,"

Rose responded.

"Let's make it even more interesting then. I win, I get a kiss."

Rose chuckled. "Real amusing. You don't have anything that I want."

"My sworn secrecy."

Rose missed the meaning. "What?"

"I won't tell anyone about the weird things that happen in your pants. That could be a serious condition, you know. You might want to get that checked out."

"Ooooweee! You're going to get a beatdown! Wait until I see you," Rose blurted, brandishing her fist like a very large weapon. "On that note, I should be going. Bye."

"You better run!" Rose argued, just before Justin hung up. She turned around but didn't make it a step before she was face to face with Sasha.

"Why are you being so nosy?" she queried, almost flinching out of her heels.

"It's my job to be nosy."

"Says who?"

"Chris, of course. I'm the one that has to deal with him if you get your heart broken."

Rose was frustrated. She was tired of her independence being stepped on. "Why does he treat me like a kid? I probably wouldn't have to deal with this type of thing if my real parents were alive."

"That's where you're wrong. Where do you think you got your charming disposition?" Sasha responded with heavy sarcasm.

Rose folded her arms and rolled her eyes.

"Your mother was as stubborn and strong-willed as anyone. She was the one that kept Chris in check, whenever his wife Melissa wasn't around."

Her latter statement pulled joyful curiosity from Rose. "Really? Oh man. I would have loved to see that. Did she ever hit him?"

"More times than I can count. I think he was actually scared of her."

"Noooo! That is hilarious. What about my dad? What was he like?"

"Arturo? Complete opposite. The biggest sweetheart in the world. It took many years and every sappy pickup line ever made for him to finally woo Candy."

The weight of the conversation caused Rose to sulk for a moment. Her recollection of the prior night was the only thing that kept her from a place of sadness that could have gripped her for days, had it taken hold.

"Did they ever mention leaving something for me?" she asked.

Sasha was puzzled. "Not to me. Why would you ask that?"

"Look at this." Rose pulled up the balance on her comm-watch.

"Twenty-million units! What the hell, how'd you get that?"

"It was already here. When I tried to create a new account, it said I had already been registered."

"Let me see." Sasha toggled a few keys, pulling up the date the account had been created. "2035... This account was created the year you were born."

"That was soon after the world broke. There's no way the WTP existed then," Rose concluded.

"The system we run here already existed beforehand. The government wanted all Project employees independent from the rest of the free world. This includes employment data, pensions, banking, tax filing. You name it."

"So, they made this much money when they were alive?"

"Your parents were always thinking ahead. They must have predicted the Project facilities would play a big role in our future. We were all at Project 047 when it happened. We restored power to the place pretty quickly, because of its independent grid. We stayed a few months, but 047 was strictly a research and training facility, so there were very few supplies to begin with. The upper floors were also severely damaged. After you were born and Candy was strong enough, we headed out to look for a better place to survive. They must have taken your retinal scan before we left and transferred their savings to it. It's been collecting interest ever since."

Tears pooled in the wells of Rose's eyes. "They really did love me?" she sobbed.

"Of course. Why would you think different?" Sasha comforted Rose with a hug.

"They sent me away. My tios told me it was for my safety, but growing up, part of me always wondered if they really cared."

"They loved you with everything they had. Your aunt and uncle too. They all died protecting you. We cried together so many nights, because we had to be away from you and Cory, but it was all worth it, because you both are alive, honey."

At last, there was time for closure. Both women took the time to cry out their feelings, embracing the pain together. The release, after so many years of tension, felt marvelous.

"Red alert," Rose announced, rubbing away the moisture from her face. Her senses had detected the enemy approaching. Sasha hurried to clear her own tears, when the predicted knock sounded at the door.

"It's open," said Rose.

Chris stampeded inside, fists clenched. "Where is he? I'm not going to kill him. I'm just going to make him wish I would have," he claimed.

"What are you talking about?" asked Sasha.

"That boy. I felt her crying, so don't try to lie for him."

"What is wrong with you?"

"With me? She's crying, but something's wrong with me?"

"She was crying because we were talking about Candy and Arturo, you asshole!" Sasha shouted.

It was Chris' turn to be embarrassed. "Ohhhh. I should probably leave before she shoots me," he decided, backing for the door.

His words of possible violence jarred an idea loose from Rose's mind. "You're not going anywhere," Rose informed him. "You owe me for being a dick, and you're paying up tonight!"

"First off, watch your mouth. Second, we have to work on this mission plan tomorrow, so the only thing my black ass will be doing tonight is sleeping."

***

"I can't believe my black ass is not sleeping," Chris complained, in full Lazer gear. The suits were repurposed ICA combat training armor. Outfitted with precision laser sensors, an accurate shot could be registered from more than 300 meters, with a margin of error only a half inch wide. Chris' was colored gold, denoting the team he was a member of.

"I think you look hot in your war stuff, Mr. Cringle," Tiffany complimented.

"Please don't ever call me that again. Chris is fine. Besides, I don't like you, Tiffany."

"Me! Why? What did I do?"

"You turned my baby into a... a... a..."

"A what!" Rose hissed, preparing to hand out a walloping.

"A grown-up! I mean, look at you. You're... you're..."

"I'm what!"

"Beautiful, god damn it!" Chris spoke in a manner that somehow took the complimentary feeling out of the compliment.

Sasha rested her head in her hands. "You have serious issues," she complained.

Rose figured it was the best she would get. "Thank you. Us women are going to change now," she spoke smugly, prancing off to the locker room, accompanied by Sasha and Tiffany.

"Not a single word," Chris said to Cory.

The women didn't take long to emerge from the changing room. In the same moment, Justin showed up with a quartet of the monstrous-looking sort, already in full battle rattle. A layer of shiny paint labeled his group the silver team.

"That's your team? That's not fair!" Justin cried. "You've got two of the greatest soldiers that ever lived."

Rose had complaints of her own. "Three of the greatest soldiers that ever lived," she corrected. "Besides, look who's talking? It would take two of me to weigh up to one of them. And we have Tiffany... No offense," Rose added, not intending to hurt her new friend's feelings.

Chris wasn't as sensitive. "Oh, there should be offense," he jabbed. "The girl is holding her damn weapon upside down."

Tiffany looked like a complete amateur. "Oops," she said, flipping the rifle into the correct orientation.

"Hey Mrs. Truman," said the largest member of Justin's team.

"Hey Tree. How's your mother?"

Tree was 6'9 and weighed around 265 pounds. Tattoos covered just about every inch of his ripped arms and torso. In addition to his towering stature, a smooth demeanor and the color of Egyptian sands made him one of the most eligible bachelors around.

"She's doing okay. She wanted me to thank you for putting a rush on that maintenance order for the leaky pipe. Says Mike would have taken forever, otherwise."

"No problem. Happy to help when I can."

"That is a big ass kid," said Chris. "You know him?"

"I know all of them," she replied. "Of course, there are thousands of citizens here, so I can't know every single one personally, but these kids are training to be a special operations unit for the WTP."

"This old man is the great Chris Cringle? I was expecting a god to be more... well, you know... godly," said one of the young men. He was a bit bigger than Chris, standing 6'3, 230 pounds.

"First of all, there's only one God, and it sure as hell ain't me." Chris turned to Sasha and asked, "What's that one's name?"

"That would be Robin Lewis, better known as Patch," she informed him.

The young man was smiling as much as his mouth would allow.

"Congratulations, Robin. You've just become my number one target. Maybe they'll write a story about you.

The kid who was shot down by an old man in less than ninety seconds."

Patch's smile disintegrated. "Ninety seconds?"

"Course is about two hundred yards in all directions. There's twenty people per team and perfect visibility, so yeah. Ninety seconds is me being generous." Chris calculated. "Also, Robin is a girl's name," he added as an additional insult.

The other two members of Justin's group laughed. "That's what you get for always running your big mouth," said the only woman of the young bunch. She was a giant as well, being 6'4, 220 pounds of chocolate beauty.

"Shut up Mona. You too Bobby. I'm not scared of him or the made-up stories about him. Disappearing cars, dodging bullets, and stopping time... I stopped believing fairy tales in elementary," Patch ranted.

"Whatever you say, Papi. We'll see on the course, won't we?" Alex replied. He was originally from the Dominican Republic and his heavy accent showed. He was also the bulkiest of the five, nearly matching Tree's weight at 260 pounds, but four inches shorter.

"Speaking of that," began Justin, the smallest of the crew, at 6'2, 225 pounds, "we are going to play this fair, right?"

"What's that supposed to mean?" Sasha was insulted that the honor of her and her loved ones was being questioned.

"No powers is all I mean."

Patch was agitated. "Not you too. You actually believe in that stuff? Look at him. He's a person, just like us!" he exclaimed.

In an instant, Chris vanished, then appeared behind Patch. "Boo!" he yelled in his ear.

"Ahhh! Shit!" Patch shouted, dropping his Lazer rifle on the ground. The rest of his friends had a similar reaction, only not as dramatic.

Tiffany may have had the most outrageous response of them all. She screamed at the top of her lungs, hiding behind Rose.

"You didn't tell me the stories were real!" she

stated, knees shaking.

Now sufficiently entertained, Chris agreed to Justin's premise. "No powers," he confirmed. "Not like we'll need them anyway."

"We? The legends didn't say anything about anybody else," said Tiffany, still cowering behind Rose, who decided to have fun at her expense.

"That's because I got mine later," she said, turning around with her eye sockets completely illuminated in the deepest blue imaginable.

The tiny woman bolted, taking cover behind Sasha. She held up her pointer fingers in the form of a cross.

"Ay, Dios mío. Tan fácil," Rose laughed.

Her change of language caught Alex's attention.

"Hola, mamita. No me dijo que hablabas español," he said.

"¿Esperé... Él habló sobre de mí?"

"Él entero día. No podemos convencerlo que se calle."

Justin followed Rose's and Alex's body languages. He perceived excitement, though he didn't understand a word of Spanish. In turn, his own involuntary facial expression was easily read.

"Relax, papito. It's not every day I get to speak to somebody in my own language. Besides, I'm not interested in young doe. I'm big game hunting," said Alex, redirecting his gaze to Sasha.

Catching his subtle advances, Sasha's cheeks grew rose. "Excuse me? I'm old enough to be your mother," she informed him.

"That's fine. I can call you mamá if you like." Alex puckered his lips at her.

"Ooowwweee!" Rose exclaimed, covering her mouth while instigating the situation.

Chris doubled over from the pain of gut-wrenching laughter. He regretted it when Sasha whacked him across the back of his head. "Damn! Why do you always have to hit me? He's the one that's trying to help you get your groove back," he complained. When Sasha balled up her fist, he recoiled, "Put that thing away! I see you were around Candy and her devil spawn over there too." Chris indicated Rose as secondary blame.

"Do you see it?" asked Mona.

Patch had been observing as well. "Yep. They're doing each other," he concluded.

"What did you say?" Sasha shouted angrily.

When things seemed about to get out of control, two more guests arrived.

"Hi guys," said Ari, next to her mother. They had just gotten their day started after sleeping through the morning. Their fieldwork had taken a lot out of them.

"Heeey," greeted Sasha. "Everyone, this is Chris' wife Yesha and his daughter Ari," she introduced, with a hint of awkwardness in her voice. Not everyone picked up on the small inflection, but Rose was one of the few that did. Suspicious, but realizing the inappropriate nature of the topic, she stored the data in her mind for later conversation.

"Hey daddy," said Ari.

Chris kissed her forehead. "Hey Baby Girl. You learn anything out there?"

"The ocean levels have risen nearly two hundred feet off the coast here. If it's the same worldwide, that means most of the glacial ice has melted, and the rest is in the process."

"That doesn't sound good."

"It isn't. Without that ice, a lot of species will go extinct, and there won't be ice to reflect sunlight. Instead, the oceans will absorb it, making them hotter. Hotter oceans, hotter world," Ari explained.

"Sheesh. I don't know if I should be proud of you for being so smart, or worried about your chance at a future."

"The first obviously, because I'm going to fix it."

Chris hugged his daughter pridefully. "That's my Baby Girl."

Cory had been quiet a while, but Ari's presence engaged him. "Are y'all joining the squad?" he asked her and Yesha.

"No sir," Yesha declined. "Only here for emotional

support."

The buzzer sounded, signaling the ten-minute warning of the coming battle. It was time for both crews to line up with the rest of their teammates, a random assortment of fifteen others per squad. "Gotta go, love. Wish me luck," said Chris, blowing a kiss to Yesha, before turning away.

"Always and forever," she responded, returning the favor.

Rose held her side weapon—a combat baton that would serve as an instant kill on contact during hand-to-hand combat—high in the air, letting out a battle cry.

"You're taking this way too seriously," Cory commented.

Rose smiled and literally skipped away like a schoolgirl, replying, "Nobody asked you," in her sweetest voice.

"Good luck," said Justin, parting ways with his troupe.

"You're the one who's going to need it," Chris replied. "Ninety seconds, big boy," he reminded Patch.

The young man snickered. "Nobody's afraid of you without those powers," he replied, sounding unsure of himself.

"You mean the ones you thought were fake just a few minutes ago?" Mona prodded.

"Shut up. You just pull your own weight. I'll take care of the old man," Patch argued.

Mona laughed. "Whatever you say."

***

Rose's team headed down a walkway with a steep incline. The entire structure was pure concrete with steel framework. Only enough light to sufficiently traverse the path was available.

"The course is back there. Why are we going this way?" asked Chris.

"We're using the above-ground course," said Sasha.

"What happened to the whole Lola problem? You're

not worried about her showing up?"

"No. We're not hiding from her. As long as she can't just pop up in the heart of our home, we're OK. Besides, they're not the only ones with special people anymore."

"Sure as hell aren't," Rose clearly articulated.

"When the hell did your language become so bad?" Chris questioned.

Rose crinkled her face. "When I became a grown woman. Plus, you just said the same damn thing. Stop being such a hypocrite all the time!"

"You better get her, Sash'. Ever since she met that boy, she's been trying me. Let's see how much he likes her when I shave her ass bald."

"You'd better not!" shouted Rose.

"Keep on then. Just keep it up and watch."

Rose rubbed her precious hair and closed her mouth. She had pressed her luck with Chris many a time, and it never ended in her favor.

"Can you two focus? The moment we get outside, the horn will start things, and I'm not losing to a bunch of buff, snotty-nosed twenty-year-old kids," said Sasha.

The course turned out to be an old college football stadium. Its oval, outer perimeter was walled in with twelve-foot-high fencing. The grounds within stretched north of two hundred yards at its widest, and just above one hundred fifty feet at its narrowest. Various obstacles, large and small, populated the battlefield. This ranged from large concrete pillars that grasped for the heavens to mirrored walls and rusted automobile frames.

The least foreseen part of the arena, for the newbies, was the packed audience. At the sight of the participants, they erupted into an anticipatory frenzy.

Rose gawked expressively. "Holy..."

"Rose!" Chris interjected, correcting her language beforehand.

"I wasn't gonna say it," she mumbled, awe-stricken at all of the people.

Sasha relished the presence of the fans. The adrenaline rush she got from them fine-tuned her concentration and alertness. "Hope none of you have stage fright," she said.

Cory was shell-shocked. "It's always like this?"

"Uh... not like this. Not ever," uttered Tiffany. She was definitely the most affected of the huddle. She clenched tight onto Chris' arm.

"What are you doing? Get off!" he demanded, trying, but failing, to pry her from his chiseled limb.

Cory was still unsettled. "What do you mean, not ever?" he asked.

"I've been to these plenty of times. There's always people watching, but never this many. There isn't a single empty seat," a young man informed Cory.

"Guess this is what happens when news spreads that four living legends are participating," said another stranger of their team. "Time for us to see how much of the legends are real."

The starting horn blared resoundingly. Everyone poured onto the battlefield, howling their grandest cries of war.

"Will you release me, you... tiny woman!" Chris yelled, still attempting to shed Tiffany's grasp. Her grip was shockingly firm for such a miniature person. Chris flailed his arm about, sliding her feet back and forth across the dirt.

"Instant karma," laughed Sasha, trotting out onto the field. "Enjoy your girlfriend."

Precious seconds were ticking away. "Screw it," mumbled Chris as he hauled Tiffany from her feet, carrying her like a human football. "What are you, like ninety pounds?" he muttered, dashing for the nearest form of cover.

It was evident that most of the contestants didn't have a lick of combat experience. They were friends and families just looking for a good time. Neglecting the use of cover, tactics, and even simple aim, they barreled at each other full speed, yanking on their triggers at random.

"If you're going to hitch a free ride, you can at least shoot someone," Chris said to Tiffany. Bobbing around must have loosened the nervous panic cinching down on her. She aimed her weapon, holding down the trigger. The simulated recoil jarred the barrel in every direction, but she failed to hit anyone. At last, making the last few feet to cover, Chris returned Tiffany to her own devices. They crouched behind a concrete blockade.

Tiffany sat on her rear end, staring at her gun, laughing like a maniac. "Wow!"

Chris was lost. "What is wrong with you?"

"I love this thing! I wanna shoot somebody!" Tiffany exclaimed with excitement.

"Then do it and stop looking like a madwoman." Chris looked up at the scoreboard-mounted clock. He had wasted about thirty seconds dealing with Tiffany. If he was going to complete his task, he had to get to it.

"I need you to cover me," he said.

Tiffany looked befuddled. "What's that?"

"Brace your weapon on top of the concrete and shoot at anybody not wearing gold."

"I can do that!"

"OK... go!" Chris gave the order, simultaneously bursting into action. He hopped over the partition, transitioning into an all-out sprint. His adept parkour skills permitted him to float over, around, and under obstacles with ease, not stopping to pick off the easiest of the fray. Two fell to his precise shots. The third took Chris' baton across the torso, as he slid under his legs and smacked it against his back.

The crowd erupted with an uproar for the ages. Such skill had never graced the battleground. What was more, it was happening all over the arena. Sasha, Rose, and Cory were accomplishing graceful feats of carnage, as well as their counterparts—Justin, Tree, and Alex.

Seventy yards or so from the starting point, Chris finally eyed his target. Patch had taken cover behind the frame of a car with three others, including Mona. They spotted him as well, so Chris knew it would take a bit of creativity to finish them off.

"Running out of time, old man. Clock says twenty seconds left. So much for the legend," Patch shouted arrogantly.

He was unaware that Chris had already mentally

checkmated him. He slid his rifle to adjacent cover. It served two purposes: to shift the eyes of his opponents, even if only for a fraction of a second, and so that he could move swiftly, without hindrance. Chris' forty time was still on par with Olympic champions. He dashed towards his weapon, then dived so that his body was completely parallel to the ground. From midair, he banked a Lazer grenade off a nearby mirrored wall.

Patch and Mona saw the fear in their own eyes as they tracked it to the reflective surface. Their hardened training made their reaction time superb. They flipped over the car before the game-ending light exploded in all directions. Their companions weren't as fortunate. They flung their weapons down in the dirt, frustrated from defeat.

The audience was pure electricity. Their eyes swiveled around, eager for more. Patch and Mona, seamlessly, rolled into kneeling positions, rifles at the ready. It took less than a second for them to locate Chris and pull the trigger. Their weapons clicked uselessly. During their effort to escape the Lazer explosive, Chris had retrieved his rifle and shot them both.

"Adiós. That's Spanish for bye. My daughter taught me," Chris teased. He winked and scampered away to assist his team with finishing the job.

Patch was irate. He looked up at the scoreboard and read "78 seconds." The fury led him to chuck his gun against the side of the car frame, shouting, "Damn it!"

"You know Sasha's gonna make you pay for breaking that?" Mona stated.

Patch left the field of play. "Shut up, Mona."

Chris parked himself behind a series of hay bales to survey the landscape. From what he could tell, all that remained were the six he expected to be.

"I'll save you, Mr. Cringle!" yelled Tiffany. She fired her weapon on the run.

"Ahhh, damn it! I almost had him," said a disappointed young woman, who had been sneaking up on Chris.

Tiffany hunkered down next to him behind the

265

blocks of hay. "You're still in? I underestimated you, I see," Chris admitted.

"You should have seen me, Mr. Cringle. I was running and jumping. This one guy jumped out, and I shot him! I was like ahhh, pew! Then, I kept running, but the funny thing was, I never got tired. I never work out on the count that I'm already small, so I don't need to, but my cardio is horrible. I guess it's all the adrenaline. I love this stuff. Can you teach me one day? I can be a soldier. Not in these ugly uniforms, though. I love fashion too."

"If you call me Mr. Cringle again, I'll shoot you myself. You should probably straighten up your glasses too," Chris interrupted, while internally formulating his next strategy.

"Sorry," Tiffany apologized. She adjusted her custom, prescription frames. "I get carried away sometimes."

The humid heat and activity had started to tease out drops of sweat. Beads of moisture traced the bulges and divots of Chris's swelling muscles. His exposed shoulders and biceps puffed slightly from increased blood flow.

Tiffany's heart rate quickened at the sight. "Do you find me attractive, Mr. Cringle?" she asked.

"What? What kind of question is that?" he asked, not really paying much attention to what she was asking.

"I think you should take me out on a date."

The bold statement garnered Chris' full attention. "Tiffany, you're a kid," he stated.

"Actually, I'm twenty-one. That means I've been an adult for a full three years. Also, I'm very mature for my age, so I'm like thirty in mental years."

"That's a stupid argument, plus I'm married. You just met my wife."

"Divorce happens all the time. Actually, the rate of failed marriages is three to five in all of the WTP colonies combined. So, chances are, you'll get one eventually. Then, you can take me out," Tiffany explained. "Or stay in," she added, suggestively.

Chris was disturbed. "That's really dark," he stated. Just then, his peripheral caught exaggerated movement.

He turned to see Rose behind cover, flailing her arms around to get his attention. She was calling for them to join her.

"We're moving. Don't follow until I stop," Chris instructed Tiffany. "Move quick, so they can't get an easy shot."

With that, Chris managed to run across without being tagged.

"Well, he didn't say no," Tiffany muttered under her breath, convincing herself she still had a shot with him. She fled across, also making it safely.

"What were you guys talking about that was so important?" asked Rose. "I was trying to get your attention for like a whole minute. I had to risk getting closer just to flag you down."

"Strategy," Chris deflected. "We have the numbers. It's five on three."

Cory and Sasha cursed out loud and kicked their rifles across the ground. A well-placed Lazer grenade by Justin had taken them both out.

"So, it's just us," Chris said, correcting himself.

"Patch and Mona?"

"Seventy-eight seconds."

Rose laughed. "That's what he gets for being so arrogant," she said.

"What now?" asked Tiffany.

Rose looked to Chris.

"Nope," he said. "It's your show. No more training wheels. You're the main course from now on. I'm just the side dish."

Rose nodded, then ran through a series of scenarios in her head. The crowd was pumping louder than ever, but she was able to focus and drown them out. That is, until they were responsible for her next idea. "Everyone's here for the legends. That includes them," she remembered, referring to the enemy.

"Huh?" Chris uttered.

"As weird as it sounds, Tiffany just became our strength."

"I did?" she responded.

Chris needed details. "Explain," he said.

"Those three are clout chasing. They want to be the ones that took down the legends. We can use that to our advantage," Rose expounded. She and Chris bounded backward across the course, tactically. As they suspected, their opponents applied the pressure. Each time they moved to retreat, Justin, Bobby, and Tree covered an equal distance forward, firing along the way. The lust to appease the audience, and their own egos, led them to be unaware that Tiffany was still in play.

"They're going to run out of room. Keep pressing," Justin ordered. His team pushed right past Tiffany, who was still hiding behind the same barricade where Rose had hatched her scheme.

"Hi guys," she said, waving exuberantly.

They turned around, hailing her with fire. She was down, but the damage was already done. Tiffany had been the sacrificial lamb. Both of her Lazer grenades burst at their feet. The victory horn blasted, but the roar of the crowd outmatched its level. The noise was maddening.

Tiffany stood up and waved out to the pleased spectators. A cheer began to spread among them. They were chanting her name over and over.

"Thousands of people calling her name for winning a war game. Can't make that one up," said Chris.

Rose removed her safety helmet. "I think you just created another legend," she said.

"Me? No. All I did was shut that smug Patch kid up. This one is all you."

***

Packs of people filed into the above-ground district of the Project 002 settlement. It was a large, open area with healthy, green grass, picnic tables, and various outdoor activities. Flavor was converted from taste to smell, as sweet smoke from several active grills surfed the breeze to meet the awaiting. The sound of sizzling meats only added to the appetizing array of sensory information.

"I know that ain't barbecue," said Chris, taking a seat at a table with Yesha and Ari. The familiarity of his favorite local cuisine teased out the hidden southern drawl in his speech.

"Yes it is," Sasha replied. She sat at a table a couple of feet away, and was assisted by Cory.

"They don't know what they're doing with them ribs."

"Says who? They learned from the best."

"Who?" Chris chuckled.

"Uh, what's funny? Don't forget that I'm from Memphis too, just 'cause I'm a white girl."

"Mmhm. Get me a plate and let me judge that."

"Me? No. That's what we had kids for. To do things adults don't wanna do. That means you, Cory. Go get momma a plate," Sasha ordered.

"Man, alright," he whined, breaking away from engagement with his new comm-watch.

Chris and Yesha stared at Ari. "Alright, fine. I'm going," she said lethargically, then accompanied Cory on their mission.

"Ever since I gave him that thing, his face is always stuck in it. It's getting annoying. I want to spend time with my baby," Sasha vented.

"They don't work outside, right?" said Yesha.

Chris snickered. "When it comes to electronics, rules don't apply to that kid."

"I'm learning that very quickly," said Sasha.

Rose appeared, taking a route to another nearby table. Tiffany, Justin, Mona, Patch, Bobby, and Tree were all walking with her, laughing and conversing with one another. She pointed and said a few words and the four men grabbed two tables, then began to carry them toward Sasha, Chris, and Yesha.

"Looks like the gang's got a new alpha," Sasha pointed out.

Yesha looked over. "She's a natural leader. Look at her. They're all glued to her and don't even realize it."

Chris's jealousy kicked in. "Ever since she got that boy, her face is always stuck in his. It's getting annoying," he complained.

"Leave him alone," Yesha demanded. "He's a good

kid."

"Oh yeah? Cory's a good kid too. Look how your daughter is over there drooling all over him right now."

Whatever joke Cory told Ari must have been hilarious. She buried her face in his shoulder, cracking up.

"Girl, hurry up with that food!" Yesha yelled, attempting to interrupt their affectionate interactions without being too obvious.

"Mmhm. That's what I thought," Chris gloated.

The group of youths arrived with their tables in tow, shoving them together to make one large surface.

"Hey, daddy," said Rose. Her kiss met Chris' cheek, then Yesha's and Sasha's.

"Hey guys," she added.

"Daughter," Chris replied with a suspicious look on his face.

"What's up with him?" asked Rose.

Yesha grunted. "What do you mean? He's just being Chris."

"Good point."

Everyone passed around greetings, then dug into a plethora of topics. Food made its way around, filling bellies to the brim. Eventually, the expected subject of discussion crept its way in.

"Soooo, how does it feel to be a loser?" Rose taunted.

"Here we go," said Justin. "I knew this was coming."

"Of course. You talked trash. You and Patch both, but you couldn't back it up."

"Yeah, yeah. Rub it in while you can. You and the old guy."

Chris remained straight-faced. "Don't have to."

He got the desired result. Not engaging with boasting infuriated the youngster.

"You got lucky," he said. "I'm bigger than you. I'm stronger, faster, and younger than you. I can beat you in anything, anytime." Patch was on a tirade.

"Is that so?"

"Damn straight!"

The Lord must have been listening, for a challenge presented itself in that very moment. A basketball bounced from the outdoor court, rolling to a stop at Chris' feet. He picked it up, spinning it on his finger.

"How's your game?" he asked.

"Immaculate."

"Three on three. Two's and three's to eleven."

Patch stood up. "This is going to be light work. Justin. Tree. Let's go," he said.

"Hey kid. You mind if we use your ball for a second?" Chris asked the child who had been shooting around when he lost control of it.

"Go ahead," he replied.

Knowing the drill, Cory got up and started to stretch.

"I can't play. I'm wearing heels," Rose advised Chris.

Sasha looked down at her feet. "We wear the same size," she said. "Take mine. I've got to see this."

Rose laced up, buttoned the top of her shirt, and rolled up the sleeves.

"You owe me for this. I just got these new clothes, and now I have to sweat them up," she said to Chris.

"Oooo! That means we can go shopping again!" Tiffany blurted out.

The concrete had been freshly paved and repainted. The rims were also in perfectly good condition, nets absent of holes or tears.

"Your ball. Check up," said Chris. Patch passed him the ball, then Chris bounced it back.

"I'm seriously guarding him?" asked Cory, struggling to defend Tree. "He's almost got me by a foot."

"Stop complaining and play ball the way I taught you," Chris demanded.

Patch dribbled the ball a short time, feeling out Chris' level of defense. Satisfied that he could take him, he drove towards the basket, then jammed on the brakes, stepping back for a mid-range jump shot. His form was good, but the well-contested attempt ricocheted off the back of the rim. Tree moved Cory to the side easily and secured the rebound. The following one-handed dunk was an attention grabber.

"Oh no!" Ari cried, watching the devastation rain down on Cory.

Whoops and hoots drew in a growing group of people. Most were the very same from the arena that had come to celebrate with the legendary warriors. "They're at it again!" yelled someone, calling in yet an even larger band of spectators.

"That's two, zero," said Patch. "Looks like everybody's coming to see you take the ass whippin' that you should have earlier."

Chris didn't respond. He dropped down into his defensive stance for more work. The next possession, Justin inbounded the ball to Patch, then cut to the basket, losing Rose, who was defending him. Not receiving the pass, he vacated the post for the three-point line. Patch had decided on isolation again. He faked the same move as before, but this time, instead of pulling up for the jump shot, he pump-faked to get Chris in the air, then leaned in for a high-arching floater. Cory rotated over and successfully contested the shot, causing it to bank off the glass and rim out. Tree negated the good defense by tipping the ball back up and into the rim.

"That's four, zip," Patch noted.

"Don't lose possession," Chris warned him. "You do, the game's over."

Cory was growing impatient. "Anytime you're ready, Pops," he said. "That old Chevy should be warmed up by now."

Patch faked one direction, then shifted the other way with a sharp, killer crossover. It appeared the move had frozen Chris in his tracks. The athletic young man lifted off to finish the play with a flashy slam, but was surprised by the manner in which he was thwarted. Chris had permitted him to blow by, but followed closely behind, waiting to time his jump with Patch's. The moment he left his feet, Chris did so as well, plucking the ball from his grasp with both hands, then tapping it against the glass on the way down for show.

The newly gathered audience cheered at the

spectacle. Rose floated to the corner, escaping Justin, who was caught watching the ball, therefore didn't see her get open. Chris found her the moment he returned to Earth, connecting with a bounce pass. Rose rattled in the long-range shot. She looked a bit disappointed for having made the shot. "A little rusty," she said.

"What do you mean? You made the shot," said Justin, befuddled.

Rose winked at him. "You'll see," she replied.

"Shit. What did this idiot get me into?" Justin mumbled, sensing trouble.

Cory inbounded to Chris on the block. He posted up, leaning his weight against Patch. "I told you don't lose possession, didn't I," he reminded him.

"Last time I checked, we're still up."

"Not for long."

Cory went across to set an off-ball screen for Rose. She faked a dive to the basket, then spun back to the perimeter, wide open again, but this time at the wing. Chris zipped the ball with one hand, not to where she was, but to where she would be. Rose caught the ball in motion. It was in the air as soon as she set her feet. It slipped through the net like butter.

"There we go," said Rose, smiling with her follow-through still in the air.

Chris went up top. "Six, four." He passed Cory the ball.

Cory abused his match-up. Tree was quick for his size, but there are levels to speed. Cory drove to the bucket, getting Tree on his heels, then yanked the ball behind his back. Tree recovered, lunging forward, but Cory immediately spun right around him and down the baseline. Patch rotated down to prevent an easy layup. Cory passed the ball to Chris through the defender's legs. Justin reacted by coming down to guard the open Chris, but he had already gotten rid of the ball as soon as he got it. Justin attempted to recover to Rose, but she was way out near the half-court line. Her stroke was pure. Even from beyond thirty feet, the ball sailed through the hoop, unscathed by the rim.

"Whew. Girl has range just like her momma," said Sasha.

Yesha pursed her lips. "Her mom could shoot like that?"

"Sorta. She didn't play ball, but she was a hell of a shot with a rifle. Probably the best long-range shooter that ever lived."

"Game point, big boy," Chris taunted. He checked the ball up, then passed it to Cory.

Cory waited for Chris to set the screen for Rose. Once Rose sprinted for the three-point line, he fed her the ball for the winning basket. This time, Justin was able to fight over the screen to contest. Rose responded by pump-faking. Once Justin flew by, she took off down the lane and floated the ball high and hard off the glass. Chris snatched it from the air, tucked it under his own leg, then banked it from the backboard the same way he found it, all before landing again.

Tree did his best to disrupt the play. He reached to retrieve the ball but put himself into harm's way by doing so. Cory bounded overhead, catching the alley-oop with two hands, but finishing with one. He banged it so hard over Tree's head that the giant tumbled to the ground.

"Good game, big fella," said Cory, walking off the court.

Yesha and Sasha jumped up, applauding like maniacs. The entertained spectators joined in with them. Ari rushed over to Cory.

"I didn't know you could play ball like that," she said.

"Pops taught us. He put together a court in the back of the house where we lived."

"You were amazing out there," she complimented, hugging him, which she immediately regretted. "Ew!" she exclaimed, contaminated by his sweat.

"Nope. You're all in now," he said, refusing to let her go, so that she became further disgusted.

"You're so disgusting!" she shouted, slamming her foot on top of his.

"Ow!" he screamed, letting go. "You're so violent.

Wonder where you got that from..."

Chris had yet to have his moment to gloat. He waited until everyone had made it back to the tables to speak.

"Immaculate, huh? You weren't responsible for one bucket," he noted.

The comment really ruffled Patch's feathers. "You didn't score either," he retorted.

"See... that type of thinking is why you won't ever win against us in anything, or win in the hardest situations life has to offer. I didn't say score. I said responsible for, as in responsibility. My role was to assist. I knew my team's strengths and used that knowledge to put them in positions to succeed. You, on the other hand, neglected the obvious mismatches available to you. Tree could have buried Cory in the post. He even set the screen to assist you, and you turned it down to take me one-on-one. Justin didn't even touch the ball. A teammate that doesn't feel involved won't play hard for you." He shifted his words to Justin, Tree, and Alex. "During the Lazer tag battle, your entire team was so focused on looking good, you three neglected the details so you could chase down Rose and me. You see how that ended. Learn how to be a unit, then you might have a chance to be great. Until then, you'll always be average," he explained, choosing to pass on knowledge rather than gloat.

Dead silence followed, as the weight of what Chris said sunk in. It was a real moment that everyone in earshot could apply to their lives in some form or fashion. It would only require a search in the mirror for signs of selfishness.

"Now that that's out of the way, who's getting me another plate? I'm hungry again," said Chris, switching gears. If it was possible to become more silent, the group had figured it out. Chris looked around, but no one would make eye contact.

"I raised three kids out here. I know one of them better be getting me some ribs," he said.

"I did it the first time," Ari complained.

Rose wasn't having it either. "I'm grown. I don't do grunt work anymore."

Cory put in his own excuse, telling him, "I'm your favorite."

Upset, Chris came up with a solution. "All three of you are going to go together. How about that? Since you already got me a plate, Ari, you can get my pop. My favorite idiot can bring a slab of ribs, and grown-ass can bring me some napkins."

"You want me to go all the way over there for some napkins, when you could just have one of them do it?" Rose moped.

"That's what I said, didn't I?"

"Uggg!" she grunted, storming off.

Cory and Ari followed suit.

"Don't send my baby on errands because you wanna be lazy," said Sasha.

"It's the only way to teach them some work ethic and responsibility. It's not like they can have a nine-to-five in this shell of a world."

Sasha had an idea. "Actually they can," she said.

"Elaborate."

"Everyone here does something, remember. I can assign them all somewhere."

"Oooo! Rose can work at the restaurant with me," Tiffany suggested.

"Actually, I was considering something new for you. We're working on expanding, since the population is still increasing. One of the new stores will be a clothing store targeting younger people. You would manage it, and Rose and Ari could be your first employees. Cory will fill your old position."

"Really!" exclaimed Tiffany. "Fashion is life. I have so many ideas. We can dress the mannequins in custom designs. Can I make the work uniforms? I could make some really good stuff. You know, I've been sewing as long as I can remember and—"

"Tiffany!" everyone yelled in unison.

She looked embarrassed. "Sorry. I was doing it again, huh?" she said.

"How about we discuss this in the morning, after we get to that Faction business?" Chris proposed. "I'd like to spend the rest of the day with Yesha and Ari."

Yesha wore an unsure expression. "About that."

Chris sighed. "Aw, what now?"

"I'm the one heading the design and construction for the new additions. I have to leave shortly to the settlement in Baja to supervise the equipment and material transfer. I was going to tell you when we were alone, but we haven't been at all today."

"Why do you have to leave today? You literally just got back. Go tomorrow. I haven't had one day with you in what, eight years?"

"I know, but this is important. If we don't expand, overpopulation could run our resources dry. We need to excavate a new reservoir, till new land for farming, and construct new habitats for people to have a home. This is important, Chris."

"And I'm not?"

"You know that's not what I said."

"Didn't have to. It shows."

"You take that back!" Yesha shouted.

"Or what Yesha? You gonna punish me by leaving?"

"So, this is how it's going to be?"

"Stop talking to me and just leave," Chris demanded angrily.

"You're so damn selfish. You made this whole speech about teamwork, then two minutes later you're only thinking about yourself and your little wee wee."

"We both know there ain't nothing little about it. Get out of my face with that."

"Fine!" Yesha yelled. "Let's go, Ari. We're leaving." She stormed off, not giving their daughter an opportunity to say goodbye.

Rose arrived with her task complete. "What was that about?"

Cory set the can of soda on the table in front of Chris. "Take it back and bring me something with alcohol in it," he said.

Rose prevented Cory from compliance. "No. He's not contributing to your inability to cope with problems and neither am I. Get it yourself. Let's go, Cory. I need to go get out of these sweaty clothes anyway, and you do too."

Their peers got up to leave as well. Tiffany scampered close to Rose and whispered in her ear, "He really hasn't been with his wife in that long?"

"Why is that your business?" she murmured in response.

"It's not, but I'd be all over a man like that."

Rose rolled her eyes and sucked her teeth. "Whatever girl. Go for it," she stated satirically.

Sasha was the only one that remained seated. "I could use a drinking partner," Chris said to her.

"Are you serious, after last night? My nana still hurts."

"Come on. Neither one of us wanted that. It won't happen twice."

"I know it won't," Sasha replied, standing up. "Because I'm never drinking with you again. Besides, Rose is right. You should find a better way to deal with your shit. This is a constant theme with you. Later." She kissed him on the forehead and left him alone.

Chris didn't move for a spell. He sat back and watched the sun head over the horizon. When the orange skyline dimmed further, he realized he was the only one still outside. The can of soda was sitting in a pool of water. It dripped off the end of the table, after flowing across to the other side. Chris stared at it. "Always follows the path of least resistance," he mumbled to himself. Finally making up his mind, he left the beverage to fend for itself in the dark of night and headed underground.

13

Choices And More Choices

In the very same seat as the night before, celebratory drinks had become tools of culling pain and disappointment. Chris had just sat down with the first serving of his drink of choice: whiskey and vanilla cola. Tiffany walked in and took the stool next to him. It was observable that she had been home to bathe and change. Her hair was puffed into natural curls, glimmering with a thin sheen of moisturizer. The feature of her outfit was a long-sleeved top that completely covered one shoulder but angled down to leave the other completely bare. Its crochet-styled, toffee-colored material ended high enough to display her pierced belly button and buttery skin. A thigh-length, khaki skirt, together with strapped heels snaking up the calves, completed the artistic piece.

"Hey, Mr. Cringle," she said, crossing her legs like a proper lady.

He sighed, wishing to be left alone. "How did you get in here?" he asked.

"Adults are allowed to go where we want," she said, with emphasis on "adult."

"Hey, Tiff. The usual?" asked the bartender.

"Yep. Thanks, Ralph," she replied.

Chris was surprised. "You drink?"

"Another thing that adults are allowed to do." She was certainly trying to drive home the point of her maturity.

"Why are you sitting here? That should be a question you can give a real answer to."

"Hmm. For the record, adults are also allowed to sit where we want to sit, but in this case, I'm sitting here because of you."

"Look, I've already explained this to you..."

Tiffany held up her hand to halt Chris' words. "To lend an ear," she further elaborated. "Or is there a sin in talking and sharing a drink?"

"No. As you keep repeating, you're an adult," Chris answered, though reluctantly. He noticed that her demeanor was somewhat different. There wasn't an epic change in personality, but she was perceptibly less giddy and hyper.

The bartender served Tiffany her drink. "Sex on the Beach."

"I'd love to," she replied, meeting eyes with Chris.

Chris squinted his eyes, then finished off his first drink. "What's up with you?" he cross-examined.

Tiffany dropped a straw into her glass to avoid smearing away her lip gloss. "Depends on what you're asking."

"There's something different about you. Earlier you were more, um... energetic."

"Oh, that. I've been told that I tend to get a little hyper and talkative when I'm uncomfortable."

"You're not uncomfortable now?"

"Nope. I'm familiar with everything and everyone here. I usually get that way when I meet new people. That, or when I'm in a packed stadium shooting lasers at people for the first time. That sure got the juices flowing."

Chris signaled the bartender for a second round.

Tiffany sipped from her beverage. "Can I ask you something personal?"

"Are you going to go away if I answer it?"

"Earlier you said you hadn't been with your wife in eight years. That's weird. Did you break up or something?" Tiffany interrogated, completely ignoring Chris' previous response.

"Do you really think I would talk to you about that?"

"Well, you obviously could use someone to talk to. As God would have it, I'm the only one that happens to be concerned enough to be here."

"Are you really? Or are you just being fast?"

"Fast women will be with anyone that chooses them. I choose who I'm with, if anyone at all."

"So, all the young men around here and you'd rather be here listening to my problems?"

"Clearly you haven't met the options around here."

"There is this one guy they call Patch. I think you'd be perfect together."

Tiffany giggled at the thought. "So, there is some humor in there somewhere," she said. Her face straightened. "You don't look as old as the textbooks say you are."

"Those books don't know anything."

"How old are you exactly?"

"Not your business."

"Come ooon. Humor me."

Chris sighed, then took a drink. "Thirty-five... forty... forty-five. Who the hell knows? Time's funny that way."

Tiffany shoved small talk to the side, diving directly into the deep questions. "Do you love her?"

Chris was caught completely off guard. What astonished him more was that he didn't have a clear answer. "I think..." he said. Tiffany's reaction showed that his response shocked her more than it did him. She had to quickly retrieve a napkin to catch the drink dribbling down her chin, preventing it from ruining her top. "You think?"

"I wasn't finished. I think that question is too complicated to answer."

"It shouldn't be. What's marriage without love?"

"You're speaking as if the rules of the normal world apply. None of those things apply to me or my situations. Time doesn't apply to me and my situations. Everything is all messed up."

Tiffany finished her first drink, then waved for a second. "Enlighten me," she suggested.

"How do I make this short? My abilities are tied to time and space. Somehow, we ended up living in two separate realities at once. In the other, I've known her many years, and I love her with all my heart. But in this one, I met her once about eight years ago, so in some ways, she's a complete stranger."

"That's what that argument was about," Tiffany surmised.

"I just want time that she isn't willing to give right now. Her work in this world is more important than our relationship in it."

"Part of you is there now, living your other life?"

"Always."

"Is she there with you?"

"No, she's working. There's some new project at 047 that she's leading."

Tiffany was seeing a picture that Chris wasn't. "How often are you alone in that reality?"

"Never. Ari's always with me."

Tiffany smacked her lips. "You know that's not what I'm asking."

"Never thought about it."

"Do you have the same feelings of doubt with your daughter?"

Chris didn't hesitate a second with his answer. "No. I love my daughter more than anything."

"I'm starting to think your doubt about Yesha isn't exclusive to this reality. She seems the type though."

"What type?" Chris asked defensively.

"The type to be married more to her work than her actual husband. She seems like a good woman, so don't think I'm bashing her. I'm only saying that you have to know exactly what you're investing in. Everyone you love isn't necessarily for you, nor you them. She's a worker. Workers work, and there's nothing that will convince them to do otherwise. If you can live with that and be happy, then you're where you need to be. If not, then you have some tough choices to make."

Chris gawked at Tiffany, dumbfounded. Suddenly, he saw a woman. A mature, fully functioning, and aware woman, rather than the oblivious, ignorant kid he presumed her to be. His gaze traced over her petite person, stopping at her legs. It was always the legs for him. The skin of her thighs was radiant and supple. It took everything in him to pry his eyes away, back up to her doll-like face.

"Sorry, I was babbling again, wasn't I?" Tiffany concluded, catching his blank stare.

"Actually, no. I was just wondering where all that wisdom came from."

Tiffany sipped more of her drink. "It's always been here. You aren't the first person to misjudge someone by what they think they see. I don't have much of any memory before the world broke. Small things here or there, like birthdays pop up, but not much else. Most of my life, I was raised in the Baja settlement by a foster family that took me in, but the moment I turned eighteen, I moved here on my own. I work, pay my own bills, and depend on myself. That kind of responsibility makes you grow up pretty quick."

"I definitely did misjudge you," Chris replied. He was beginning to feel an intense attraction to Tiffany. It wasn't clear if it was because of the increasing alcohol content in his bloodstream or his elevated perspective and respect for her mind. Either way, he realized it was best to abort and leave. "Um... I should probably go," he said, preparing to head out. "I haven't showered yet, and even I can smell myself."

"Awww. Things were going so well," Tiffany pouted.

Chris closed his account with the bartender, using the comm-watch provided courtesy of Sasha. "That's the problem," he said.

"Guess I have no reason to be here then."

"You haven't even finished your drink."

Tiffany sucked down the remainder of her cup. "Now I have. Ready to go?"

"I'm going to my place. You're going to yours."

"It just so happens that I'm passing your place on the way to mine. We can finish our conversation on the way."

"Your place is not on the way to mine," said Chris, calling Tiffany's bluff.

"I didn't say it was. I said I'm passing yours on the way to mine, and you know what?"

"Let me guess. Adults can take whatever route home that they want to."

"Yay! You catch on fast, Christopher."

"What did you just call me?"

"You said don't call you Mr. Cringle, and everyone else calls you Chris. I like to be original."

"You're original alright," Chris replied, walking out.

The two chatted nonstop on the way back. The walk took much longer than it felt because the closer they got, the slower they walked. The subconscious behavior was triggered by an internal desire for the talk to continue. Finally, at his door, Chris bid his drinking buddy goodbye. "You really are a special girl. You'll make someone a good wife one day," he said.

"Awww. Thanks," she said, reaching for a hug. It lasted longer than required. Neither really wanted to let go.

"Enough of that," said Chris, pulling himself free.

"Can I use your restroom really quick?" asked Tiffany.

Chris was suspicious. "Can't you hold it until you get home?"

"No. This alcohol is really running through me. I have to go bad, and it's a long walk."

He was hesitant but relented. "Fine. The guest bathroom is over there. I'm going to shower. You can leave when you're done."

"OK, thanks. I'll be quick," said Tiffany, speed-walking away.

The shower was a godsend. Stressors cascaded from Chris' brown sugar skin and down the drain along with suds and water. He emerged a little more sober and better for it. Now alone, he felt no cause to overdress.

Boxer briefs were sufficient enough. Shredded quads pressed out on the breathable fabric, free from restriction.

Before bed, Chris made a detour to ensure that Tiffany had locked the door behind her. He was relieved that she hadn't stayed, although he did leave the door of the master bath open, in case she did—a sign of a conflicted mind. The lock of the front door clicked as Chris engaged it. He turned around to find that the wrong wish had come true.

"Oh, my bad. I thought you had already left," he said to Tiffany.

"I can, if you still want me to."

Chris found words that were most honest. "I don't, but you should."

Tiffany rubbed her hands down the center of Chris' chest, then through the crevasses of his statuesque abdominals. The tingle of her fingertips caused him to clench, bulging them like golden loaves of fresh-baked bread. "I don't wanna go," she said.

"You should, more for you than me. I'm not good with love. I hurt women. You don't deserve a man like me."

"I'm a big girl. I can handle myself. And maybe if you had a woman that checked every box, you wouldn't wander." The first time they locked lips was charged and fervent.

"One condition," said Tiffany, licking the side of Chris' neck. "I don't need you to make love to me. I need you to fuck me like it's the end of the world because it is."

The couch rocked when their entangled bodies crashed on top. Chris flung away the decorative pillows as Tiffany scrambled to kick off her heels and slip out of her dress. Underneath was a black, lace, two-piece with red trim. Her boy-short bottoms permitted her true figure to take center stage. Chris took a moment to admire her delectable allure.

"Custom design. I made it just for you," said Tiffany, flaunting her entirety.

"Looks good on you," he complimented.

"It'll look better on the floor."

"One way to find out." Chris watched her do away

with them.

Tiffany's high-pitched moan was enough to induce shivers as Chris made her fruit his dessert. She palmed his head and dug her painted nails into the cushions. Appetite appeased, Chris slid safe into home. He drilled deep into Mother Earth, fulfilling Tiffany's one stipulation. There was no love involved, only pure satisfaction.

Her clenching told plenty. She was past her second orgasm. Her pushing told more. She was in sweet pain. Escape was too easy, so Chris adopted a new approach. He turned her face down and found his way back to home plate. Tiffany's wails were louder. The more they were so, the further it energized Chris. He was on a mission: seek and destroy at the command of his master. The grip on Tiffany's waist was firm, nearly unbreakable. When she attempted to flee, Chris would reign her in again. At last, able to shed custody, Tiffany flipped over the arm of the couch.

"Where you goin'?" Chris asked, breathing heavily.

Tiffany was breathing harder. "Just catching my breath, that's all," she replied.

Chris made a beeline to reengage. Tiffany held up her finger in a gesture to plead for more time but was denied the luxury. Before she knew it, her legs tied around his waist, and her back met the wall. No mercy was desired, and none was shown, nor would it be for as long as both parties could hold out.

***

Just next door, Rose was enjoying her first private time with Justin. She had invited him over after parting ways to handle hygienic duties.

"Right there, right there!" Rose instructed him. She groaned, tilting her head back in complete euphoria. Justin adjusted the pressure to focus deep into her soft tissue.

"Ahhhhh," Rose softly moaned as the tension evaporated from the arch of her foot.

"I'm glad one of us is enjoying this," Justin said. "My fingers are killing me."

"Less talking, more rubbing."

Justin eased from arch to heel, then stroked from calf to thigh, then on to the border below her gray cotton shorts. The gentle touch introduced Rose to sensations she didn't know existed. A brush of the lips was the next natural step, also the first of its kind for her. She did what felt like instinct, quickly graduating from a peck on the lips to one of the French sort.

Rose's hands found the small of Justin's back, slipping underneath his shirt. The muscles flanking each side of his spine felt like iron posts. Before she knew it, her legs hooked around his hip. It was beyond her control.

Things were escalating quickly. Rose's top was gone, then her bottoms kept them company. Visions like this had evaded Justin's imagination. Rose lay before him, a platter of perfected woman that couldn't be drawn up by the most creative of artists. Her bikini-styled panties were sheer everywhere but her most sensitive area, permitting the curviest parts of her hips to be appreciated. Her silky skin glowed in the light, only interrupted by her matching, angel white brassiere. It also did its best to leave most of her uncovered, aside from her most privates.

Rose and Justin tried to focus on the movie, but the noises next door kept breaking through the thin walls. Every now and then, they exchanged amused glances, both shaking their heads at the over-the-top sound effects from Chris and Tiffany's "activities." "Man, they're not even trying to be quiet," Justin commented with a chuckle. "Seriously. It's like they don't care who hears," Rose added, laughing despite herself. She leaned back on the couch and sighed, trying to block out the noise by munching on more popcorn.

"I bet you never imagined this when you invited me over," Justin teased, nudging her with his elbow. "Not even close," Rose replied, rolling her eyes playfully. "But I guess every family's got its quirks." Justin smirked. "Yeah, but this one takes the cake." After a while, the sounds started to die down, and the movie finally regained their attention. The awkwardness of the moment was fading, replaced by the comfort of each other's company. Though their earlier moment had been intense, both were now settled, finding a rhythm that was comfortable   and   warm. "You know," Rose said, breaking the silence, "for all their craziness, they're still my family."

14

Boom

Being underground so much was at times disorienting. Half the time, no one could tell day from night, without checking the time. Yesha, along with her team of engineers and architects, had come up with a creative solution. Six inch diameter tubes were built in each room, reaching from the roof to the surface, allowing natural light to travel down. This gave some semblance of time awareness.

Piles of illumination trickled down into the bedroom, peppering Chris and Tiffany with circular spots of warmth. Her head rested on his chest. She could feel the steady thump of his heart. "How long have you been up?" she asked, turning just enough to see that Chris' eyes were wide open.

"Pretty much all night."

Tiffany rubbed his chest, then laid her head back down. "What are you thinking about?"

Chris exhaled after a deep breath. "About everything you said yesterday."

"I said a lot of things yesterday."

"I'm not sure if I jump woman to woman because

I'm searching for some perfect blend of something, or simply because I'm selfish."

"A selfish person wouldn't care to wonder why, now would they?"

Chris tangled his fingers in Tiffany's hair. "Guess not," he replied.

"Is that all you were thinking about?"

"Yesha and Ari too. Every decision I make affects them."

"It's good that you're considering the happiness of the people you care about, but that street works two ways. You should have a serious discussion with Yesha. Find out if you and your daughter are number one, or her work. If it's the latter, that's when your choice gets easier. At the end of it all, happiness in a relationship is a shared responsibility. Unless, you don't mind spending the rest of your life with someone, knowing you're not the focus of their world."

"That advice would have been a lot better coming from you before last night."

"Before last night, you wouldn't have taken me seriously enough to listen."

"You sure you're only twenty-one?" Chris interrogated.

"As sure as anything is possible nowadays." Tiffany sat up on the bed, adjusting the waistband of her translucent lingerie to a more comfortable position. "Let's do an exercise," she suggested.

"I'm not exactly in the mood for more sex."

"A mental exercise silly."

"Do I have a choice?"

"You always have a choice."

Chris couldn't think of an excuse. "Fine."

"How many women do you think you've been with?" Tiffany asked, very directly.

Chris leaned up on his elbows. "Is that a serious question?"

"I'm trying to help you, not judge you. Just play ball. You'll see where I'm going with this."

Chris scratched his chin, thinking. "That's not really

possible to answer honestly. I went through a phase of women and alcohol after my first love died."

"Of those you can remember, think of the ones that stand out, then focus on the best and worst traits of each of them."

Chris checked his memories. Bethany was her own woman, capable of being a full partner in every aspect of life, but lived the dangerous life of a soldier, which led her to pay the ultimate price. Melissa was unapologetically confident in who she was, but at times lacked tenderness and could lack creativity in bed. On the contrary, Lola was gorgeous and an animal in bed, but out of her mind. Yesha was intelligent and sweet, but a workaholic and Sasha was never his. What happened between them was a big mistake.

Tiffany consolidated Chris' dream woman. "So your heart desires a sweet, beautiful woman that is all your own. She's balanced; independent enough to take care of herself, but not to the detriment of your relationship. She's self-confident and clinically sane, but also a complete freak and wise enough to help you find out what exactly you want in a woman," she concluded, obviously angling for herself at the end of her summary. "Doesn't seem too unreasonable. You just have to wait for her and stop settling for the person that just happens to show interest in you at the time."

Again, Tiffany had outpaced Chris' expectations, but he had a question for her. "Have you done this already?" he asked.

"Yep. Sure did," she replied.

"And?"

"Well... My dream guy is a strong, black man that carries himself like a king. He's ambitious and a natural leader. Firm when he needs to be, but soft when it's necessary. He has to speak his mind and always take care of his responsibilities, even those created from mistakes. Most importantly, he has to have taken a carpentry course, because I need the wood laid regularly," Tiffany explained.

"Oh, you do huh?" Chris suggestively retorted.

Tiffany mounted his abdomen, groping his gaudy

undercarriage. "I am an F-R-E-A-K," she spelled out. "Wouldn't be wise to be with a man who doesn't give me what I need."

Chris gripped her tiny waistline, working her underwear lower.

"Nope," Tiffany denied, smacking his hands away. "Another one of my biggest desires is honesty. You don't get anymore of this until you figure out if you're going to settle, or if you're going to dream. You should also tell her everything, if you want to break this cycle."

"If I choose you, what would people say?" Chris worried.

"Why do you care? I don't."

Tiffany was about to get up to get dressed and leave, when the bedroom door flung open.

"You piece of shit!" Yesha shouted.

Tiffany rolled off of Chris and covered herself with the bed sheet. "What a minute Yesha," he yelled out.

"Don't talk to me! I'm taking Ari and we're moving to another colony. Don't you dare try to find us," she replied, storming out. Chris fumbled through his drawer, trying to get dressed.

"Well, if you were going to tell her, you don't have to now," said Tiffany.

"Don't do that. Either way, I wouldn't have wanted her to find out like this." Chris trudged out of the door with his shirt in his hand, still trying to jam the second shoe on his foot. His belt jingled, not yet buckled.

When he made it out into the hallway, Rose was standing in her doorway with Justin. "What the hell is going on?" she asked. "Did you see which way Yesha went?" he replied, slipping his shirt on.

"That way," Rose pointed. "Looked like her and Ari were headed outside and they were moving pretty quick. You two arguing again? We heard y'all nasty selves making up last night."

Tiffany stepped out, trying to see what was going on, still dressed in only her women's private wear. She dragged the bed sheet out with her, attempting to cover her body, but failing, as she stepped on the trailing section pulling it down.

"Oooowweee!" Rose exclaimed, seeing her new buddy only two steps from nude, coming out Chris' doorway. "You little skank. That was you last night?" She wasn't angry at all, but actually rather amused.

"What? You told me to go for it," Tiffany replied.

"I was being sarcastic. I didn't think you actually would... I didn't think he actually would."

Passing Rose's door, Chris' peripheral vision kicked in. "What the hell is he doing here this early? Did he spend the night with you?" he asked, freezing in his tracks.

"Are you really on my case after you just got caught ramming my best friend?"

"I'm your best friend? Yay, I have a best friend," said Tiffany.

"Best friend? You've known the girl for two days," Chris pointed out.

"So! I'm making up for all these years without one. Mind your business anyway. As a matter of fact, you'd better catch up with your business, before she leaves with your kid," Rose advised.

"Shit," Chris grunted. He ran down the hall, yelling at Rose, "I'm killing you and that boy when I get back!"

"We didn't even do anything," Rose pouted.

"Speak for yourself," said Justin, wagging his tongue around.

Rose whacked him in the chest. "Shut up," she demanded.

"Ouch. I'm already gonna die. At least I'll die a happy man though."

Tiffany caught every bit of the back-and-forth banter. She gasped, covering her mouth. "You didn't!"

"Relax," Rose whispered, checking if they were alone. "Nothing happened. I made him stop."

"Nope. I'm not buying it. I know what I just heard."

"Seriously." Rose glanced around again, then whispered, "He only licked it a little."

Tiffany broke into hysterical laughter.

Chris made it to the surface, but he wasn't alone. Sasha and Cory saw him speeding down the corridor and followed to see what was happening. Rose and Justin had also let their curiosity draw them outside.

Chris finally caught up to Yesha. "Will you give me a second?"

"What can you say to me, huh? What could possibly be a good enough excuse for sleeping with her?"

Sasha was overcome with grief. "It's not all his fault. We drank too much and didn't know what we were doing," she said defensively, unaware that Yesha was actually pointing at Tiffany, who had arrived and was standing behind her.

"What are you talking about?" Yesha questioned.

Rose covered her mouth to keep it from hitting the ground. "Oh my God! You didn't!"

"Mom, you didn't!" said Cory, equally as mortified as Rose.

Chris threw his arms up, defeated. "Not you, Sasha. She wasn't talking about you."

"Daddy!" exclaimed Ari, filled with disappointment.

"Ohhhh. She's the one that wasn't supposed to happen," Tiffany mumbled to herself.

"None of you are helping!" Chris shouted.

Yesha wept, "Her I understand. She doesn't owe me any loyalty, but I can't believe either of you would do this to me."

"Quiet," Chris yelled.

"Are you seriously telling me to shut up, you asshole? You know what? I'm leaving."

"I hear it too," said Rose. "What do you think it is?"

The sky parted with familiar cracks of electric bursts. Before anyone could react, ballistic missiles rained from portals between the clouds. Violent impacts sent seismic ripples through the earth, toppling everyone over. Chris and Rose made an effort to redirect as many of the bombs as they could, using their own abilities, but there were too many.

"It's Lola!" Sasha screamed. "Everybody get back inside!"

The emergency siren's distinct wail sounded. There was a mad scramble to retreat underground. Above ground turrets returned fire, but there wasn't an actual target to aim for. The shooters just pointed for the sky and held down the triggers.

Chris froze the time, so that he and Rose could corral their friends and family to safety. He was floored to find it instantly reversed. He asked himself if Lola had become that powerful, but didn't have time to reason. Yesha and Ari were huddled together, too shocked to move. Chris made a dash to save them, but quickly realized that running wouldn't be enough.

Strategy shifted to magical means. Chris blew open a portal behind them, then manipulated the space ahead to kick them through. A missile hit the dirt a short distance off, sending fire and shrapnel in all directions. Chris closed the portal hurriedly, to prevent any from following them in, simultaneously creating them an exit within his reach.

He was horrified, as they fell through, knocking him on his back. A stray piece of metal had gotten through. It sheared Yesha's head cleanly from her body. Chris sucked in air to scream her name, but never succeeded. Another explosion turned his lights out.

15

Bet You Didn't Expect This

It was completely dark. The only sliver of light came from the part of the burlap sack around the neck area. "On your knees," said a man, kicking Chris in the back of his knee. Lack of knowledge of the situation he was in was the only thing that prevented Chris from attempting escape. As soon as he could figure things out, he would adjust his tactics accordingly.

"You too," said another voice. The statement informed Chris that he wasn't alone, making things far more delicate. The hood was ripped from his head, revealing that his assumption was correct. He wasn't alone. Rose, Cory, and Ari were all kneeling at his side, with their hands zip-tied behind them.

Further observation uncovered a grim setting. They were being held in a gigantic sewage drain pipe. Contaminated water soaked their pants from the knees down, running through a metal grate at the end. It would be an understatement to say that the odor was repulsive.

"I missed you so much, bae," said Lola.

Chris cringed at the sound of her voice. "I missed you too," he replied.

His children looked at him, disgusted.

Lola kissed him, and he kissed back. "If you missed me so much, then why didn't you come to find me?" she asked.

"I thought you were dead. No one should have survived that crash."

"I thought you were dead too. Well, not at first. When I found out that you passed your gifts to us and that's what saved our lives, I thought you might be alive too. I searched for a long time. After a while, I gave up. Can you imagine the joy when I found out you were alive all along?" Lola's smile morphed into a deranged scowl. "Until I found out you were with that bitch, Sasha."

"What did you do to my mom?" yelled Cory, concerned for her safety.

Lola paced back and forth as she spoke. Her four guards stood watch. "I tried to kill her. Slippery rat got away again. Got the other little whore, though," she said.

"You did what?" Chris questioned.

"Do you think I'm stupid? That one's your daughter," said Lola, singling out Ari. "She has that same stupid nose, and I can smell your blood in her. What I can't figure out is how our beloved friend Candy's daughter got it. You fucked her and got her pregnant too?" Lola aimed her gun at the front of Rose's head.

"No! It was a blood transfusion," Chris explained, sure that Lola would kill Rose if she thought he had any sexual past with her. "She almost died, and I gave her my blood. That's how she got it."

"Hmph. Blood transfusion. I guess that makes sense," Lola reapplied the safety on her weapon. "What's your daughter's name?" she asked Chris.

"She has nothing to do with this. None of them do. I'm who you want. You already have me, so let them go home."

"Answer the question, unless you want to see her head lopped off like her mother's."

"I'm going to kill you!" Ari vowed, struggling to free herself. Her anger swelled, drawing on a power that she had no control of. Her eyes began to glow, but suddenly her body seized, falling over like a wooden board.

"Ari!" Chris cried out. "What's wrong with her?"

"Relax, drama king. She'll be OK. Just a little shock from those things on your wrists. Any of you try to use your powers and you'll get a good jolt. Wouldn't advise you to try and remove them either. It'll take your arm off."

Chris scooted on his knees to Ari's side.

"Don't touch me!" she yelled, tears streaming. "It's your fault Mom is dead. You did this."

Lola was eager to correct her. "Actually, it's my fault. Couldn't let her live after she fucked my man. Today, tomorrow... I would have gotten her eventually." Seeing confusion across their faces, Lola laughed louder. "You didn't think that was a random piece of metal, did you? You were trying so hard to save her. Almost did too, but nothing a little nudge can't fix." She waved her hand, lifting Ari back to her knees, with that same skill she used to fling the steel sheet that ended Yesha's life.

"Ahhhh!" Ari screamed out. Her body seized again, but this time she willed herself to remain upright.

"Wow, bae. She's got your willpower for sure. I see potential in her. She might not have to die today. Our daughter might like the idea of meeting her sister anyway."

"We were having a son. I saw the ultrasounds myself," Chris reasoned.

"I've learned a lot since we've been apart. One of those things is how wonky time travel is. Somewhere on our way here, things got mixed up. You should have seen my face when Courtney was born."

"On our way here? What are you talking about?"

Lola grabbed Chris by the chin. "You really don't know anything, do you?" she asked, looking into his eyes for possible deceit. She saw none. "When you interfered with the LOGOS during takeoff, like an idiot, you fried the computers. We skipped across the universe and made it to Atlas in less than a second. Problem was, we came out of space travel in the middle of the atmosphere. The ship spun out of control and crashed."

"If that was true, we wouldn't be here on Earth."

"There isn't a difference, smart ass!" Lola yelled.

"Atlas is Earth."

"What? Atlas is in a whole different galaxy."

"Nooo, it isn't. Things aren't always what they look like from far away. There is no Andromeda. There is no Atlas. Our telescopes looked through space, but we learned that space is one with what?" Lola held her hand out, with body language that signaled Chris to fill in the blank.

"Time."

"Bingo! Tell him what he's won, boys," Lola said to no one. "He's won an explanation. We were, in actuality, looking at ourselves in the future."

"Atlas had a purple-looking atmosphere, and Andromeda is way bigger than the Milky Way," Chris pointed out.

"Ever heard of red shift? Red plus blue equals what?"

"Purple," Chris mumbled. "That still doesn't explain the size of the galaxy and position of stars."

"Eh. That's boring stuff. Distortion, a single plane of reality splitting off into multiples, everything that can happen does happen, yada yada yada. Simply put, we knocked the planet off its course, shot across the universe, and arrived five years into one of an infinite possible futures."

"That accounts for that memory gap," said Cory.

"Sash and Scottie's. The only one of us here with pure muggle blood," said Lola.

"What about them?" Cory challenged, referring to her guards.

"Them? Oh, they're nobodies. You, on the other hand, are today's sacrificial lamb."

"Lola, just send them home. They're kids," Chris begged.

"So you can ruin everything like last time? No. I don't trust you anymore. But, you are about to have your chance to earn it."

Rose was brewing. "I'm going to kill you. Even if I have to come back from the dead to do it," she threatened.

"Be quiet, Rose," said Chris, trying to keep control

of the situation.

"You don't tell me what to do! If you wouldn't have been banging everybody, we wouldn't be in this situation."

"You just lost your virginity to a boy you've known for two days, if you were even one to begin with. You and Cory make me wonder sometimes," Chris argued.

Cory was angry. "What the hell did you just say?"

"You heard me. It's not like you're real brother and sister."

"So, you destroy the planet fucking this psychotic bitch, screw his mom, my friend, then you think you have a right to talk to us like this?" Rose contended.

"A couple more years, and I would have fucked you too, you ungrateful slut," Chris shouted venomously.

Rose tried to overpower her suppressing unit, but it shocked her to the ground.

"That's what you deserve," Chris stated.

Ari was appalled. "Who are you?" she asked. "You're not the father in my memories."

Chris was seething with hatred. "Exactly. That dude lives in another dimension. I don't even know you. You're just some little strange girl, and these fake memories don't change any of that. I'm just glad Lola found me and showed me how useless all of you are to me," he divulged. "Cut me loose and give me a gun," he demanded of Lola.

"Why would I..."

"That wasn't a fucking suggestion. You're the one that wants me to earn your trust. Give me a damn gun and cut me loose," Chris repeated, cutting Lola off.

At first, she hesitated, but then nodded for one of her men to do so. "If you try something stupid, they all die," she reaffirmed.

Chris rubbed his tender wrists and stood up. "Gimme that," he said, snatching the pistol from the guard's hand. "I'm sick of following everybody else's rules and getting treated like shit for it, but you don't have to kill them. They're already dead." The gun flared two times as Chris blasted a single hole in the center of Rose's and Cory's foreheads. Their lifeless bodies thudded against the concrete tube.

Ari howled, full of despair. She laid down on Cory's remains and curled her knees to her stomach.

"Stop your whining," Chris told her. "We're going to get this soft shit out of your system real quick." The barrel was still smoking as he spoke. "You two. Take my daughter to a free room and make sure she doesn't leave," he commanded Lola's men.

They didn't move.

"Give me your helmet," he said to another of them.

He didn't move either.

Chris punched him in the stomach and yanked off his helmet. A shot through his eardrum finished the job. "Do what the hell I said, or both of you are laying down beside them!" he shouted.

The remaining men hustled to do as he bid.

"Let me go!" Ari struggled as they carried her off by the arms.

"If she loses a single hair on her head, I'll gouge your eyes out," Chris warned them, tucking the gun in the small of his back.

Lola clung to his arm. "That was dramatic," she said.

Chris responded with a loving embrace. Lola stood on her tiptoes, but still, her head rested on his chest, a side effect of her short stature. "Take me home, then get naked," he hunched over and spoke into her ear.

"What about them?" Lola asked.

Chris released her and gazed back at the bodies of Rose and Cory. "What about them?" he said.

16

Never Good Without A Plan B

Chris walked out of the shower, patting his shirtless torso dry. In the process of waiting on his return, Lola had dozed off, sprawled completely naked across the bed. Her state informed Chris that he had done his job, but he had to be sure that he had done so thoroughly. Lola's eyes sprang wide open. She groaned as Chris got straight back to work.

"Wait, wait, wait!" she laughed, attempting to backpedal away. "You're cheating. I'm not ready."

Chris attempted to keep at his job, but suddenly Tiffany popped into his mind. "You're not getting any more of this, until you break the cycle," her voice said.

"Why'd you stop?" asked Lola. "I don't need your damn pity. I need your dick."

Chris shook the thought from his head. "You're the one whining. Shut up and take it, or put your mouth to use some other way," he said. Speaking so brash was uncomfortable for him, but he had to get used to it if he was going to keep Lola under his spell.

The war raged on until Lola tapped out, knowing she would have difficulty moving around pain-free the following day. This time, her heavy snoring signified complete exhaustion. Chris quietly began to get dressed. A wall mirror caught his attention and drew him in. He gawked into his own eyes, seeing through to his soul. Things had come full circle. Chris' strength had been born from powers through a glass mirror, but he could barely stand to look at himself within one.

A revelation came to him in that moment. The man beheld in his reflection was what he'd permitted himself to become. An addict, reliant on sex and alcohol. His vices had run amok, first inside of him, then spilling out for everyone else to witness. Things that were meaningless in the bigger scheme of life had destroyed it all. "Today we man up," Chris said to himself.

***

Word quickly spread through the ranks of Lola's army that Chris was in charge and more volatile than she, due to Chris' prior actions. This allowed him to creep out of Lola's abode and move freely. Sewage water sloshed around, agitated by his feet. Soon the bodies of his children came into view. "God, this has to work," he prayed.

Without time to waste, Chris dragged Rose and Cory to a dryer portion of the tunnel. He saw clumps of who knows what in Rose's hair. "Aw man, she's going to kill me for that," he grumbled. Holding his hands over the wounds of their heads, Chris summoned lightning from his fingers, as he focused his control on the bullet-sized pockets of space and time. The bolts of electricity stabilized into tangible strings, extending from hand to mortal injuries.

Chris got up slowly, intent on keeping focus. The energy-packed threads stretched longer as he clenched onto them like rope in hand. Finishing his maneuver would require a free hand. Chris moved his right over to his left, combining the tips of energy together. With his newly liberated appendages, his gun was now accessible. He retrieved it, then aimed it down at the corpses of his beloveds.

After a deep breath, Chris slammed the electrified current into the barrel of his weapon. The spent ammunition shot in reverse, back down the rifling. One by one, both empty shells sprang up from the ground, returning through the ejection port, becoming whole again.

Rose and Cory popped up into a seated position, sucking in lungfuls of air. They coughed, then vomited from inhalation of the disgusting fumes. Chris shook his fists to the sky, thankful for success. "I'm so glad to see you guys," he said, attacking them for a group hug.

They both stood up, gawking around, stupefied.

"Did you shoot us? You fucking shot us!" shouted Rose, pounding away at Chris, like she had reverted to the fighting style of a toddler. Frustrated with him slapping her fists away, she kicked him in the shin.

"Ow!" he screeched. "I had to. It was the only way to earn her trust."

"It was actually genius," Cory admitted, after running the logic through his gifted mind.

"Don't you dare take his side!" Rose scowled. "Don't you remember all the shit he said before he shot us?"

"It was obviously part of his plan."

"I had to make her believe I hated you guys. If I just shot you for no reason, she would have been suspicious. You really think I would try to hurt you?"

"You didn't shoot Ari in the face. Just us rejects. She's your real daughter. I see the way you look at her. You don't look at me like that anymore. You haven't for a long time," Rose argued emotionally. She started to tear up.

"I don't give a damn about paternity. Do you think I would hound you the way I do if I didn't love you? You're right, I don't look at you the same. I look at you as a woman, cause that's what you ask of me, but anytime you need to be my little girl, I'll drop anything for you."

Rose wept like she hadn't since she was an emotional teenage kid. Chris' shoulder was right there to lend her support. Cory joined in, and they held one another a while.

"We love our families and spouses for what they give, or what they do. We love our parents for raising us. We love our children because they exist. Before you guys found me, I was lost without a real reason to live. You gave me purpose again. I will die loving you both. I promise I'll do better. No more alcohol. No more women. I'm going to be someone you'll be proud to call your father," Chris reassured them.

Rose's cries subsided to whimpers, her whimpers to calm. "You still shot us in the face," she joked.

"I unshot you, didn't I? So, actually, it never happened."

"What's the plan?" asked Cory. "I know you wouldn't have come until you had one."

"It's simple actually. Rose, you're going to port back to Project 002. You'll find Sasha to assemble an assault team, the biggest you can get, then port everyone just out of view of this facility at exactly this time tomorrow. Cory, you'll need to draw on everything I've ever taught you. You have to be a ghost. I need you to disable every bit of artillery, anti-aircraft guns, and whatever other heavy munitions they have defending this place, without alerting anyone. After that, get into their armory and blow the entire thing up. Without the big guns, they'll be vulnerable. We take the facility, then use the equipment to fix the planet." Chris pulled out a map for Cory. "Here's a map. I snuck it out of Lola's room. Set a timed detonation. Whatever you need to get the job done should be in the armory. Get here before it blows." Chris pointed to the map.

Cory noted where his finger signaled. "Food storage? Why there?"

"Nobody is thinking about a tuna melt after an explosion," Chris argued. "You have to get there no matter what, or you're probably dead. You don't have my blood, so I can't locate you."

"You got that map from her room?" Rose interrogated.

"Look, I'm doing my part to save the world. If that requires me to sacrifice my body for the greater good, then that's what I have to do."

"Sounds like he's changing to me," Cory commented.

"I am. I swear. Once we do this, I'll be a faithful man." Chris gestured a cross on his chest.

"Wait, how am I supposed to port out of here with this thing on my wrist?" asked Rose.

Chris flashed his empty arm.

"How'd you get it off?"

"It's actually genius. She designed it so that only a jolt of our kind of energy from outside the band can unlock it. Since all of us had them on, none of us could take them off, except her. I swayed her to take mine off."

"How would you have done that, I wonder?" Cory was insinuating more indiscretions committed by Chris.

"Hey, don't get mad cause your daddy can lay some pipe. You pickin' up what I'm puttin' down?"

Rose cringed. "Ew! You are so disgusting."

"Just give me your hand, so we can do this."

Chris zapped the wrist piece, and it disengaged, falling into his hand. "One last thing," he said. "That uniform's for you, Cory. It'll allow you to move around easier."

"You want me to strip a dead man naked and wear his shit-covered suit?"

"Boy, if you don't stop cursing and put on the damn suit and do your job, I'll shoot you again."

"Shall we work?" Cory replied.

"Let's work," said Rose, ripping open a portal and vanishing into the darkness.

***

Lola woke up, relieved that Chris was still sleeping at her side. She grabbed her robe and headed for the shower. "Hey, bae," she called out.

"Yeah?" Chris replied.

"Come join me. I need you to wash my back."

Chris mimed frustration, smacking his palm against his forehead. "I just want to lay down," he said, attempting to avoid another sexual encounter with Lola. As loco as she might be, she was still extraordinarily beautiful, and equally as gifted using her body. Getting in a shower with her was not a good way to prevent doing so.

"Stop being a pussy and come on!"

"I could really use an assist on this one, Lore," Chris whispered to the sky. Just as he spoke, there was a knock at the door. "Thank you!" Chris mimed, before yelling, "I have to get the door," to Lola.

"To hell with them. They can wait!"

Chris ignored her and opened the door.

"Your daughter wants to see you, sir," said one of the guards he had placed on Ari's detail.

"It's my daughter. She wants to see me. I'll be back," Chris yelled to Lola.

"You know you have another daughter, right?"

"You can take me to see her when I get back."

"Fine. Hurry up," Lola said, impatiently.

The guard walked Chris to a nearby room and unlocked the door to let him inside. "Leave us alone," Chris ordered him.

Ari sat on the bed, weeping with her knees to her chest.

"Aw, Baby Girl. Come here, don't cry," said Chris, attempting to comfort her.

"Don't touch me!" Ari shouted. "You're a monster. I just want you to let me go home, then I won't be your problem anymore."

"It's not what you think."

"What I think? You practically told me I'm not your daughter. You killed Rose and Cory right in my face! That's not what I think. I saw it with my own eyes. Then, you just locked me in here like an animal."

"Rose and Cory aren't dead," Chris whispered.

Ari wiped her eyes on her sleeve, but the tears kept on running. "What are you saying? You shot them in the head and left them there."

"Keep your voice down," said Chris. "Rose is back at 002 with Sasha and Cory is handling something for me. Later tonight, we're taking over the place so that we can fix everything."

"You're lying. That's not possible."

"Have you seen what we're able to do? Nothing is impossible. Everything that happened in that sewer was a decoy to get Lola to trust me. I went back and reversed what I did, then sent them on missions."

"What about what you said to me and what you did to Mom with Sasha and that girl?"

"Sasha and I made a mistake, which is why people shouldn't drink the way we did." Chris looked at the floor, embarrassed to say what he was about to, but he thought honesty was best for starting over. "As for Tiffany, I have to admit that I knew exactly what I was doing. Your mother neglected me, both in this life and the other. I wasn't happy. Tiffany gave me what I needed, and I'm not talking about sex. That was more of a side effect. What I said to you last night was all for show. You're my Baby Girl and I love you with everything I've got. Our memories are the most precious gift a father could have."

Ari was young, but not stupid or blind. "I could always see the sadness in your face, even as a little kid. I felt that same sadness because she wasn't there for me much either. Always put her work first, but she's my mom and I miss her." Ari broke down, sobbing inconsolably. The image of her decapitated mother was seared into her brain for all eternity.

Chris sat on the bed and coddled the hurt of his baby. "I know, Baby Girl, I know. I'm sorry. I'm so sorry. Daddy's not going anywhere. You just get some rest. I'll still be here when you wake up," he promised.

Ari laid on his broad shoulders, closed her eyes, and cried herself to sleep.

***

Barely an hour passed before Lola opened the door. She cleared her throat loudly, accomplishing her goal of waking Chris and Ari.

"What are you doing?" she asked him.

"Sleeping. What does it look like?"

"You said you were coming right back."

"Well, I lied. You have a problem with that?"

Lola poked out her lip. "Whatever, let's go," she ordered.

"Why are you rushing me? I'm not going anywhere. I live here now, remember?" Chris combatively stated.

"It's fine, Daddy. You can go," said Ari, trying to be helpful.

"You sure?"

"Yeah. Do what you have to."

Chris used a hug to disguise a message. "Don't leave this room until I personally come to get you, no matter what you hear outside that door," he instructed.

After a kiss goodbye, Chris headed for the door.

"You didn't kiss your other daughter goodbye, you bastard," said Lola.

"Don't do that," Chris argued. "I didn't even know I had another daughter until yesterday."

"If you didn't blow up the damn ship, you would've been here with her."

The two argued out the door and down the hall.

17

Do You Love Me Or No?

The outside of this particular door was unique, compared to the rest throughout the building. It was wooden with intricate carvings and paintings on the outer surface. The engravings seemed to tell a story of the life of an angel.

"Well, open the door, stupid," said Lola.

Chris picked her up and held her upside down. "Who's stupid now?" he said.

Lola struggled to get free. "Boy, put me down before I hurt you," she threatened.

The door opened. The girl standing in the frame was much taller than Lola, only a few inches shy of Chris. She shared his bronze skin, full lips, and distinct nose.

"What are you doing?" she asked, annoyance written all over her voice.

Lola was still upside down but stopped squirming to tell her, "Oh, this is—"

"My father. I know," Courtney interrupted. "I could sense him the moment you brought him in the building last night." She walked back to her room, leaving the door open.

Chris returned Lola to her feet and eased his way in. She attempted to follow him in, but he cut her short. "I need to do this alone," he said, his voice filled with gravel.

Lola knew this usually happened when Chris was at his most serious. "OK, I'll be back later," she responded.

Chris closed the door behind himself. He admired Courtney's room. It was excessively neat. Everything from the remote control to writing utensils was squared away with the edges of the tables upon which they sat. The walls were decorated with several beautiful paintings. They ranged from the abstract to landscapes and portraits.

"You did all these?" Chris asked, peeping a box of expensive paper on a desk in the far corner.

"Yeah," Courtney replied. "They're my favorites. I think my latest is the best though."

"Can I see?"

Courtney stepped to her easel and removed the protective tapestry over the top. The piece was unbelievable. There must have been a million shades of blue. Every stroke was with random purpose. Dark shapes blended with light bands to form the distinct features of a face.

"That's me," Chris said.

"Yes."

"When did you do this?"

"Yesterday, when you got here."

Chris was astonished. "How did you know what I looked like?" he questioned.

"The air told me. I just felt the difference between the molecules touching your face."

This further stunned Chris. "You did what?"

Fearing that Chris would think she was an oddball, Courtney explained why she was the way she was. "Mom makes me practice a lot. My earliest memories are of her pushing me to squeeze out as much as she could from my abilities."

"That how you knew who I was?"

"Yes. I can feel the power in you. It's pure, unlike the rest of ours. You're the original."

"That may be true, but I never dreamed of being

able to do the things that you can do."

"I can feel her too. She's my sister, right?"

"Ari? Yeah."

"She feels sweet."

"She is."

"She also feels sad."

"She just lost her mother."

Courtney took a seat on her bed. "I hate her," she said.

"What?"

"Lola."

"But, that's your mother."

"And I love her for that, but I hate her for what she is," Courtney reasoned. There was a brief, awkward silence.

"She told me stories about you," she continued.

"What kind of stories?"

"She said that you were the love of her life. You were the only man she'd ever been with and would ever be with. Sometimes she would get angry though. When she got angry at you, she'd curse at me and send me away for looking like you." Courtney looked deep into Chris' eyes. "So, which stories are true? The good or the bad?"

"A bit of both, I'm afraid. There's a lot of things to discuss about your mother, and we will one day, but I don't think now's the time to get into that."

Courtney began to lose the battle of holding back her tears.

"What's wrong?" Chris asked.

The young woman struggled to get her words out, finally asking, "Do you love me?"

"Of course I do," Chris reassured her. "Why would you ask a question like that?"

"I'm not a little girl that you can just pop up and grow with. I'm just some strange woman to you. How could you love me when the people that have been around me my entire life don't?"

"Look, I know things won't be that easy for us, but you're important to me. There wasn't a day that I didn't wonder what you would have been like. I thought you were dead for a long time. It tore out a piece of my heart. Your older brother too. I'll never see him again, but the Lord has brought you back to me, and I'll do whatever I can to make up time with you."

Courtney's posture collapsed in on itself. Her heart was weighing down her shoulders. It was time to be a real father. The poor girl hadn't felt love over the span of her life and was radiating hopelessness. Chris stepped in, ready to accept his duty.

"Would it be OK if I held you?" he asked.

Courtney was still too emotional to speak, but nodded yes. Chris sat with his back against Courtney's headboard and reeled her close. She squeezed him like she feared she would never be held again. Chris could feel her sorrows evaporating away.

18

This Means War

Laughter resonated through the door and rumbled down the entire walkway. Lola popped in the door, prepared to be a sourpuss.

"What's so damn funny?" she asked.

It took an effort to get the words out, but eventually Courtney said, "Dad was telling me the story about you and your old boyfriend Turner."

"He was not my boyfriend!" Lola screamed.

"He may not have been your boyfriend, but you sure as hell were his girlfriend," Chris teased.

"Shut up! You've been in here long enough. We're leaving."

"You're going to start by lowering your voice, and then you're going to say hello to our daughter like you miss her. After that, you're going to stop talking to me like you're my boss. I'm back, and I run shit here, you got it?"

"Who told you that?" Lola combated.

"When have you ever known me to be a follower?" Chris asked her, still fully enveloped in his role. "Not ever, and you won't be the first person I follow. Now, how about you shut up while I say goodbye."

"Hurry up!" Lola yelled, sulking.

"I'll be back as soon as I can, so we can talk more. I've got to go do nasty things to your mother, so she can stop being so damn uptight," he said.

Courtney laughed. "You could've kept that information to yourself," she said.

"See you later, queen," he said affectionately. "I love you," he added, knowing how important it was for her to hear it as much as possible. His words caused Courtney to smile ear to ear.

"So damn mushy," Lola insulted. "Don't turn my daughter into a sucker like you."

"Suck these nuts. How 'bout that?"

***

"Get off! Get off!" Chris shouted.

Lola was decisive with her response. "Fuck no! I'm... I'm... Ahhhh!" she screamed.

Chris screamed with her. "Ahhhhh."

Lola fell back on the bed, an exhausted heap of woman.

"Oh God, I missed your thingamajig so much. None of the women since you've been gone compare to you."

"You expect me to believe you haven't been with a single man since the last time you were with me?"

"You can believe whatever the hell you want, but you're the only man I could ever be interested in."

"Mmhm."

"I have a question," said Lola.

The fact that Lola actually might have a good question sparked interest. "Ask it."

"Why did you try to pull out?"

Chris was caught off guard. "The question is why you didn't get your ass up. I've had enough trouble with kids. You damn sure don't need another one. There's gotta be some day-after pills around here."

"Don't I get a say?"

"Uh, no you do not," Chris replied decisively.

"You sure about that?" asked Lola, getting up to turn on the radio.

Chris laid there and stared. "What did you do that for?"

Lola stood up on top of the bed. "I'm changing your mind," she replied, dancing around.

"So, twerking like a stripper is supposed to make me want to have another kid with you?"

"Is it working?"

"Uhhh, not from that angle. Turn around and do that again."

Lola did so and put her back into it, gyrating with complete control.

"Aye, aye, aye!" Chris chanted, enjoying the show.

The thing with people is that nothing is black and white. Chris was beginning to discover that fact for himself. What we consider to be a good person isn't without evil, and those that live in harmony with Satan aren't lacking good somewhere in their heart. It wasn't clear when Lola became what she was, but Chris still loved her a great deal. No matter what, she would always be the mother of his child, and good times like this gave glimpses of who she had the potential to be, and how life could be with her.

Genuinely enjoying Lola's company, Chris forgot that he may potentially have to kill her to save everyone else. Reality returned the next instant. Everything shook violently, knocking over trinkets on tables and walls. The sound from the explosion was deafening, even from the living area clear across the facility.

"What the fuck was that?" Chris shouted, pretending to be worried.

"How the hell should I know? I'm here with you, idiot!" Lola hopped out of the bed and got dressed as fast as she could.

"Stay here," she said. "I'll see what these dumbasses did this time and telepath you if I need you. This is the second time they've blown something up this year, and if they're not dead already, I'm going to kill them." Lola walked through a portal as easily as an open doorway.

As soon as she disappeared, Chris threw on his clothes and did the same. He reappeared in the designated meeting place for him and Cory.

"Come on, kid. Where the hell are you?" Chris mumbled, searching the underground warehouse.

There were cardboard boxes stacked to the ceiling on rows of metal shelves. Chris ran up and down the aisles searching for where Cory could be hiding. At last, Cory materialized around the corner, causing Chris to react by slamming him into a cardboard case of breakfast cereal. The marshmallow pieces poured over both of their heads.

"Damn it, Cory! Why would you sneak up like that?" Chris yelled, whispering at the same time.

"What did you want me to do, call your name out loud like in the movies?"

"We don't have time to make fun of cliché movies. Let's go. Rose and Sasha should have gotten the signal and started assaulting the building by now."

Chris searched for Rose's distinct signature. Once locked on to her location, he opened a doorway for him and Cory to step through. What they walked into wasn't exactly what they were expecting. A full-scale battle, the likes of which neither of them could have dreamed up, was raging atop the ruins of what used to be the surface building of Project 001. Small arms fire accounted for much of the discord, mixed with screams, shouting, and localized explosions. Thunder boomed piercingly, not one to be outdone by mere humans.

"Cory, watch out!" Chris yelled, tackling him out of the way of a tumbling Humvee. They toppled down a slope of broken concrete into a shallow, mud-filled hole. Recovery was immediate, and it needed to be.

"Shit! I don't have a weapon," Cory announced.

Chris clotheslined a Faction soldier, who was running nearby, and caught his rifle out of midair. After popping two rounds into his head, he handed Cory the rifle.

"You cannot die, do you hear me?" Chris said to him, worried.

"I don't plan on it," he replied.

Chris hugged him tight. "I'm going to find Roe. Maybe together we can end this quickly."

With those words, the two parted ways. Chris locked on to Rose again, then dashed toward her location. He unleashed havoc on the opposition every step of the way. Bullets ricocheted at the fan of his hand as he used waves of compressed air like a deflective shield. Realizing bullets weren't working, a Faction soldier swung his rifle at Chris like a major league batter in a home run derby. Chris slid across the rain-coated mud and flung the soldier a hundred feet away.

Tens more fell at Chris' hand before he got an eye on Rose. She was levitating massive, multi-ton concrete blocks from the old building, using them as bludgeoning weapons. When one crumbled to pieces from overuse, she would pluck another from the ground and continue her slaughter.

A handheld rocket was fired in Rose's direction. Chris whipped it around, right back to the sender. The resulting explosion took out several more Factionees.

"This wasn't what we were expecting!" Rose yelled, still fighting. Her rain-soaked hair danced as she scuttled about.

"Neither was I," Chris replied. "They must have had another cache of weapons somewhere."

"What now?"

"What do you mean, what now? Kill them and don't let them kill you."

"You zig."

"You zag."

Chris and Rose moved together, a sweet symphony of grace. They had trained together almost her entire life for this kind of fight. One would open a portal, then the other would dive through. When one defended against gunfire, the other played offense.

"Where's Sash'?" Chris asked.

Rose picked up an abandoned rifle and mowed down several of the enemy. "She's somewhere around here."

"That doesn't help."

"What do you want me to do? I'm kind of in the middle of something."

Cory had managed to fight his way to Chris and Rose, but he wasn't alone. "I brought support," he said.

"We thought you were dead," said Justin.

"Not yet," Chris responded.

"Looks like we're winning," Tree pointed out.

"Don't count your chickens yet," said Chris. "Lola won't go down easy."

Patch looked to the sky. "You mean that evil-looking bitch floating in the sky?" he asked.

Lola had appeared on the battlefield, fully dressed for combat. Her one-of-a-kind red, bulletproof vest made her stand out, even against the black, rainy setting. She hovered tens of feet up, calling lightning from the sky at her bidding, flinging the charged bolts at helpless targets on the ground.

"Oh my God!" Mona exclaimed at the power Lola wielded.

Alex peered across the landscape. "There's Sasha," he said.

Unfortunately, Lola had picked her out among the sea of people as well. She wound up, preparing to make Sasha an unremarkable, black smudge on the turf.

Running was useless and porting was too imprecise. In a fraction of a second, Chris solved the mystery of flight by recalling his meeting with Director Steed. The LOGOS ship worked by compacting space ahead and expanding it behind. A sonic boom sounded with its two distinct bangs as Chris broke both the sound and light barriers at the same time. He absorbed the bolt of lightning through one hand, then redirected it back at Lola, knocking her from the sky. She crashed into one of the few pillars still standing, pounding it into powder.

"This was your goddamn plan?" Sasha ridiculed when Chris landed beside her.

"Criticize me later. We have to finish this now," he replied.

Everyone gathered around Sasha and Chris, having been guided through a portal by Rose.

"Guess the whole family's here," said Justin.

The comment racked Chris' memory. "Not

everyone. Ari's still inside," he said.

"What do you want us to do?"

Chris thought for a moment. "We can kill two birds with one stone. You guys go and get my daughter, then locate the equipment and research that we need to fix the orbit. Since Ari will be with you, I can ping your exact position and port the stuff back to 002. That'll kill the need to keep this up. Too many people are dying. Rose and I can hold things together out here."

Chris ported everyone into Ari's room, minus Rose and himself. Without warning, she was sent flying in one direction and he in the other. "I knew you couldn't be trusted," Lola said to Chris. The shock had done a great deal of damage, burning the side of her face to a charred crisp.

Nearby, Courtney had tackled Rose. The two young women were in a desperate clash to best each other in combat. Rose was technically sharper, but she was struggling to match Courtney's sheer power. Born with her abilities and drilled endlessly, the creativity of her use of power was immeasurable.

Chris burst from the ground toward Lola. She caught him by the neck, then slammed him through a concrete slab. Her grip tightened around his larynx.

"Since you couldn't live with me, you can't live at all," she said. The burns on her face started to disappear as she slowly rolled the cells back to a time before the damage. Her age also seemed to roll back years, to her most prime state.

Chris fumbled his hands around until one grasped hold of a rock big enough to do bodily harm. He smashed it into Lola's temple, knocking her over. A kick to her downed body skipped her across the moist sediment, as if a smooth rock across a lake.

Whenever Courtney pushed hard, Rose pushed back harder. The response led to ever-increasing destruction. Courtney gravitated soccer ball-sized stones and used time to erode them into thin skewers. Rose dodged some and was able to deflect many more while still rushing forward. A new batch of the stone arrows proved to be too much, as one tore through the meat of her left bicep.

"Ahhh!" Rose screamed in agony. She fell to her knees, a few feet from Courtney, all but yet defeated. She expected some evil villain speech, but there wouldn't be one. Courtney was lining up for the killing blow.

The calm before almost certain death penetrated Rose's mind. She finally understood the one lesson that had eluded her from Chris' teachings. He always told her that she pressed too hard to overcome things, rather than thinking them through. It was truly evident now that she had run into someone who was both an immovable object and an unstoppable force rolled into one. Finesse would be required to elude death.

This time, when Courtney released her flurry of darts, Rose was prepared. She redirected them all, picking off surrounding Faction soldiers who were still engaged with members of the WTP forces. The maneuver diverted Courtney's attention, as it was designed to do, but not for long. She was already lifting more rocks to reload her arsenal. She didn't see the single, slim spike that Rose had sent around the long way. It looped in a complete circle, cutting clean through the side of Courtney's thighs.

Lola bounded back from the ground as quick as she had landed. She dashed toward Chris, but his counter was already set up by Rose. The spike was intentionally sent toward the spot he stood. Its arrival and Lola's were simultaneous. Chris snatched it from the air and stabbed it through her shoulder.

Lola reacted as if she didn't feel it. She leapt into the air, forming dense balls of energy around her fists, pounding down on Chris repeatedly. He was able to form an energy shield of his own, but each blow he absorbed dug his feet deeper into a widening crater. He didn't know how much longer he would be able to stand.

Rose walked over to Courtney, who was flat on her back, mounted her, then dazed her with two right hands. Groggy from the hits but still conscious, Courtney grabbed hold of Rose's hands. Blood dripped from both her nostrils.

"This is for my father!" Rose shouted, sneaking an

elbow through Courtney's guard.

"This is for me!" Another fist landed home.

"And this is for being your mother's daughter!" Courtney went limp.

Lola continued to rain down pure anger and hatred. The relentless pounding, driven by her fists, caused Chris to buckle to his knees, giving his all to hold her at bay. Everything came full circle. Chris stared down at a pool of collected raindrops filling the crater. There was his reflection, staring at him again. He vanished through a mist of blue, leaving Lola to pound the pavement.

"Get out here, before I kill that little bitch!" Lola hollered, confused and frustrated that her target was nowhere to be found.

"You mean that bitch that just kicked your daughter's ass?" Rose replied, antagonizing her.

Lola pounced for her. Chris tackled her from an adjacent path, but was countered and shed off violently. Sick of the games, Lola pulled from all her inner power, then her body seized up. She fell flat on her face. "What did you do? Get this thing off me!"

Chris had clamped her own power-sealing device on her wrist, rendering her abilities useless.

This further enraged Lola. The electronic bracelet beeped at an increased rate as she tried to overpower it, but the design was impregnable. The wearer was the power source. The more Lola put out, the more efficient it became. It sizzled until her body shut down, and she passed out.

*∗∗

At daybreak, the battle was done, and the war was close behind. The remaining Faction soldiers had surrendered. Rose, Chris, and the WTP rounded them up among the smoldering rubble that was once Project 001.

Sasha and the others resurfaced from below ground.

"Dad! I thought you were dead when you didn't come for me," said Ari, running into Chris' arms.

"Not dead, just a little busy, Baby Girl," he replied,

nodding to Lola and Courtney, who were shackled with zip ties, sitting in the mud.

"It took three of us to drag her out of the room," Cory complained.

"He told me not to leave unless he personally came and got me!" Ari shouted.

"I'm pretty sure we were the exception."

"Will you people shut the hell up? Either that or go ahead and kill me," said Lola.

Sasha punched her square on the jawline. "You shut up!"

Lola spit a glob of blood from her mouth and cackled loudly.

"Mom!" Courtney called out in concern.

"Shut up, or you'll get one too," Sasha threatened.

Chris wasn't having it. "Hey, chill out on my daughter," he demanded.

"She's the one that killed Scott! I saw her do it. That little bitch is just like her mother."

"It was her?" Cory aimed his gun at Courtney.

"You'd better think about it before you pull that trigger, son," Chris warned him.

Cory was beyond rationality. "So, you're choosing her over us?"

"I'm choosing right over wrong. Revenge is easy, but you don't know her story."

Lola laughed louder. "Kill her already. The dyke couldn't even serve her purpose. All you had to do was win your father over and make him stay with us. You're worthless!" she berated.

Courtney stared at the ground, ready to embrace her fate. Life without love had no value anyway, so she was ready to die.

"Untie her," Chris ordered.

No one moved.

"Untie her!"

Ari walked up to Cory and snatched the blade from his sheath. She then approached Courtney, cut the zip ties from her wrists and ankles, then helped her to her feet. "I'm your sister, Ari."

Courtney tried to make eye contact but stared back at the ground, bashful and embarrassed about what her mother had turned her into.

Ari grabbed her hand, guiding her to stand with her behind their father. "Anybody takes a shot at her, you'd better make sure you kill me first, we clear?" Chris barked.

Silence was his only answer.

"Did we get the equipment?"

Cory and Sasha were too pissed to answer, so Justin stepped up to give the report. "We looked where the map said it was stored, but it wasn't there," he said.

"You're so damn predictable," laughed Lola. "You think I didn't know what the hell you would look for if you turned on me again? I had it moved."

"Moved where?" Chris asked, intensely.

Lola cackled like a witch. "To the armory, you dumbass. You blew it up."

"Fuck!" Sasha screamed. She grabbed Lola by the collar and banged her fist into her nose until she felt better.

"Enough!" said Chris. "Is there some other equipment out there?"

"No," Sasha answered. "That was it. It was experimental, so it was the only equipment in the world. We just messed up our only chance at saving the planet."

"Not exactly," said Courtney.

"Shut up, you fucking traitor! You'd better not say another goddamn word!" Lola fussed.

"Gag her," Chris ordered.

"Finally something we can agree on," said Cory, shoving a muddy cloth in Lola's mouth and tying it down.

"Go on, baby. Tell me," said Chris.

"Our powers are connected. It's the reason we can all feel each other's locations, moods, and things like that," Courtney began to explain.

"What does that have to do with repairing the orbit?" Rose quizzed her.

"Nothing. We can't fix the world, but we can go back in time and stop it before it breaks."

Now everyone was interested. "We can go back in time almost twenty years? This bitch really is crazy," said

Patch.

"OK, I'm zapping the next person that disrespects my daughter to the top of the atmosphere and watching them fall all the way back down," Chris threatened.

Courtney continued. "Technically that's not how time travel works. You don't just travel around time like it's a location, meaning you can't just show up five years ago and meet yourself. Time is stitched together in a fabric. When my parents and I traveled here to the future, it was more like hitting the fast forward button, but we ripped a piece of the fabric in the process. That's why so many things are out of whack. We opened parallel timelines, altered people's state of beings, and the universe itself."

"So what does all that mean?" Chris asked.

Courtney singled out a point in the sky. "There. That's the direction we have to go to get back to our Earth."

"We don't have the LOGOS anymore."

"We are the LOGOS. You, me, Ari, Rose, and Mom. We have the same power as the ship. Together, we can generate enough power to go back to the time before the world broke, fixing everything."

"Your mother won't help us."

"She doesn't need to. A comm-watch doesn't ask a battery for permission to use its energy. If you plug it in, power flows. Same concept."

Rose was convinced. "It's worth a shot."

Chris agreed. "When should we try it?"

"Now," said Sasha. "Let's not give her time to escape."

"I agree with her," said Courtney. "No need to wait."

Sasha rolled her eyes. She must have spoken the moment into existence because Lola had been working while they were all distracted. A blade was hidden between her body and her armor, in the small of her back. She had managed to slip it out and sever her thumb from her hand, creating just enough room to slip from the band that imprisoned her power.

Rose could see the telltale sign of her glowing eyes charging for action. Mentally she was ahead, but Lola already had the jump on everyone, using her ability to trip them of their weapons, flinging them well beyond reach.

Reality slowed to a crawl. The next few seconds would determine the fate of the world. Rose reached her hand out like she was waiting on something. Indeed she was. A golden handgun with mahogany trim fell from a hole in the sky, a gift courtesy of the Faction themselves. Rose caught the weapon and emptied its small, six-round arsenal.

Lola was dead. Rose's tight grouping punched a hole through the heart of her light armor.

"Damn it! Now what?" Chris shouted. "We might not have enough energy."

Courtney didn't show much regret at the loss. "Her body still works," she said. "Gather around her and let's go."

"Wait," Chris said. "What happens if this doesn't work?"

Cory calculated out loud. "It's only theory, but you could rip through the fabric of spacetime, or fall into a place completely void of time altogether. Creating a singularity is also somewhere on the list of possibilities."

"In other words, we'll just speed up the inevitable death of the planet," Courtney plainly stated.

"And you guys still wanna try this?" asked Mona.

"What other choice do they have?" Tree replied. "Damned if they do, damned if they don't."

"I guess we should say our goodbyes in case," Rose suggested.

"No time. The soul is in the mind. In less than a minute, my mom's won't have enough oxygen and her cells will start to die. That happens, we might not have enough power to get all the way back before the world broke," said Courtney.

Rose didn't want to wait around to find out. "Let's hurry then. What do we do?"

"Link hands in a circle around my mom."

Rose, Courtney, Ari, and Chris clasped hands, encircling Lola's body.

"Dad, you're the only one of us old enough to

remember where we want to go. Make your connection and we'll all feed off it. If everything works, you can take us back and change our future. It's all on you."

Chris nodded, then closed his eyes. He imagined a time before he allowed himself to fall into Lola's web of temptation. Maybe if he never slept with her in the first place, she wouldn't have latched on to him the way she did.

Pebbles floated around first Chris, then the rest of the quintet. Visible strings of current followed, intertwining around their linked limbs. Brilliant radiance blazed, unable to be contained by their eyelids. Sasha yelled out to the others, and they ran for cover. The ground shook beneath them as they sped off in all directions.

The potent energy was too much for a single doorway. The bodies of the powerful compensated by releasing more through gaping mouths. Lola's wound spewed blue as she began to hover. A vortex swirled, gaining momentum. It reached past the stratosphere, punching a route through the clouds. Thunder roared, and then there was dead silence.

19

Settle or Dream

Chris shouted in pain. His soul was blasted back into his body, tipping him over backward in his office chair. Lola clenched her legs tighter on his waist. She bounced harder and screamed along with him, reaching her climax. "Oh my Lord! I didn't know sex with a man felt that good," she said, collapsing onto Chris' chest.

Chris was still reeling, oblivious from the disorientation of his journey through time. As he gained his bearings, he realized that he had missed his target by mere minutes. "You're pregnant... Fuck!" he grunted, upset with himself. He didn't mean for Lola to hear, but she did.

"You think so?" asked Lola, rubbing her flat stomach. "I wonder if it'll be a girl or boy. Oh well, let's do this again soon."

"I'll pass."

"Like you could turn all this down." Lola went to the restroom to clean herself up, pulled on her coat, and left.

Enough time passed, giving Chris time to think and reflect on his journey and what was to come. He was determined to deviate from the boy he saw in the mirror, to become a man of character. "Come in," he said, still seated at his desk.

Sasha entered with her face scrunched. "How did you know I was out there?"

"I know a lot of things."

"Well, did you know Lola was still in the building?"

"Yeah," Chris replied. "I just had sex with her."

Sasha's chin dropped past her knees. "You did what? You're getting married! You have a kid at home! What the hell were you thinking?" she shouted.

"I wasn't. Oh yeah, she's pregnant too." Chris spoke monotone, as if he was in a daze.

"There's no way you can know that."

"Yet, I do. Actually, there's a whole lot more than that. You should probably have a seat because this is going to take a while. A long while."

Chris told Sasha everything. Who Lola was, what she did, and how the resulting world was doomed to perish. He spoke of Cory and of Rose. Not a single detail was left out.

"You expect me to believe all of that?" Sasha questioned. "It's impossible."

Chris levitated his desk in front of her. "Sasha, I can do shit like this. Do you really want to sit here and tell me about what's possible and what's not?"

Sasha rested her head on his desk, heavy from the news she had been trusted with. "And we had sex... me and you?"

"Yes."

"Us?"

"Yes."

"I'm never..."

"Partying with me again? Yeah, I know. You said that already, several times."

"So what are you going to do?"

"I'm going to tell Melissa what I did."

"You know Melissa. She'll never take you back."

"I know," Chris said, "but I made the bed, so I have to lay in it."

As expected, Melissa held to who she was. She and

Chris would never again be more than friends who shared a child. Still, he was content, for at least she had forgiven him due to his honesty. Melissa had chosen to go her own way and leave him with the house built on his grandmother's land. The place felt empty. Chris roamed the interior, stopping at her old closet.

Through the crack of the door, an orange shirt was visible on the floor. Its presence tugged at Chris, until he gave in and went to retrieve it. "My old U of M shirt," he said, holding it up to see the tiger across the front. Suddenly, it hit him. Destiny had momentum, and this momentum was carrying him to his true love. Chris bolted down the steps, knowing exactly what he was supposed to do.

Shelby rumbled to sleep outside of Melvin's place. Chris practically ran inside.

"Why you runnin' in my place like you done lost yo rabbit-ass mind?" asked Melvin.

Chris panned around the venue. "I'm looking for someone," he said.

"I don't know where you bumped yo damn head, but it's da middle of da afternoon. Ain't nobody here but me. It ain't never nobody here but me at dis hour."

Chris rubbed his chin. He must have been missing something. Yesha told him she met him in an orange tiger shirt, outside what he concluded was Melvin's bar.

"You do know dat shirt look tacky as hell on you, right?" Melvin insulted.

"Outside!" Chris shouted. "It was outside the bar near Shelby." He ran back through the door.

Melvin shook his head. "That stockin' stuffin' mofo done lost his damn mind," he mumbled.

Chris crashed through the door and ran into Yesha, knocking her cup from her hand. "I am so sorry," he said, not yet seeing her face.

"It's OK," she replied. "It was only water."

Yesha's voice gave away her identity. Chris smiled at her. "I still apologize. I'm Chris, by the way," he said, introducing himself, with his hand extended.

Yesha took it, then replied, "Yesha. Your face looks

familiar."

"You familiar with Project 047? I'm the head of the ICA unit that trains there."

"Oh really? I was a structural engineer there."

"Was?"

"Yeah. I'm moving to Paris for a new gig, but weirdly, something has been telling me to consider staying."

Chris' attention was abruptly drawn elsewhere. Another familiar face was seated at an outdoor table outside of a café, two buildings down. "Can you excuse me for a second?" he said, walking away.

"Tiffany?" he said. He couldn't believe the odds of her being at that specific spot, at that specific time. The bigger shock was that she was exactly as she was, nearly twenty years in the future. She must have been one of the time anomalies that Cory and Courtney spoke of all along, he thought.

The young woman looked up and lowered her glasses slightly to look over them. Her freckles were accented by the dark frames. "Yes, that's me. Have we met?" she asked, curious how he knew her name.

Picking up her skepticism, Chris thought on his feet. "No. Your name's on your student ID," he pointed out.

Tiffany smiled, feeling a little silly. "Oh, right. I'm sorry. I can be a little ditsy at times," she said.

Chris glanced back, remembering he had left Yesha standing there. She was already walking away.

"Would you like to sit with me? I could actually use the company," said Tiffany. "I need a break from working on my designs for fashion week. It's part of my finals this semester."

Chris had a moment to make the choice of his life, and again, all decisions have momentum. The one he picked would likely ripple through time, altering the path of not only his future, but the future of everyone in his path, born and unborn.

Tiffany's voice of a long-lost future echoed in his mind. "Figure out if you're going to settle, or dream," she said.

***

Chris was both happy and distraught about his decision. The year was a long one, but he and Tiffany's relationship was as strong as one could wish for. However, a side effect of his choice was the nonexistence of his daughter Ari. Her absence left a gaping hole in his heart.

Tiffany ran downstairs, screaming at the top of her lungs. Chris yanked Retta from his holster, ready to protect her life. Nothing was there, but she kept on shouting.

"What the hell, Tiff?" Chris exclaimed.

"This morning I was feeling bad. I didn't know why, so my friend told me I should buy this thing, so I did. I bought the thing and I came back home, then I went upstairs to the restroom, then I did the thing on the thing, and..."

"Deep breaths, bae. You're doing it again."

"I'm sorry, but I can't help it!"

"You only talk this much when you're nervous, so what is it?"

"I'm pregnant!" she screamed. "We're going to have a little girl."

Chris used logic to suppress his joy. "How do you know? The baby doesn't even know what it's going to be yet."

"Well, I know it. I can feel it in my bones." Tiffany was so sure of herself. "We're having a girl and her name is going to be Ari."

Chris was floored. Tiffany knew nothing about his escapades in the future that never happened. He was the lone person that showed any signs of active memory of the alternate time. "I guess His will happens no matter what," he concluded.

EPILOGUE

After further investigation, Lola was imprisoned when involvement with her mother's initial plot was suspected. A surprise guilty plea accelerated her sentencing, which was long but fair. Chris thought it should be much harsher than it was, but the Justice Department concluded that they couldn't punish a person for crimes that they hadn't yet committed, much less in a future that now would never happen. The can of worms that type of justice would open wasn't worth dealing with.

"Daddy. Aunt Sasha's here. She says she needs to talk to you," said Ari. Her personality was truly her own, but her appearance was very different, lacking the genes of Yesha's Indian heritage. Early on, Chris found it weird to hear her voice, then match it with the wrong face that was in his mind. As time passed, this issue faded.

Chris went to the foyer to meet Sasha. "Come on

back," he said. "You can have dinner with us."

Sasha seemed to be a little on edge. "I can't. I just need to tell you something."

"What's up?"

"I haven't told Scott yet, but I'm pregnant."

"Congratulations. You wanna do something to surprise him?" Chris smiled.

"No... He's not the father."

Chris looked around the room to be sure no one was eavesdropping. "What the hell, Sasha... You didn't learn from my fuck-ups?"

"I didn't cheat on him, asshole. The baby's yours."

Chris was in denial. "Nope. I don't believe it. Nope. We never had sex. That future doesn't exist, remember? Nope. You wouldn't remember. I'm the only person in the world that remembers anything from that future, because IT NEVER HAPPENED!"

"Stop yelling. Do you want Tiffany to find out about this before we figure this shit out?"

Chris had a question, praying that Sasha's response didn't cut the mustard. "How do you even know the baby's mine? I'm sure you and Scott bang all the time."

There wasn't a verbal response. A gleam of blue rippled across Sasha's eyes.

"God damn it, not again!" Chris shouted.

About the Author

Lasheckia Lyons is an emerging entrepreneur and talented writer hailing from Memphis, TN. with roots in Flint, MI. She is dedicated to enriching the literary world by introducing readers to innovative and creative stories that offer fresh, unique perspectives.

Alongside her role as a devoted prison wife, Lasheckia collaborates closely with her husband on various writing projects, blending their experiences and insights into compelling narratives.

Lasheckia's dedication to exploring diverse voices and stories underscores her commitment to making a meaningful impact through her work

9 798330 470464